THE WEIPA CROCODILE
Part 1

Murders in the Outback

Victoria Reiby

This is a work of fiction. Names, characters, places, and incidents either are the product of the author's imagination or are used fictitiously. Any resemblance to actual persons, living or dead, events, or locales is entirely coincidental.

Copyright © 2024 by Victoria Reiby

All rights reserved. No part of this book may be reproduced or used in any manner without written permission of the copyright owner except for the use of quotations in a book review.

First paperback edition October 2024

THE WEIPA CROCODILE

"It's always the crocodile you don't see you have to worry about." Jeremy Wade

TABLE OF CONTENTS

CHAPTER 1 1

CHAPTER 2 8

CHAPTER 3 17

CHAPTER 4 25

CHAPTER 5 32

CHAPTER 6 44

CHAPTER 7 55

CHAPTER 8 67

CHAPTER 9 78

CHAPTER 10 88

CHAPTER 11 90

CHAPTER 12 103

CHAPTER 13 108

CHAPTER 14 112

CHAPTER 15 116

CHAPTER 16 127

CHAPTER 17 135

CHAPTER 18 143

CHAPTER 19 153

CHAPTER 20 162

CHAPTER 21 177

CHAPTER 22 183

CHAPTER 23..201
CHAPTER 24..214
CHAPTER 25..218
CHAPTER 26..227
CHAPTER 27..237
CHAPTER 28..243
CHAPTER 29..251
CHAPTER 30..260
CHAPTER 31..265
CHAPTER 32..273
CHAPTER 33..289
CHAPTER 34..293
CHAPTER 35..298

CHAPTER 1

Bruce Hudson descended into a restless slumber, his imaginings taking on a vivid, otherworldly quality. Amidst the swirling visions that danced through his mind, a ghost-like figure emerged in the distance, shrouded by the relentless curtain of rain, drawing his attention like a moth to a flame. As the form drew nearer, his senses sharpened, and he recognised the familiar gait and silhouette of one of the ancients, Tali, a revered elder who had long since passed.

The storm, marking the arrival of the wet season, began with a ferocity that he had not witnessed before. Tali stood firm, his eyes gleaming with the ancient wisdom of the Dreaming, meeting Bruce's in a transcendent gaze. There was a silent understanding between them, a knowing that belied words. They had shared countless moments like this, where the elements themselves seemed to conspire to reveal the path that must be taken, and he felt a sense of awe at his mentor's reappearance.

Without a word, the older man approached Bruce, his steps deliberate. He reached out and touched his shoulder, a gesture that bridged the physical and spiritual divide, acknowledging and affirming their connection. Together, they stood in the heart of the storm.

The rain began to relent, gradually transitioning from a deluge to a gentle shower, mirroring the changing currents of their dreamscape. The thunder and lightning receded, replaced by the rhythmic symphony of dripping leaves and the distant song of awakening birds, merging the boundaries of fact and fiction.

Tali broke the silence, his voice resonating like the call of a wise old owl, an echo of the wisdom of generations. "The land speaks to us. It whispers its truths in the language of the elements. You have listened well; it is time to heed its call."

Bruce nodded, his heart pounding with anticipation. He knew this was the moment he had been preparing for, the culmination of a lifetime of learning and communion with the land, a convergence of the historical and the spiritual. In a symbolic gesture, the ancient presented him with a small, weathered pouch containing a collection of deadly nightshade berries, a potent symbol of duality, creation, and dissolution. "These are the tools of your journey," Tali said, "They carry the essence of our ancestors and the spirits of this land. Use them wisely, for they will guide you."

With a nod, he accepted the pouch and responded, "I understand, my Wisdom." He felt the weight of responsibility settle on his shoulders, a duty he knew he must fulfil.

He understood the gravity of the task ahead, a mission that carried not only the wisdom of his people but also a debt to be paid, an obligation to confront and reconcile as he embarked on the path before him.

Earlier that day, he had entered the clearing alone, a place familiar to him, the same area where the sorry business for "Barlang" had been carried out many moons ago. He had located the deadly nightshade bush and collected a bag of berries. With an eerie certainty, he consumed a feast of the berries, understanding that this marked a pivotal moment of reckoning; the ancients would decide his fate. Anticipating the imminent onset of hallucinations, he ventured into the encroaching darkness, acutely aware that the convergence of nightfall and the potent effects of the toxic berries would soon engulf him.

Moving purposefully, Bruce made his way to the middle of the clearing; in the darkness, he walked silently, navigating the terrain with an instinctual knowledge that transcended the need for illumination. His bare feet moved noiselessly, a testament to the skilled tracker within him. Pausing in the heart of the clearing, he stood at the juncture of liberation and the unfamiliar, absorbing the surroundings, tuned into the primal cadences coursing through the age-old terrain.

A vitality about the outback stirred the senses, infusing the air with a soft rustling as leaves from giant eucalyptus trees released their fragrance into the night breeze; scent and memory were entwined, summoning recollections from long past.

Two hours after the daring ingestion, he became immersed in a surreal experience within the serene clearing. Animated by the hallucinogenic effects, the once-static elements of nature – animals, trees and rocks alike – came alive in a kaleidoscope of vibrant colours, defying the prevailing blackness of the night. In this altered state, Bruce conversed with the seemingly animated entities, transcending the boundaries between reality and the fantastical realm he had willingly entered.

He found himself amidst a nocturnal menagerie, where the creatures of the night awakened with a symphony of sounds. In his altered state, Bruce perceived a surreal transformation of the animal kingdom; the sugar gliders murmured, "Follow the whispers of the wind, seeker. The unseen paths await your discerning steps."

"In the shadows, secrets unfold. Listen, for the night speaks of wisdom as old as time," the tawny frogmouths declared.

"Change approaches, swift and unyielding; brace yourself, for the dance of fate begins," the possums hissed.

The kookaburra, once a spectator in the night's play, now engaged Bruce in a cryptic dialogue, "Ha-ha-ha, traveller of dreams, do you sense the impending reckoning in the rustle of the leaves?"

Confused and disoriented, he found himself on the precipice of profound reflection. The years unfurled before him, each moment contributing a pen stroke to the tome of his life's journey. There was much to be proud of, but his pride was not born of vanity; it was the quiet satisfaction of a man who walked through fire and emerged, not unscathed, but transformed. Every trial he faced seemed to function as a forge, refining the essence of his character. Rather than weakening him, each obstacle acted as a catalyst for growth, infusing him with a steely resolve.

Bruce's recollections danced like ethereal fireflies, glowing on his canvas of consciousness. He stood as a solitary figure in a small clearing, barely visible beneath the expanse of the ink-black sky above. His senses were finely honed through years of immersion in this untamed realm. His every breath revealed the secrets of the bush, the whispers of the land, and the stories written in the fragrant script of nature. He could sense the approach of rain, a subtle shift in the air's temperament, a moist promise carried on a gentle breeze.

Upon reaching the clearing, he felt the initial drops of water caress his face, and soon, the arrival of the wet season was announced by an unrestrained tempest, its sudden and fierce onset taking him by surprise. The atmosphere erupted, unleashing torrents of rain that cascaded down upon him. Lightning streaked across the darkened sky, illuminating his world in brilliant, jagged veins of electric white. Simultaneously, thunder roared with a mighty voice reverberating through the landscape. Under the shroud of darkness, he knelt in a field of earth, rich and ochre-hued, a sacred expanse he now called his own.

He pressed his hands into the drenched soil with reverence, then raised them heavenward in homage to the weeping skies, the ancients, and all the unseen forces conspiring to bring him to this pivotal juncture. He felt a profound sense of vindication surge through him, an exhilaration swelling and pulsing with the rhythm of the storm. This would be his truth-telling.

He rose to his feet, arms outstretched, a bridge connecting the terrestrial realm with the universe above. It was a moment of profound elemental communion, a sacred dance linking his memories with the spiritual realms of his ancestors, enveloped by the rhythmic caress of the natural world. The heaven's tears baptised man and soil in a cleansing downpour.

He arched his head back and released a triumphant laugh. His teeth gleamed like polished ivory, a stark contrast against the ebony velvet of the night sky. His body was engraved with the scars of his journey. Ceremonial paint adorned his weathered skin, each symbol representing the stories carved into his bones. In his presence, one could feel the heartbeat of generations past echoing through the core of his existence. He was a living vessel, carrying forward the legacy of those who came before him.

The rain poured over him, a sanctifying deluge cleansing his soul, leaving him reborn—an indomitable and unyielding lone figure in open country in the Australian outback. Defined by the lightning's fleeting illumination, his silhouette, outlined against a backdrop of land reclaimed through sweat and tears, spoke of battles fought and victories won. Draped in the sacred folds of an Aboriginal "possum" loincloth, he wore his heritage like armour.

Dangling from his neck was a totemic crocodile tooth secured by a delicate strand of kangaroo leather—a talisman imbued with the ancient understanding of his ancestors. In the days of his youth, amidst the sage counsel of revered elders and the company of his tribal kin, this animal was chosen as his totem, a creature of power and stealth, a living emblem of the ancient spirits coursing through the land. The pendant represented continuity—a lineage passed down through the ages, destined to find its way to the next chosen one, a successor bound for greatness within the tribe, a conscience kindred to the cunning and predatory temperament of the crocodile.

Lifting his eyes towards the sky, he searched for the constellations. Underneath the tumultuous, storm-laden skies, their presence eluded him. Yet, years of dedicated practice had equipped him with the precise knowledge of where to gaze to locate Orion—the celestial canoe, its stars steadfastly gleaming akin to the eyes of a soul mate. This luminosity persisted within his thoughts, even in the encompassing darkness that now enveloped him. A broad and contented grin spread across his face, mirroring the tranquil satisfaction of a crocodile basking in the sun. In this moment, Bruce and his totem intertwined, forever bound by the clandestine knowledge they shared.

His silver-white beard flowed like a cascade, a river of wisdom dancing in the wind. It was an uninterrupted extension of the natural world, an outward manifestation of his deep connection with the earth and sky. The wind whispered secrets to him, and the earth cradled his every move. At this moment, Bruce was one with nature. The world around him vibrated with life, and he, too, pulsed with it.

In the calm of advancing years, he welcomed the role of a revered elder, once a distant ambition in the recesses of his adolescence, deferred by a cruel blow. This painful strike, a harsh amalgamation of his actions, naivety, and the unreserved trust often accompanying the innocence of youth, was a lesson cut into the essence of his being, a stark reminder of the power of choices made in haste and the painful consequences they wrought.

Once a mere whisper in the wind, his voice evolved into a resonant echo, carrying the weight of ancestral learning and the cadence of a lifetime steeped in acquired knowledge. The mantle of elderhood rested upon his shoulders with a grace that spoke of a destiny fulfilled. Bruce stood tall. His shoulders squared, his expression confident, a guardian of liberty, a personification of the price man is willing to pay in exchange for emancipation from the suffocating constraints of a society that seemed alien and hostile. A spirit refusing to be tethered to a world that did not recognise its worth.

    A realisation settled deep within him, a quiet certainty that his moment had finally arrived. Then, amidst the palpable anticipation, Tali materialised from the dense scrub, gracefully stepping into the clearing. The air seemed to hold its breath as their eyes met, a pivotal moment that would alter the course of Bruce's life.

CHAPTER 2

Ten years earlier

In the dimly lit room, the air hung heavy with the stench of decay as the lifeless body lay sprawled on the bed. The sickening hue of mottled green painted a gruesome scene, reflecting the surrounding putrefaction that whispered secrets of a nasty demise. The skin stretched taut over bloated limbs, glistened with a nauseating sheen of sweat and bodily fluids. Upon the exposed torso, foul blisters erupted, their contents oozing like macabre tears, leaving a chilling trail down the man's trunk.

It was a lazy Sunday afternoon when the local Weipa police were first alerted to the disappearance of Walt Henry, Cape York's wealthiest man. He hadn't been seen at his usual haunts, which was uncommon. Being a man of habit, he was always seen at the local Albatross Bay Hotel, or the "Alby", every Friday and Saturday night when he was in town.

The local police officers were Senior Sergeant Phil Roberts and Sergeant David "Davo" Smith. Phil had been stationed in Weipa for the last decade. His face displayed a weariness that only years of observing the worst aspects of humanity could carve. A weathered man, his empty eyes spoke volumes of the darkness he'd witnessed. He yearned for the sanctuary of his police pension. At fifty-eight, he had devoted almost forty years to the force, and the fatigue ran deep in his bones. He had traversed the remote corners of Cape York, from Cooktown to Pormpuraaw, a remote outpost five hundred kilometres away from Australia's northernmost point, known affectionately as "The Tip" by the locals. Retirement was within his grasp, tantalisingly close. He could practically taste the freedom, envisioning himself kicking back on his verandah with an ice-cold beer, savouring the sweet release of a lifetime of service.

Davo was new in town. He arrived six months ago after receiving his promotion to Sergeant and was still young enough to be full of enthusiasm. In his early thirties, with a mop of curly blonde hair and eager blue eyes, he was not yet tainted by the rigours of the job. He was still to encounter the visions that struck at the very heart of a police officer's existence.

Phil was at the station when Brendan, the manager at the Albatross Bay Hotel, called. "Hey Phil, Brendan here."

"G'day Brendan, what's up? Another fight at the Alby?" Phil laughed at his joke. He was called there often to break up drunken brawls.

"It's probably nothing," Brendan replied cautiously. "It's just Walt Henry. He didn't come in for the Friday night meat tray raffle or the Saturday rump steak and jug special. I did give his mobile a call, but no one answered. I just thought someone ought to check on him and see if everything is okay. Whenever he's been in town, he has never missed a single weekend at the pub."

"Sure thing, Brendan. Davo and I will take a look at his place now."

"No worries. Maybe he's just gone away for the weekend with another of his floosies," said Brendan light-heartedly, stifling a chuckle.

"You could be on to something there, mate. We'll go around and take a look. I'll give you a buzz when I find Walt."

"Thanks, mate. Seeya." Brendan ended the call.

Phil called out to Davo. He was out the back filing paperwork, "Hey Davo. Walt hasn't been seen at the Alby for a few days. Brendan just rang; he wants us to check it out."

"Sure thing, I can finish this later," he replied, stacking the remaining paperwork neatly in one corner of his desk.

They locked the station before driving to Walt's house to investigate. The billionaire's planes were parked on his private runway, but no other vehicles were in sight. The triple garage doors were down and appeared locked.

The two police officers stood before the front door, drenched in unsettling silence and sweat. The pre-monsoon heat was stifling, and the short walk from the car to the front door was enough to soak their shirts. Call it cop's intuition, but Phil sensed something was amiss. Everything was just a little too quiet. He had hoped the house owner, Walt, would be waiting on the other side, happy to welcome a visitor, but there was no response to his persistent knocks.

Optimism and caution battled within him as he retrieved the spare key from its hiding place under a pot of vibrant scarlet geraniums, a secret known only to a select few. He inserted the key into the wooden door, which boasted intricate lead glass windows. It opened effortlessly, revealing the lavish foyer that lay beyond. Phil and Davo cautiously crossed the threshold, their hands gripping their weapons with white-knuckled intensity, wary of potential intruders.

The air hung thick with the unmistakable stench of death, a sickening combination of rotting flesh and metallic tang mingling with the heavy tropical humidity. In the oppressive silence, every soft footfall on the gleaming entrance hallway's polished floorboards sent shivers down Davo's spine.

With his gun held firmly at the ready, Phil's senses heightened to a razor-sharp level. He scanned the surroundings, his gaze darting from shadow to shadow, his instincts urging him to ensure the house remained clear of lurking intruders. The weight of the mission pressed upon him, his trained mind calculating every possible threat.

As they cautiously ventured deeper into the house, their footsteps now muffled by the thick carpet beneath their feet, Phil's focus remained unwavering. The vacillating light streamed through the stained-glass window of the front door, creating an eerie dance on the ornate walls, adorned with a collection of lavish-looking paintings. The officers began to navigate the mansion with disciplined precision; their steps were measured and deliberate.

Phil Roberts indicated to the junior sergeant to take the left side of the house while he took the right. Each room they entered told a story of wealth and privilege, the trappings of a life well-lived yet now tainted by a sinister presence. Phil moved cautiously through the loungeroom before sliding along the walls, clearing each bedroom of the house's first floor. Davo did the same on the left.

After clearing the house's ground floor, the two officers proceeded upstairs, maintaining a vigilant stance with their guns ready. The putrid odour assaulted Phil's senses, an unmistakable stench of decay growing stronger with each step. He followed the repulsive scent, his heart pounding in his chest. The sickly, sweet aroma led him to the main bedroom, where darkness engulfed the room like a shroud.

With trepidation, Phil flicked on the light switch, casting an unnerving luminosity upon the scene awaiting him. The room was steeped in an atmosphere of morbidity. He raised his sweat-soaked shirt to cover his nose, attempting to shield himself from the overwhelming stink.

His gaze fell upon the bed, and what he saw seared into his memory. The oppressive heat and the man's large amount of body fat had accelerated the natural processes of decomposition, releasing a pungent haze that hung heavily in the air. The stench, an offensive blend of rot and decay, clung to every surface, invading the senses with its nauseating potency. His once recognisable features were distorted and obscured; the deceased's eyes, still wide open, had sunk deep into their sockets, leaving behind hollow, empty voids staring into the abyss.

Despite the horrific transformation death had imposed upon him, Phil recognised the unmistakable contours of that bulky physique. The tattoo of a mine shaft sketched on Walt's right forearm and the two missing fingers on Walt's left hand confirmed his identity, leaving no room for doubt.

A bleak guise settled in Phil's eyes as he called out to his partner, "Are you ready for this one, Davo?" His voice echoed through the room.

His pulse racing, the younger officer nodded quietly before taking cautious steps towards Phil's voice. Anticipation mingled with nervous energy. As he entered the bedroom, the sight greeting his eyes elicited a visceral reaction, an overwhelming surge of disgust and horror. A wave of nausea washed over him, propelling him towards the nearby bathroom, where he retched violently into the toilet. The nature of the scene before him was unlike anything he had encountered, and it shook him to his very foundations.

After rinsing his mouth and splashing cool water on his face, Davo mustered the courage to return to the bedroom, his voice trembling with vulnerability. "Sorry about that. I've seen my fair share of dead bodies, but never something so bloody horrible."

His expression, a blend of understanding and experience, Phil offered a knowing reply, "Not the first time a young bloke has responded like that, and it won't be the last. The sights we see in this line of work can consume a man if you let it." His words held a sinister sincerity, a cautionary reminder of the price they paid in pursuing justice.

The two officers combed through every inch of the house, exploring every avenue in their search for clues that could shed light on the mysterious death of Walt Henry.

Their trained eyes scanned each room, scrutinising for any signs of disturbance or evidence of foul play. Yet, to their perplexity, there were no apparent indications of forced entry, and the house's interior appeared surprisingly intact and undisturbed. The sole oddity was the back door on the lower level was unlocked. Phil didn't attach much significance to it; various explanations could exist.

The Senior Sergeant's mind raced, attempting to piece together the baffling elements of the investigation. The lack of forced entry and the absence of any visible signs of struggle confounded him. The pieces didn't fit, even though he possessed a sixth sense honed from years of experience. He couldn't shake the feeling that something was off.

With a sense of frustration, Phil holstered his gun. The absence of immediate danger allowed him to shift his focus to the next crucial step—calling for assistance. He reached for his radio, pressing the button firmly as he summoned the local paramedics.

"G'day Gladys," he said after the ambulance dispatcher answered.

"What's up, Phil? I haven't heard from you in a while. Business must be a bit slow," she laughed, finding humour was the only non-destructive way of coping as a first responder.

"Afraid I've got some bad news. It looks like old Walt Henry is dead."

"You don't say," Gladys gasped, audibly upset yet intrigued, "How did he die, Phil?"

"I don't know, but I do know Davo and I are going to investigate."

"Geez, Phil, I'll get the paramedics onto it immediately."

"Thanks, Glad, you're a real gem."

As the paramedics arrived, their faces mirrored concern and curiosity. The undeniable truth was apparent: the individual before them had passed away some days before, requiring only a doctor's confirmation to certify the obvious. The paramedics called the Weipa Hospital, inquiring whether one of the two doctors on duty could spare some time to certify the deceased body. Dr O'Connor responded promptly, offering his assistance. He was acquainted with Walt's medical history and had seen him as an outpatient several times; the doctor arrived at the house without delay.

Phil and Davo greeted the doctor and led him to the grim scene awaiting him in the upstairs bedroom. Unperturbed, the doctor performed the necessary checks to confirm the patient's death. Using a pocket torch, he examined the pupils, finding them fixed and dilated. Next, he retrieved his stethoscope, listening to the left side of the chest, and detected no heartbeat. He also noted an absence of respiratory sounds. After recording these findings in his notes, he announced Walt's death, concluding with "R.I.P." following the citation.

Despite the advanced stage of decomposition, the physician observed no signs of physical trauma. Considering Walt's medical background, which included obesity, hypertension, high cholesterol, intermittent angina, diabetes, and a long history of cigarette smoking, the local medic expeditiously completed the death certificate, attributing the cause of death to acute myocardial infarction secondary to coronary artery disease. It seemed like a straightforward case of natural causes leading to death. As Walt's regular doctor, he identified the body as belonging to one Walt Henry, aged sixty-five years.

Meanwhile, back at the ambulance station, Gladys took out her earpiece and went to the tea room. Needing a break, she found a secluded corner. Learning of a local's death in such a tight-knit community was never easy, but when it was someone as lively, renowned, and benevolent as he was, it deeply saddened her. Her hands trembled as she reached for her worn, cracked and heavily stained coffee mug on the shelf above the sink, seeking stability in its familiarity.

Here, she needed to settle her frayed nerves and regain control of her emotions in the face of this unfathomable news. After making herself a cup of coffee and sitting at the corner table of the tea room, an undeniable urge gnawed at her. She desperately wanted to share this newfound knowledge with her best friend, Judy. After all, what was gossip if not an escape from the bleakness of reality?

She glanced around cautiously, ensuring no prying eyes observed her. She took out her phone and dialled Judy's number.

On the first ring, her friend answered, instantly recognising the unique ringtone she had set for her closest companion—the chorus of Queen's "You're My Best Friend."
"G'day, Glad. What's up?"

"A lot, mate, a lot. I have so much to tell you, but I better keep it quick. I'm at work, darl," replied Gladys.

"Spill the beans. Please don't keep me in suspense. What is it?"

The dispatcher hesitated, her voice calm and laced with apprehension. She whispered the shocking revelation to Judy, "Seems like old Walt Henry is dead."

"Dead? How?" Came the concerned reply.

"No one knows yet. I just took a call from the top cop, Phil. He seemed pretty shaken up."

"Gee whiz. Think of the possibilities. He did have a few enemies. Maybe he was murdered; now that would be some goss!" Replied Jude, her voice laced with excitement. "Are they sure it's Walt?"

"Pretty sure, I have to go, love, the phone's ringin' off the hook. Looks like a busy day for Weipa," she paused before adding, "I finish at five. Do you want a quick drink at the Alby this afternoon, and we'll talk more about it? It's the most exciting thing to happen here in years. Not that I wished the old bloke harm. It does make ya think, though, doesn't it?"

"Oh, the possibilities. Say six p.m. at the local; we could have a drink and then a meal. It wouldn't surprise me if this had something to do with Bruce's actions at the pub last weekend. Those indigenous fellas and their hoodoo. You might know a bit more by tonight!" Judy responded a little too enthusiastically.

"You might be onto something there. I never thought of that. It was a bit of a spectacle last weekend, wasn't it?" she replied, "Gotta get back to work, seeya love, talk later."

"Seeya, thanks for giving me the heads up. When this gets out, it'll spread like wildfire. I can't wait to see you tonight."

"I'm looking forward to it," Gladys said, concluding the call and returning to her station to operate the phones.

CHAPTER 3

Despite the exclusive title of the largest town in Cape York, Weipa, with its fluctuating population of approximately four thousand people, depending on how many miners and campers were in town, was still considered an isolated coastal community by the locals. Not a lot changed in Weipa. The average temperature swung between nineteen and thirty-six degrees year-round. The town had only two seasons, "The Wet", which ran from December until April and "The Dry" between May and October. Rio Tinto, a leading global mining group, was the town's major employer. Its shopping precinct, if one street could be called that, consisted of a Woolworths, a Beer Wine and Spirits (BWS) and a couple of fishing tackle shops. While the town's central streets were sealed, the roads in and out consisted of lengthy stretches of dusty, dirty, corrugated roads extending for hundreds of kilometres.

Most people visiting Weipa were campers or caravanners, stopping overnight or even for a few days to fish in its bountiful river estuaries and restock food and fuel supplies before heading north toward Australia's northernmost tip—the tip of Cape York.

Despite his faults, Walt was a "big man" in Weipa, not just in size and stature but known for his generosity and regular donations to support the local community. He was six-foot-four and weighed in at around one-hundred-and-fifty kilograms. Walt was a good time bloke who blended in naturally with the people of Weipa, seen regularly at The

Deck restaurant and bar at The Albatross Bay Resort on most Friday and Saturday nights. He loved a cold beer and a steak just as much as the next man. Not one to shy away from helping anyone in need, Walt was generally regarded as a great bloke by the locals. He sponsored the local Weipa Raiders Rugby League Club, even buying them a bus to travel to remote locations across the Cape and greater Queensland to compete against other rugby league teams.

Earlier that year, when floods caused the Arthur River to overflow, police were forced to close the Peninsula Development Road between Coen and Weipa. Walt used his private chopper to bring food and alcohol supplies to the town and his private jet to transport indigenous students, stranded at Horn Island, to Cairns to continue their studies at various boarding schools located in the city. Walt wanted the small coastal community to survive, thrive, and prosper; he did everything he could to ensure it did. Many considered him a local hero. The people of Weipa were not quick to judge a man of his nature for the occasional fling. They forgave quickly and considered this just part of Walt's larger-than-life personality. He loved life, he loved his community, and he certainly loved the ladies. Even Carol, his recently estranged wife, mostly forgave him for his dalliances, as, just by being in Walt's company, his big-hearted nature, raucous laughter and ability to laugh at himself and others were contagious.

Walt's journey began in the modest setting of Georgetown, Western Queensland. Despite the simplicity of his early life, he held a deep understanding of his place in the world. Humility was his companion, which earned him widespread respect within the community.

Born into a family of five siblings, Walt was the eldest. He experienced the joy of a happy but straightforward life until tragedy struck at the age of twelve. It was a day etched into his memory with indelible ink, altering the course of his existence.

The quiet town of Georgetown stood witness to a heart-wrenching incident when Walt's father met a tragic end. It was a day when the Etheridge River, on the outskirts of town, unleashed its fury, trapping two men in the relentless floodwaters. Without a second thought, Walt's father leapt into action, attempting a heroic rescue.

Walt's vivid memories of that day still haunt him. Standing on the riverbanks, he screamed desperately, "Dad! Dad!" The cries echoed in the rain-soaked air, but they were futile. The roaring waters swallowed his pleas as he watched, helpless, the two men vanish beneath the unforgiving current. Then, with a heavy heart, he witnessed his father succumb to the merciless torrent.

In that heart-wrenching moment, with rain pouring down like tears from the heavens, Walt's father surfaced briefly for a gasp of air. Locking eyes with his son, tears mingling with raindrops, he silently conveyed his love. It was a fleeting connection, Walt's last gaze with his father.

Seated on the riverbanks amidst the relentless downpour, Walt cried until his eyes ran dry. The pain that gripped his heart seemed insurmountable, a wound that he knew would never fully heal. The loss of his father left an indelible mark on his soul, shaping his character and influencing the trajectory of his life in ways he could scarcely comprehend at the time.

He wearily trudged back to the familiar embrace of the family home, the weight of devastating news clinging to him like an oppressive shroud. As he faced his mother, her intuitive gaze pierced through the facade he tried to maintain. Her heart sank, recognising the depths of sorrow etched across her son's vacant, tear-stained eyes.

A guttural cry, laden with anguish and disbelief, erupted from her trembling lips, echoing through the walls of the once-happy home. "Nooooooooo!!!" The desperate wail hung heavy in the air, a mournful symphony of a mother's worst fears realised. Without warning, she crumpled to the unforgiving floor, her hands clutching at her head as if to contain the overwhelming pain that now consumed her.

Uncontrollable sobs wracked her body, each heave of breath a painful reminder of the unexpected tragedy. Walt, grappling with his sorrow, moved closer to his mother. In the smallness of his young heart, he sought solace in the only gesture that felt right – a hug. It was a feeble attempt to mimic the comforting embrace of his absent father, now thrust into the role of the eldest male in the shattered household.

The community rallied, organising a search party with hopeful whispers that perhaps, against all odds, there might be a glimmer of hope. Yet, deep down, everyone understood the futility of their efforts. The relentless waters had claimed everything in their path, leaving behind a void that seemed impossible to fill.

Walt's mother gathered her five children around, their faces still bearing the weight of recent events. Amid their collective grief, she addressed them with a sombre yet determined tone, "We've got no future here without your father. We must pack up and head to a bigger town, where jobs can be found. I'll have to find work, and Walt, you'll have to lend a hand. Maybe, if luck is on our side, I'll find a good man willing to marry me and take us all in."

The children, their expressions a mix of sorrow and uncertainty, nodded in silent agreement. The gravity of the situation hung heavily in the air, and the prospect of leaving their familiar town was daunting and necessary.

"Now, they say Charters Towers is thriving. There's talk of gold still waiting to be discovered, even to this day," she continued, trying to infuse a glimmer of hope into their uncertain future. "I'll make inquiries and take in washing, ironing and sewing repairs initially while I search for a decent job."

The move to Charters Towers marked a turning point in their lives. Walt's mother, resilient and determined, found love again. Her new husband, a geologist, played a pivotal role in shaping Walt's future. One day, with a twinkle in his eye, the stepfather took Walt to prospect for gold in the town's bushland.

Walt started working at the Charters Towers gold mine when he was fifteen, soon after beginning his studies to become an assayer. Four years after gaining his qualifications, he undertook employment with the Geological Survey branch of the Queensland Department of Resources. This job took him to Weipa, where he befriended a local man, Bruce Hudson. This man led Walt to the discovery of commercial quantities of bauxite on Aboriginal lands. After further exploration, Walt staked his claim on the sacred land and initiated talks with the Comalco mining company for a potential sale.

From this point forward, Walt's life was on the up and up. He explored and profited from other mineral-rich regions in Western Queensland. Regardless of his increasing wealth, Weipa would forever remain Walt's true home. There, he found solace and, most importantly, he first encountered Carol.

Their romance began when Walt, working to repair a fence on his cattle station, ended up with a cut on his right thumb requiring stitches. Carol, overseeing the local nursing station in Weipa before the construction of the hospital, entered the picture. She exuded vivacity, a playful flirtatiousness, and possessed an appealing touch of youthful plumpness. Her cheeks were always rosy, and her ever-present smile gave her a charm few could resist. Walt could not take his eyes off her; he knew this was the woman he would marry, and in a bold proclamation, Walt declared, "Carol Whitman, mark my words; one day, I'll make you my wife. I'll see to that."

With a twinkle in her eye and a playful giggle, Carol responded, "Now, will you just... Many men have tried, but all have failed to date. You'll have to chase me pretty hard." Her laughter echoed in the air, and the timbre of that giggle resonated irresistibly with Walt.

Despite the age gap, the two shared common interests like country music and quiet nights sitting outside on the verandah enjoying a cold beer together. At the same time, they chatted away endlessly about any topics that came to mind. A life together felt right; they were in love, and there were no two ways about it. After a whirlwind romance, they were engaged a mere fifty days later and married at Merluna Cattle Station two months following their engagement. It was a big event for Weipa and the neighbouring towns. Everyone from all the surrounding communities was invited to join in the festivities. The local CWA and Indigenous elders put on a great spread, and Walt arranged a refrigerated vehicle to ship in all the necessary beer and wine to make this day special for everyone. Most people camped overnight on the farm or fell asleep in their vehicles. The festivities lasted an entire three days. It was an event to remember.

As the decades of their marriage unfolded, Walt's reputation as a "ladies' man" became a whispered euphemism, a cheeky acknowledgment of his wandering eyes and penchant for pursuits with younger women. The passage of time did little to curb his habits, and Carol, a decade his junior, found herself grappling with the repercussions of his affairs.

Nearly thirty years into their union, the strains of Walt's infidelity had worn Carol down to a breaking point. On a seemingly ordinary day, she decided to confront him. Her voice, tinged with frustration and hurt, cut through the air, "I've had enough, love. I just can't take it anymore. Either tell me I am the only woman you'll ever need and you don't want all those other women in your life, or leave." It was an ultimatum.

Walt, caught off guard by the severity of her tone, bowed his head in shame. "I can't help myself; you know I love the ladies," he mumbled, his admission laced with remorse.

Despite his pledge to try his best, Walt's efforts were in vain. Carol, the pain etched on her face, discovered through the local gossips, Gladys and Judy, that Walt had been seen once again with another younger woman in Weipa. The news was a final blow, the breaking point she could no longer ignore. Love for him clashed with the self-respect she owed herself.

"That's it," she declared, a heaviness in her voice. "I can't go on like this despite my love for you." The decision was made, and it led to their separation just two months before the unexpected passing of Walt.

She dated John Granger for several years in her younger days. He was the eldest son of the owner of one of the largest cattle stations in Cape York, Watson's River Station and was due to inherit the farm upon his father's passing. They had a substantial bond and were once engaged for three months. However, the winds of fate shifted when Carol crossed paths with Walt. The moment their gazes met, she recognised him as the singular lodestar of her heart. The magnetic pull was irresistible, and it became unequivocally clear Walt was the man who ignited the flames of her passion.

Despite the breakup, John and Carol remained steadfast friends. She would drop by for a visit and a heartfelt chat when her travels led her near Watson's River Station, a tradition she still upholds. Yet, through all the years and nostalgic encounters, Walt remained the North Star guiding her heart. She knew it with unwavering certainty from the moment they first locked eyes.

While his mining empire grew and Walt was away from home on increasingly frequent business trips, she became a dutiful housewife while raising their two children. As his wealth grew, and with the arrival of his cherished children, he took prudent steps to ensure their future. He drafted a comprehensive will in the early years of their marriage, designating Carol as the primary beneficiary of his vast holdings. Moreover, he established individual trusts for his beloved offspring, securing their financial well-being.

CHAPTER 4

Bruce came into the world as a member of the Wik mob, an indigenous Australian tribe. During his youth, he acquired tracking abilities taught by the group elders. He also excelled in hunting and fishing. With an intense fascination for bush skills, he soon recognised most local plant species by their names. He knew which plants were suitable for consumption and which ones to steer clear of due to their harmful or potentially deadly properties.

Amidst the Wik community's vast expanse, his presence was as bright as the sun-kissed sands. He effortlessly forged bonds with those around him, his trusting nature drawing people in. His openness, though, some would say, bordered on naivety, a trait that would eventually be proven correct. Yet, his demeanour was that of a keen learner, absorbing the world around him with an eagerness that set him apart.

From the tender age of four, Bruce would sit cross-legged in the company of his revered elders, gathering in a circle upon the warm, dry, crimson soil. Their worn fingers delicately sketched fleeting tales of the land onto the dirt canvas.

The eldest and most revered elder spoke first: "Young Bruce, you gotta listen to the old stories, our ancestors talkin'. The land, she shows ya, full of bush tucker and animals." His tone was sincere, and his eyes locked onto the young boys to display the significance of this newly imparted knowledge.

"Look here," said a second elder, carving and stamping patterns into the dry earth, "Tracks of emus, all kinds of kangaroos, cheeky wallabies, sneaky echidnas, and the winding paths of lizards and snakes. Bush tells them stories, right here in Country."

"I see, Elders," the young boy nodded, "I'll keep these shapes in my head, stitchin' my spirit to this land." His reply was earnest. Even as a young lad, Bruce was an intellectual figure.

With these whispered secrets, he ventured into the surrounding scrub, diligently searching for the trails he had learned intimately. Upon his return, the first elder spoke again, "With these secrets in ya, you'll start to see the tracks. In time, you'll learn how to track people too."

"The Wik mob sees ya got a sharp mind, you pick up wisdom quick," the second elder said, "We'll take ya deep into the bush, right to the heart."

The two men and the boy stood as the revered men walked with him, leading him deep into Wik-Mungkan country amidst swaying grasses and towering trees; the elders pointed to subtle shifts in the landscape.

"See that twig flipped over, that tiny thread hangin' on the branch, the way the grass been pressed down." As he spoke, the most revered elder's face bore the weight of wisdom and authority, etched with deep lines that spoke of countless experiences and the passage of time. His eyes, though weathered, glinted with a keen intelligence that commanded respect.

The young boy turned to the two men, "Thank you for sharin' the old people's wisdom; I'm real honoured." His round, expressive eyes sparkled with innocence and curiosity; a bright, genuine smile played on his tiny lips, showcasing his joy and pride in expressing such a grown-up sentiment.

During his numerous days wandering the surrounding scrub, Bruce's young eyes followed the human trails, committing each detail to memory. He gauged the person's weight by the depth of shoe or foot impressions in the sand, estimated their height from the impact on nearby grasslands, and discerned their gender from the size and contours of their footprints.

Bruce's heart pounded as he discerned the faintest signs. In this symphony of nature, he danced, playing intricate games of hide-and-seek with his peers. Each relied on newfound tracking skills to uncover the concealed.

By the tender age of eight, he possessed an uncanny gift—the kind that set him apart in the quiet, sun-drenched outback. His world was not one of schoolbooks and structured lessons but of open skies and the orchestra of avian voices gracing the land.

In his budding understanding, Bruce unlocked the secrets of the feathered residents of his homeland. He marvelled at the artistry of their song. To him, the very air carried the delicate trills of life. The high-pitched "pee-pee-pee" and "tsip-tsip-tsip" of the Australasian pipit, a serenade to the heavens, resonated within his keen ear. These lyrical notes adorned the bird's aerial displays and territorial disputes, a language dancing upon the wind.

The resplendent plumage of the Gouldian finch entranced him. Often referred to as the rainbow finch, this avian beauty earned its name from the dazzling array of colours adorning both males and females. Their feathers displayed a vibrant black, yellow, green, and red spectrum, with the females possessing a slightly more subdued brilliance. In the mating season, he was a connoisseur of sweet and musical notes, the male Gouldian finch's serenade to prospective partners. He cherished this serendipitous song heralding love's bloom. Yet, in the face of danger, he could discern the finch's call to arms—a sharp, high-pitched alarm, a clarion call of vigilance for the fellowship it held dear.

His discerning ear was not confined to one finch alone. Though the red-browed finch and the double-barred finch shared the same world of chirps, they bore distinctions only he could unravel. The double-barred finch painted its chirps with sharper strokes, a staccato rhythm contrasting the red-browed finch's soft, tinkling lullabies.

Among his cherished observations were the fairy martin and tree martin, master architects of the bush and grasslands. They, too, spoke in the language of design and devotion. Bruce held a special affection for the fairy martin's bottle-shaped mud nests. As the birds embarked on their northward migration, a precursor of summer's wane, he felt the world change around him. The lengthening shadows whispered the approach of shorter days.

Amidst the verdant grasslands, the young lad found joy in the aerial ballet of the tree martin. Their acrobatics enthralled him, an exquisite dance of life against the boundless azure canvas above. His gaze was drawn inexorably to their plumage—black against white, white against black—as if nature tumbled dominos from the heavens, a grand spectacle of order and chaos intertwined.

But the true opus of his life began to unfold when the elders invited him to delve into indigenous astronomy. At the age of nine or ten, they approached him. With reverence, the eldest of the men spoke, "Bruce, we reckon you now ready to learn the rhythm of the cosmos."

The second elder spoke, "The single stars, the mob of stars and them planet bodies up in the sky. They mean a lot in our ways. They follow the seasons, show us when tucker's good to be picked, and when the daddy emu's sittin' on the eggs, so we can go fetch them. The night sky up there guides us through the bush, the seas, and the waters around us. They tell us when it's time for our ceremonies and corroborees." Their stories whispered to him reverently, bridging the gap between sky and earth.

His essence trembled in recognition of the cosmic kinship, feeling the heartbeat of all existence. As stories wove, the tale of "The Canoe in the Sky," or, as the white fellas called it, "The Orion" constellation, entranced the young man. He marvelled at the connection between the heavens and life cycles below. His heart resonated with the ancient rhythms, and understanding these celestial motions guided the seasons of sustenance and ceremony.

A third elder spoke of the Orion saga, "Bruce, my son, one day, y'know, three bruddas from a nearby clan; they thought 'bout goin' fishin' in their canoe. When the day was done, they only caught a min wunkam, a rock cod. The bruddas got hungry and decided to go against our cultural law and eat that rock cod. Strangely enough, the rock cod was the youngest brudda's totem, you see. When the sun woman saw, she got real mad. She sent a strong wind, taking those three bruddas and their canoe into the night sky. Now, them three stars in the Orion belt, they're the three brothers in their canoe. And that big star in Orion's sword, that's that rock cod them brothers ate. The bright stars on Orion's shoulders and foot are like the two ends of the canoe gettin' drawn into the night."

A young man with an insatiable curiosity, he delved deep into the art of waterway navigation. Like life-giving veins coursing through the land, the rivers became his hunting grounds. He embarked on dug-out canoe journeys in the company of seasoned elders seeking the local barramundi fish in the waterways in and around his ancestral homeland. With time, the expanse of the Arafura Sea beckoned. Now a masterful mariner, he answered the call, becoming a hunter of the deep, seeking out sea turtles amidst the song lines and ancient constellations that held his trust.

These ancient song lines, woven into the fabric of tradition, found voice in the haunting strains of Dreaming Tracks. The elders, keepers of time's secrets, wove tales of cosmic architects shaping the world's personality during the Dreaming, the primordial genesis of Earth. They unravelled the land's mysteries - ancient monoliths, sacred pools, coursing rivers, consecrated trees, and the boundless expanse of sky and sea - through the rhythmic cadence of song and dance.

Moonlit nights found Bruce enraptured by constellations, his gaze reaching beyond the veil of stars. To him, they weren't distant firelights; they were ancestors watching over them, casting their blessings upon the earthbound. At fourteen, the mantle of maturity draped his shoulders. Paintings and stone alignments became his tools for time-keeping, handed down from generations past. As he studied these markers, the realisation dawned that over two hundred and fifty diverse mobs spread across the land, each with its language and dialect. The communication exchange followed the current of shared celestial stories, cave art, and handcrafted rock formations, bypassing the need for a shared language.

It was time for the first elder to speak again, his brow furrowed, and he looked at Bruce earnestly, a powerful spiritual connection forming between the man and the boy, "It be the time now, young fella. Yer standin' right there at the edge of becomin' a man. Yer totem, the salt-water crocodile, be given to ya by our mob and elders." He draped a crocodile tooth, bound by a leather cord, over the teenager's neck. Bruce bowed his head and bent his knees in reverence to accept this ancient gift, "See, you got this way 'bout ya, quiet but sharp like a tracker who knows things that the wind whispers. It's a bond, that is. A bond that echoes the quiet strength ya got as a hunter. This creature, it be in ya, woven in yer very soul. This necklace should serve as a reminder of that. So ya take hold of it. Yer to hold back from eatin' its flesh, mate. 'Cause eatin' it, it's like takin' a piece of yer own spirit." The elder then turned to the other two respected tribe men, "He got that deep truth, fellas. His eyes and heart got filled up with the wisdom our old ones handed down." The others silently nodded in agreement.

Bruce looked straight at the elder, right into his eyes and thoughts, soaking in this moment. His young mind cementing this milestone occasion. "Thank you," bowing his head in respect, "This story, this totem, it be bestowed upon me by the first elder, the one we all look up to. It is an honour." His eyes looked toward the ground as his lids closed, taking this moment and etching it into his consciousness. It was a profound moment in his life that was never forgotten.

Like the ebb and flow of desert winds, his existence was destined for greatness, a respected figure within his mob. As he ventured into the untamed wilderness of manhood, his skills as a tracker and hunter flourished, transforming him into a vital provider for his clan.

His innate connection with the land bore fruit, often in such abundance that it overflowed, and the surplus was freely shared not just amongst his clan but also among fellow mob members. He couldn't have imagined a more gratifying existence in those moments of communal feasts, laughter, and gratitude. His enthusiasm soared with each successful hunt, and his heart swelled with pride, for he fulfilled his role with utmost devotion.

But, as life often unfolds, destiny can alter its course with a single twist. It was a fateful day when Walt Henry, a white fella with the allure of places beyond the horizon, appeared on the fringes of Bruce's world. With a presence seeming to challenge the essence of the outback, Walt wove himself into Bruce's life, gently at first, then with a grip tightening like the coils of a serpent.

CHAPTER 5

Walt's arrival brought a subtle transformation that slowly unravelled the bonds of trust within Bruce's mob. The stories he told, the ideas he planted, and his apparent genuine interest in the mob's culture and ways of life had the power to captivate and bewitch. Soon, the whispers of ancient secrets, hitherto guarded fiercely, found their way into Walt's ears. Secrets passed down through descendants, stories stamped into the sacred landscapes of the Dreamtime, now threatened to fall into the hands of a stranger.

It had been over three decades since Bruce first crossed paths with Walt, a meeting fixed in his memory as if it unfolded just yesterday. The sands of time failed to erode the vividness of that moment, and the recollections, like repulsive relics, remained remarkably preserved in his mind's eye.

At thirty-one, Walt worked with the Geological Survey branch of the Queensland Department of Resources after completing his qualifications as an assayer. While initially sceptical of Walt and his intentions, Bruce, at eighteen, gradually developed a sense of trust towards him. Being so far north, encounters with white fellas were rare, and they usually only appeared for their gain. However, this outsider displayed a genuine interest in the ways and traditions of the indigenous tribes from the time he first set foot in the town. Bruce thought this man went above and beyond, utilising his four-wheel drive to provide local children with rides to school and offering assistance to their community whenever someone fell ill, whether providing financial aid or arranging for a doctor to visit their remote settlement. He recalled how Walt asked him to teach him the ways and language of his people. The young man readily agreed and efficiently instructed him in his mob's local dialect. Walt quickly grasped the intricacies. In the brief span of one year, Walt became adept at communicating with the indigenous population of Weipa and beyond, wherever the mob's influence extended.

One fateful day, Bruce made the decision that still haunts him, recalling the time as if it happened yesterday. He deeply regretted his choice, for he shared something significant with this intruder. It was a secret rooted in his mob's cultural heritage and entrusted to only a few. A decision that would turn his life upside down and enrage his kin.

Bruce approached Walt. "Ya know, I reckon you're a true mate to me. You've earned me trust and the trust of me people. I reckon it's time to share somethin' sacred with ya. There be a special place in Cape York, hidden away, known only to our mob. It's where the spirits of our ancestors dwell. A holy site with rocks that carry these beautiful spirals, like nothin' else ya ever seen."

"Spirals, you say? What sets them apart? What makes them so special?" Walt appeared captivated, a glint in his eye.

"These here stones, mate, hold a power like no other. As a people, we reckon our connection to this land, the trees, the rocks, and the critters runs as deep as our bond with one another. We are the land, and the land is us. Them swirls, they burst with colours, like the rainbow serpent herself. White, grey, red, yella and brown. They been bringin' healin' to our tribes for generations. It's a place where our people find peace and feel the presence of our ancestors," he explained. He was sharing a piece of his heritage with this outsider, a dangerous move typically, but Bruce felt he could trust his youthful instincts.

Walt responded humbly, "I feel honoured that you're willing to share such a sacred place with me. How far away is it, mate?"

"It be a long way, fella, no doubt 'bout it. The sacred place lies deep within our ancestral lands. It's a protected spot. It's time for ya to experience it to find a deeper bond with our land and its people."

"Thanks a lot," Walt expressed, his voice tinged with genuine gratitude. His smile radiated warmth, reflecting his sincere appreciation for the opportunity that lay before him. The significance of the impending journey filled the air with a palpable sense of enthusiasm. "To witness something of such immense importance means a great deal to me," he remarked, his head bowed in reverence.

Walt's eyes met Bruce's once again, and they shimmered with curiosity and eagerness as he spoke, his genuine interest evident in how he hung on to every word. With a touch of anticipation, he inquired, "Is there anything I should be mindful of or prepare for as we embark on this venture?" His openness to guidance echoed through his words, demonstrating his readiness to embrace whatever lay ahead.

"Ya gotta show respect for our sacred place. Approach it with reverence and humility. Understandin' and honourin' the cultural significance it holds for me people is key. We gotta tread lightly and leave no mark behind, ya hear?" Bruce emphasised. "And never, I repeat, never take any rocks from our sacred place. Those who do so are sure to face a horrible fate." He looked Walt directly in the eye as he spoke; this was not a decision he had undertaken lightly, and he wanted to know that this white man understood the significance of the invitation.

Walt extended his hand, displaying his sincerity. "You have my word," he said, and they sealed the agreement with a firm handshake.

As arranged, the men made their way to the sacred site two days later with Bruce behind the wheel. After two hours over rough terrain and journeying via dirt tracks, they came to a clearing. Bruce bowed his head and silently slipped out of the vehicle. He led Walt to a large stone wall covered in vibrant spirals and gently touched the rocks, closing his eyes as if soaking up the energy from within.

Bruce felt a profound connection transcending the physical realm in the sacred embrace of the land and its ancient spirits. The wisdom of ages whispered through his veins, imbuing him with a sense of deep peace and serenity. For a moment, his connection with the spiritual realm wavered, and he reluctantly opened his eyes, catching a glimpse of a sparkling expectation in his new friend's gaze. Amidst this ethereal communion, he couldn't help but notice a change in Walt's focused gaze. A flicker of something different stirred a separate current of thoughts within him.

Walt's gaze fell upon the sedimentary rocks before them. A wry smile crept onto his face, and his pupils dilated.

"What ya thinkin', brudda?" asked Bruce.

"No wonder you picked this place as sacred. It looks like high-grade bauxite to me," came the speedy reply. Walt reached out and touched the wall, not in the serene way Bruce had, but taking a more academic approach. A broad grin now spread across his face, his eyebrows raised in excitement.

While the younger man remained blissfully unaware of Walt's true intentions, a subtle shift in the air pricked at his senses. There was now an aura of foreboding, a premonition of things to come. His intuition detected this subtle change but struggled to decipher its meaning. Unbeknownst to him, Walt yearned to confirm his suspicions and unlock the boundless financial possibilities concealed within the rocks.

On the drive home, both men were reticent; Bruce strongly suspected he should never have shown this white fella his sacred place. He noticed the gleam in his passenger's eyes and regretted his decision immediately.

"You okay, fella?" he asked.

"Yeah, mate, just dandy," came the reply, his eyes sparkling. Bruce could see the dollar signs in his eyes and was overcome with deep regret.

He later discovered Walt had returned to the site that evening and collected small rocks and scrapings from the area. The samples confirmed high-grade, commercial deposits of aluminium containing bauxite. The outsider quickly staked his claim, securing his entitlement to the valuable land. However, in a shrewd manoeuvre, Walt omitted Bruce's name from the mining claim application. It was a calculated move, one that would carry enduring repercussions. This action unfolded within the context of an era where such actions by a white fella were not uncommon, transpiring long before the enactment of the Aboriginal Land Rights Act in Queensland. The prevailing sentiment of "finders, keepers" dictated the course of land acquisition, often marginalising the rights of the original inhabitants.

While seemingly advantageous in the short term, Walt's strategic decision laid the foundation for a defining chapter in their relationship. The consequences of this omission would unfold over time, shaping the trajectory of their connection in ways that neither could fully comprehend at that pivotal moment.

After learning of this news, Bruce's fury smouldered like a raging inferno in his mind. The revelation scorched his ego, a betrayal of the deepest kind. His so-called friend plunged a dagger into the heart of their tribe, a wound that cut through generations. The sacred and revered land was stolen from them.

With the weight of injustice pressing upon him, Bruce sought counsel from the eldest of his kin. Bruce's voice was booming as he addressed the council of three, ancient wisdom echoing through the air, "A grave injustice has been wrought upon us," he growled, eyes smouldering with unquenchable fire.

Their brows furrow in deep thought; the council deliberated in hushed tones. It was decreed that Bruce must attempt to reason with the betrayer, to plead for redemption and sanity amidst the desecration. It was a last chance for Walt to heed the call of the ancients and spare the sacred site from further violation.

A foreboding satisfaction twisted Bruce's lips as he embarked on the mission. He sought Walt out, and, in a clandestine meeting at the white man's home, he laid bare the will of his people, the echo of ancestral voices reverberating in the air. "Y' gotta put a stop to this disrespect," he commanded, his voice tinged with the steel of ancestors past. "When you take what ain't yours; when you steal the rocks, it ain't just bauxite. It's a sacred place, a haven for our spirits and peace."

Walt's response was a cold gust, slicing through the air like a dagger. "The die is cast. I've staked my claim, and the land is now solely in my name. I have the freedom to do with it as I see fit," he sneered, the arrogance of a conqueror exuding from every pore.

Bruce's eyes narrowed, his voice dripping with a chilling premonition, "Ya keep walkin' down this path of destruction, understand this: them elders, they got power beyond what you can imagine. They might take up the bone, channelin' the anger of a thousand generations straight at ya. It's a curse. A payback that'll stick to ya 'til your last gasp."

The words hung like a shroud, a portentous omen. Bruce's warning was not to be taken lightly, a harbinger of doom for the man who dared defy the sacred. Walt was quick to dismiss the threats. He harboured scant reverence for Aboriginal traditions, holding little faith in their mystic potency. At that moment, the die was indeed cast.

Two years elapsed, and the fruits of Walt's astute investment manifested when he made a lucrative deal with

Comalco, selling his mining claim for a staggering $2.2 million. The company recognised the area's untapped potential and spent little time initiating commercial mining operations. Comalco's endeavours proved immensely successful as time progressed, prompting the eventual sale of their mining interests to industry giant Rio Tinto.

Bruce was distraught. He'd tried to reconcile with Walt, to allow him to right his wrongs. The man refused to listen. Leaving Bruce with no other choice, he consulted his elders again. The tribe's men gathered on law grounds for a significant ceremonial gathering, a corroboree. Together, they deliberated on the appropriate course of action to address Walt's grievous acts. Not only had he defiled their sacred place of healing, but he had also sold their land from underneath them.

The wise elders decided to seek justice and restoration for the wrongdoing. After much deliberation, they concluded Walt should be "sung" or have the bone pointed at him by Bruce, the harshest of all punishments. They initiated a process involving crafting a kangaroo bone into a pointed tool, carefully coating its tip with resin. While performing sacred chants and rituals, they imbued this instrument with potent mystical powers, intending to bring about severe consequences or even death to the one responsible for the desecration.

In addition, they fashioned a pair of unique footwear known as kurdaitcha, carefully constructing a thick pad of emu feathers intertwined with the blood of a young tribal man. The intricate design included a network of human hair, symbolically representing the collective wisdom and strength of the tribe's elders. Due to the immense negative energy contained within these items, it was paramount that they remained concealed from the women and children.

Following the completion of the shoes, by their customary practices, the foremost elder respectfully asked Bruce to take a seat. The elder gently softened the joint with a heated stone to the base of Bruce's smallest right toe with precision and caution. In one swift motion, the elder dislocated the joint, causing Bruce to recoil in pain. Despite the discomfort, Bruce remained composed, aware of the importance of adhering to the established rules and traditions. Following the ceremony, he returned home, each step a painful journey along the familiar path leading to his dwelling in the settlement. A haphazardly constructed and overcrowded tin shed awaited him.

The following day, he set out to find Walt, driving to his house in Weipa, before placing the kurdaitcha upon his feet, his right toe still throbbing from the recent dislocation. Silently, he walked through the scrub surrounding his betrayer's house, intending to curse and confront him. The front door was open, and silently, Bruce shuffled in. His newly acquired footwear was designed not to make a noise or leave a trace.

He found Walt in the kitchen and immediately took out the cursed bone from his trouser pocket, pointing it directly at the traitor: "I curse you! You wreak havoc upon my boodja, my people, and our sacred places, brudda. To think I once called you kin," his words resonated with the weight of his people's pain. His face etched with fury, his nostrils flared, and his brows were drawn together in a fierce V.

"If this is about the mining contract, don't worry, mate. You'll get your share," Walt replied, taken aback by the sudden confrontation.

"No bloody money can fix what ya done to our sacred site. Ya wrecked it good, mate. Now ya cursed, the land cursed, and the spirits, they're fumin'," Bruce's voice surged angrily. "Now ya gonna pay, pay with ya life. I curse ya, Walt Henry. I curse this house and ya whole fuckin' family." His words carried the echoes of his ancestors, the ache of a violated legacy, and the righteous fire of his people. The depth of betrayal fuelled Bruce's will to bring justice and ensure the consequences of this man's actions echoed through his existence and his kin.

"Settle down, mate. Here's what I'll do: give you two hundred and twenty thousand dollars. That's quite a bit of money. You could do a lot with that. Help your mob out; buy a bus for the kids to get to school."

"Ya bloody snake! Ya made a promise. You promised not to touch our sacred place, fella. We sealed it with a handshake, eye to eye, ya bastard," Bruce's voice seethed with frustration.

Consumed by a profound sense of vengeance, he stood solid in Walt's house, pointing the bone directly at him. The ancient incantations rolled off his tongue with an unnerving intensity, each syllable laced with a potent mixture of anger and retribution. The room echoed his words as only the walls bore witness to the enormity of the transgression fuelling his wrath.

Walt appeared trapped in stunned disbelief, finding himself at the mercy of this dark ritual. In this chilling encounter, the ancestral spirits invoked seemed to respond, lending an otherworldly presence to the unfolding ritual. The atmosphere crackled with an electric tension. In that instant, destiny was set to unfurl its unforgiving hand.

Bruce returned to his community with a profound sense of closure. He had carried out what he believed to be the necessary reckoning for the desecration inflicted upon his people and their sacred land. Justice, in its raw and unbending form, had been enacted.

The following day, Bruce stirred from his slumber with anticipation and trepidation. As the dawn's light gradually illuminated his surroundings, he couldn't shake the heavy burden. Uncertainty clung to his heart like a suffocating fog, reminding him of the bone-pointing ceremony and its impact on Walt's life. The significance of that event lingered in his mind, refusing to fade away. Soon, a palpable presence tainted the air around him. He knew Walt was not far away.

His senses heightened as the traitor drew nearer to the mob's grounds. The air crackled with tension, the undercurrent of emotions almost tangible. He could practically taste the remorse emanating from Walt. This stirred a whirlwind of emotions: bitterness mingled with curiosity, anger clashing with a flicker of longing for reconciliation. This encounter could redefine their relationship, either deepen the wounds or offer a glimmer of redemption.

Joined by two tribal elders, the young man stood his ground. Walt spoke humbly and bowed regretfully before looking directly at Bruce, "Please listen. I come here today seeking your forgiveness and reconciliation."

With a sombre expression, Bruce responded, "You know what you done, eh? Hurt real bad, them wounds still cuttin' deep. Ain't healed yet, them scars still fresh. I can't forgive ya, not now."

"I understand your position. My heart aches, as it should." Walt said, his shoulders slumped, his eyes downcast.

One of the elders turned to Bruce, "Listen, son. Our mob been through it 'cause of him. You been hurt bad, real bad."

"I been hurt real bad, real bad," he replied nodding in agreement."

It was then the most senior and respected elder of the tribe who took it upon himself to speak to the betrayer, "We hear you sorry, but that hurt you caused, it don't just go away like that. We need time to heal up, time to get that trust back."

He gently responded, "I understand, and my heart grieves. We have much to work through. I respect that. I can offer you money."

"Forgiveness don't come easy, nah. Tjukurpa says so. No money gonna bring back our sacred place," the first elder spoke again, his tone challenging.

"I understand, and I respect the laws of the land," he responded, his shoulders slumped, his sad eyes filled with remorse.

With that, Walt returned to his car and drove away. He never kept his promise to regain the trust of Bruce or his mob. Little did he know the surreal twist of fate awaited him a mere forty-eight hours later. Returning to what he now dubbed the "quarry," Walt carefully arranged sticks of dynamite, attempting to break the bauxite-rich ore into submission. Yet, from some unseen realm, a capricious spark materialised, an evil phantom that, in a deafening crescendo, callously severed the fourth and fifth digits of his left hand and left him completely deaf in his left ear.

From that fateful moment onward, a creeping unease enveloped his consciousness, an unshakable wariness that cast a shadow of doubt over his Aboriginal acquaintance and his enigmatic, sorcerous powers.

In the wake of the calamity, the rage consuming the mob was a storm of betrayal, ancient bonds sundered by an act of perceived treachery. To them, Bruce violated an unspoken pact standing since time immemorial: the solemn covenant never to share their sacred heritage with those outside the sanctified bloodline. The wisdom of the land, the secrets of survival, the sanctity of the Dreamtime—all were meant for the chosen few, the guardians of their hallowed ancestral legacy.

Despite the elders' rejection of the money, Bruce, trapped by the siren call of wealth, eventually yielded. The promise of an abundant bounty proved too enticing to spurn, and he claimed his share without a moment's pause, forging a rift that would echo through the corridors of their once close-knit community. As the murmurs of dissent grew louder, the elders of the mob convened in solemn council, their decision echoing through the ages. The young man's fate was sealed with the weight of tradition, a verdict that carried the harshest of sentences—exile. His place among his people was forfeited, his name a whispered curse.

He found himself adrift, the shackles of his past haunting him like a relentless ghost, far from the untamed Australian bush that had once been his sanctuary. He retreated to the claustrophobic space of a makeshift dwelling far from his mob, seeking solace in the numbing embrace of alcohol, his dreams of eventually rising to the status of a revered elder now nothing more than fading embers in the darkness. The man who had once been the pride of his clans was now a solitary figure, a stranger to himself, drinking himself to death on the unforgiving outskirts of Weipa.

With each passing day, Bruce's life spiralled further into decline. The bottle became his steadfast companion, numbing the pain and fuelling his inner turmoil. The unresolved rage, stemming from the betrayal he endured, consumed him from within. Stripped of purpose and haunted by the grudges he held, he soon found himself completely disengaged from his mob, existing on the fringes of society.

As the years followed, alcoholism and pent-up rage consumed him. He now lived in a shanty on the outskirts of town, relying on government handouts for survival. Decades came and went. His hair flowed untamed, untouched by scissors, while his once ebony beard surrendered to the wintry touch of age, resembling a cascade of snowflakes. His humble abode, a weathered shanty, bore no allegiance to modern comforts, no running water to quench his thirst and no connection to the pulsating currents of town electricity. On the infrequent instances when he sought respite in the cleansing embrace of a shower, it was within the confines of a public restroom nestled in town or through a covert escapade into the hidden corners of the local caravan park, veiled by the darkness of night. An indefinable yet ever-present musty scent wafted about him, a testament to his solitary and bare existence.

CHAPTER 6

One week earlier

An extravagant and quintessential Australian party, the epitome of indulgence, unfolded as the sun dipped low on the horizon. Walt's sixty-fifth birthday celebration was no ordinary affair; it was a magnetic lure to everyone in the town and surrounding areas. They flocked to "the Alby" with eager hearts, lured by the promise of the finest Australian cuisine money could buy.

The anticipation in the air was palpable, drawing the curious, the hungry, and the gourmands alike. The alluring whispers of free-flowing booze and lavish feasting traversed far and wide, capturing the imagination and desire of all. There was, however, one notable exception, and that was Davo. As the junior of the two police officers in town, duty called, and someone had to remain behind to watch over the station.

As guests arrived at the venue, they were greeted by a scene that seemed like it had been plucked from the pages of a grand novel. Enormous marquees, adorned in vibrant colours and balloons, hosted the evening's culinary spectacle. Within these luxury tents, the heart of the feast unfolded.

Spit roasts showcased succulent pigs and lambs, slowly revolving above hot coals, sending the scent of sizzling meat wafting through the air. Within the marquees, enormous seafood platters overflowed with fresh prawns from the Gulf of Carpentaria, oysters flown in from South Australia, Tasmanian smoked salmon, seared scallops, and delicate slices of tuna and salmon sashimi. Whole baked barramundi, delicately seasoned with lemon myrtle, bush pepper, and succulent lobsters, their tender flesh bathed in a decadent butter sauce infused with the finest caviar. Plates were piled high with mud crab claws, lovingly prepared, glistening with zesty lime and chilli butter, delivering an irresistible kick of spice to complement the sweet, delicate meat within.

The Country Women's Association (CWA) played a central role. Their dessert plates were garnished with pavlovas that crumbled with a whisper, lamingtons with coconut-dusted allure, and finger foods beckoning with temptation - homemade sausage rolls and mini quiches; each bite an exploration of taste and texture. Among the tireless members of the CWA was Carol, who had recently separated from Walt but was still deeply entrenched in his life. She played a significant role in the association since its inception in Weipa, and her expert touch was evident in every delectable morsel on display. She knew his palate better than anyone else.

The spectacle did not end with the entrancing spit roasts or the delectable desserts. Drizzled with a velvety truffle-infused olive oil, roasted root vegetables brought a comforting warmth to the table. Their earthy sweetness harmonised with the succulent meats and seafood, creating a symphony of flavours that danced on the palate.

The wine flowed freely, with each bottle carefully selected to complement the diverse array of tastes on offer. The wine selection demonstrated the sommelier's expertise, from crisp, mineral-laden Chardonnays to robust, velvety Shirazes.

Guests were presented with a seemingly boundless array of culinary options. Platters of salads spanning the spectrum from Caesar to green, potato to fruit, painted a vibrant and flavourful picture. Crisp, fresh greens mingled with creamy dressings, while fruits brought a refreshing sweetness to the palate.

This extravagant Australian banquet was more than a feast; it was a celebration of indulgence, a reminder that the bonds of community and shared experiences are as enduring as they are nourishing. Walt's sixty-fifth birthday would become an unforgettable chapter in the town's collective narrative for more than one reason.

For Bruce Hudson, this moment shimmered like an iridescent sliver of destiny, a long-awaited chance to face Walt, whose actions carved profound scars upon his heart and his kin, stretching back through the jumble of years. This was the juncture he'd longed for, an opportunity to unmask the true essence of this respected figure in the eyes of the entire town.

Thirty-five years ago, Bruce had brandished the pointed bone, an ancient and formidable tool of power, aiming it at Walt as an act of mystical retribution. Today, seasoned by the passage of time and emboldened with Dutch courage, he nurtured a desire to fully harness the bone's immense power, ready to unleash its profound consequences. This time, he vowed to summon every ounce of the bone's magic, ensuring justice was unquestionably served.

The scent of stale alcohol enveloped him like a poignant whisper, serving as a bitter remembrance of the potent elixir that both bolstered his mettle and honed his unwavering commitment to the mission. The weight of his past injuries pressed upon him, etching lines of conviction onto his face as he delved into the recesses of his memory, reliving the events that unfolded more than three decades ago.

As he steered his vehicle toward the Alby, the engine's hum harmonising with the thudding of his heartbeat, his intentions blazed like a wildfire within him. Every detail and emotion flooded back with vivid intensity, freezing the present moment and transporting him back to those days when his life changed forever.

Now, making his way to the pub to confront Walt on his birthday, he placed his right hand deep within his pocket; his fingers closed around the sharpened kangaroo bone, its edges honed to a deadly point. This bone symbolised his lingering anguish, something he held onto for all these years, a physical manifestation of his desire to bring Walt to justice. The bone was clutched tightly, almost as if it were an extension of his very being, a testament to his unwavering vow to see this mission through.

The alcohol coursing through his veins was a volatile catalyst, fuelling his assurance and granting him a fleeting sense of fearlessness. He placed his kurdaitcha upon his feet and silently walked toward the tavern. As he pushed open the doors of the Alby, the air thick with anticipation, he prepared himself to unleash the full force of his conviction.

As his eyes scanned the room, he caught sight of the man in question, Walt's laughter echoing raucously as he enjoyed a pint with some mates at the bar. The swing band on the stage set the atmosphere alive, and the dance floor pulsed with vibrant energy. Bruce's pent-up fury surged within him, urging him to take action.

He retrieved the bone he was clutching, his knuckles turning pale as he held it with a strong, firm grip, its sharpened edges glistening with an ominous gleam. This bone, a forceful symbol of ancestral heritage and unspoken grievances, embodied the weight of his suppressed anger.

With a mix of torment and disdain visible upon his face, he confronted Walt, releasing a torrent of accusations, laying bare his deepest frustrations, "Ya deceitful bastard!" Bruce's voice cut through the festive ambience, carrying the raw intensity of his emotions. His words reverberated with a unique cadence, "You were never me brudda, just a treacherous presence in me life. I cast upon ya a curse, a reckonin' ya can't escape. Your time is limited, for ya must be held accountable for the atrocities ya committed against me mob. Ya stole our ancestral land, desecrated our sacred site, and now, ya finally gonna face the consequences."

Unwavering in his quest, he held the bone steady, its jagged tip aimed directly at Walt's heart, leaving no room for doubt regarding his intent to inflict harm. His gaze, an intense vortex of tenacity, delved deep into the man's soul as he began reciting ancient incantations, his voice resonating with a primal power that seemed to transcend time.

As the invocations flowed from his lips, he slipped into a trance-like state. His eyes, previously filled with fire, now showed only the whites as they rolled back into his head, giving him an otherworldly appearance. The power of the bone surged forth, coursing through Walt's body like a torrential river carrying the weight of ancestral wounds and a solid quest for vengeance.

In the room, an uncanny silence blanketed the witnesses, their collective focus entirely fixated on Bruce's lone figure. The air grew thick with the palpable aura of his desire for reprisal and his longing for redress, creating an atmosphere pregnant with tension and anticipation.

Once a mere instrument, the bone underwent a profound metamorphosis, evolving into a tangible embodiment of retribution. It absorbed and channelled countless kith and kin's accumulated fury, its presence in the room exuding an invincible force. Fixed unwaveringly upon Walt's heart, it bore witness to unwavering purpose, a symbol that the transgressions of yesteryears would never fade into the annals of forgotten history.

Bruce's exit from the chamber was a measured ballet of purpose, a deliberate pivot resonating with the weight of a mission fulfilled. He departed, leaving behind an atmosphere charged with formidable authority. None present could claim to have witnessed a spectacle of such magnitude before. The memories of the event would linger.

A collective enchantment seemed to hold the entire populace, a momentary trance where words lay dormant. Their gazes flitted covertly between one another, rousing briefly from the shared reverie. A pervasive sense of bafflement descended in its wake.

As the seconds stretched on, Gladys dared to break the silence. Her eyes widened with disbelief, her mouth agape like a doorway to the unknown. "Well, what da ya know?" she blurted out. Her rough, unrefined voice echoed through the room like the raw, untamed rush of a river. "Wasn't that the strangest bloody thing you've ever seen?" Her words hung in the air.

As Bruce's car hummed in the distance, its sound growing fainter with each passing moment, he retreated to his shanty, leaving a trail of unanswered questions. The mystery of the motive behind this confrontation on what should have been a joyous occasion lingered, etching itself indelibly in the minds of all who bore witness to this inexplicable event. The pub's patrons, their voices stifled by the weight of the unspoken, couldn't help but exchange furtive glances conveying their shared curiosity and unease.

Having broken the silence, Gladys gazed around the room, taking in the bewildered faces surrounding her. She could sense the unspoken questions hanging heavily in the air, and her inquiry merely scratched the surface of the collective intrigue.

Judy, her best friend, leaned in closer, her eyes gleaming with fascination. "Ya reckon Bruce's got somethin' to do with Walt's missin' fingers, Glad?" she whispered, her voice carrying a trace of fear, "Ya reckon somethin' bad's gonna happen to the birthday boy now?"

Gladys shrugged, her eyes fixed on the door through which Bruce exited. "Hard to say," she replied in a hushed tone. "But somethin' tells me this ain't the last we'll hear about it."

It was now Walt's turn to take action. Over the years, the man often bore the brunt of rumours and innuendo in the small, tight-knit community. No one was privy to the circumstances leading to the loss of his two left-hand fingers, with speculations permeating the air that the accident was somehow related to a confrontation between Bruce and him many years ago. Still, Walt never deigned to confirm or refute these reports.

He strode purposefully to the stage, his every step reverberating through the hollow wooden floor. Upon reaching the platform, he approached the microphone, intending to address the crowd and diffuse the tangible tension in the room. Like every community member, he recognised that speculations would fester and spread if he failed to confront the proverbial elephant in the room, further complicating an already delicate situation.

"Now, this is not the speech I intended to give on my birthday," Walt began, his voice echoing through the vast space as he reached into his pocket, retrieving a crumpled piece of paper. Still reeling from the shock, the onlookers held their breath in hushed suspense as he tightened his grip on the paper, his fingers forming a vice-like hold. Then, with a sudden, purposeful motion, he let go, and the paper unfurled in the air. Its crisp sound, akin to the rustling of dry leaves stirred by a gentle breeze, resonated as the sole noise in the room—a stark contrast to the previous profound stillness blanketing the space.

"Before I begin, I want to say I don't want to hear a bad word about Bruce," his voice projected to the attentive audience. "This is all on me. I brought this upon myself. I did him a great wrong, and I deeply regret it." He bowed his head in remorse as he spoke, his eyes glistening with the weight of his repentance.

Walt stood before his fellow townsfolk, his rugged face fixed with a deep sense of purpose. He decided it was time to break his silence and reveal the truth behind the bone-pointing confrontation, a revelation that would lay bare the mysteries that had haunted the town for far too long.

Walt's weathered voice cut through the tension-laden air as he recounted the story that remained locked within the depths of his being for decades. His tale unfolded like a well-worn map, revealing the secrets of the past, and as he spoke, the room seemed to hold its collective breath. "It all started long ago," Walt began, his eyes scanning the faces of his neighbours, friends, and fellow townsfolk. "I was young, much younger than I am now, and I ventured deep into the heart of this land, seeking riches I believed would be found within its sacred soil."

He continued to speak, his words weaving narrative-like pages turning in a novel, "I journeyed to the remote reaches of Far North Queensland with Bruce as my guide. He led me to a concealed cave known only to a few indigenous elders. Inside that cave, Bruce shared with me the stories of its ancient wisdom and mystical powers. That encounter changed everything for me." He paused momentarily, collecting his thoughts, "I was young and naive," his voice carrying the weight of guilt, "Even though Bruce impressed upon me the profound importance of this sacred site to his mob. I dismissed their traditions as mere superstition, thinking them irrelevant. I ignored his earnest advice not to disrupt their hallowed ceremonial ground; all I could see was the lure of wealth. I saw commercial-grade bauxite, which blinded me."

His head hung low as he contemplated the harm his actions wrought. "I trespassed upon land that was considered sacred and claimed the land as my own, unwittingly shattering a delicate balance that had endured for thousands of years. Bruce came to me early on and warned me of the risks of proceeding. He implored me to stop. I ignored him, continuing to explore the hallowed site. Two years later, I sold the title to Comalco for a sizable profit. In response, the elders of Bruce's Wik-Mungkan mob implored him to have me sung, point the bone, and curse my name."

There was a haunted pause as the gravity of his words sank in, "Bruce came to me mere days after I sold my mining claim; all this business unfolded over three decades ago. He stood in my house wearing nothing more than a loin cloth, body paint, ornamental beads in his hair, and shoes made of feathers, human hair and blood. At that time, I dismissed it all as nonsense, just a bunch of mumbo-jumbo. Yet, to my astonishment, just two days later, an unexplainable spark erupted while I stood at that quarry, preparing dynamite to fracture the bauxite. It cost me two of my left fingers and deafened me in my left ear as if the spirits swiftly exacted their retribution." Walt continued, his voice laden with reflection, "But what I failed to grasp at the time was the deeper significance of it all. The bone-pointing served as a warning, a means to impart the vital lesson of respecting the land, its traditions, and its people. I now know I was lucky only to lose two fingers. The events that unfolded tonight have left me deeply unsettled, and I solemnly vow, in the presence of every one of you here, that I will find a way to make amends to Bruce when the moment is fitting. You have my word, and all of you are now witnesses to this solemn pledge."

Once more, the room descended into a profound silence, but this time, it was a silence imbued with comprehension. The townsfolk, once confused and distrustful, now collectively realized the situation's significance. Walt's revelation opened the door to a mutual understanding of their intrinsic connection with the land and its indigenous stewards. It also shed light on the mystery of Walt's absent fingers and clarified Bruce's enduring resentment over the years.

"Now that we've got that out of the way," Walt chimed in, his cheery disposition adding a touch of down-to-earth charm to his words, "Let's crack on with the party! There's no point in lettin' all this top-notch grub and grog go to waste. We're 'ere to have a bloody good time!" He raised his half-empty schooner of XXXX Bitter beer in the air, "Cheers!"

A thunderous eruption of applause and jubilant cheers shattered the tension gripping the packed pub and surrounding grounds. It was as if the revelry, temporarily suspended, surged to life with newfound vigour. For now, the impact of the speech and the weight of its implications slipped into the recesses of collective memory. That could be pondered on another day, for tonight was Walt's—a night destined for merriment and celebration.

The night wore on, the stars painted the sky with their twinkling canvas, and the celebration at Walt's birthday party grew livelier. Laughter and music filled the air, and the clinking of glasses and hearty cheers echoed through the balmy night.

Walt, the man of the hour, moved from one group to another, sharing stories, trading jokes, and clapping his mates on the back. His voice reverberated with warmth and camaraderie as he regaled his friends with tales of their shared adventures and mishaps over the years.

Meanwhile, the pub's band struck up a lively tune, and the dance floor quickly filled with merrymakers, their feet tapping and bodies swaying to the rhythm of the music. Couples twirled, friends linked arms, and even some elderly folks couldn't resist joining in, their faces lighting up joyfully.

As the hours slipped away and the clock neared the wee hours of the morning, the party showed no signs of slowing down. Walt, the life of the party, led the charge, his mind fixed on making this night one for the history books. In this small community, birthdays were more than just milestones; they were an opportunity to strengthen bonds, forge memories, and celebrate the essence of mateship, defining them as Australians.

Over the coming days, the story of Walt's missing fingers was recounted multiple times, and the bizarre confrontation with Bruce continued to cast a long shadow over the residents of Weipa. Murmurs of conjecture and hearsay about what would transpire next swirled in an unending cyclone, each rendition ballooning in size and extravagance with every retelling.

Amidst the persistent intrigue, Walt pressed on with his customary routines, devoting his days to leisurely pursuits on his expansive property at the town's periphery. His absent fingers an enduring reminder of that distressing day, but also a symbol of his reluctance to unveil the mysteries shrouding the bone-pointing incident. He managed to maintain this silence for decades, guarding those secrets with unwavering willpower, until his sixty-fifth birthday, when fate finally turned the tide of revelation for his hand and the truth it concealed.

Gladys and Judy often discussed the strange occurrence during their regular visits to the Alby. Each time, their conversations drifted toward the inexplicable, their curiosity unabated. The two friends couldn't help but wonder if hidden forces were at play, which had yet to reveal their true intentions.

Meanwhile, Bruce kept a low profile, seemingly content with his abrupt exit from the hotel that night. The ever-watchful community couldn't help but speculate about his next moves. Some believed he returned to his hut to seek protection from the unknown forces he provoked, while others thought he might be planning something even more mysterious or malicious.

CHAPTER 7

In the wake of their grisly discovery of Walt's body on Sunday afternoon, Phil and Davo settled to divide and conquer, enabling them to cover as much ground as possible before the information was distorted by local gossip. Phil assumed the responsibility of notifying the next of kin while he suggested Davo undertake a discrete ring around before making enquiries at the local caravan park.

Among all the people Phil knew, Walt's ex-wife, Carol, held the closest connection to him. He told Davo, "I'll drive to see Carol and tell her the bad news. It might take a while, so I'll meet you at the station when you finish your calls and enquiries at the campground."

"Sure thing, boss," Davo replied, happy to be relieved of his administrative duties.

Phil turned to his junior officer once more, his voice laden with urgency, "Mate, we've got to dive headfirst into the heart of this community and extract every morsel of local wisdom ASAP. Today's shaping up to be a busy day. It might seem like Walt's passed away from natural causes, but there's a deeper game afoot, mark my words. People like Bruce and Carol have interests that aren't as straightforward as they seem. Bruce's behaviour down at the Alby was mighty peculiar, and as for Carol, with billions potentially in the balance, it doesn't sit right with me. My instincts tell me there's more to this story than meets the eye."

Davo nodded, fully understanding the complexities at play, "As you suggested, I'll start making a few calls, hit the caravan park and then meet you back here to discuss our next steps."

"Sounds good. We need to establish a timeline, mate. Who last saw Walt, who spoke to him? You know the deal."

"Sure do, boss," he responded eagerly.

His first call was to the Albatross Bay Hotel, "G'day Brendan, Davo here."

"What can I help ya with, mate?"

"I'm trying to establish a timeline of Walt's whereabouts last week. When did you last see him?"

"The last time I saw him was on his birthday last week. I think the whole town saw him then. He looked well and was in fine form—his usual self. I've had four days off and only started working again on Friday night. Why? Did you blokes find him?" Asked Brendan.

"Sorry, I can't say too much at this stage. Can you do me a favour and ask around the pub? I want to hear from anyone who saw him in the last week or so."

"Sure, no worries," came Brendan's hesitant reply. He could sense something was amiss.

"Thanks, mate."

Following the conclusion of his telephone conversation, Davo drove directly to the Weipa Camping Ground. There, he encountered Shirley, a woman in her mid-thirties, whose appearance was captivating. She possessed long, black hair cascading gracefully down her back, eyes as dark as the depths of a moonless night, lips endowed with a generous allure, and a countenance bearing the gentle caress of the sun's affection. On this particular day, her husband had embarked on a fishing expedition, and with the caravan traffic trailing off as the wet season approached, she found herself trapped by boredom's grasp, eager and willing to engage in conversation.

Davo addressed the receptionist, "Hi Shirl, got any gossip?'

"I dunno, Davo, depends on who ya talkin' about," she said with a grin.

"I'll cut to the chase. Has Bruce been seen around town recently?"

Shirley replied dubiously, "Yeah," after a prolonged silence, she asked, "Why ya askin'?"

"Just making some enquiries," said Davo.

"I heard Big Walt's missing," Shirley declared, her eyes traversing Davo's face, seeking any hint of a concealed truth or unsettling revelation.

"How did you hear that?" he inquired.

"Word's out," she responded, her words carrying a weight of uncertainty. "Brendan over at the Alby mentioned Walt was a no-show on Friday and Saturday, which isn't like him at all. And then there's Bruce; he was spotted at the BWS just two days back, loading up on his usual weekly provisions. After the ruckus he caused at the pub last week, it's got folks speculatin' that somethin' ain't right."

Davo replied, "I can't say too much at this stage. I'm just trying to put together a timeline of Walt's movements from the last week or so."

She continued, her voice laced with a tinge of concern, "Ya see, when Brendan let slip Walt hadn't appeared for a couple of days, the whispers started buzzin' like a swarm of flies. First, folks reckoned he might've been feelin' a bit under the weather on Friday, or perhaps he yearned for a quiet night at home now that he's, well, you know, gettin' on in years. But when Satd'y came and went without a trace of him, the gossip reached fever pitch. Was he alright, they wondered? Maybe he'd skedaddled off to Cairns for a weekend getaway with a new flame? Or perhaps he'd finally up and vanished with one of his mistresses. This mornin', as I drove to work, I couldn't help but notice his chopper and that fixed-wing plane of his still parked on the runway over at his Marina Road estate. Once me hubby gets back from his fishing trip later today, I'll have a word with him. If he's as clueless as the rest of us, I'll ask him to put the word out and see what he comes up with. Don't fret, Davo; I'll do me best to gather as much info as possible and get back to you."

"Have you noticed anything peculiar 'round these parts lately?" Davo asked in a somewhat absent manner, deploying an open-ended query that occasionally revealed more than anticipated.

Shirley responded with a wry grin, her eyes glinting with mischief. "Well, mate, you know how it goes 'round these parts. You might say we've got our fair share of oddballs, Wolf Creek types. Plenty of nooks and crannies to stash away secrets in the Cape," she chuckled. "Oh, and speaking of peculiar, Mad Maureen visited us a few days back. We had to give her the boot again for tryin' to turn her van into a makeshift brothel. We've stopped ringin' you lot about it; it's become downright routine. That, and someone rummaged through the RFDS doctor's kit after last week's clinic. The doc was stayin' in one of our units up front by the beach."

Maureen's last name was a mystery to all; she was simply called "Mad Maureen." She embodied the untamed, possessing piercing green eyes appearing to jut from her face and a perpetual squint. With a vibrant mane of black hair flowing down her waist, she personified an unruliness that was hard to ignore. Being of mixed Aboriginal and white heritage, she was caught between worlds, never truly fitting into the white or indigenous communities. Consequently, she settled on the outskirts of society, soliciting herself around Cape York in exchange for food, accommodation and a few extra bucks for "essentials".

Shirley said, "Other than that, mate, it's been quiet as a church mouse round here."

That reminded Davo he and Phil must look further into the report of stolen medicine from the doctor's bag; now, there was an unexpected death. It probably wasn't related, but they had to follow all avenues. They fingerprinted the bag when it was first reported being broken into, took DNA samples for completeness and made a formal report. Meanwhile, Dr O'Leary, hailing from the Royal Flying Doctor Service (RFDS), promptly notified the Australian Health Practitioner Regulation Agency (AHPRA) and Queensland Health regarding the missing medications, ensuring every relevant authority was apprised of the situation.

Davo diligently jotted down the details while Shirley shared her recollections. His quest was to piece together the puzzle of Walt's last known whereabouts and the individuals who interacted with him in those crucial moments. As the officer moved to part the fly door and exit the reception area, Shirley's voice carried after him, a nugget of potentially valuable information. "I do recall, you know," she called out, "Walt had a visit from the clinic nurse last Wednesday, the one now workin' with the RFDS. I didn't lay eyes on 'em together, mind you, but I did spot that unmistakable RFDS vehicle parked outside his residence. Might be worth lookin' into if that helps."

"Much appreciated, Shirl," he acknowledged warmly, a friendly smile gracing his features as he departed from the reception area. He couldn't resist casting a parting look in her direction, his grin broadening, and he playfully added, "Catch ya later, love," accompanied by a casual wave. Inwardly, he couldn't help but admire her; he considered her a striking woman and thought her husband was a lucky bloke.

Upon returning to the station, where he patiently awaited Phil's arrival, Davo took the initiative to reach out to the RFDS base in Cairns. After a brief exchange with the dispatcher on duty, he conversed with one of the doctors, Stephen O'Leary. Dr O'Leary confirmed he had overseen a clinic in Weipa on the previous Wednesday. Though he hadn't personally laid eyes on Walt, he assured Davo their nurse, Cindy, undertook a house call to visit the man.

In his unmistakable Irish lilt, Dr O'Leary explained, "I was conductin' the clinic inside the local hospital, ye see, and as it was a standard check-up, Cindy, our nurse, was more than willing to make the drive to Mr Henry's residence," his words carrying a musical cadence. "Regrettably, she's not here today, but I'll retrieve the pertinent file. Bear with me a moment." Following a brief pause, he returned to the conversation, apologising, "Sorry for the wait, officer. I've got the file in hand now. Accordin' to her nursing notes on Wednesday, everythin' seemed to be in order with Walt Henry. His heart rate was regular, his blood pressure was good, and his blood sugar levels were within the normal range. The patient did not have any pain or health issues to report."

"Thanks for that, doctor; very useful. When will you be back in Weipa again?" asked Davo.

"I'll be runnin' another clinic on Wednesday, and Cindy will be joinin' me on that day as well. I'm sure she wouldn't mind if ya asked her a few questions then," he replied, running his hands through his jet-black hair, his Irish green eyes always twinkling, thinking a bit of mischief might be in the air.

"Yes, we'd like to speak to her," replied Davo, "She might be able to fill in some gaps for us."

"No worries at all, I'll let her know when I see her," replied Stephen, "And sure, there's one more thing I reckon ye should know, although it might not be of much interest. She was away from the clinic for a good two hours that day, ye see."

"I'll note it down," replied Davo, "By the way, we haven't had a chance to look into the report of the stolen medications from your doctor's bag yet. We'll run the fingerprints through the database this week and see if we get a match. We're unlikely to find the culprit, but we might find a match if they have a criminal history."

"Take yer time now, no harm done, I hope. The medications have been replaced, and the incident has been reported to the relevant bodies. Probably just some young lads messin' about."

"That's the most likely explanation," replied Davo, "By the way, what were the medications that went missing?"

"Ten fentanyl patches, two-hundred, thirty-milligram codeine tablets, and two two-hundred millilitre bottles of liquid morphine called ordine, strength 1 milligram per millilitre."

"Okay, doctor, thanks for that. I'll catch up with you on Wednesday."

Stephen replied, "My pleasure. Until then," though a sense of curiosity lingered in his thoughts, and he wondered about the purpose of this inquiry.

*****

Once Phil settled into the driver's seat of the police car, he felt a wave of apprehension wash over him. He knew he had a difficult task—delivering unpleasant news to Carol. To buy some time and postpone the unenviable position he found himself in, Phil reached for his phone and dialled Gladys' number.

"G'day, Phil," she said, "You got any more info on the big case yet?" He could sense the excitement in her voice.

"Not yet, Glad. I need to know if any emergency calls were made from Walt's house or anyone else reporting anything suspicious in the last week or so."

"I checked the call log soon after we last spoke. No emergency calls were made in the ten days before Walt's death. It's been pretty quiet around here lately."

"Thanks, Glad," said Phil and ended the call before driving to Carol's house.

Phil knew he couldn't deliver such grave news over the phone; it must be done in person. Having shared nearly three decades of life with Walt, Carol remained the person closest to him, at least to the best of Phil's knowledge. He pulled his police vehicle to a halt along a quiet street in the suburb of Nanum, Weipa, and walked along a path flanked by majestic Birds of Paradise plants leading to her front door. Their bold display starkly contrasted with the sombre news he was about to deliver.

With each step, he steeled himself emotionally, knowing the weight of the words he bore. Standing before the ornate, keenly polished brass knocker, he finally arrived at the doorstep. Walt's ex-wife answered his knock promptly, instinctively aware something was wrong. In the quiet enclave of Nanum, where familiarity and neighbourly connections thrived, visitors rarely resorted to knocking on doors. Everyone knew her door was always open, a welcoming haven where a warm cuppa and heartfelt conversations awaited any visitor.

Phil's fortitude wavered momentarily as he stood before Carol, his gaze meeting hers. "Hello, Carol," he began, his voice tinged with formality and gravity. His countenance took on a grave demeanour, reflecting the weight of the news he carried. "May I come inside?" he continued, his words punctuated with urgency. A distinct air of sadness enveloped him, mirrored in the gentle downturn of his eyes and the subtle crease between his brows.

"Sure, Phil, this must be pretty serious," she acknowledged, sensing the seriousness of the situation. Wanting to provide comfort amidst the impending news, she offered, "I'll make us a cuppa, and we can sit in the lounge."

A few minutes later, she entered the cozy lounge room, placing two steaming cups of tea, perfectly sweetened with milk and sugar, alongside a plate of homemade biscuits on the coffee table. The atmosphere was tinged with anticipation as she settled herself, her eyes fixed on his furrowed brow and concerned expression.

"What's up?" she inquired, her voice betraying worry and curiosity. "Has something happened to Walt?" Her keen perception detected the depth of his unease.

Phil hesitated, "I'm afraid to tell you," he confessed, his voice tinged with sorrow. "I don't even know how to tell you."

Her patience wore thin, her urgency evident as she said, "Just spit it out. I know it's not good, so let me have it," she steeled herself, prepared to confront the truth behind his troubled expression.

As Phil gathered the courage to break the devastating news, he took a deep breath and addressed her, "I'm sorry, but Walt's dead," he solemnly announced. "Davo and I found him in his house this morning."

Carol sat stunned, the weight of the news settling heavily upon her. After a few seconds of silence, she cradled her head and whispered in disbelief, "Oh, my God."

Phil, aware of the immense pain she was experiencing, sought to provide some solace. "We will do everything possible to discover what happened," he assured her. "It appears he passed away peacefully at home, in his bed."

Overwhelmed by grief, tears streamed down her face as she began to weep. "He was too young to go and so vibrant. How could this have happened?" Her voice shuddered with sorrow and disbelief.

"I don't know," Phil admitted, reaching out to place a comforting hand on her knee.

"I spoke to him on Saturday morning," Carol said, "He mentioned having a stomach issue and feeling a bit crook, but I didn't think it was serious. If it had been, I thought he would've called me."

Concerned, Phil inquired about Walt's condition during their last conversation. Carol paused to compose herself before responding, her voice filled with regret. "He didn't sound entirely well, but I thought it was just a bout of gastro. People get sick like that from time to time. I didn't think much of it. Oh, God, I should have gone to check on him. I thought he would be fine." Her eyes became bloodshot, and a glum expression lingered as tears continued to flow down her face.

"I have a couple of other questions," said Phil, "You organised the food for the party for Walt?"

"Yes, that's right?"

"Did you cook anything?"

"Yes, I oversaw every dish and made the pavlovas myself, just as Walt likes 'em," she replied, somewhat distantly.

"Did anyone else get sick after the party?" Phil continued his enquiry.

"Not that I know of. I haven't heard any negative reports back from the food. Everyone seemed to think it was great," she replied, a suspicious look on her face, wondering where this line of questioning was going.

The reason for this line of questioning suddenly dawned on her: "Oh no, I feel terrible. What if it was the food at the party? I may be responsible." Her reddened eyes widened at the thought.

Phil offered words of reassurance, trying to ease her burden of guilt. "It's not your fault, Carol. We can't change what has already happened."

Overwhelmed by emotion, she continued to weep, feeling as though she abandoned her ex-husband and closest friend in his time of need and may have inadvertently killed him. Through her tears, she made a heartfelt request. "May I see him?"

Phil's response was measured and cautious: "I would strongly advise against it. The heat hasn't been kind, and the body's condition is not something you would want to witness. Besides, the local doctor has already confirmed the body's identity as Walt's."

Despite Phil's warning, Carol expressed her desire to see him, driven by her love for him. "I want to see him. I need to make sure it's my Walt. Despite his flaws, I loved him. I still do. We only separated two months ago, and the divorce hadn't been finalised. I hoped for reconciliation, that he would realise his mistakes and commit to a faithful relationship with me," she confessed, her eyes swollen from crying. Anxious anticipation filled her as she clasped her hands together, preparing herself for the difficult task ahead.

Phil and Carol left in the patrol car with heavy hearts. Delivering bad news was never easy. He turned to her as they reached Walt's house, "I hope you're ready for this, Carol," he said, "It can be confronting."

The stench on opening the front door was overwhelming. Phil led her upstairs. She only needed to go as far as the threshold of the bedroom. She'd recognise that physique, the rotund face, his tattoo and missing fingers anywhere. "That's him; that's Walt," she said, her eyes welling up as she stared at the hollow sockets where his eyes used to be. How could she forget those laughing eyes, dancing as he recounted bush legends and urban myths? So many years together, so many memories.

"C'mon love, I'll take ya home," said Phil. They exited the house and walked to the patrol car for the short drive to Carol's house, "Is there anyone I can call to sit with you for a while? I don't think you should be alone right now."

"Thanks, Phil. I'll call my daughter and deliver the bad news. She'll let the rest of the family know and will happily stay with me for the next few days." Carol exited the vehicle and reached for her phone, strolling inside, her head low.

Phil turned the engine back on and was ready to drive back to the station when she tapped on his driver's side window, "You know, I bet that Bruce has something to do with this," her eyes narrowed, and there was anger in her tone, "With all his carry on at Walt's birthday last week. Stealing the show, bringing up shit from more than thirty years ago. I'll kill the bastard!"

CHAPTER 8

As anticipated, Dr Stephen O'Leary and his nurse, Cindy Newman, arrived Wednesday morning to commence their clinic at Weipa Hospital. Dr O'Leary utilised his extensive knowledge of tropical medicine to care for individuals who found it inconvenient or too costly to visit a specialist in Cairns. He dedicated significant efforts to treating the local indigenous population, who were still grappling with the high prevalence of tuberculosis in this region of Australia.

Meanwhile, the clinic nurse primarily focused on administering childhood vaccinations, conducting blood tests, and tending to wounds. Occasionally, she would make home visits to individuals with severe impairments or people such as Walt, who exhibited a lack of motivation to attend the clinic personally. Walt had ample financial resources at his disposal, and in the event of a severe illness, he could hire a pilot to fly one of his private aircraft to the Emergency Department at Cairns Base.

Dr Stephen O'Leary, a seasoned veteran of the Royal Flying Doctor Service (RFDS), brought a wealth of experience to the organisation, having dedicated many years to serving remote communities. In contrast, Cindy was a relative newcomer, working as a locum nurse and traversing Australia to fill essential positions in remote areas. This marked her second opportunity with the RFDS, and she had commenced her current assignment with the Cairns division a little over three weeks prior. She was committed to a four-week locum term while two other regular nurses took a well-earned break.

A vibrant woman in her late thirties, she sported a stylish pixie cut accentuating her delicate facial features. Her short blonde hair perfectly framed her friendly smile, adding to her undeniable congeniality and making her an instant hit among those who crossed her path. Embracing her warm and engaging nature, she seamlessly integrated into her team, breathing a refreshing sense of positivity into the workplace. Her willingness to share amusing anecdotes about her outback adventures and infectious laughter created a vibrant atmosphere within the team.

However, her culinary talents truly endeared her to her co-workers. Her baking became a cherished tradition in the office, brightening up otherwise mundane workdays and fostering a sense of camaraderie. The aroma of freshly baked goods wafting through the corridors created a comforting and welcoming environment, drawing people together for moments of delight and indulgence and a well-deserved break from their often-hectic schedules.

Before joining the RFDS, she undertook various locum positions in remote Aboriginal communities across Western Australia and the Northern Territory. Her dedication to delivering healthcare in underserved regions led her to a recent assignment at the local hospital in Tennant Creek, where she committed to a six-week stint. However, unexpectedly, she abruptly left after just four weeks of service.

Within the community, hushed conversations circulated, hinting at a distressing incident involving the nurse. It was whispered she was the victim of a brutal assault and gang rape, allegedly perpetrated by a group of local Indigenous teenage boys. Despite the pervasive rumours and speculation, no charges were ever filed, and no individuals came forward to admit culpability. The truth remained elusive, concealed beneath a blanket of silence and uncertainty. Cindy never disclosed any details about the incident; instead, she hastily packed her belongings and departed two weeks earlier than planned.

It was said the local mob in Tennant Creek, following their tribal traditions, administered their brand of punishment upon the alleged culprits. This "tribal justice" was rumoured to involve penalties far more severe than those imposed by mainstream legal or "white fella" systems.

Phil and Davo wanted to talk to the nurse about her home visit to Walt last week. As Dr O'Leary pointed out, she had been missing for two hours from the clinic last week when she said she would only pay a quick house visit to Walt for routine observations. The police officers arrived at Weipa Hospital around 10 a.m. and asked to speak with her. As far as they knew, she was the last person to have seen Walt alive.

Shortly after, she reached the reception desk, her nervousness evident. Sensing her hesitation, the police officers led her into a private room in the hospital. A table and three chairs were already set up for the interview.

Phil initiated the conversation with formal introductions, adopting a precise and professional tone, "Good afternoon, Nurse Newman. Thank you for taking the time to speak with us. I am Senior Sergeant Phil Roberts, and this is my colleague, Sergeant David Smith. We are here to discuss some matters regarding Mr Walt Henry's condition last Wednesday."

"Good morning, officers. Please call me Cindy," she smiled warmly at them both, "I appreciate the opportunity to speak with you."

"We are grateful for your cooperation. We have a few questions regarding your home visit to this man last week," Phil began the questioning.

At this point, the nurse hesitated, "Yes, of course. What do you need to know?"

"We've discovered you were scheduled for routine observations at Mr Henry's home, but it seems you stayed there for a significantly longer time, nearly two hours. Can you shed some light on why that was?" Davo took it upon himself to speak.

The nurse's response was careful and veiled, "Well, it... it ended up taking more time than I had anticipated. I had some personal matters to attend to," she cautiously stated.

"Personal matters?" Phil responded, his tone subtle but suspicious, "Could you provide more details about what these personal matters entailed? I would consider it somewhat unusual to have private errands to run during a scheduled visit for routine observations."

She looked toward the floor, avoiding eye contact with the officers, "They were tasks unrelated to Mr Henry's condition. They bear no relevance to what happened."

Davo immediately picked up on the nurse's evasiveness: "There's no point messing about, love. It might look like a very open-and-shut case, but Mr Henry was wealthy and influential in these parts. There could have been any number of people who intended to harm him. Can you be more forthcoming about these personal matters?"

Her tone grew louder as she shifted her weight in the chair, responding, "I've already mentioned they were personal. I did what I had to do, and then I left. I assure you they had nothing to do with what happened to Walt."

Phil took over the questioning, his voice firm and steadfast, "Can anyone vouch for your whereabouts on these so-called tasks? Did anyone see you?"

"No, well, not that I know of. As I have already explained, they are private matters I had to attend to."

Phil persisted in seeking the truth, "Your hesitancy and evasiveness are evident. We have a responsibility to uncover the truth regarding Mr Henry's situation. I can sense you connected with the victim personally, considering you referred to him as Walt. Please grasp the seriousness of this matter and answer our questions with complete honesty."

Her voice trembled with guilt as she spoke, "I... I've already shared everything I can. There's nothing else to disclose. Can we please move on to a different topic?"

Davo spoke with scepticism, "Miss, we cannot dismiss these inconsistencies. Our investigation requires thoroughness. Your demeanour and responses are raising my suspicions. We must uncover the truth about Mr Henry's passing." He could sense her responses were becoming more assertive, almost aggressive.

"I assure you, I have been truthful. I've provided all the relevant information. I understand the seriousness, but there is nothing more to add. I am a registered nurse and take my professional duties very seriously; if you are done, please let me return to work. I have patients waiting for me."

"Miss, we may need to revisit this line of inquiry later. The signs we've observed and your reluctance to cooperate fully indicate there may be more to this story. We won't rest until we find the truth." Phil replied firmly, seeing this interview was going nowhere fast.

"I've already answered your questions. I'll do my best to respond if you have any other queries, but I've been honest. I have nothing to hide," she replied, "Absolutely nothing. Now, if you'll excuse me, I have patients to attend to," rising from the table, she left the room.

The interview room door closed behind the nurse as Senior Sergeant Roberts and Sergeant Smith concluded their questioning. Her mind was still reeling from the intense scrutiny and the weight of her concealed secret. Exiting the room, she found herself face to face with Dr Stephen O'Leary, who was waiting just outside.

Dr O'Leary's keen eyes quickly scanned Cindy's appearance, observing the lines of worry in her face and the subtle tremor in her hands. Concern filled his expression as he recognised her obvious distress. Without hesitation, he touched her arm gently, offering support.

"Cindy, is everythin' grand?" Dr O'Leary asked, his voice laced with genuine concern. "Ye seem a wee bit flustered. Is there somethin' troublin' ye?"

Her heart skipped a beat, momentarily taken aback by the doctor's unexpected presence and perceptiveness. She hesitated, grappling with whether to divulge the truth that weighed heavily on her conscience. With a deep breath, she knew she couldn't keep it inside any longer.

"Oh, Dr O'Leary," she replied, her voice quivering slightly. "I... I'm just a bit overwhelmed with everything that's been going on."

His concern deepened as he listened attentively, his professional instincts urging him to delve deeper into the source of her distress. He maintained a gentle grip on her arm, providing a reassuring presence.

"I understand it's a difficult time," Dr O'Leary said, his voice filled with empathy. "But if there's anythin' I can do to help, or if ye need someone to talk to, please know I'm here for ye."

She felt a wave of gratitude wash over her, appreciating the doctor's genuine concern and offer of support. She knew she couldn't hide the truth, especially from someone she respected and trusted.

"There is something I need to tell you, doctor," she admitted, her voice quivering with anxiety and relief. "It's about Walt."

Stephen's eyes widened in surprise, his expression betraying the unexpected nature of her revelation. He maintained his grip on her arm, silently encouraging her to continue.

"Walt and I... we were having an affair," she revealed, her voice barely above a whisper. "It had been going on for the past four weeks."

The doctor's initial surprise transformed into a mix of understanding and concern as he absorbed the significance of her confession. He realised the complexity and potential implications of such a revelation in the context of the ongoing investigation.

"I see," Dr O'Leary responded carefully, his Irish accent colouring his words. "That's a bit unexpected, now. But why didn't ye mention this earlier?"

Her gaze dropped to the floor, ashamed of keeping this secret. She mustered the courage to meet his gaze, her voice filled with sincerity, "I didn't want anyone to know," she confessed, her voice laden with vulnerability. "Walt and I had plans to start a new life together in Port Douglas. It was meant to be a secret, and I didn't want it to affect my work or how people saw me. It was only a short affair, but we were in love. I couldn't help it. It just happened."

The doctor's expression softened as he understood the situation's complexity and the weight the nurse was carrying. He tightened his grip on her arm, conveying a sense of support and reassurance.

"This is a mighty revelation," he acknowledged, "It does complicate matters, ye see. But honesty is crucial, especially in situations like this. We need to ensure the investigation is thorough and impartial. Have ye shared this information with the police?"

She shook her head, her eyes filled with fear and remorse. "No, I haven't," she admitted. "I was afraid of the consequences and how it might affect me personally and professionally. But I understand now it's important to be truthful."

Stephen nodded, his green eyes conveying his support and understanding, "I appreciate yer honesty," he reassured her warmly. "Sure, it couldn't have been easy for ye to admit this. I urge ye to share this information with Senior Sergeant Roberts and Sergeant Smith. It may shed new light on the situation, and it's essential for them to have all the relevant details, ye know."

The nurse nodded, her fear slowly transforming into gratification. She appreciated Dr O'Leary's understanding and guidance, finding solace in his support during this trying time.

"Thank you, doctor," she said, her voice tinged with relief and vulnerability. "I appreciate your understanding. I'll do what needs to be done."

He offered her a heartening smile, his grip on her arm easing as he stepped back slightly. " You're not alone in this, love. Me and the rest of the team are right by your side, you see."

Resuming her clinic duties, her heart was weighed down by her recent disclosure to the doctor. The intensity of the atmosphere enveloped her as she pondered the consequences of her words. Having only worked with Dr O'Leary for a brief few weeks during this stint and the prior one with the RFDS, she couldn't help but feel a creeping discomfort, questioning her decision to reveal anything. The urgency to keep the affair concealed until the opportune moment gnawed at her every thought, shrouding her actions in a mystery.

Two weeks before her locum assignment in Weipa, she had arrived early to acquaint herself with the area and put some distance between herself and Tennant Creek. In a meticulously orchestrated encounter at the local supermarket, she crossed paths with Walt, leading her journey down an unexpected course. Like most, she knew well of his background—a billionaire mining magnate with a penchant for women, an egotist who mistakenly believed love could be bought. Cindy took the initiative to introduce herself, recalling the spark in his eyes as their gazes first met.

From that moment, a profound desire grew on his part, and the nurse took the lead in getting to know him. She sensed his instant attraction, prompting Walt to invite her to his home for dinner that evening. The opulence and grandeur she encountered there thrilled her senses, overwhelming her. As night fell, she took the initiative, slowly undressing before him. She chose expensive white lace lingerie, a garter belt, and stilettos for the occasion. He couldn't tear his gaze away; the hunger in his eyes was palpable, a fierce and primal intensity that spoke of a deep, gnawing desire. She skillfully used her feminine wiles to maintain her sway over him. Subsequent visits became a regular occurrence. He practically begged to see her almost daily.

It only took a few weeks for Walt to reassure her of his commitment to her well-being, with a heartfelt promise that if anything were to happen to him, she would be well cared for in the future. He professed his love, leaving no room for doubt in Cindy's mind. Her belief in their relationship was unwavering. He instructed her to cancel all the locum positions she had previously arranged for the next six months. He insisted this was not a passing infatuation but a genuine, undeniable love. She remembered looking at him with feigned sincerity, mustering a smile and replying, "Yes, you're right, Walt, my darling."

The days leading up to Walt's passing would remain in her memory forever. It was the week before his demise on a Monday afternoon. Cindy, finishing her shift earlier than usual, decided to surprise him at home. Little did she expect the heartrending but opportune scene awaiting her.

Upon opening the bedroom door, she was met with the devastating sight of Walt with another woman. She feigned shock, overwhelmed and heartbroken. She sobbed and fled, hands cradling her face. She could still vividly recall the mixture of terror and regret in his eyes. He leapt from the bed, completely naked, pleading for her forgiveness, insisting it was a momentary lapse in judgment, reflecting his ingrained unfaithful tendency. But Cindy remained resolute. She needed him to believe his words offered no comfort.

Without a second thought, she left the house, leaving him shocked. Feigning astonishment at the sight of him came naturally to her; his physical form repulsed her.

Later that evening, he desperately attempted to mend the shattered pieces of their relationship. He reached out, his voice tinged with regret, but she remained firm, refusing to entertain his pleas. Tuesday afternoon brought another call from Walt, a last-ditch effort to bridge the widening gap between them. He implored her to come over, a request she reluctantly granted.

Upon her arrival, Cindy was met with a revelation that sent shockwaves through her. The words spilling from his lips held a promise she had dearly hoped for all these weeks, but she hadn't anticipated such generosity. A mixture of surprise and inner conflict stirred within her.

With earnestness, he confessed he took decisive steps to rectify the wrongs of his past, beginning with a profound alteration to his will. He spoke of her tenderly, declaring her to be the paramount love of his life. He sought to bestow upon her a substantial sum to safeguard her financial future in the event of unforeseen circumstances. She could still vividly recall when he retrieved an envelope from his back pocket, holding it out to her with vulnerable sincerity.

"Consider this my form of atonement," he offered, his voice tinged with apprehension and hope. "It's yours, without any strings attached. You have every right to leave, but I would be grateful if you chose to stay. I love you, Cindy. There's simply no other way to put it."

With hesitant acceptance, she took the envelope from his outstretched hand, her fingers trembling slightly as she gently pried it open. What lay inside was nothing short of astonishing—a bank cheque bearing a staggering sum of ten million dollars. It rendered her momentarily speechless, the weight of its significance settling in.

Yet, there was more. He pledged to mend the fractured relationship with Bruce Hudson, a promise holding substantial significance given their tumultuous history. Walt extended her a copy of the amended will, urging her to keep it for her records. However, as she took it in her hands, bewilderment washed over her. She couldn't believe her luck; a couple of million, yes, but this extravagant gesture? It was beyond her wildest expectations.

In addition to her generous gift, the notion of inheriting an additional fifty million dollars left her incredulous and adrift in a sea of emotions. The enormity of this gesture was implausible, filling her with a profound sense of gratitude and, simultaneously, an unease at the magnitude of the change that was now set into motion.

As the days passed, Cindy found herself in a precarious position, burdened by the secrets she now held. She chose to keep Walt's final wishes to herself, fearing revealing them might implicate her in his sudden demise.

The investigation into Walt's death was ongoing, and the authorities were piecing together a complex puzzle. As Cindy watched the events unfold, she couldn't help but feel the pressure mounting. She knew sooner or later, she might be called upon to reveal the truth about Walt's last wishes, and the thought left her anxious and apprehensive.

Cindy felt a heavy burden settling on her shoulders, knowing this newfound information could potentially cast her in an unfavourable light. The weight of this secret and the tangled emotions she harboured left her torn between loyalty and self-preservation.

CHAPTER 9

As the community grappled with the lingering shock of Walt's untimely demise, investigations into his death yielded no suspicious leads. Much to Phil's unease, the case seemed to be a closed book. Phil and Davo, back at Weipa police station, resumed their routine duties, delving into the familiar realms of petty theft and domestic disputes—the bread and butter of their lives as law enforcement officers in Weipa.

It was a regular Monday morning, and the two men were engrossed in completing the paperwork from the weekend's callouts. As they settled into their routine, Phil's phone pierced through the quiet with a shrill ring. With a sense of urgency, a frantic voice erupted from the other end, "They're dead! Both of 'em!" The woman's voice quivered, tears mingling with her words. "I dunno what to do. Can ya come out?"

To calm the woman down, Phil responded in a measured voice, "Take a moment, catch your breath. Who am I speaking to, and where are you calling from?"

"I'm sorry, Phil. It's Diane Granger 'ere, John's wife," her voice trembled.

"All right," Phil said slowly, "Tell me what's happened, and we'll get onto it as soon as possible."

Diane spoke slowly, still shocked, "I came home from a weekend in Cairns with me girlfriends this mornin'. I couldn't see me husband or Noel, the station manager, anywhere on the property as I drove up the drive. I thought it was a little unusual 'cause normally they'd be doin' work around the farm, feedin' the cattle, repairin' fences, that sorta thing," she went quiet, taking a moment to compose herself.

"Take your time," Phil replied softly.

"Well, when I couldn't find 'em, I parked the car and entered the house, callin' out John's name. It was only when I went to the kitchen to put me bag down on the bench that I," she started crying again, "I found 'em," her tears turned to guttural sobs, "Please help Phil. This is just bloody awful. I dunno who else to call. We've got no neighbours for miles."

The complexity of the situation deepened as Phil absorbed Diane's words. Watson's River station was a sprawling two-hundred-thousand-acre cattle farm nestled one hundred and fifty kilometres from Weipa. Phil's mind raced with the implications of the gruesome discovery.

With a composed voice, Phil inquired, "Have you touched anything yet?"

Diane's response carried a grave tone, "No," she whispered, "I haven't stepped past the kitchen bench. I'm on me mobile just starin' at the two of 'em. Oh God, it's just bloody awful," she choked back her sobs. "I can see John face down on the table. He's not movin' and looks pale. Noel might have fallen from a chair and is now lyin' on the ground. Oh, Jesus, neither of 'em is movin'. I can't see 'em breathin'. I'm certain," she paused, trying to regain her composure, "they're dead."

An unsettling silence followed Diane's words. Phil carefully considered the situation, aware that this incident called for immediate action. He instructed Diane, "I need you to stay where you are, Diane. Don't touch anything else. We'll be there as soon as possible. Stay strong, love. Can you call someone to come and be with you right now?"

"Yeah, me daughter's livin' not so far away. Just a hundred clicks. I'll call her and let 'er know what's happened. Perhaps I can stay with her tonight?

"I know that right now you just want to get away," Phil replied, "But we need you to stay where you are. This may well be a crime scene."

"I understand," said Diane, "I'll just sit outside on the verandah and give me daughter a call; shouldn't take 'er long to get 'ere."

"That's great, love. Thanks for your co-operation. We'll be there soon."

Phil knew both men; it was hard not to know everyone in a small community after working there for a few years. The owner of Watson's River Station was fifty-eight-year-old John Granger. The second man was presumably Noel Manson, the farm manager, a forty-three-year-old who was handy in the saddle and came to earn John's trust over the fifteen years they worked together. Starting as a ringer, Noel soon worked his way up to the position of head stockman. Over the years, a deep bond formed between the two men, and while John took long, exotic holidays all over the world, Noel managed the daily operations of the cattle farm.

Phil turned to Davo, his expression puzzled. "What's up?" the junior officer asked.

"You won't believe this," came Phil's reply.

"Go on, try me."

"Looks like John Granger and Noel Manson are both dead."

"Jesus! Who was that on the line?" Davo asked, reeling from the information he had just received.

"Diane. She's just returned from a weekend in Cairns and found both men. She says they're not moving or breathing. Can you get on to Careflight and the RFDS? I'm not sure which one services the station, but hopefully, someone is free to get a doctor out there ASAP."

"On to it, boss," came the swift reply.

As Phil sat at his desk gathering the necessary paperwork before heading out to the station, he received an update from the doctor who arrived at the scene. "Hello, Senior Sergeant Roberts; this is Dr Shelby Wright of the Careflight team. I've examined the two men and found them both to be deceased," she continued, "It seems very suspicious two relatively young men should be found dead at the same time and in the same place. There are no external signs of trauma. I think the matter should be referred to the coroner. Not knowing either of the men, I cannot write out a death certificate as I am uncertain as to the cause of death. I believe the best thing for me to do is fill out form 1A and alert the coroner," she said confidently.

Phil understood the gravity of the situation and the need for a thorough investigation to bring justice to those who lost their lives, "Suits me, Dr Wright. Thank you for your timely assistance."

"No worries, Sergeant," replied Shelby, "I'll do that from the air. We have another call out."

"Have a safe journey, and thanks again, doctor," replied Phil in a subdued tone, still in shock at the sudden turn of events.

Half an hour passed, and Phil's phone chimed once more. It seemed as though his phone had transformed into a nexus of communication. On the line was the coroner. Phil welcomed him warmly, and the coroner began, "Just now, I received a call from today's Careflight doctor, Dr Shelby Wright. She apprised me of a concerning development - two men have been discovered deceased at Watson's River Station. The circumstances appear highly suspicious. I've taken the initiative to inform the local forensic pathologist and have requested her immediate involvement in scrutinising the case. Would it be convenient for her to contact you on this number?"

"Sure," Phil replied, a tone of gratitude resonating. "That arrangement works perfectly. Thank you for your prompt attention to this matter."

Phil's mind raced with questions. What sinister force was sweeping through their region, claiming the lives of innocent people? Who would want Noel and John dead? Could these incidents be linked to Walt Henry's recent passing? He sensed the need for assistance and intended to ensure the proper authorities took charge of the case. With that in mind, he rang the Aurukun Police Station south of Weipa. Both stations were an equal distance from the potential crime scene. While smaller than its Weipa counterpart, this station played a vital role in upholding regional law and order. It was staffed by two dedicated junior officers, Constable Mark Doomadgee and Constable Wayne Reed.

Constable Doomadgee, a local indigenous man, deeply understood the community's dynamics and cultural nuances. His connection to the Weipa mob and a shared dialect allowed him to navigate complex situations with empathy and cultural sensitivity. His presence at the station comforted the Aboriginal community members as they saw a familiar face serving and protecting their interests. Vitality coursed through his veins, a show of his strength and resilience. But not merely his physical prowess that endeared him to their hearts; it was his innate ability to lend an attentive ear, a skill he honed to perfection.

On the other hand, Constable Wayne Reed, the son of English immigrants, recently graduated from the police academy and was embarking on his first rural posting with the Australian Police Force. Wayne's arrival in Aurukun marked a significant milestone in his career, as he embraced the opportunity to learn about the diverse communities of Australia and contribute to their well-being. Youthfulness was his companion, tall and lean; his frame exuded an aura of promise. Mousy brown hair bordered his face, and his ever-watchful and considerate brown eyes held the potential for understanding and connection.

Constable Doomadgee was the first to pick up the call. He recognised the number, "G'day Phil, what's up?"

"More than you probably want to know, Mark," replied Phil, "We've just taken a call from Watson's River Station; two blokes have been found dead."

"Anyone I know?" asked Mark.

"Unfortunately, you do know them. It's John Granger and Noel Manson. Noel's the station manager, one of your mob, I believe. I just got a call from Diane saying she came home to find them both dead," Phil relayed, giving Mark a moment to process the news. "I suppose you heard about Walt Henry two weeks ago?"

"I don't reckon there's a person in Cape York who hasn't heard the news yet," replied the Constable, highlighting the widespread awareness of the recent events.

"That's three dead bodies in two weeks. It all seems odd to me," Phil's tone filled with anticipation. "You haven't heard anything down your way?"

"Just rumours, fella, just rumours. I reckon it's widely known 'bout that old bugger Bruce's performance at the Alby on Walt's birthday. That's some powerful magic, and now another brudda is dead, plus a white fella. It just doesn't add up," Mark replied.

Upon receiving the distressing news about the two men found dead at Watson's River Station, Mark informed his colleague, Wayne. After a brief discussion, they acknowledged an investigation of this magnitude was beyond their current capabilities. However, they were eager to lend a hand and learn from the experience. Recognising the importance of their involvement, they agreed to meet Phil and Davo at the cattle station to initiate the investigation.

As Phil drove, Davo sat beside him in the passenger seat. They were looking forward to meeting up with Mark and Wayne. A couple of extra pairs of eyes never hurt in such a situation. Their collaboration, combined with their varying expertise and perspectives, would be instrumental in navigating the complexities of the investigation. Each of them contemplated the challenges they would face and the potential implications of the rumours surrounding the recent deaths in the area. Both men remained committed to approaching the case with an open mind.

The four officers arrived within minutes of each other at Watson's River Cattle Station. They all greeted each other warmly before heading toward the homestead. Diane sat on a sun-bleached wooden rocking chair on the verandah, her daughter, Veronica, holding her hand, sitting in a similar chair beside her. Next to them was an old picnic-style table flanked by bench seats on either side. Both women had been crying.

"G'day, Diane, Veronica," he greeted, his gaze shifting downward to meet each woman's eyes in succession, "I am so sorry about this," said Phil, his voice brimming with compassion. "Is there someone I can call to be with you both? You shouldn't be alone at a time like this," he leaned forward and touched her shoulder gently.

"Thanks, Phil," she replied, her eyes filled with tears. "Ronny's here now." She smiled at her daughter and gently squeezed her hand. "I'll be all right to sit 'ere for a while. I need some time to process all of this."

As the officers entered the house, the air seemed heavy with unspoken tension as they took in the sight before them—the two lifeless bodies lying motionless in the kitchen dining area. Phil grew more assertive, convinced that three dead bodies in two weeks demanded a thorough investigation. Retirement loomed, and he knew he couldn't afford to leave this case unsolved. He did not want to leave any loose ends before quitting the force.

Stepping into action, the officer's extensive years of experience informed his decisions. He promptly recognised the need to cordon off the area. An unmistakable shroud of suspicion surrounded the entire situation, leaving him uneasy. His phone rang, and he handed it to Davo, preferring to secure the potential crime scene instead.

The forensic pathologist from Cairns called for an update on the situation. "Hi, this is Dr Catherine Reynolds. How can I be of assistance? I have just got off the phone with the coroner, and I understand there are two deceased men at Watson's River Station."

Davo spoke in hushed tones, relaying the situation to the pathologist. His face grew more serious as the conversation progressed, mirroring the shocking nature of the circumstances under which the men were discovered. Busying himself with securing the site, Phil anxiously awaited the outcome, knowing the pathologist's insights could be vital to unlocking these deaths' mystery.

Dr Reynolds, momentarily pausing the conversation, gently motioned to her assistant. She requested another cup of coffee with a tired glance, hoping to shake off her drowsiness. She had been up most of the night attending a domestic violence scene that had turned lethal.

"Three unexplained deaths in two weeks seems unusual," she remarked speculatively.

Davo replied detachedly, "It sure is. First, Walt Henry was a mining magnate and Cape York's richest man. One week, he was celebrating his birthday, fit as a fiddle. The next week, we found him dead in his bed."

"How old was he? Any medical conditions?" asked Dr Reynolds.

"He'd just turned sixty-five; sure, he was obese and suffered high cholesterol as well as diabetes and some minor heart problems, but no one expected him to go so suddenly."

"Could easily be attributable to a heart attack. He may well have died in his sleep. But, now you say you have found two more deceased men?"

"Yes, Ma'am. Senior Sergeant Phil Roberts and Constables Doomadgee and Reed from Aurukun station are here with me at the cattle station right now," replied Mark, "John Granger, the owner, was fifty-eight, and Noel Manson, the manager, forty-three. They are the ones who've passed and were both found near the kitchen table. John was face down on the table, and it looked like Noel fell from his chair and ended up on the ground with the chair on top of him. From what we've been told, they were both in good health before this happened.

The forensic pathologist sensed something was amiss. It was uncommon to encounter deaths outside the broader Cairns region, as most were typically handled by the local police and settled straightforwardly. Three deceased individuals in two weeks struck her as highly unusual. Recognising the urgency, she realised immediate action was necessary.

"I will see if I can arrange a flight later today. This situation appears peculiar and warrants a comprehensive forensic investigation. We could potentially be dealing with a highly skilled killer. Have you already contacted the homicide squad in Brisbane?" she asked, emphasising the importance of involving the specialised team.

"No, doctor, we are not even sure the three deaths are homicides; we were hoping, with your knowledge and assistance, you could shed more light on the situation before we call them in from Brisbane," replied Davo.

"I understand," she replied contemplatively. "Thank you for the information, and I'll hopefully see you later today."

"Please let us know your flight details, and we'll meet you at the airport," added Davo.

"Thank you, Sergeant. That would be much appreciated. There is a lot more to this situation than meets the eye. Seal off the homestead as a crime scene."

"Senior Sergeant Roberts is already onto it."

"A couple more questions before you go," she remarked. "Has Mr Henry been buried, and has someone cleaned his house?"

"Unfortunately, yes. His funeral occurred a week ago, and his ex-wife cleaned the house, preparing it for sale. She wanted no part of it after what happened there."

"All right, we can address that at another time. Let's focus on the current situation, the two men at the Cattle Station."

"Sounds good. We'll expect your call when you have your flight details."

"As soon as I know, you'll be informed," she replied before bidding goodbye.

Davo pressed the end call button on Phil's phone before returning to the group. There was a slight tremor in his voice as he shared the information he just received. "Dr Reynolds believes this case demands urgent action. She expressed concerns about the circumstances surrounding the deaths and stressed the necessity of a comprehensive forensic investigation. She also recommended cordoning off the area as a crime scene immediately."

Phil's eyes narrowed with concern. He understood the severity of the situation; he needed all available resources. He spoke to his team. "We're contacting the homicide squad in Brisbane. This is bigger than us, and we need their expertise. We must act now." Having said that, he reached for his phone and punched in the number for the homicide squad.

CHAPTER 10

In the shadowy recesses of Brisbane city, a simple ring, its design unassuming and its purpose unremarkable, seized Detective Graves's undivided attention. With a deft swipe, he activated the "Accept Call" feature on his mobile phone and, with an air of tension, announced, "Detective William Graves speaking.

On the other end of the line, the voice of Senior Sergeant Phil Roberts crackled with the weight of foreboding. "Detective Graves," he began, the importance of his tone palpable, "It's Senior Sergeant Phil Roberts of Weipa Police Station speaking. I urgently require your assistance regarding a matter that unfolded at Watson's River Station, east of Weipa, earlier this morning. Two men, same time, same place, discovered by the landowner's wife upon her return from a weekend in Cairns with friends."

"Thank you, Senior Sergeant Roberts," Detective Graves replied, his tone official and measured. "I've received preliminary information from the Cairns coroner. I'm assembling a team, and we'll depart for Weipa tomorrow on the first flight available. Upon arrival, we'll proceed with the briefing and expand our resources as necessary."

"Excellent. Your expertise is imperative in this matter. Something's not right, Detective. The situation doesn't quite add up; three relatively young men meeting their end in a fortnight and no tangible leads or solid motives to trace back to any suspects."

Detective Graves wasted no time replying, "Senior Sergeant, rest assured. My team is primed and ready. We'll be there as soon as we can."

"Once again, thank you. Time is of the essence in cases such as this. This event is our top priority."

Grave's voice sharpened, a solemn edge taking hold. "I understand. Now, I need your utmost attention. Under no circumstances, and I emphasise **under no circumstances**, should anyone tamper with a single element of the scene. We will operate as a unified front – you, the other local police, the forensic experts, all of us. Our greatest focus should be on preserving the integrity of the site."

With a weighted breath, cognisant of the intricacies that would ensue, Phil replied, "I understand and am already onto it. You have my contact details. Ring me just before you depart from Brisbane. Sergeant David Smith and I will rendezvous with you at Weipa airport, guiding you to our location."

"Indeed, I shall," the detective affirmed before severing the connection.

CHAPTER 11

Following a call from Dr Reynolds in the afternoon, Sergeant Phil Roberts was informed she had secured seats for herself and her forensic photographer for the next flight bound for Weipa from Cairns.

"We're scheduled to touch down later this afternoon, around one," she relayed with palpable anticipation. "You can brief me upon my arrival. And what about the homicide squad? When are they planning to join the scene?"

"Tomorrow morning, hopefully," Phil replied, exuding a proficient demeanour. "Detective Graves, dispatched from Brisbane, has assembled his team. They aim to arrive tomorrow as soon as flights permit."

"That's great," she replied warmly, "That way, you can inform me of what you already know before the Brisbane squad arrives, and we can continue the investigation early tomorrow morning, working as a team."

Earlier that day, the officers had initiated measures to safeguard the homestead. They were keen on formally interviewing Diane and, if he hadn't cleared out, Bruce. They aimed to gather as much local intel as possible before the forensic pathologist and the homicide squad rolled in.

Pulling out his notebook, Phil gently approached Diane. "I understand this is a difficult moment for you, but we need to ask you some questions," he said, settling into a seat at the picnic table alongside her and Veronica on the homestead's verandah.

Diane broke down in tears. "This is so overwhelmin' Phil. I dunno what to say or think. Can you give me some time to get me head together? Perhaps we can talk later this arvo? It's all a bit much now." She held her head in her hands as she rocked back and forth in her chair, tears streaming onto her white cotton dress adorned with sunflowers, her sun-kissed face now blotchy and red.

"I hear what you're saying, love," replied Phil kindly, "I know this is hard, but I will need to see your airline tickets and hotel bookings, plus take a look at your phone for any calls you might have made to John or others, and any photographs you took in Cairns during the weekend."

"Here, have a look at me phone now," Diane choked through muffled tears. She took out her phone and handed it to Phil. He scrolled through the happy photos of her with her girlfriends on the esplanade in Cairns, sharing drinks and meals at various restaurants. Her call log revealed she last called John Friday night.

"I see you called your husband on Friday. Was he all right then?" asked Phil.

"Yes," she said, "Fit as a fiddle. He'd been working mendin' fences most of the day. He said he was tired and was gonna take it easy. Have a few beers with Noel, cook a nice steak and then relax. That was our last conversation." Her grief-stricken eyes showed the extent of the pain of her sudden loss.

Phil could sense Diane was near breaking point. He brought a large thermos of coffee and a packet of scotch finger-biscuits designed for such occasions. He was a seasoned veteran and knew when witnesses and potential suspects required a moment's respite. "How about a cuppa coffee and a biscuit, love?" he offered gently. "We can continue our chat once you've had a moment to gather yourself. We'll need to ask you questions about what transpired here before you set off for Cairns."

"I understand, Phil," she replied, her voice holding a hint of gratitude. "I need a bit of a breather, and then I'll be right as rain. I gotta know what happened, and I'll do everythin' in me power to assist ya." With gratitude, she smiled through her tears and accepted the thermos lid filled to the brim with piping hot black coffee, sweetened just as she liked it, and a single biscuit.

Phil and Davo retrieved the thermos and settled into their police car. They had a pair of camping mugs on standby, relishing a much-needed break for themselves. The tasks ahead loomed large, and they'd soon have to go to the airport to meet Dr. Reynolds.

Once they'd drained the last of their coffee, the mugs still warming their hands and the rich, nutty scent clearing the fog from their troubled minds, Phil and Davo rejoined Diane on the verandah and settled on the well-worn picnic-style bench beside the two rocking chairs. Davo was at Phil's side, ready to transcribe the forthcoming conversation. Phil was the first to speak, "Are you ready to answer some more questions, Di?"

She nodded, her eyes weary from hurt, "No worries. Ask away."

"Could you tell me your departure time for Cairns," Phil asked, "And the most recent update you received about the farm before your departure?"

"I left around noon on Friday," she replied. "Everything seemed pretty normal then. John and Noel were workin' on some fence repairs, and I'd been helpin' out with some chores around the house. I made sure the blokes had some beers and steaks for the weekend. Didn't notice anything unusual at the time."

"All right," Phil said while Davo was scribbling notes in his notepad. "Did anyone call you about the incident?"

Diane took a deep breath, trying to steady her emotions. "That's the thing, no one called; normally, at least one of the farm hands checks in on the homestead, even if it's to share a beer with John or Noel. They're all good mates. I couldn't believe it when I came home today and found 'em both dead." She started to cry. "It was an absolute shock. I went to find Bruce in the donga and let him know. He was genuinely upset, ya know, grieving' for his brudda and John at the same time."

Phil and Davo exchanged glances, sympathising with Diane's anguish. "We understand this is a tough time for you, but any information you can give us might be helpful. The farm hands, are they always here?"

"Basically, yes. John employs a lot of local indigenous people. They like the work, and we like having 'em around. There's always somethin' to do on a farm. It never stops."

"Tell us more about the farm hands, if you don't mind," urged Davo.

"They all live off-site. Not far from 'ere. We have absolute faith and trust in all of 'em. They've all been workin' here for over a decade. None of 'em mind a bit of hard work. Mabel cleans the house; more recently, her eldest daughter has come on board to help with the new bed and breakfast. We've employed a couple of blokes to drive the cattle trucks to the slaughterhouses and help around the station. They dig in and help with whatever needs doin': gardenin', feeding the livestock, drivin' the tractors. You name it."

"Did John or Noel have any enemies or disagreements with anyone recently?"

She shook her head, tears welling up in her eyes. "No, not that I know of. John and Noel were mates and always got along fine. Can't imagine anyone wantin' to harm 'em."

"Fair enough," Phil said, offering her a reassuring smile. "We'll look into everything. Did you notice anyone else on the station while you were here? Maybe any strangers or unfamiliar faces?"

Diane thought for a moment, wiping a tear from her cheek. "Well, a coupla backpackers stopped by Frid'y arvo after I left, Bruce told me; they planned to free camp on one of our back paddocks on their way to the Tip of Cape York. They must've been passin' through, takin' in the sights, I s'pose. Can't say I saw anyone else out of the ordinary."

"Backpackers, huh?" Davo chimed in. "Did you catch their names, by any chance?"

Diane scratched her head, trying to recall. "Ah, now let me think. One of 'em was named Jake, I think. The other one, I can't quite remember. But they'd left by the time I came home. I doubt they had anythin' to do with it. You can have a look for yourselves; they left their names in the check-in book near the front gate."

"So, did you set eyes on them?" pressed Phil.

"Nah, we don't interfere too much with the free campers. Inspecting the log books when I return is a bit of a ritual. The road to the homestead cuts through that paddock. And you'll find a sign on the highway, just near the turnoff, offerin' a free spot for the night to anyone who might want or need it."

Phil absorbed this information, his brow furrowing in thought. "Were there any other visitors or campers out here at the same time?" he asked, his interest still keen.

"Well, ya see, it must've been a busy weekend on the station," Diane began, leaning back against the chair, the wide brim of her Akubra hat casting a broad shadow over her face. "Mad Maureen, she's a bit of a wanderer. She was campin' in one of the paddocks 'round here when I left on Frid'y, but I reckon she's moved on now. She's got a peculiar way of talkin' and them funny eyes, but she's harmless."

"Who was helping with the fences? Anyone new?" asked Phil.

"Just Bruce Hudson was helpin' when I left. He's a hard worker when he's not on the bottle. Noel and John are pretty handy, but occasionally they need a bit of a hand; they often call on Bruce, have done for years," Diane replied, tucking a loose strand of greying blonde hair behind her ear.

"What about the free campers? Do they normally help out if they are camped on the station?"

"Yes, of course. It's all hands on deck at times at this place. Everyone sees it as a payment for the free use of our land," Diane casually replied.

Phil asked, "Did John and Noel have a good relationship with Bruce? Did they ever have any barnies?"

"Oh no, never, he's a good bloke, he is. Known 'im for years. He's been workin' on and off at the station for quite some time now. Helps out with odd jobs when needed; you know how it is. But nah, he's a decent sort. Can't see 'im doin' no harm to anyone."

"Is Bruce still around?" asked Phil

"Probably; he normally sticks around for a week or two when needed. I guess he'll be leaving now. As I said, he was the first person I told when I found John and Noel. He was shaken up and real upset. You'll find him in the donga near the old abattoir if he's still here."

"We'll keep that in mind," Phil said. "Thanks for your cooperation, Diane. We'll do our best to get to the bottom of this," Phil said, "Thanks for sharing what you know, love. We'll keep working on this case and hopefully get to the bottom of it soon."

As they strolled away, Diane said, "You know, Phil, you lot can always bunk up in the old homestead for a few nights. Saves ya the trouble of driving back and forth to Weipa ev'ry day. It's quite a roomy place, recently spruced up by yours truly. Even if I do say so meself, it's pretty comfortable," she paused, offering a warm smile through her tear-stained face, "If that's of any help to ya."

"Thank you, Di. We might take you up on that offer. It would be great to have a central place out here, close to the scene. That way, we can ensure no one else enters the property. I am much obliged," responded Phil.

After leaving Diane to grieve, Phil and Davo exchanged solemn glances. They knew there was much ground to cover in their investigation. Stepping purposefully forward, they made their way toward Constable Mark Doomadgee and Constable Wayne Reed, who just concluded their search around the farm for any additional evidence, potential witnesses, or fellow campers who might be of assistance.

The four huddled together, exchanging notes, theories, and speculations. They discussed the possible involvement of free campers, curious if anyone might have witnessed or heard something that could shed light on the tragedy. It was an isolated area, making gathering information all the more challenging. Mark and Wayne told the two sergeants there was no sign of Mad Maureen; she left the farm late on Friday night, according to one of the farm hands, and the two campers signed the check-out book early Sunday morning.

As Phil checked his wristwatch, he realised it was time to begin the hundred-and-fifty-kilometre drive back to Weipa airport. The morning slipped through their fingers, and the clock hands were past 1 p.m. Instructing Davo to remain at the station with vigilant eyes, he designated the old homestead as their makeshift command centre, at least for the next few days. Wayne would continue his examination of the station's surroundings before regrouping with the other officers and the forensic pathologist come evening.

Turning to Mark, Phil spoke thoughtfully, "I reckon you, Constable Doomadgee, are the best man to have a yarn with Bruce. You both speak the same lingo, part of the same mob. Di mentioned you'll likely find him in the donga near the old abattoir out back. Does that sit right with you?"

"It fits perfectly, Phil. I'm grateful for this chance," Mark responded humbly.

As Phil climbed into the car and headed back along the rugged, mostly unpaved road to Weipa airport, Mark approached the donga. He couldn't help but feel a mix of emotions. The enormity of the situation weighed heavily on his heart. John and Noel, their friends, were gone, and the circumstances surrounding their deaths were shrouded in mystery.

Mark knew if Bruce hadn't shot through already, he would be the best bloke to shed any light on the situation. However, he also understood this fella might be considered a suspect. Despite this, he felt compelled to step forward and take charge. He believed through their connection, he would be able to get the most out of him.

As the officer approached the dimly lit donga, he recognised Bruce sitting quietly inside, lost in his thoughts. Upon seeing him, Mark let out a sigh of relief. At least he was still here. He greeted Bruce with a nod of familiarity and respect. Being from the same mob meant they shared a deep bond, a connection through their culture and heritage.

"Hey, brudda," Mark began gently, "I heard what happened to John and Noel. It's a terrible thing, mate. How ya holdin' up?"

Bruce looked up, his eyes reflecting the pain and confusion he must have been feeling. "I can't believe it. They were good blokes, always there for us. And now they've gone, and I dunno what 'appened."

Mark nodded, understanding his sentiments all too well. "I'm here for you, mate. We all loved 'em, and we'll find out the truth together. But I need your help. Can you tell me anything about what might have happened?"

"Well, the fellas asked me to swing by the homestead on Satd'y night. They wanted to have a few brews together after chowin' down on their steak dinner. But, ya know, John and Noel, they started feelin' proper crook that night, eh? Vomiting and all. Must've been somethin' they ate or drank, I reckon. They were keen for an early night, too, which ain't our usual way. Satday ~~Satd'y~~, we usually get proper into it, and Sund'y, well, that's our day of restin'. But then, Mond'y comes 'round, and I hear from Di both of 'em are dead," he concluded with a heavy sigh, his eyes downcast as he spoke in hushed tones.

Mark suggested they move the conversation outside because of the lack of natural light inside the donga. Just as he was preparing to leave the dimly lit abode, his perceptive gaze caught a glimpse of something amiss amidst the barren desolation. Atop the mantelpiece lay an array of peculiar items. Approaching deliberately and cautiously, he subjected each object to scrutiny. There sat six pristine fentanyl patches, still untouched. Beside them, a small plastic container bore the label "ordine," yet, to Mark's dismay, the container was hollow, its contents long depleted. His search then turned to the four boxes of thirty-milligram codeine tablets; upon closer inspection, two boxes were empty.

He stepped outside to join Bruce. The afternoon sun was now high in the sky, casting golden light on the men's faces as they spoke. They sat together on the battered wooden porch of the donga, their faces etched in sorrow. Bruce's eyes were weary, a deep sadness lingering in their depths, while Mark's brow was furrowed, his features a portrait of concern.

"Now," said Mark, getting straight to the point, "I seen them medications inside ya donga, mate. How did ya come across those?"

"I'll be straight up with ya, brudda. Mad Maureen was camping out 'ere. She sold 'em to me. Didn't say how she came across 'em, but I expect they were stolen,' he paused before adding, "Given her reputation." He looked up to see Constable Doomadgee looking at him quizzically, a concerned frown clouding his expression. "I needed 'em for me back, fella. It's been playing up real bad. All those years of shearing and mending fences takes its toll on a bloke my age."

"Do you know where Maureen is now?" asked Mark, looking intently at Bruce.

"Nah, she took off real quick. Vanished in the blink of an eye, soon as she sold me them drugs late on Frid'y night. Didn't say where she was headin'."

"Tell me what happened after you left Noel and John?"

"After the drinking session ended earlier than expected, I came back to the donga and went to bed. No point staying up if ya got no one to 'ave a few drinks with."

"And what about Saturday night?" pressed the constable.

"I went out huntin' kangaroos in me ute. Got a few good-sized ones; used the best bits for me tucker that night, the back straps. I was buggered, so I ended upending sleeping most of the next day. Had some tea, then called it a night. Was gonna call in on Noel and John later this mornin' when Diane came rushin' over in her car to tell me the horrible news."

"Did you see anyone or go hunting with anyone else?"

"Yeah, brudda, one of the other campers drove the ute, and I stood in the back behind the spotlights, shootin' the roos."

"Can you remember their name?"

"I think Jake. Said he was with his girlfriend, spendin' a coupla nights campin' out 'ere. I said I'd give him some 'roo meat if he helped with the driving. Seemed a fair deal to both of us."

"Anyone else?" asked Mark.

"Yeah, Carol, Walt's ex. She was good friends with John and Diane. Came out on Frid'y arvo and brought the blokes some pavlova. She knew Di was goin' away for the weekend and wanted to see the fridge was stocked and they had some good tucker to eat."

"Any other people on the station?" asked Mark for completeness.

"There's always a few farm hands hangin' about. Other than them, not a soul."

"You've been a great help, brudda," Mark's hand came to rest on Bruce's shoulder, a comforting gesture that spoke volumes. "Just one more question for curiosity's sake – did you share food with the two blokes?"

"John offered me some, but after they both said they was crook, I had me reservations. I didn't want no part of any food that mighta made them fellas crook. I seen the pav in the fridge when I helped meself to a second beer. There was only 'bout half left."

"Thanks for your cooperation, mate," said Mark, "I've gotta be honest with ya, though. Things aren't lookin' too rosy for ya right now. We've got two deceased blokes with no obvious cause of death, and you admitted you were probably one of the last to see them. You've also acknowledged purchasing hefty amounts of regulated medications you suspected were stolen and still have some in your possession. We've yet to check out your alibi, and the empty bottle of liquid morphine is not helpin' either. Those other coppers, they're bound to raise an eyebrow, and I can't exactly turn a blind eye to it meself. Add to all that you pointed the bone at Walt just a week before he kicked the bucket. I'm afraid there's a fair bit of evidence pointin' squarely at you."

Bruce wiped a tear from his cheek, his voice a mix of defiance and anguish. "I know, Mark, but Walt, he had it comin'. He took our land and desecrated our sacred sites. Can't carry a grudge forever, brudda. Gotta do somethin' 'bout it, or it eats away at your insides. I was drunk, seething. He was rubbin' his wealth in our faces, the whole community."

Mark's eyes held understanding as he nodded solemnly. "We're all stayin' put on the farm tonight. Phil's gone back to Weipa to meet the forensic pathologist and bring her out here. We have a lotta work to get through, and we'll need your assistance until we sort this all out. You'll need to stay here till then, mate."

Bruce gave a weary nod, his gaze distant as he stared at the ground. "No worries, Mark. I ain't goin' nowhere. John and Noel, they were mates, ya know? Noel was part of our mob. This sorry business gonna stretch on for days. Grief, it's like a shadow that don't leave our side. But let's call him Barlang for now. Them white fellas, I know they gotta use his rightful name for this investigation, but, us bruddas, we gotta show respect."

Mark's hand squeezed his friend's shoulder gently, his voice soft yet firm. "I hear ya. I'll spread the word, but we'll keep the meetin' away from this place. Gotta preserve the potential crime scene."

He looked up at Mark, gratitude and conviction mingling in his gaze. "Fair enough, brudda. I'll gather the mob for the sorry business. Barlang, he's been part of this land for years. It's his home, true and proper."

Mark's gaze met Bruce's, a shared understanding passing between them. "You do that, fella. I'll make sure word gets around, too."

Bruce replied, his face solemn, his eyes downcast, "This land, it's seen too much hurt. Maybe this funeral, this sorry business, it'll mend what's been torn. I've changed me ways too, mate. No more grog for me. Family is what matters now. I'll start looking for a place for the sorry business tomorrow morning."

"Before I take off," the police officer said cautiously, "I reckon it'd be good to give Phil a ring. Let the fellas hear your side of things rather than just goin' by what I say. You alright with that, brudda?"

His head bowed low, eyes weary and bloodshot, Bruce replied, "Sure."

Mark dialled Phil's number, and after a brief exchange, they both concurred hearing Bruce's account directly was the wisest course of action. This would prevent any potential confusion or misinterpretation down the line.

"You reckon you can walk with me to the old homestead, mate? Phil and the other two officers wanna hear it straight from the horse's mouth. Keep everything on the level." Mark said to Bruce.

"Sure thing, brudda. I reckon a bit of distance from this place would do me good. Feel like there's a darkness settlin' in me heart right now."

As Mark left the donga with Bruce, he couldn't shake the feeling this was just the beginning of a complex and challenging investigation. He knew he must tread carefully, balancing his duty as a police officer with his loyalty toward his mob and Bruce.

CHAPTER 12

At the stroke of 3 p.m., the silhouette of Dr Reynold's plane made contact with the earth, its tyres meeting the runway with a gentle thud; Phil stood ready to greet her. As the doctor and her photographer disembarked from the small Bombardier DHC-8-400 8Q, a seventy-four-seater plane dwarfed by the vastness of the outback, they were immediately thrust into a storm of red earth. Despite the recent sealing of the runway, the relentless outback's rust-coloured dust, like an aggressive assailant, attacked her from all angles. It infiltrated her senses without remorse. The red dirt invaded her nostrils, permeated her ears, made her eyes gritty, painted her skin and clothes with an ochre hue, and left her with the surreal sensation of literally chewing earth. The grit even found its way into the crevices and gaps between her teeth as if intent on claiming every inch of her being.

With a knowing smile, Phil offered a friendly warning, "Shoulda warned ya 'bout that," he chuckled, his eyes crinkling at the corners. "Follow me, Dr Reynolds. I assume this is your forensic photographer?" Phil inquired, scrutinising a middle-aged, portly man with a shiny bald head and a weary look.

"Please, call me Catherine. And yes. Senior Sergeant Phil Roberts, meet George," she confirmed. George extended his right hand to Phil, who shook it firmly, their grips connecting.

"You'll both have to collect your luggage outside the terminal. That's the way we do things 'round these parts."

With a nod, he directed Catherine and the photographer towards the car park, signalling for them to follow him to Watson's River Station after picking up their rental car. The group reached the isolated cattle station around five p.m., and the forensic pathologist immediately surveyed the area. The homestead was meticulously cordoned off, securing the potential crime scene for further investigation. Davo sat outside on the verandah and warmly waved to Dr Reynolds.

"Would you like me to accompany you inside?" Phil asked.

"No, thank you, Sergeant. I'm confident I'll manage," she responded, reflecting years of experience and her ability to detach emotionally from potentially distressing scenes.

"I'll return to the homestead and chat with the other two officers. Davo will still be on watch when you're finished," Phil informed her.

"Thank you. I'll be in touch soon," she replied, her tone somewhat distant.

Aware that her keen eye for detail was crucial, Catherine methodically scanned the surroundings, keenly attuned to anything appearing amiss or deviated from the norm. Diane and Veronica were still on the verandah, and despite the dreadful findings inside, they both gave Dr Reynolds and George a warm smile. They were grateful for their time and assistance.

One by one, the forensic team cautiously crossed the threshold into the solemn homestead by slipping under the yellow crime tape. As Catherine made her way through the eerily quiet rooms, her footsteps echoed on the polished floorboards, breaking the silence. The sight greeting her in the kitchen rendered her speechless. A Caucasian man slumped motionless on the kitchen table, and a younger

Indigenous male lay sprawled on the floor, pinned beneath a fallen chair. George silently followed, camera at the ready.

Catherine opted to stay a secure distance behind the kitchen counter. Her photographer mirrored her movements closely, poised for guidance. In the waning light of the day, she examined the two motionless figures with a blend of clinical detachment and deep reverence for the stories their remains could tell.

In a calm tone, she addressed George, "Could you capture both wide-angle shots of the scene and some detailed close-ups?"

A simple nod from George sufficed, a response that suited Catherine just fine; she found his calm presence reassuring. As daylight surrendered to the embrace of night and shadows danced around the lifeless figures, Catherine knew her work was far from done.

Arriving at the old homestead, Phil placed another call, this time to Davo. He instructed Davo to return to the homestead with the forensic pathologist once she was prepared. Phil also asked Davo to reassure the doctor and her photographer that there was ample space for everyone, ensuring everyone could have their own room during this initial investigation stage. He acknowledged this might shift once the homicide squad arrived, but for now, Phil was aware of the importance of providing a space for everyone to process the day's events and get a good night's rest before an early start tomorrow.

A few hours later, hearing the approach of footsteps, Davo turned to see the pathologist and her photographer emerging from the homestead. He rose from his seat, his voice slicing through the silence as he neared her. "Dr Reynolds?"

"Yes," she answered evenly.

"Would you like an escort back to the old homestead? Phil's keen on a sit-down with the lot of us, Bruce included.

Wants us all readin' from the same hymn sheet, if you catch my drift."

"Sure," she replied, her thoughts racing as she formed a plan for the investigation's next steps. She trailed behind Dave, and George followed some distance behind, their steps leading them to the cusp of the front door of the old homestead. She raised her gaze to find the trio of officers gathered around the kitchen bench, a large, weathered table dominating the centre of the dining room.

"Evenin', Dr Reynolds," the three officers greeted almost in unison.

"Please, call me Catherine. If we're to work together as a cohesive investigative team, let's dispense with formalities. I've found fostering a more personal connection builds trust, which is crucial in our line of work," she replied sincerely, a marked departure from her clinical demeanour at the crime scene. Instantly, the men seemed to warm to her. She held a hand out to indicate the forensic photographer, "This is George. He will be documenting all the evidence we accumulate."

The men directed nods towards George, and then Phil spoke, "Choose a room and make yourself comfortable, George. We'll call you when dinner's ready. Take some rest. The rest of us will review today's events and resume the investigation tomorrow."

George, head down, quietly slipped into the hallway. Catherine briefed the officers, "He always brings his own food. He has several food intolerances, so he's always prepared. George values his own company. Don't worry too much about him. I'll communicate with him directly as necessary."

The night unfolded its velvety canvas, a silver crescent moon ascending briskly, casting a haunting glow across the expansive landscape. Wearied from the day's relentless pursuit of leads, the officers exchanged knowing glances. It made little sense to embark on a gruelling one-hundred-and-fifty-kilometre drive back to Weipa or Aurukun in their current state. Instead, they decided to accept Diane's earlier offer and remain at the station for at least a few nights, ensuring they remained near the potential crime scene. A proper rest would be their most potent asset in the trials of the days ahead.

As the homicide squad's imminent arrival approached, a pervasive weariness settled in. Yet, Phil couldn't dismiss the insistent pull compelling him to be thoroughly briefed on all developments before they settled in for the night. With a dogged tenacity, he called for Catherine, his fellow officers, and Bruce to convene this meeting before the need for rest took over.

Phil knew the value of a down-and-dirty round table session, a raw exchange of insights from the depths of the potential crime scene. He sought to ensure everyone was in lockstep, bound by the collective knowledge that could make or break this case.

CHAPTER 13

Seated around the weathered, substantial oak dining table at the homestead, on heavy oak chairs that groaned and creaked under their weight, Senior Sergeant Phil Roberts, Constable Reed, Constable Mark Doomadgee and Sergeant David Smith delved into the mounting evidence. Catherine and Bruce joined them at the table, silently absorbing the knowledge gleaned from the investigation's progress.

Once again, Phil assumed command of the proceedings, "All right, team," he addressed them as one, "We've got a possible double murder on our hands, and we must approach this with utmost professionalism. Mark, I appreciate you for bringing Bruce into the fold; Catherine, your expertise is invaluable."

Catherine remained silent and acknowledged the sentiment with a nod of gratitude.

Turning to Bruce, Phil's gaze met his, a shared understanding in their eyes. "Your dedication is clear, and Mark tells me your insights have already proven valuable. Please recount everything you've observed for the benefit of our team. Every detail counts." He turned and looked at his fellow police officers to ensure everyone was listening.

Returning to Bruce, he looked him straight in the eye, "This is a formal police interview, and all your responses will be recorded. Please state your name and address for the record."

After stating his name and place of residence, Bruce leaned forward, his worn hands, those of a diligent worker, resting on the table's weathered surface. With a deep, steady voice, he began to recount the events he observed at the station in the days before the discovery of the two bodies. His descriptions were clear-cut and precise; there was no embellishment.

Catherine listened intently, occasionally interjecting with questions or seeking clarification on specific points, "What time did you come to the homestead to have beers with Noel and John?" She asked, "What time did you leave?"

Bruce answered earnestly, "I went over to their place 'bout eight p.m. and only stayed an hour or so. Musta been back at the donga by nine-thirty p.m. at the latest Satd'y night."

"And tell me about the empty ordine bottle containing potent strengths of liquid morphine and the missing fentanyl patches," she pressed.

"I tasted the ordine meself at the donga after Maureen sold it to me on Frid'y. It tasted shockin' and didn't make me feel any good, so I chucked it down the drain. Them patches and pills gave me some relief, so I decided to take a couple over to John and Barlang," he paused before using the deceased man's birth name, "Noel."

"I see," came her measured reply. Her brow furrowed as she processed the information, mentally piecing together the puzzle before them.

Bruce began to speak again as Phil watched the room, gauging the reactions of each team member. The sergeant could sense the collective determination in the air, a shared understanding they were facing a challenging case. It was pitch black outside now; the once vivid hues of the evening were now muted, swallowed by the encroaching shadows.

Once Bruce finished, there was a moment of reflective silence. Phil broke it, his voice resonating with purpose. "Thanks, Bruce. Your account is helpful," he turned, looking warmly at the man who had so far appeared direct and invaluable in gathering new evidence, "Can we give you a lift back to ya donga?"

"Nah, thanks. I don't mind a bit of a walk. Stretch me legs and clear me head, fella."

"Before you go, Mr Hudson," Catherine interrupted, "You say the men offered you food that evening. Can you tell me what was in the fridge?"

"Sure. A few beers, some steaks, a few veggies in the crisper and a half-eaten pavlova," came the immediate reply, accompanied by a shrug.

"Any what was on top of the pavlova? Cream? Yoghurt? Fruit?"

"Not sure if it was cream or yoghurt, but there were three types of berries."

"Three?" asked Catherine, "What sort?"

"Looked like raspberries, strawberries and blueberries to me," replied Bruce hesitantly.

"I see," replied Catherine, taking a mental note of Bruce's reply. "Those are all my questions for now. Thank you, Mr Hudson."

"No problem. Is there anything else?" Bruce asked, scanning the expressions of the pathologist and the officers.

Phil surveyed each individual, receiving subtle headshakes indicating they had no additional queries. "That covers it for now, Bruce. Thanks again for your cooperation."

Mark turned to Bruce as he exited the old homestead through the front door, "I'll meet ya back at the donga at ten tomorrow. We'll continue our talk," he said, rising from his chair and seeing Bruce to the door. "Seeya then, mate."

"Okay, brudda, I'll be waitin' for ya."

As Bruce returned to his lodgings, Phil turned to the rest of the group, "Now," he began, "Let's discuss our next course of action. Once the homicide squad arrives, I suggest we adopt a collaborative approach and allow Detective Graves to lead and assign roles to officers with nothing else to do. Mark will continue his questioning and evidence collection with Bruce tomorrow. Catherine, you clearly understand your responsibilities in this investigation and will have a one-on-one conversation with him. I have a few phone calls to make, starting with Carol. But it's too late to call her now. Wayne and Davo, are you comfortable following Detective Graves and assisting him and his team wherever necessary?"

"Yes, sir," Wayne affirmed while Davo nodded silently.

The team convened in spirited discourse, exchanging ideas and weighing potential leads. Catherine's expertise in forensics proved pivotal, steering their approach. "I propose we collaborate closely with the homicide squad when they get here," Catherine suggested, glancing at her colleagues. "I'm well-acquainted with them; we understand our roles and how to navigate without hindering one another. We are adept at playing our parts in a thorough investigation like this. I've worked with Detective Graves on numerous occasions previously."

As the clock neared midnight, the team concluded their discussions. The air was thick with fatigue, urging them to surrender to their beds. They dispersed to their respective rooms, seeking solace from the unrelenting demands of their duty. The stillness of the outback surrounded them, a sanctuary of calm amid a world brimming with unanswered questions. Despite this, sleep eluded them; a whirlwind of thoughts and reflections consumed their minds.

CHAPTER 14

As the first rays of the morning sun kissed the horizon, Bruce stirred from his cot and made his way on foot to a quiet part of the station, far from the homestead. He had a stubborn glint in his eyes. He wanted to set up an area for the sorry business, where grief could be shared, and healing might begin.

The burden of profound grief weighed heavily upon his mob, a community that had witnessed an abundance of pain. The sorrow ran deep within him, an ache that called for acknowledgment and resolution—this moment presented a pivotal juncture for him, an opportunity to mend the rifts within his kinship and regain the favour he once held. In the stillness of the morning, he envisioned a sanctuary where the echoes of shared pain could be transformed into the foundation of communal resilience, turning the tide towards a brighter and more united future.

As he stumbled through the bushland, he was hit by the pungent smell of a the deadly nightshade bush. Glancing about, he noticed their dark berries standing out against the morning light. Bunches were missing and seemed freshly picked, and small shoe prints were visible in the soil. His heart ached as he recalled the knowledge passed down from his mob, skills learned in his formative years as he tracked and hunted for sustenance.

He trailed the series of shoe prints until they intersected with the road, his gaze shifting to the ground, where he observed three tyre tracks. The tracks appeared fresh, likely imprinted on the earth within the past few days. Scanning the surroundings, he noticed the point where the shoe prints abruptly ceased, and one of the tyre tracks momentarily paused before resuming; a vivid scarlet droplet of dried blood adorned a patch of cut grass near the driveway leading to the recently constructed homestead. It might not have been much, but his sharp eyes didn't miss this subtle yet crucial detail.

The mine's impact on his people was profound, erasing their traditional ways and leaving a void. During his formative years, Bruce acquired his formidable tracking skills from his people, a skill set rooted in trailing for sustenance. The intrusive presence had halted the indigenous people's age-old hunting and gathering practices. Ironically, the mining company claimed ownership of the land, stripping away the rights and heritage of the traditional landowners.

Anger still burned within him. Walt Henry and Comalco had destroyed so much of his people's traditional ways of life that it tore his mob apart. He resented that members of his community were forced to work in the mines to support their families.

Maybe John Granger, the wealthy pastoralist who bought multiple shares in the company, was also to blame. As for Barlang, he was a traitor. He had worked for the mines before joining John on the cattle station. Still, Barlang was part of his mob, and the sorry business must be carried through.

After walking for over an hour, Bruce arrived at a spacious area enclosed by towering eucalyptus trees and vibrant yellow wattles in full bloom. Within him, Bruce felt a profound sense of knowing this was the exact spot he had been looking for; it echoed in his bones. He set about painstakingly clearing the land, designating it as the sacred site for mourning. He ensured it was free from any obstructions or distractions, adorning it with his paintings and carvings.

This carefully curated space would serve as a solace where the community could come together to grieve, remember, and find strength in their shared heartache. He envisioned every member of his mob feeling the profound embrace of their collective sorrow, finding comfort in the unity they drew from one another. Bruce's endeavour went beyond mere physical preparation; it was a profound gesture of solidarity. He yearned for the acceptance of his people after years of living on the outskirts of society. This was an opportunity to finally find a place of belonging after years of isolation.

Mark Doomadgee echoed the call for unity as the news rippled through the community that morning. He spoke to elders, sent messages through the bush telegraph, and contacted neighbouring communities. The response was heartening; people expressed their willingness to travel to be present in this profound loss.

A solemn hush, an uncharacteristic stillness, settled over the land as Bruce diligently continued his task of clearing away any remnants. He kindled a fire carefully, encircling it with stones amassed during his morning's endeavours. This fire held a multifaceted purpose: it provided warmth, a means to prepare sustenance and a conduit for the cleansing ritual.

Bruce created a place to welcome his extended family with open arms. Standing solitary in the heart of this cleared expanse, he took a moment to pause, the weight of his responsibility mirrored in his eyes. He knew this sorry business was not just for them but for the generations that came before and those yet to come. Together, they would honour the memory of their ancestors and find strength in their shared grief.

Following Barlang's passing, he wanted the homestead to become a sanctuary for healing. He yearned for the moment when narratives would be exchanged, melodies would fill the air, and ceremonies would be enacted, each thread interweaving to craft a vivid mosaic of recollection and fortitude. The earth would stand as a silent sentinel, bestowing its unwavering endorsement upon this community, knitted together by a shared chronicle, blood, and an unshakeable sense of harmony. His lineage and kin were as intrinsic to the landscape and heavens as to him.

CHAPTER 15

As the first rays of dawn brushed over the timeworn homestead, Phil was the first to wake, effectively transforming the aging abode into an impromptu headquarters. Sleep had been elusive, his mind a storm of thoughts and considerations. As the first light touched the weathered window panes, he sat at the aged wooden dining table, bathed in a luminous embrace. With deliberate movements, he prepared a fresh cup of coffee, allowing its comforting heat to mirror the cadence of his reflections.

Before him lay an expanse of information, an assortment of details systematically gathered by his team. The sheer volume of facts inundated him, demanding his unwavering focus and astute analysis. He yearned to weave these threads into a coherent tapestry of understanding, eager to convene with Catherine and the three other officers for another round of discussions before Mark reengaged with Bruce.

A short while later, Catherine strolled into the dining room, clad in sky-blue scrubs serving as makeshift pyjamas. Settling in beside Phil, she offered a cheerful morning greeting. Her eyes flickered briefly to the faint shadows beneath his, noting, "Looks like you got as solid a sleep as I did." A playful smirk tugged at her lips. With a languid stretch, she raised her arms above her head, an inevitable yawn slipping past her.

Phil turned to Catherine and detected the telltale etchings of fatigue beneath her eyes. "Yeah, my mind would just not shut off."

"I know the feeling all too well," she replied with a knowing smile.

In the distance, the faint sound of showers running echoed from a few rooms away. Mark was the next to join them, followed shortly by Davo and Wayne, as they all gradually emerged freshly bathed, scrubbed clean and prepared to confront the day ahead.

The clock had just ticked past eight a.m., and the ancient homestead was bathed in light, the dining area, now aglow with the promise of morning, rapidly warming under the sun's touch. In the absence of air conditioning, the atmosphere was becoming stifling, causing beads of sweat to form on the foreheads of the investigating team despite the whirring fan above.

Phil had given Diane the okay to stay with her daughter the previous evening, understanding that she did not want to be near the deceased bodies of her husband and their close mate, Noel. Prior to her departure, in her characteristic considerate manner, Diane had replenished the fridge, freezer and cupboards in the homestead from her own kitchen, guaranteeing the team wouldn't go hungry. This allowed them to channel all their energies into the inquiry, unburdened by the mundane chore of shopping.

Phil prepared a satisfying meal of toast, crispy bacon and scrambled eggs as Catherine and the three officers converged around the sturdy dining table. As they gathered, Catherine and the officers braced themselves for the long day ahead. For Phil, the lingering silence on the phone weighed heavily. The anticipated call from the homicide squad remained elusive, postponing their commencement. It meant a late kick-off, with the added inconvenience of the squad flying from Brisbane to Cairns before catching a regional flight to Weipa, perhaps precipitating further delays.

Cooking was a refuge for Phil, a moment to gather his thoughts before immersing himself in a tangle of discussions. He studied the expressions of those gathered around him as he prepared to revisit the details of the investigation; his gaze moved from Catherine to the three other officers, noting the combination of weariness and unyielding dedication evident in their faces. A contemplative silence enveloped them.

Catherine was fully cognisant of her role in this investigation. The other officers patiently awaited Phil's words, poised to follow his lead.

"All right," Phil began, breaking the pensive silence with a gravelly cadence commanding attention. "We've gathered some pieces to this puzzle, but we must fit them together. Let's go over what we know so far."

"First up," he continued, his eyes narrowing as he ticked off points on his fingers. "Bruce, our prime suspect, had himself an empty bottle of liquid morphine and a stash of those fentanyl patches. Claims he got them on the cheap to ease his chronic back pain. But we'll keep a close eye on that."

Davo, his brow furrowing, added, "Mad Maureen is said to be the one who supplied Bruce with those meds before she scarpered off the station on Friday night."

"Exactly," Phil affirmed, shifting his attention to each officer. "Maureen's possession of those medications likely ties into the recent incident involving stolen meds from the RFDS doctor's bag in Weipa last week. Fingerprints were lifted, but we'll need to return to that later with the whirlwind we're currently in. At least we took the fingerprints and the DNA samples. We can easily cross-check the prints with Dr Stephen O'Leary and his nurse, Cindy Newman, who we know both had access to the medication bag. As for any other fingerprints, we already have Mad Maureen's on file. Might be an easy one to solve."

Constable Reed leaned forward, his eyes gleaming with a flicker of insight. "Diane, she seems to have an alibi that lines up, right? Timing's snug for both those men's demises."

A thoughtful silence settled over the room as they contemplated Diane's possible involvement.

Mark Doomadgee's deep voice resonated next. "Carol, she swung by the station and dropped off a pavlova for our departed mates. Might've been a friendly gesture, but it's worth keepin' in mind."

Phil leaned back in his chair, steepling his fingers. "And as it stands, apart from a handful of passersby, our suspect pool seems pretty shallow. I think we can dismiss the possible involvement of the young free campers. Bruce's story about them checks out with the log books, and Diane said there was no sign of them when she arrived home on Monday. I think we can rule her out too, her photos from Cairns and flight times all check out."

The room fell into a contemplative hush, the weight of their discoveries settling in. Phil broke the silence, his voice steady and resolute. "We're making progress, team. But we can't afford to let our guard down, not even for a moment. We'll regroup here tonight and keep pluggin' away at this investigation. Right now, I'm leaning towards a bleak outlook for Bruce. Mark will have another chat with him in the donga as planned to see if we can dig up anything else. Meanwhile, I think the..." His words trailed off, swallowed by the abrupt ring of his phone.

"Sergeant Roberts, Detective Graves speaking," came the stern, slightly impatient voice on the other end. "Our flight's been delayed. We're leaving Brisbane at 10:30 a.m. With the connection, we should be in Weipa by around 6 p.m."

Time hung heavy in the air. "I understand. These things happen. We hoped your team would arrive earlier so we could continue our investigations with the benefit of your expertise," Phil replied, his brow furrowing in concern.

His voice was indifferent as if he tempered his expectations. "Do you have any updates for me?"

"In fact, I do. It appears Mr Bruce Hudson had access to a significant quantity of presumably stolen opiates. We discovered an empty bottle of liquid morphine, two depleted and two intact packets of codeine, and several fentanyl patches in his donga."

Graves absorbed this information with deliberate consideration. "I see," he responded slowly, his thoughts churning. "And what are Catherine's initial thoughts on this?"

"She hasn't had a chance to thoroughly examine the victims yet."

"Well then, I strongly recommend she commences her examinations immediately. Given the prevailing weather conditions up there – the heat and humidity – we need the evidence to be as fresh as possible. We're in dire need of answers, Sergeant," the detective asserted firmly.

"Yes, I'll make sure of it," Phil replied with a hint of irritation.

"May I have a word with the pathologist, please?"

"Of course," Phil said, covering the microphone and turning to Catherine. "It's Detective Graves. He wants to talk to you," she nodded and Phil passed her the phone.

"Hello, Detective Graves, Dr Reynolds speaking. How can I assist you?"

"Hello, Catherine. I'm relieved to know you're on the case. We go way back," came his slippery tone.

In reaction, Catherine shut her eyes, rolling them beneath her closed lids, before retorting, "Indeed, Detective. I had hoped for a more peaceful life when I left Brisbane. It seems that's not the case."

"What time did you arrive at the station?" He asked.

"Yesterday, around 3 p.m. I managed a brief look at the deceased before night fell. I was hoping to start fresh this morning."

"That sounds like the best course. What about the other officers and their plans before we arrive?"

"Sergeant Phil Roberts has assembled a solid team. He's a seasoned pro. Knows his stuff," she praised, lowering her voice discreetly. "Then there's Constable Mark Doomadgee and Constable Wayne Reed from Aurukun station, young but eager. And Sergeant David Smith, who's been in Weipa for six months. They are a good bunch. Mark plans to speak with the suspect again this morning. Phil plans to continue coordinating with us until your squad arrives, and Wayne and Davo will likely scour the station for further evidence."

Detective Graves chuckled. "Already on a first-name basis, I see. You have a way of putting people at ease, Catherine."

"Old habits die hard, Detective," she smiled to herself.

"So, is the suspect still on the station?"

"Yes, Bruce Hudson. He's from the same mob as Constable Doomadgee. He's been cooperative so far."

"Excellent. It sounds like you've got a handle on this. We'll catch up later tonight," replied Detective Graves.

"And, by the way," Catherine responded, "Diane Granger, the wife of the deceased station owner, has offered the old homestead, now a B&B with ten rooms, for us to use as a makeshift command centre. Should be spacious enough for all of us, depending on the size of your team."

"Thanks, Catherine. I'll see you tonight and meet the rest of the team."

"Indeed, you shall," she ended the call and handed the phone back to Phil. "You heard most of that, I assume?"

"Hard not to, Catherine. You do have a voice that, how shall I put it... carries." Phil chuckled, "I hope I haven't offended you."

"Not at all, Phil. I've heard worse. Now, I'd like to get started at the new homestead." She checked her watch. It was a quarter to ten, "I assume Mark is about to talk to Bruce?"

"Yes, he is. I think I'll go with Mark this time. Bruce is a focal point of interest; having an additional perspective might uncover even the smallest detail that could prove crucial. Following your advice, I'll assign Davo and Wayne to review the station again. Did you hear that, lads?"

"Yes, sir," came the immediate replies.

The idea of revisiting Bruce and the surrounding station with fresh eyes resonated with all of them. Each of the investigating team members was eager to contribute to the discussion planned for later that day. As one, the officers rose from the table.

Considering the information, Phil furrowed his brow and led the other officers and Catherine to the front door, "Okay, so, is everyone clear on their roles? Mark and I will go and speak with Bruce. Catherine will initiate the forensic investigation at the new homestead. Davo and Wayne, it is imperative you leave no stone unturned. Even the seemingly minor details, please document and photograph. Let's regroup for lunch around 1 p.m. How does that sound?"

The team agreed with the assigned roles and set out diligently to accomplish as much as they could in three hours.

As promised, Mark drove from the old homestead and arrived at the donga at ten a.m. This time, Senior Sergeant Phil Roberts accompanied him.

He found Bruce sitting on the doorstep, a sorrowful gleam to his dark, deep-set eyes.

"How you holding up, mate?" Mark asked.

"Been sorting out a place for the sorry business this morning. Got me real riled up 'bout the past and all the mess those white fellas caused among our mob."

"I get ya, brudda, but we can't change the past. You find a good spot away from the homestead?"

"Think I did," replied Bruce, a bit downhearted. His heart appeared heavy, not just for his friend's passing, but, his land, and his kin. Mark could see the pain etched on Bruce's weathered face and his tired, inflamed eyes.

Phil intensely scrutinised Bruce, his keen eyes darting over every nuance of the man's expression. He was on high alert, attuned to even the faintest suggestion Bruce might be holding back crucial details. It wasn't just the words Bruce expressed but the unspoken language of his behaviour and mannerisms Phil was attuned to, searching for any elusive sign that would betray an incomplete narrative.

"That's good news, fella. Did ya notice anything else on the way out there?" Mark inquired, not anticipating the response that was coming.

"I did, actually. Caught me by surprise. Might be somethin' important," Bruce said.

"And what's that all about?" inquired Mark.

"Well," he began, pausing briefly to collect himself. "When I was searchin' for a decent spot, I stumbled upon a deadly nightshade bush teemin' with ripe berries. Looked like some of 'em had been picked recently. Noticed some small shoeprints, too, likely belongin' to a woman. Used some of them old tracking skills to follow those prints in the dirt, right up to the road leadin' back to the new homestead."

Phil's interest was now piqued, and he leaned closer to avoid missing a word.

"Keep goin'," urged Mark, leaning in with a furrowed brow, his curiosity evident.

"Sure thing, mate. After that, I spotted three sets of fresh tyre tracks. Figure one could've been Diane's, seein' as she left just Friday. One might belong to Carol, though I ain't seen no other visitors 'round this weekend. And those marks were brand-spankin' new, happened within the past few days."

Phil's gaze intensified as he processed the information. "You know I've got a duty to investigate this case thoroughly. You've been on the homestead, and the timing of those fresh tracks raises questions."

Bruce's eyes held a mix of frustration and understanding. "I get it, Sergeant. But I swear on our ancestors, I had nothin' to do with those deaths. I might've found those tracks, but that don't make me no killer."

Mark turned to Phil, studying his expression for guidance on the next steps. Phil nodded subtly and gestured with a slight head tilt towards Bruce, signalling for Mark to continue the conversation with him. Mark leaned back, his expression thoughtful. "I believe you, brudda. I've known you for years, and I know you're not capable of such a thing. But you need to help me understand what you found."

Bruce nodded, a sense of relief washing over him. "Like I said, I followed those fresh tyre tracks back to the homestead. They led straight to the main building. There was somethin' strange about the whole thing. Looked like someone was tryin' to cover their tracks, but not too well. The dirt around those marks was disturbed, like someone has been sweepin' it to the side."

Mark's eyes narrowed. "Covering their tracks... Could be someone tryin' to divert suspicion. We need to take a closer look at those tracks ourselves," he glanced at Phil for affirmation. Once again, Phil nodded, signifying to Mark he should lead the conversation. "Anythin' else ya seen that might be of interest?"

Bruce scratched his head, thinking. "Yeah, as I got closer to the homestead, I could see some blood on the cut grass near the house, past where the footprints went. It ain't much, but it's there."

Phil's jaw tightened. "Blood... We're gonna need to get forensics on this ASAP. Bruce, I need you to stick around and answer any more questions we might have. We'll clear this up together."

Bruce nodded solemnly. "I ain't goin' nowhere, Sergeant. I wanna find out what happened as much as you."

Mark reached out and clasped Bruce's shoulder in a firm grip. "Thanks, brudda. We'll get to the bottom of this, and justice will be served."

Phil swiftly extracted his phone from the top pocket of his sweat-stained shirt, punching in the digits for Detective Graves. The seconds dragged like hours, hoping against hope the officer hadn't yet boarded the plane. The hands on his well-worn watch sneered at him—ten minutes to eleven.

A wave of relief washed over Phil as he finally heard the dial tone. Graves' voice crackled through, irritation dripping from every word, "Yes!"

"Oh, good, you haven't left yet," said Phil, sighing.

"Damn planes, never on bloody time," came the gruff retort.

"I need to know if you've got a botanist in tow. We're in need of an expert's eye out here. Seems like someone's been foraging fresh deadly nightshade berries in the past few days, and there's more..."

Before Phil could complete his sentence, the Detective interrupted him, "We've got one on the team. Standard procedure in these sprawling cases. We cast our net wide and keep our minds open. Apologies, Sergeant, we're boarding now. Catch you tonight." The line abruptly fell silent, leaving Phil feeling disrespected, his brow furrowed in irritation. The abrupt end to the conversation left him with a lingering sense of contempt from Graves, as if the urgency of his departure took precedence over the importance of their discussion.

CHAPTER 16

Forensic Pathologist Dr Catherine Reynolds knew the importance of meticulous preparation. The stakes were high, and amidst the unforgiving expanse of the arid and dusty outback, she exercised utmost caution, acutely aware of the perilous Northern Queensland rural environment surrounding the scene, threatening contamination.

As she pulled up to the new homestead, the air was heavy with anticipation. Catherine's mind raced, considering what awaited her as she approached the deceased men. This case was unlike any other she had encountered – two relatively young men, both gone, their deaths likely linked to this very place, in a timeframe that paralleled eerily. Leads were scant, leaving her to rely on her instincts and professional expertise.

The harsh mid-morning light cast eerie shadows amongst the red earth and surrounding dust as she drove with George to the scene in the unassuming rental car. The air was heavy with suspense. She knew a single slip-up could unravel the entire crime scene.

With great care, she retrieved a bag filled with sterile clothing and accessories from the back seat and placed it on the homestead's recently constructed expansive, wooden decked verandah. The stark contrast between the pristine gear and the rugged outback setting reminded her of the fine line she walked.

She transformed herself into a picture of sterility outside the homestead. Her change was disciplined, dressing from head to toe in protective, disposable clothing – booties to guard against any trace evidence, a hair net, a full-length gown flowing like a ghostly curtain, and a face mask, protecting her from any particulate matter as well as preventing any inadvertent contamination. The ensemble was her armour against the elements and her aide in the relentless pursuit of truth. George donned identical attire from the shared bag, mirroring her every step, his timing precise to ensure they approached the house as a unified force.

With attention to detail, she performed a final act of caution. Before passing under the yellow crime tape, Catherine swabbed her hands with alcohol wipes, ensuring her touch remained untainted. She then slipped on sterile purple latex-free gloves, each movement unhurried, each detail a safeguard.

It was a far cry from her sterile haven at Cairns base hospital, where every surface gleamed and the scent of antiseptic hung in the air. There, the tools of her trade were born from a world of automation and technology – a no-touch sink responding to motion, multiple autoclaves for disinfecting equipment, ensuring every step was calculated and clean.

But here, in the heart of the outback, Catherine's instincts were her greatest asset. The environment was punitive and unforgiving, but she was resolute. This was where the truth lay, waiting to be unearthed from the dust and shadows.

Entering through the threshold, she stepped down the hallway toward the kitchen. It was the very spot where she stood behind the breakfast bar the previous night, surveying the scene from a distance. Now, she understood the criticality of her vigilance. Each piece of evidence required her scrupulous attention.

The sweltering air wrapped around her like a suffocating veil, the sterile attire clinging to her form. It was as though the very atmosphere conspired to impress upon her the weightiness of the situation. She slowly advanced, cognisant every step held the potential for a breakthrough. Her eyes swept over the surroundings, seeking any hint that might illuminate the puzzle of not one but two deaths. She noted the men's positions. John lay face down on the table, his head resting on his folded arms. On the other hand, Noel was found in a curled and slumped position on the floor, with a chair seemingly having toppled over him.

Reaching the two figures, she embarked on a tender exploration of the bodies, mentally cataloguing every mark, every irregularity that might unveil the secrets shrouding their demise. Her senses sharpened, tuned to the slightest nuance within the kitchen—aromas, stains, and even the faintest whisper of an alien substance. She knew clarity could emerge from even the most minute observation in this stifling crucible. The only disruption in the stillness was the gentle hum of the air conditioning unit.

Her trained eyes honed in on subtle details as she observed the two men. She lifted each of their heads to examine their faces. George remained a sentinel by her side, waiting for further directions. Remaining focused on her task, Catherine observed the faces. She took note of the resolute expression on John, the Caucasian station owner, and the vomit stain on the indigenous man's cheek, which seeped onto the red, patterned rug below. She gestured to George, indicating he should capture detailed close-ups of the men's faces alongside the customary crime scene photographs. Her expertise and experience allowed her to discern the subtle nuances that might escape an untrained eye.

Drawing on her extensive knowledge and expertise, Dr Catherine Reynolds skilfully intertwined various pieces of evidence. The presence of rigour mortis, the chilling coldness emanating from the lifeless bodies, the telltale signs of livor mortis in the dependent parts of their bodies, and the minimal degree of decomposition all indicated a relatively recent passing, likely within the last twenty-four to thirty-six hours. The icy atmosphere suggested an extended period of air conditioner use, cooling the environment and preserving the bodies in the unforgiving heat.

Catherine sought to refine her estimation of the time of death. Retrieving a rectal thermometer from her forensic toolkit, she carefully measured the core temperature of the deceased individuals. Comparing this reading to the ambient temperature, she aimed to attain a more accurate assessment of when life left their bodies. She delicately measured the temperature, mindful of the significance of this data in the quest to unveil the truth. By aligning the central body temperature with the prevailing atmospheric conditions, she endeavoured to establish a crucial timeline that would aid in deciphering the circumstances surrounding their tragic demise.

Her gloved fingers moved precisely, gently probing for any anomalies or signs of trauma on the bodies. She carefully examined their hands, noting callouses and scars hinting at their histories. As she worked, her mind raced through a mental checklist of potential causes of death, considering everything from toxicology to blunt force trauma. George, her trusted assistant, moved quietly beside her, capturing each detail with a camera and ensuring nothing was overlooked. His steady presence provided a sense of support in the midst of the glum task at hand.

The room seemed to close around them, the weight of the unsolved mystery pressing on their shoulders. The air was heavy with the scent of George's sweat and a faint undertone of decay. Catherine's keen eyes caught a glint of something glossy near one of the bodies. She plucked it up with tweezers, recognising it as a single, medium-length, fine, blonde hair. It was an unexpected discovery, and she couldn't help but wonder what secrets it might unlock. She placed it in a specimen jar for evidence and future DNA analysis.

As the minutes stretched on, Catherine's persistence remained unwavering. She knew answers were hidden within these bodies, waiting for her to uncover them. With each compartmentalised examination, she felt herself drawing closer to the truth. Initially, Catherine ruled out the glaringly apparent causes of demise one by one – no telltale signs of brutal force, no lacerations or gunshot wounds to be found. The unsettling presence of vomit left her pondering. It might be a coincidental occurrence, but it also held the potential to unveil a darker narrative – one possibly woven by toxicity or overdose. The likelihood of two men succumbing to natural causes in such close temporal and spatial proximity seemed remote, even to a seasoned specialist like her.

Finally, after what felt like an eternity, she straightened up, her gaze fixed on George. "We need to conduct a thorough toxicology screening," she instructed, her voice steady. "And notify the lab to expedite the results. There's something more to this than meets the eye."

George nodded, his expression reflecting a shared sense of urgency.

Aware that time was a critical factor, she understood once her tasks were completed and the homicide squad concluded their investigation at the homestead, she would ensure the bodies were safely transported back to Cairns Base Hospital. The duty pressed heavily upon her, as she recognised the importance of preserving the integrity of the evidence and ensuring the deceased received the proper care they deserved.

Catherine checked her watch. Was almost 1~~one~~ p.m. She hoped there hadn't been any further hold-ups with the homicide squad. She knew the flight duration from Brisbane to Cairns was just over two hours. With mixed feelings, she called Detective Graves, who picked up promptly.

"Catherine, we've just touched down. What impeccable timing."

"Yes, Detective. I'm grateful for the chance to talk. Can you spare a moment?" she inquired, her tone professional.

"Of course, we have a five-hour layover here in Cairns. Ongoing updates are always appreciated. It'll give our team time to strategise before we reach Weipa."

"I've completed external examinations on both bodies. Aside from the vomit stains on the indigenous man's cheek and the rug below, few clues point to a cause of death. Given the absence of external indications, I'm strongly inclined towards a toxicological cause, whether self-administered or through another party. I've collected a sample of the vomitus, and I'm keen to obtain blood samples from both the femoral vein and cardiac chambers for overnight screening."

"Understood. I don't want our tardiness to impede the progress of this investigation," Detective Graves replied, processing this information. "Go ahead. I hate to ask, but I assume you documented all the evidence and the scene before examining the bodies."

Catherine sighed, "Yes, Bill, George is here with me. He's as professional as ever."

"Good," came the swift response.

"I also wanted to let you know I found a fine, blonde hair beside one of the bodies. George has documented the position as well as the collection of the hair. We can run it through our DNA database, and back at the lab we'll photograph it with our electron microscope to attempt to ascertain its origin."

"Sounds like you are making great progress, as usual," Graves smiled, aware of Catherine's exacting standards, "Of course, feel free to take the samples. Just have George photograph the extraction and try not to disrupt the scene too much. Have him send the digital photos to my email address, and we can all collaborate to piece this together," he replied somewhat brusquely. He couldn't shake his frustration at the logistical challenges of the remote location. "I'd drive to the station myself if it wasn't nearly eight hundred kilometres away and the roads weren't so rough north of here," he remarked, exasperation in his voice.

Catherine, focused on her task, sympathising with Graves' predicament. "I can only imagine, Detective. The distance certainly presents its challenges. We'll do everything we can here to provide you with the information you need."

"Thank you."

"We're all eager to act swiftly. Time is crucial, as you know. I'll gather the samples with George's help and have him send you the photos. It might take a few emails due to the file sizes," she replied calmly, sensing the tension in Graves' responses.

"You're always two steps ahead. Please keep me updated if any new evidence comes to light. At the very least, it will help pass the time in this damn lounge waiting for our bloody plane to depart."

"I certainly will. The plan is to meet with the investigating officers over lunch and discuss our findings. If there is anything that might be of interest to you and your team, I shall be in touch immediately."

"I can always rely on you. I'll catch up with you later this evening," his voice held a buoyant note, almost as if he were looking forward to their meeting.

"Goodbye, Graves," came her reply before ending the call.

She systematically gathered the samples of blood and vomitus, carefully sealing them within a designated box. Prior to their dispatch, she documented each item, leaving no room for oversight. George stood ready to capture the necessary images, poised to swiftly transmit them to the awaiting homicide squad for their expert analysis. It was now half past one, and she was behind schedule for lunch and the agreed-upon meeting time at the old homestead. Rather than calling, she deemed it more efficient for George and her to return to the rental car to join the rest of the team at the old homestead.

CHAPTER 17

As Catherine and George made their way back to the homestead, the afternoon sun beat down on the sprawling landscape, casting long shadows across the terrain. As they entered the house, familiar sights and sounds greeted them — the creaking of the old wooden floors, the subtle hum of the overhead fans, and the faint aroma of leftover lunch.

To their surprise, they found Phil and the three other officers already gathered in the dining area, their voices filled with a mix of intensity and speculation. Plates sat pushed to the side, half-eaten meals abandoned in their haste to dissect the morning's events.

Catherine's sharp ears caught snippets of conversation. "Deadly nightshade," Mark murmured. Phil mentioned "Tyre marks". The words hung in the air, immediately capturing her attention. Her curiosity was piqued as she approached the group, drawing their focus.

"What's this all about?" she inquired, her tone blending curiosity and self-confidence, "Seems I have a lot to catch up on."

Phil turned to her, his expression a mixture of relief and urgency. "G'day, Catherine. We've uncovered some crucial leads. It appears we may be onto something significant. Deadly nightshade was found near the scene, and there were peculiar tyre marks. Three sets, in fact. It's all rather intriguing."

Her eyes sparkled with fascination. Deadly nightshade was not a plant one encountered by accident in this part of the country. And peculiar tyre marks hinted at potential foul play. She wasted no time joining the discussion. Once quiet and still, the homestead hummed with a renewed sense of purpose.

Phil continued, "It's no surprise you took longer than expected. This is proving to be a complex case. I assume you'll be able to give us an update on your progress after lunch, and we can go from there. This way, we'll be well-prepared before the homicide squad arrives later this evening."

Her stomach let out an audible growl. She could definitely use a meal to replenish her energy levels.

"I apologise," Phil responded, "The boys and I were quite hungry. Diane left us some beef stroganoff. I took the liberty of gently reheating it. It should still be warm, and I've cooked up some pasta to go with it. Help yourselves."

George shot the team a dismissive look and quietly retreated to his room.

"Oh, right, I almost forgot," Phil added with a self-amused smile, "Food intolerances."

Catherine served herself a portion of the fettuccine, appreciating its al dente texture, and added a generous helping of the stroganoff. The aroma was delightful—rich, creamy, and hearty. She was famished. After helping herself, she joined the men at the communal dining table. She ate with gusto, finishing her meal before the two junior officers cleared the plates and loaded the dishwasher.

Once done, the group gathered around the table to exchange their findings from the morning. Phil briefed her further on the tyre tracks, freshly picked berries, and the bloodstain. Catherine updated the team on her discoveries, "Interestingly, there were no external signs of trauma. I discovered the indigenous station manager lying face down with a chair on top of him. It appears his fall likely coincided with the time of his demise. Conversely, the Caucasian owner was found slumped over the table, his head resting on his arms."

"Please go on," encouraged Phil, "I don't want you to leave anything out. We must all cooperate and bring everything to the table."

"At this point, I'm leaning towards a toxicological explanation for the cause of death, possibly due to poisoning or envenomation. The crucial pieces of evidence were the vomit on Noel's cheek, and I located a fine blonde hair near his body. I've sent samples of both to the lab, along with central blood samples from the heart and one of the major veins," she reported, her tone devoid of emotion.

As the team absorbed Catherine's clinical report, the room fell into a contemplative hush.

Phil broke the silence, his voice resolute. "Thank you, Catherine. This information is crucial. We'll need to await the lab results, but in the meantime, let's not overlook any other leads. Has anyone found anything else of note?"

Mark broke the silence; his voice measured, "Before we proceed, is it conceivable both deaths could be linked to deadly nightshade berries? There's mounting evidence pointing in that direction—the unidentified foot and tyre prints near the tree, the freshly plucked berry clusters. Bruce's first-hand report on the half-eaten pavlova in the fridge, topped with what he insists are blueberries. Will the toxicology report shed any light on this?"

She took a moment to consider before responding, "Yes, it's a plausible theory. Any part of the plant, not just the berries but the leaves, stalks or seeds, could induce this effect. However, the active compounds, atropine and scopolamine, are rapidly metabolised by the body."

"And what does that imply, precisely?" Phil's frustration was palpable, evident in his need for further clarification. He wasn't accustomed to being embroiled in potentially complex murders, let alone double homicides. In his decade in Weipa, the cases were typically straightforward—often suicides, sometimes violent, like hangings or shootings, or clear-cut homicides with an obvious suspect.

"It means we might not be able to detect any evidence on the rapid toxicology screen. In plain terms, if the men consumed the berries on Friday, as Bruce's report suggests, then it is likely all traces of the berries would be out of their system by now, and nothing would show up on the tests conducted by our laboratory. I'll have to perform post-mortem examinations on both deceased men to gather further evidence on the cause of death."

Phil's brow furrowed in frustration. The situation was becoming more convoluted by the minute. "So, you're telling me unless there's something glaringly obvious, we might not have any concrete evidence pointing to foul play?"

Catherine nodded, "Exactly. The window for detecting those berries in their system has likely closed. We'll have to rely on the post-mortem examinations for any conclusive findings. It's not ideal, but it's the best course of action at this point."

Phil sighed, running a hand through his hair. "Alright, I guess we'll have to wait for the post-mortems. I know you will be thorough, but we do not have much to go on at the moment. Please keep me in the loop as to your findings, both on the lab analysis and the post-mortem findings. We need every lead we can get on this one."

She nodded in agreement, scribbling some notes on a clipboard.

As the late afternoon sun bore down, the room grew stiflingly warm, but Phil was eager to maintain the momentum of the investigation. He turned his gaze squarely on Catherine, his voice steady and direct, cutting through the heavy air, "What are your plans after lunch?" he inquired, not one for beating around the bush.

Her gaze was sharp, her response equally direct. "I need to speak directly with Detective Graves again. Perhaps we could set up a conference call so we can both input our findings and suspicions and confirm his flight arrival time."

"Good idea," said Phil resolutely, "We'll get onto that straight away."

"George will send the forensic photos to the homicide team, to Grave's email, to be exact. That may take some time, but George is very systematic. As there is no flight back to Cairns tonight, I suggest we charter a flight for George to return with the samples to Cairns Base for processing ASAP," she proposed, her tone carrying an air of assurance.

"Yes, of course," Phil replied, his satisfaction evident. The investigation was gaining traction, and he felt the gears of justice grinding steadily forward. "Are you happy to liaise with the forensics department to arrange that?"

"No need," Catherine assured, her confidence unwavering. "I have an expense account for matters such as this. I will arrange it immediately, and then we can make the conference call."

Phil's nod conveyed approval. He looked up at Catherine. She was undoubtedly a consummate professional, warm yet clinically detached and keen to step the investigation up a notch. She was prompt and efficient, qualities he admired in a person.

Armed with the fresh evidence that emerged earlier that morning, Phil needed to reach out to Carol for additional questions regarding the pavlova. The three recently imprinted sets of tyre tracks and the footprints near the lethal nightshade tree left him puzzled. He knew it was imperative for George and Catherine to record these discoveries before the photographer's departure. With everyone on board, the unanimous decision to press forward was set into action.

Meanwhile, Detective Graves was keenly anticipating an update on the situation as he waited in the departure lounge of the domestic terminal at Cairns Airport. He combed through the initial reports and was eager for new developments. Just then, his phone vibrated, signalling an incoming call.

"Detective Graves, it's Senior Sergeant Roberts," came the voice on the other end. "I hope you don't mind; I am here with Dr Reynolds, and we have initiated a conference call from our end to talk with you. We've all made significant progress today. Constable Doomadgee and I have unearthed what we believe to be some crucial evidence."

The detective leaned forward, his interest piqued. "Tell me everything."

Over the course of the next hour, Phil and Catherine relayed their findings. Phil discussed the three sets of tyre prints and the footprints near the nightshade tree. Additionally, he mentioned the unsettling fact that both deceased individuals, according to Bruce's eyewitness account, had fallen ill several hours after consuming Carol's pavlova. Catherine informed Graves that prior to his departure, George would photograph the area concerned, including the blood stain on the cutgrass. The blood and grass stem would be taken in their entirety for processing in their lab. They speculated on the significance of these elements, piecing together a theory about what might have transpired on the fateful day the two men passed.

Graves listened intently, occasionally interjecting with questions or suggestions.

After they finished their updates, Catherine took charge once again. "Detective Graves, I've arranged for George to charter a flight back to Cairns with the evidence. He'll have the samples sent to processing as soon as he returns."

"Excellent work, Catherine," he commended.

"And Sergeant, I need you to follow up with Carol about the pavlova. It might hold a key piece of information."

Phil nodded, even though Graves couldn't see him through the phone. "That issue has already been discussed and was on my 'to-do' list. I'll see to it right away, Detective."

A subtle agitation coursed through Phil's veins, accompanied by a burgeoning annoyance. The man in question was yet to make his appearance. So far his influence over proceedings was palpable, commandeering the very essence of operations. It was as though the toil and sweat of his team were being cast aside, their efforts relegated to insignificance.

He elected to assert himself, his voice unapologetic as he interjected, "And, Detective Graves..."

The response unfurled with a rising cadence, more a query than a statement. "Yes?"

"In light of your team's tardy arrival, might I suggest acquiring a rental vehicle from the airport? We can then coordinate our efforts once you and your team are on site." The utterance bore the weight of a directive, its query-like veneer thinly veiling its true nature. "I'll ensure a vehicle is prepared for collection upon your arrival. Will you be requiring one car or two?"

The response unfurled, tinged with a hint of bemusement. It was evident the Detective anticipated a reception and briefing upon touching down at the airport. "Ah, two will suffice. I presume the locale is reasonably straightforward to locate?"

"Yes," replied Phil matter-of-factly, "There is only one road in and one out of Weipa. Just follow it for one-hundred-and-fifty-three kilometres straight out. Watson's River Station is clearly marked on Google Maps, or if you get lost, I can give you the GPS coordinates. Phone reception is also pretty good for a place so far north."

"I am confident we shall navigate it adequately. Your guidance is appreciated, Sergeant," came the succinct acknowledgment.

"The team will be expecting you. We are all staying at the old homestead. You'll find it about six hundred metres north of the new homestead via a dirt road. Any problems, you have my number."

As Detective Graves pressed the button to end the call, a subtle crease hovered over his brows, betraying his irritation. His eyes, usually sharp and discerning, now bore a faint glint of impatience.

Beneath his composed exterior, it was clear that a storm of vexation churned. The implication of the officer's tone and instructions had not escaped Graves. He was, after all, no stranger to the intricate dance of rank and authority. The fine line between cooperation and deference had been trodden by him many a time, and it irked him when that line was not acknowledged.

The moment the call came to a close, Catherine contacted the charter service. She took it upon herself to secure a flight for George, ensuring a timely departure back to Cairns would be at his disposal once the newfound evidence was documented. She needed to stay to transport the bodies back to Cairns once the homicide squad had completed their own examination of the scene.

CHAPTER 18

As the sun in the afternoon cast a warm golden hue over the Outback, Catherine and George trailed behind Mark, making their way to the deadly nightshade tree. They took precautions, ensuring they kept a safe distance and donned complete medical-grade personal protective equipment (PPE) to shield the scene from any potential contamination.

Under Phil's directive, Davo and Wayne were tasked with the careful organisation of paperwork before the anticipated arrival of the homicide squad later that evening. The room whirred with their concerted efforts, papers shuffling and laptop keys tapping across the breakfast bench as they worked diligently to bring order to the chaos.

Surrounded by a flurry of activity, Phil maintained his stance at the unpretentious wooden table, its surface engraved with the well-worn imprints of countless family gatherings and shared meals. He cradled the phone in his hand, its weight familiar and reassuring. With a contemplative expression, he scanned his recent call log and selected a number.

As he dialled, the room's ambient sounds seemed to fade into the background, leaving only the rhythmic tap of keys and the distant murmur of voices. Phil's focus was unwavering; his thoughts concentrated on the conversation awaiting him at the other end of the line.

After a few rings, the line clicked, and a voice, thick with the nuances of the land, answered, "Carol speaking."

"It's Phil Roberts again," he began, his tone respectful. "I'd like to ask you a few questions about the pavlova you delivered to Noel and John a few days back."

A pause, and then Carol's voice came through again, slightly hesitant. "Sure, Phil. What do you need to know?"

"Can you tell me what you topped it with?" he asked, his fingers drumming lightly on the desk.

"Raspberries and strawberries," she replied confidently.

Phil's feet shifted as he glanced at his notes. "Funny thing is, Bruce is telling us he saw a half-eaten pavlova in the fridge with three different types of berries. One of the fruits, he thought, might have been blueberries."

Carol's voice held a touch of surprise. "Blueberries? Well, I never put those on."

"Someone must have," Phil muttered before continuing, "By the way, we need to ask, as a formality, can anyone vouch for your whereabouts on Friday? I'm trying to create a timeline of events."

"Sure, love. I dropped off the pav to the boys and then drove straight to the Jamboree at Bramwell Junction, as I do every year. I whipped up two desserts, one for the blokes on the station and took the other with me to the event, just the same, topped with strawberries and raspberries. I was running late, so I didn't dilly-dally. I made good time getting to the event and saw plenty of people. Give the station a bell; they'll back me up," Her voice started to quiver, and then she burst into tears. Phil could hear her distress through the phone.

He rapidly responded to this unexpected surge of emotion, "What's up love? What's happened now? Is it Walt you're missin'? That's completely understandable."

Tears welled in Carol's eyes, but she fought to maintain composure. "No," she replied, her voice trembling, "I was summoned to the lawyer's office today for the reading of Walt's will. I was named as the executrix, and Walt set up those annuities for each of the kids. But here's the twist in the tale," she took a moment, letting the gravity of her revelation hang in the air, "I discovered Walt's will was altered just a week prior to his passing. He bequeathed a substantial sum to a certain Cindy Newman. Fifty million dollars, to be precise." She paused again, letting the enormity of the sum settle, "And there's more. Walt's bank records show he wrote a bank cheque for ten million dollars, addressed to the same woman, only days before he died."

This unexpected twist took the Senior Sergeant aback. He visibly recoiled in his chair.

"And that's not all," she continued, her voice now steady though laced with incredulity, "Walt specifically designated an amount of $5000 per week for Bruce Hudson for the rest of his life. There was also a sealed envelope, bearin' Bruce's name, marked 'confidential'." The weight of the unspoken hung heavily in the room, a web of mystery and intrigue spun by a man now beyond the reach of questions.

"Well," said Phil, pausing for reflection, "That certainly throws a spanner in the works."

A baffled silence hung between them for a moment. "Cindy Newman? I've never heard of her. Walt never mentioned anyone by that name," said Carol, "Who is she?"

"She is a locum nurse with the RFDS. Does a weekly clinic with Dr O'Leary and works a few shifts at the local hospital. She's only signed on for four weeks while two regular nurses take a break." Phil's pupils dilated as he jotted down a quick note. "Strange, indeed. He left her fifty million bucks?" Phil enquired, unsure if he heard correctly the first time.

Carol's voice wavered. "Yep. Plus, the ten million he'd already given her, that's sixty million. That's," she paused, "Aa lotta dosh. I don't know anything about this Cindy person, and you say she's only in town for four weeks? Now that's what's got me thinking and all upset."

"We'll definitely be looking into her further; make no mistakes. Thanks for sharing this with me. Now you've got me thinking, too," he mused, gently caressing his freshly shaved chin, his thoughts swirling with theories.

Her gratitude was unmistakable as she responded, her voice carrying a distinct twang of a long-term resident of far north Queensland. More relaxed now, she settled into her familiar tone, "Thanks, Phil. It's been a real heady time since Walt passed, ya know? Organisin' the funeral and clearing out his house for sale – it's been a lot to handle. I don't think I'll be stayin' in that house, even though it was left to me in the will."

Phil's deep voice resonated with understanding as he replied, "No worries. We'll definitely be digging deeper into this Cindy Newman situation and taking another look at Bruce. I'm shocked at the large amounts of cash Walt was throwing around towards the end. Your information is helping pull all this together. I'll make sure to keep you in the loop."

"Much appreciated, Phil," Carol said, a tinge of weariness in her voice.

"Just one more question, love. Did you find anything unusual when cleaning out the house?"

"Well, let me tell you, that was a job and a 'alf. Now, ya ask if I found anything strange when sortin' through Walt's things."

"That's right, Carol," Phil responded attentively. "Did anything catch your eye?"

A moment of thoughtful silence hung in the air before she continued, "Well, not that I'm any investigator, but nothin' major stood out. There was the usual clutter and odds and ends. The fridge was nearly bare, except for a few tinnies and two blueberry muffins. I didn't think much of it at the time; just chucked everything out, as ya do."

Phil listened intently, his curiosity stimulated, "Thank you. Your thoroughness is greatly appreciated. Those muffins, though... That's a bit peculiar. Did you recognise them? Was it something you baked for Walt?"

Her voice held a hint of uncertainty. "Nah, not at all. They looked like regular blueberry muffins. It wasn't me who cooked 'em."

Phil made a mental note of this. It seemed like this case was far more complex than he first assumed. His voice grew more serious as he spoke, "All right, Carol. You've been a great help. If anything else comes to mind, don't hesitate to call me. We're going to get to the bottom of this. I know Walt had health issues, being sixty-five and all. Natural causes may well explain his death; after all, he did like his food and grog."

She interjected with a half-hearted chuckle, trying to introduce some light into such a dark topic of conversation, "And his women!"

"I'm sorry about all of this, love. We know he had his faults. I want you never to forget your instincts are important. You knew him better than anyone else in the world. We'll do everything we can to get to the bottom of this."

Her tone carried a mixture of hope and concern as she replied, "I'm countin' on ya, Phil. It's just that feelin' in my gut, ya know? Something doesn't quite add up. Please, do whatever it takes to figure it out."

"You've got my word," Phil assured her, his words carrying a comforting weight. "We won't rest until we've got this sorted. You take care now, and if you remember anything else, don't hesitate to give me a shout."

"Thank ya, Phil," she replied, a sense of relief threading through her voice. "I appreciate all you're doin'."

After saying their goodbyes, Phil leaned back in his chair, deep in thought. The mention of those muffins added another mysterious element to the conundrum. He needed to find out where they came from and if they were connected to the deaths of the two men at the station. As he gathered his notes, Phil made a mental checklist of what needed to be done next. Interviewing Walt's neighbours, looking into recent visitors, and cross-referencing Walt's contacts were all on the agenda.

The newfound evidence occupied Phil's mind, from its potential implications to its intricate details. With a resolute expression, he delicately returned the phone to his pocket. Meanwhile, the afternoon breeze flowed through the open windows, causing the papers on the table to flutter gently. He eased back in his chair, hands interlocked behind his head, the solid oak chair teetering on just two legs.

Despite the gritty fatigue pulling at him, he recognised the urgency of moving forward before the leads grew cold. His resolve remained unwavering. Carol had conveyed the latest developments, which included the suspicious changes to Walt's will shortly before his passing – Cindy's substantial inheritance as well as Bruce's annuity and confidential letter. Then, there was the perplexing matter of the blueberry muffins. Armed with this fresh evidence, Phil's next objective was to contact Dr Stephen O'Leary from the Royal Flying Doctor Service (RFDS) in order to locate nurse Cindy Newman.

Taking a moment to pause, Phil brewed another cup of coffee; he secured Dr O'Leary's mobile number by dialling the RFDS base in Cairns. The receptionist informed him the doctor was attending to a motorbike accident at Bramwell Station, Cape York. After concluding the call, Phil's fingers moved swiftly over his phone. He paused momentarily, reluctant to interrupt the doctor but understanding Dr O'Leary wouldn't take the call if he were occupied with something else. He dialled and reconnected with the doctor. Without hesitation, he answered, playfully quipping, "Well now, if it isn't Sergeant Roberts. What's the reason for blessin' me call log with your presence today?"

"New information has come to light, and I'm attempting to establish contact with your nurse, Cindy Newman," Phil disclosed. "We've encountered a situation involving two deceased individuals on a nearby cattle station, and fresh revelations concerning Walt Henry and Cindy have emerged. Would it be possible to speak with her?"

"Ah, I'm sorry, Sergeant, but I'm afraid I can't be lendin' a hand," responded Dr O'Leary. "She wrapped up her time with us two days ago; she did. We've got one of our usual nurses on duty this fine day."

"Damn," Phil's frustration was evident.

"Is there somethin' I can assist you with?" Dr O'Leary inquired.

"You might be able to. Can you tell me where Nurse Newman was four days ago? On Friday?" Phil pressed.

"Give me a wee moment to have a look at the notes. Ah yes, she was doin' house calls all day."

"House calls?" Phil sought clarification.

"Aye, one of our nurses pays visits to all the far-off farms and homesteads and those people that are too unwell to come into our clinic every fourth Friday of the month. She checks basic observations such as blood pressure, heart rate, and takin' any regular blood and blood sugar levels. She reports directly to me if anythin' is amiss. Why, is there a problem?"

Phil considered for a moment. "Can you tell me if she visited Watson's River Station on Friday?"

"I'll have a gander at the notes for ya. Hold on a minute," Dr O'Leary's voice momentarily faded as he attended to the task. Soon, he returned with the answer, his tone tinged with satisfaction, "Why, yes, she did. She paid a visit to Noel Manson. He's a diabetic, on medication for it. Here we go," the doctor reviewed the notes, "Blood sugar level four point three, no cause for concern, the patient reported feelin' well, all other readings were as they should be."

"In that case, any notion of her whereabouts?" Phil inquired, his anticipation hanging on the doctor's response.

"Not a bleedin' clue, I'm afraid. We had ourselves a grand send-off for her come Sunday eve." Dr O'Leary hesitated momentarily before adding, "Sure, now that I've got ya on the line, I'd be wantin' to ask, did Cindy ever come clean about her fling with Walt? She had a word with me not long after yer last interview, and she was in a right state, I tell ya. I grasp dat she shared her thoughts wit me, but it's naht quite akin to the trust between a doctor and a patient. I've 'eard whispers in da community hintin' at a potential double murder investigation in progress. Surely, dat takes precedence over the confidentiality of an in- 'ouse conversation, dahn't you reckon?"

"Is that right?" enquired Phil, perplexed by all of this new information suddenly coming to light, "Well, that explains a bit!" he exclaimed. Taking time to compose himself, Phil asked, "Do you know if she had any plans following her stint with the RFDS?"

"She did be tellin' us on Sunday she planned to start headin' north that afternoon. Not a wink of a plan after that she did let slip, mind you. She did mention somethin' about gallivantin' 'round Northern Queensland, maybe even makin' her way up to the tip of Cape York Peninsula for a bit of a leisurely break, if you catch my drift."

"Interesting," mused Phil, "Could you share any contact particulars? An email, mobile number, anything that could assist us?" Phil requested.

"Aye, I've got both at hand. I'll be shootin' them over in a wee text message, no doubt about that. But time's a tickin', ye see, as I'm gettin' a patient ready for a jaunt on a fixed-wing plane. I'll be takin' me leave for now, but I'll be hangin' up and shootin' ye the particulars as quick as a wink, mark my words."

"Thank you, Doctor. Your timeliness is greatly appreciated," Phil acknowledged, his voice reflecting genuine gratitude.

The line went dead; minutes later, Phil's phone pinged with an SMS from Dr O'Leary containing Cindy Newman's mobile number and e-mail address.

As the late afternoon hastened its descent, Phil cast a fleeting glance at his SMS messages, stumbling upon an overlooked one from Detective Graves. The message confirmed Graves' plane was punctual, and he and his squad would arrive at Weipa airport as scheduled at 6 p.m. This prompted Phil to engage in a final phone call. It was an endeavour to establish contact with Nurse Cindy, an individual undeniably relevant to this potential double homicide. A resolute exhale escaped him as he punched in her number. Yet, his hopes were dashed as he was met with the disheartening automated message, coldly stating the number he sought was no longer in service. He turned his attention to her email, harbouring a glimmer of hope for a more favourable outcome. Regrettably, the outcome remained unaltered; there was no reply.

Frustration simmered beneath his strong-minded exterior as he ended the futile phone call and stared at the unresponsive email. The urgency to gather all necessary information was escalating, and the disappearing trail of Nurse Cindy Newman was a vexing setback.

As the clock ticked towards the impending arrival of Detective Graves and his team, Phil knew little time remained to gather crucial information. He couldn't afford to let this lead slip away.

Feeling a pressing need, he hurriedly made plans to reach out to individuals who knew Cindy from her previous workplace at Tennant Creek. Realising it was almost the end of the workday, around five p.m., he opted to send emails instead of making phone calls to the local hospital and police station. He included his contact information while keeping a vigilant eye on the steadily advancing clock.

The minutes stretched endlessly as he anxiously awaited responses, fully conscious the impending investigation hinged on finding Cindy and untangling the mystery surrounding Walt Henry and the potential double homicide at Watson's River Station. He had a strong gut feeling these cases were intertwined. There were too many lingering questions. Why did Walt experience a sudden change of heart in the last week of his life? Why would he bequeath such a significant sum to a woman he presumably barely knew? Whose footprints, blonde hair, and tyre marks tainted the station? Who harvested the deadly nightshade berries? He decided he would start making phone calls if he didn't receive any updates by lunchtime the next day. He longed for answers, and he needed them sooner rather than later.

CHAPTER 19

As time marched relentlessly on, Phil could sense the impending arrival of the homicide squad at Weipa airport. They'd descend like vultures, hungry for leads and answers, the moment their plane touched the tarmac. His seasoned instincts placed their estimated arrival window between seven-thirty and eight p.m., factoring in the unpredictable nature of air travel and allowing the team time to pick up the rental cars.

Summoning the junior officers from their paperwork, Phil offered them a much-needed respite, beckoning them to gather around the dining table. The early evening light, now fading, draped the weathered homestead in a melancholic manner, paralleling the shocking events that unfolded. Mark and Catherine arrived with slumped shoulders, resonating with the collective fatigue of the entire team. George followed suit, his footsteps a weary resonance in the sombre atmosphere.

The unrelenting day demanded every ounce of their endurance, leaving them all drained. Another pot of coffee bubbled away in a corner, a feeble attempt to ward off the encroaching tiredness. The consensus was unanimous – an early supper was the order of the day. In her considerate manner, Diane left behind a treasure trove of frozen meals alongside an ample supply of expertly butchered steaks and pre-made salads. It was a parting gesture of care before she left to spend time with her daughter. Her thoughtfulness in preparing the meals was not lost on Phil. It was a small token, but it spoke volumes about her dedication to the team. He made a mental note to thank her when she returned.

Sensing the need for some time out, Phil rose from his seat, taking charge of the impromptu kitchen. With the air of a seasoned chef, he delved into inquiries about everyone's steak preferences. Davo, in turn, retrieved the carefully prepared potato salad from the fridge and set it on the table, a gesture of shared camaraderie amidst the weighty atmosphere enveloping them all.

As Phil deftly worked the sizzling steaks on the stovetop, the rich aroma of seared meat permeated the air, momentarily dispelling the lethargic mood clinging to them all. The room was filled with the sounds of utensils clinking against plates and the low murmur of conversation, a brief respite from the grim reality they faced.

Catherine's once-piercing gaze was now softened by the weariness gripping her. She leaned against the countertop, sorting and bagging the samples she had cautiously collected from the crime scene. Her eyes, though dulled, bore a glint of gratitude and anticipation as they followed Phil's movements. She acknowledged the immense value of his experience and intuition in this sinister tango with crime and was keenly aware of his thoughtfulness in preparing her dinner.

Mark, a formidable presence even in repose, occupied an old, scratched chair at the table. His broad frame seemed to slump under the weight of the investigation, a heaviness pressing on his heart. His mind churned, grappling with the unshakable unease that Bruce, a member of his own mob, his flesh and blood, might somehow be entangled in this twisted web of deceit and death. The notion gnawed at him, casting a shadow so profound it eclipsed all other thoughts. Outside, the night whispered its secrets to the wind, leaves rustling in conspiratorial huddles. It was a night made for secrets and shadows and hidden truths.

While Phil worked on preparing the steaks, he couldn't help but observe Catherine's attention to detail. She expertly packaged the samples of blood and vomitus from the deceased and the stray blonde hair, ensuring they were securely sealed within a box before passing them over to George.

She turned to George, her tone serious, "I insist you use the rental car to get to the airport. A charter flight will be ready for your departure around eight p.m. Make sure to return the car promptly at the depot. There'll be plenty of vehicles on-site for the homicide squad's transportation. It's crucial to ensure your cargo reaches its destination efficiently and securely."

The forensic photographer, a taciturn figure with an eye for detail, acknowledged the unspoken urgency with a nod. The prospect of joining the others for dinner was dismissed with a glance towards the untouched spread. Instead, he settled for a hastily assembled meal, his mind already thinking ahead to the work awaiting him in the lab. With slumped shoulders and a downcast expression, he quietly left the scene behind, the echoes of his departure barely registering amidst the intensity of the investigation.

Phil watched him make his departure. He knew every moment counted. With George on his way, Phil turned his attention back to the homestead. Wayne and Catherine were now setting the table, their movements slow and deliberate, a testament to their shared fatigue. The scent of the freshly cooked steaks mingled with the scent of the Australian outback, creating an oddly comforting juxtaposition. The fragrances wafted through the room, momentarily providing a semblance of solace in their tumultuous reality.

As they sat down to eat, the conversation was a mix of subdued reflections on the day's events and quiet anticipation for the arrival of the homicide squad. They knew the investigation was entering a critical phase, and everyone needed to be ready.

After supper, Phil retreated momentarily, seeking relief in the quiet recesses of his thoughts. The evidence they'd amassed was compelling, painting a negative portrait with Cindy at its centre. Yet, he understood the threads they held were but a fraction of the hard evidence they required for justice to be meted out. The elusive nurse remained the linchpin in this dark narrative, the key to unlocking the truth that would bring closure to the victims and their families.

Walt's demise was at the forefront of Phil's mind. Cindy's motives were clear, her opportunity glaring. Two more lives were claimed, and Dr O'Leary's confirmation of her Friday visit to Noel solidified her presence at the heart of this chilling tale. Phil's mind delved into the mountain of evidence—the puzzling tyre tracks, the sinister nightshade berries, and Catherine's discovery of a short, naturally blonde strand of hair near Noel's lifeless form.

His thoughts inevitably drifted to the innocuous blueberry muffins found in Walt's fridge, now disposed of without ceremony by Carol. Phil couldn't help but wonder if they held a more sinister truth. Were those seemingly benign berries actually a deadly substitute?

Regrettably, truth remained elusive in Walt's demise. Carol scrubbed the house clean, and Walt's remains were reduced to ash. Unanswered questions lingered, but Phil knew dwelling on the past would serve no purpose. His focus had to be on the present scene, on ensuring justice was handed down.

Yet, amidst the mounting evidence and enigmatic clues, Cindy loomed ever larger in his thoughts. Her ties to each victim were inescapable, the web of intrigue tightening with each revelation. The mosaic was forming a picture begging to be acknowledged.

He knew he must bring her in for questioning, though he anticipated a battle of wits. Cindy was no stranger to evasiveness; now, she seemed to have vanished. Doggedness blazed in Phil's eyes; he desperately wanted to uncover the motive behind these seemingly senseless deaths. Time, he knew, was a relentless adversary. Each passing moment was a potential harbinger of more tragedy; he couldn't allow that to happen. He knew he needed to act before any more lives were lost. The hunt for Cindy would begin anew, and he would see her brought in for interrogation, no matter the cost.

Following the meal of perfectly seared, medium-rare aged rump steak accompanied by a lovingly prepared potato salad, Wayne and Mark pushed their chairs back and stood simultaneously before clearing the table. It was a transition from sustenance to the next round of discussions, a seamless shift in focus. Phil rejoined the group, his presence commanding attention as they settled into a renewed fervour of conversation. Their voices wove through the air, a symphony of insights and speculations, each note harmonising with the others.

Earlier that day, Davo and Wayne embarked on an exhaustive search of the station, hunting for any additional evidence that might hold the key to unscrambling the truth. They began the day side by side, their shared mission clear. However, as the hours wore on, Davo's focus narrowed, honing in on the area where Mad Maureen temporarily sought refuge. It was only later they regrouped, their steps weary but purposeful, heading back to the homestead together. In the whirlwind of activity that followed lunch, there was no opportunity to apprise the team of their current findings, leaving an air of anticipation hanging over them.

Wayne, his eyes sharp and his demeanour purposeful, took it upon himself to provide a succinct summary of his morning's work. His efforts were channelled into a studious examination of the paddock designated for free campers, an area of particular interest in verifying Bruce's alibi and locating the elusive figures known as "Jake" and his girlfriend. Turning to the expectant faces around him, Wayne began, "First, I delved into the logbook. And there they were, signed in on Friday afternoon and checked out early Sunday morning – the names of our backpackers, Jake Griffith and Lisa Sinclair. With that confirmation in hand, I scoured the free camping paddock."

He paused, allowing his words to settle in the room. "Interestingly," he continued, "apart from a few pieces of stray rubbish near one of the old forty-four-gallon drums serving as a makeshift bin, there were no signs of recent camping activity. No disturbed grass, no trace of tyre tracks, not even the remnants of a fire or a stray tent peg."

A silence blanketed the room, each officer absorbing the implications of Wayne's findings. It was Phil who broke the quietude, his tone measured. "Perhaps," he offered, "they were simply exceptionally tidy campers?" The question hung in the air, a seed of doubt waiting for fertile ground to take root.

After a moment, Catherine raised her head, her expression thoughtful. "It's worth considering," she mused, her voice measured. "But we can't overlook the fact their names were logged in and out. That suggests they were here, at least on paper."

Wayne nodded in agreement, "Exactly. We need to broaden our search. If they didn't camp here, then where did they go? And why did they sign in and out?"

The unanswered questions hung in the air, a riddle demanding a reply. Phil, sensing the gravity of the situation, spoke up. "We need to expand our canvas. Look for nearby campsites. Talk to anyone who might have seen them."

The group nodded collectively, understanding every lead must be closely followed up.

Davo, a stalwart presence in the room, commanded attention as he took the floor. His voice held an air of authority; each word was spoken with purpose. "Wayne and I hit the ground early this mornin'," he began, his tone steady, "aiming to cover as much ground as possible. Divide and conquer, ya know? My focus was on Mad Maureen's secluded campsite. I found fresh tyre tracks and clear signs of recent habitation. There was a fire pit appearing as though it had recently been taken apart, with kindling scattered nearby. Despite reaching out to her usual haunts and contacts, I've hit a wall in locatin' her."

A collective frustration simmered in the room, a shared sense of exasperation. Mad Maureen's vanishing act seemed to defy their best efforts, leaving them grappling with a phantom.

Phil recognised their next move revolved around gathering intel on Cindy's vehicle – its make, model, colour, and, most crucially, its registration number. The VIN, that alphanumeric key, promised to track her down. She transitioned from person of interest to prime suspect in Phil's mind. He couldn't shake the creeping sense born of a seasoned cop's intuition. The three deaths were inexorably intertwined.

Mark leaned forward, his expression a mirror of Phil's formidable determination. "We need to find that vehicle. Talk to anyone who might've seen it. Put the word out. No matter how small, every lead could be the one that cracks this wide open."

Heads nodded in agreement, the room pulsating with renewed urgency. They were on the precipice of a breakthrough, and every moment now counted in their relentless pursuit of truth. The station seemed to hold its breath as the night wore on, awaiting the revelation that would shatter the silence.

Phil's mind circled back to Carol, a steadfast presence amidst the swirling chaos of the investigation. Her alibi held up under scrutiny, and her cooperation was unwavering. He could exclude her from the list of suspects with a reasonable degree of certainty. It was time to redirect his focus towards the remaining three.

Mad Maureen, an unlikely but not impossible suspect, lingered on the fringes of Phil's considerations. She had an alibi for Walt's untimely demise, but her recent activities on the farm during the other two deaths raised unsettling questions. The enigma of Bruce loomed large; his proximity to all three victims was a glaring red flag. The roster was concise: Cindy, Bruce, and the enigmatic Maureen. None of them could be definitively cleared from suspicion.

The elusive threads connecting these cases tugged at Phil's conscience. The swift, seemingly untraceable deaths of three robust men in a fortnight's span painted the eerie portrait of a potential serial predator. It was a haunting possibility Phil couldn't, and wouldn't, dismiss.

After careful deliberation, Phil issued an arrest warrant for Mad Maureen. It was a tactical move that might compel her to communicate with him or Davo, just as she had in the past when facing legal entanglements. Her history bore a smattering of minor infractions but nothing of a truly menacing nature; it was a calculated step, a beacon of hope in the quest to unveil the heavily cloaked truths of this investigation.

As the day's light rapidly faded on the station, the bulk of impending tasks settled heavily on Phil's shoulders. The arrival of the homicide squad was imminent, casting a long shadow over his thoughts. The sprawling list of duties stretched before him, a warren of leads to chase down and a web of connections ready to be forged.

Just as he was beginning to carve out a plan of action, a sharp ping from his phone jolted him from his contemplation. Swiftly, Phil retrieved the device and navigated to his inbox. There it was, an email from a locum Emergency Doctor at Tennant Creek Hospital, an unforeseen glimmer of hope in the midst of their investigation.

The doctor's message bore the promise of crucial information, a tantalising clue that might hold the key to untying the mysteries they faced. With an air of urgency, the physician offered a contact number and signed off with his name, Dr Charlie Daylight. The request for a morning call before his afternoon shift added an extra layer of intrigue, fuelling Phil's resolution.

Without a moment's hesitation, his fingers danced across the screen as he composed a reply. He thanked Dr Daylight for stepping forward and acknowledging the significance of the information he might possess. With a firm commitment, he assured the doctor he would make contact the next morning, ready to delve deeper into the revelations he held.

As the email winged its way into the digital ether, Phil's spark of hope ignited. This unexpected correspondence had the potential to be a breakthrough, a flare of light in the shadowy maze of their investigation. He made a mental note to compile a list of probing questions, eager to extract every ounce of insight that might lead them closer to the truth. The night, once draped in uncertainty, now held a glimmer of possibility.

CHAPTER 20

As the team sat together, cherishing the brief respite, the evening air was disrupted by the faint, distant hum of tyres against gravel; the homicide squad finally arrived. Phil's demeanour shifted, a well-practised facade of composure descending upon him. His nod of acknowledgment to his team marked the conclusion of their fleeting respite. Their dedicated efforts would commence anew, now at an elevated level, with unfamiliar faces joining in.

As the night unfolded, a canopy of stars emerged, sprinkling the sky with their distant, glimmering light. Detective William Graves, a seasoned figure in the world of such investigations, led his dedicated unit to Watson's River Station. Their rental cars rolled in, the engines humming quietly against the serene backdrop. The clock edged towards eight p.m., and Graves, following the detailed instructions provided by Phil, guided his steps towards the weather-beaten homestead.

Each footfall was purposeful, a proclamation of his arrival, culminating in the gentle push against the creaking hinges of the front door. Before Phil could fully process the situation, he found himself face-to-face with a figure shattering his assumptions. Standing on their makeshift command centre threshold, this seasoned investigator carried the weight of years with unexpected grace, momentarily catching Phil off guard. There was an air of authority about this new man on the scene, an unspoken assurance that he was accustomed to navigating the intricate web of crime and punishment.

Phil rose from his seat, a well-practised poise settling over him as he extended a firm hand in greeting. His countenance remained grave.

"Detective Graves, welcome to Watson's River Station," he intoned. His voice bore the weariness of relentless dedication. A subtle arch of his brows betrayed a hint of surprise, a witness to the unforeseen energy the detective exuded.

The hardened detective, ever the astute observer, fixed his discerning gaze upon his elder counterpart. "Senior Sergeant Roberts, you seem somewhat taken aback. Is there something amiss?" Graves' words carried a tone of perpetual vigilance, an indication of his keen instincts.

If Phil was candid, he might have remarked on the detective's unexpectedly youthful appearance, a vitality defying the rigours of their shared profession. Instead, he offered a subdued murmur, his words a modest brush-off. "Oh, nothin' of consequence. Just tired, I guess."

As their exchange unfolded, there hung an unspoken understanding between the two men. Each harboured a depth of experience, a shared understanding of the toll the relentless pursuit of justice could exact. In this pivotal moment, they stood united, ready to embark on the challenging path ahead. The air was charged with an unspoken fortitude, a tacit acknowledgment that the journey before them would demand nothing less than their absolute best.

Beside Phil stood the younger and more spirited Davo, his disposition a stark contrast. His face was graced with a welcoming grin as he extended a warm greeting, "Good evening, Detective. We're at your disposal, ready to lend our full support. The potential crime scene has been cordoned off, and a perimeter has been secured. There's much to discuss with your team; say the word when you're good to go."

Detective Graves, a man of few words and eyes that missed nothing, ushered the rest of his team inside. He gestured for them to find a seat, the room's atmosphere electric with anticipation and trepidation. His gaze, sharp as a blade, settled on Catherine first. "We meet again, Dr Reynolds," he greeted warmly, a glint of something unspoken flickering in his eyes. His excessively affable tone sent shivers down her spine.

"Yes, Graves. I've laid it all out for you," Catherine affirmed, her tone steady, the weight of her discoveries hanging in the air like a hidden truth yearning to be unveiled, "George has taken custody of the samples. I trust you've had a moment to peruse the photos of the potential crime scene on the way here?"

"Your efficiency never ceases to amaze me," the detective acknowledged, a wry smile playing at the corners of his lips. His eyes held a glimmer of admiration, not just for her professionalism but also for her striking looks and feminine energy. His gaze lingered upon her a little too long for Catherine's liking.

His regard slowly shifted towards Phil. The warmth gracing his features now gave way to a more intense, probing scrutiny. "Senior Sergeant, have there been any significant strides since our last conversation?" he pressed, his voice carrying the weight of expectation.

Phil met Graves' look squarely, a sense of purpose in his demeanour and tone, "Actually, quite a bit," he confirmed, the words hanging in the air, pregnant with anticipation.

"I'm eager to lay eyes on the scene. Is it crucial you relay this information to me now, or can it be deferred?" the detective inquired coldly, a trace of impatience seeping into his tone.

"I think you may be very interested in what I have to convey. The devil may very well be in the details for this one," Phil affirmed, a sense of seriousness underscoring his words.

"Then, let's not squander a moment. Lay it out for me," Graves ordered, his posture resolute, his single-mindedness slicing through the charged atmosphere.

Phil took a deep breath, his voice a steady anchor amidst the brewing storm. He recounted his conversation with Carol. "I had a conversation with Walt Henry's ex-wife, Carol, today. She confirmed that she indeed delivered a pavlova to the two deceased men on Friday before heading off to a Jamboree. I've verified her alibi, and it checks out. Now, here's where it gets intriguing; she insists she only topped the pavlova with strawberries and raspberries. However, we have an eyewitness account from Mr Hudson, located here on the station, stating the dessert had three types of berries - strawberries, raspberries, and what he believed to be blueberries," he let that sink in before continuing, "Now, it might appear trivial to some, but to me, it hints at concealed motives and hidden truths, especially in light of the recently discovered deadly nightshade berries."

Graves was absorbing the information, nodding his head in encouragement for Phil to go on.

"Then, Carol informs me she was summoned to the lawyer's office today. Here's the twist. She was shocked to discover Walt altered his will just days before his passing. In addition to bequeathing her fifty million dollars, he wrote a bank cheque for ten million dollars to Nurse Cindy Newman in his final days."

Graves raised an eyebrow at this latest revelation.

"And that's not all," Phil continued.

"There's more?" the detective asked incredulously, his pupils dilating and eyebrows lifting.

"Yes, indeed. In revising his will, Mr Henry also left Mr Bruce Hudson an annuity of five thousand dollars a week, along with a mysterious sealed envelope labelled 'Confidential'," Phil revealed.

This last piece of information truly ignited the detective's curiosity.

As Phil's voice resonated in the dimly lit room, the walls seemed to inch closer, conspiring to stifle the truth lingering in the air. The thick fog of intrigue and unanswered questions hung heavily, casting a shadow over the two men who sat locked in a dance of secrets.

Detective Graves leaned in, his steel-grey eyes fixed on Phil's. They were windows into the storm of uncertainty raging around them, the seriousness of their mission pressing upon their shoulders like a thunderhead on the brink of unleashing its fury. He remained a sentinel of attentiveness in the ominous silence, his ears attuned to every word Phil uttered. His gaze never wavered, a glint of intrigue dancing in those calculating orbs.

"Very interesting, Sergeant," Graves remarked, his voice low and measured, like a man who'd navigated the treacherous alleys of crime countless times, "That's a lot of information to process."

Phil seized the moment, eager to unveil their investigation's tangled web of deceit. "And there's more, Detective. Dr O'Leary from the RFDS informed us Nurse Newman admitted to an affair with Walt Henry in the weeks preceding his death."

Graves reclined in his chair, his mind a maze of possibilities as he absorbed the deluge of revelations. The room bore witness to his silent contemplation, save for the occasional whir of the overhead fan, as if it, too, awaited the unravelling of this enigma.

"Thank you, Sergeant," the detective finally uttered, his words laden with intrigue. "This is quite the web we're untangling here," his voice was a symphony of restraint and caution, like a masterful conductor leading an orchestra through a complex composition, "It appears we have a complex set of connections. Nurse Newman's inheritance, Bruce's annuity, and this sealed envelope marked 'Confidential' are all fascinating elements."

Phil nodded, acknowledging the intricate web of deceit and scheming they were slowly pulling apart. "Yes, Detective. It most certainly is."

"And the affair with Walt Henry," he answered, "That's a significant revelation. It could shed light on possible motives," his sharp eyes fixated on a distant point beyond the window as if searching for answers amidst the passing shadows.

"Yes, sir," Phil affirmed, "Dr O'Leary assured us Nurse Newman was quite forthcoming about it."

Detective Graves straightened in his chair, his features carved from granite, self-assurance impressed into every line of his face. "We'll need to delve deeper into all of this. Our first priority is locating the nurse. Following that, I'd like your team to schedule formal interviews with Carol, Bruce, and anyone with a potential role in this situation."

Ever the diligent assistant, Davo swiftly transcribed the Detective's directives onto a notepad, his pen scratching against the paper as if it were a code to unravel. Meanwhile, Phil's mind raced like a finely tuned engine, formulating strategies for the upcoming phases of the investigation.

"Understood, Detective. I'll make sure everything gets underway," Davo replied eagerly.

Phil cast a stern yet appreciative look toward Davo, his unspoken message clear. "Of course, I'll discuss it with Senior Sergeant Roberts before taking any action," the junior sergeant quickly added. The delicate dance of procedure and protocol was one they must master, for in the realm of crime-solving, even the slightest misstep could prove disastrous.

"This is getting complicated," Graves remarked, "We need to scrutinise each suspect individually in light of the evidence we have so far. Have you made any headway in locating this nurse?"

"As for her whereabouts, no, not yet," replied Phil, "But I did receive an interesting email from a locum doctor at her last place of employment, Tennant Creek Hospital."

"I need to know everything, Senior Sergeant Roberts, every last detail," he responded, placing emphasis on his final three words, his brows knitted in deep contemplation. He wore the expression of a man peering into the abyss of a mystery yet to be fully comprehended. "I assume all of this has been thoroughly documented?"

"Yes, it certainly has. Constable Reed and Sergeant Smith have been hard at work on the paperwork for most of the afternoon. Everything should meet your exacting standards. It's just the last few phone calls I need to detail," Phil explained, a hint of weariness creeping into his voice. He pressed on, dedicated to seeing this through. "I plan to track down the make, model, and colour as well as the registration number of Cindy's car and follow up with the Tennant Creek doctor early tomorrow morning."

Graves considered the wealth of new information, his concentration firm, his brow furrowed in deep contemplation, "Thank you, Senior Sergeant. I understand it's late, but as you so aptly emphasised earlier, time is not on our side. I'm keen on not wasting a moment and would like to commence the investigation of the potential crime scene as soon as possible. We've brought all the essential equipment to work through the night: lights, lenses, filters for detecting blood and other potential contaminants. Our evidence bags are at the ready, and each of us is equipped with personal protective gear. We're prepared to begin the painstaking process of collecting evidence this very evening."

"I see," Phil replied, his voice steady and professional, though a sense of irritation simmered beneath the facade. "I want to assure you, we will fully cooperate."

"Thank you," Graves responded, a glimmer of gratitude softening the stern lines of his face. The corners of his mouth curled upward ever so slightly, a rare display of warmth. His gaze then shifted to the assembled team, a sea of faces behind him, each one a cog in the machinery of justice.

"You all know the drill," he declared, his voice steady and commanding, a guidepost of authority in the gathering dusk. "Senior Sergeant Roberts and Sergeant Smith will lead us to the homestead, and we can kick off the evidence collection." His words hung in the air, a call to action for each member to step into their role in this investigation.

Turning to the botanist, Graves continued with a deliberate tone, "Henry, I'd like you to accompany Constable Mark Doomadgee to the reported deadly nightshade tree. Confirm its species and genus. We need to be certain." The desire for precision was palpable in his words.

Detective Bill Graves had cemented his position as the one firmly at the helm of this intricate investigation; his gaze now fixated on Catherine, a silent directive coursing through the room, "Catherine, I assume you'll want to arrange for the bodies to be transferred for autopsy at Cairns Base Hospital as soon as possible?"

"Absolutely," Catherine responded, her voice steady and resolute. She was a pillar of practicality in this sea of uncertainty. "That's the most prudent course of action. After you've compiled all the essential evidence tonight, I'll coordinate the transportation of the deceased to Cairns tomorrow morning. This will enable me to carry out the forensic autopsies. Additionally, I anticipate receiving the overnight lab results, transported by George, back in Cairns by tomorrow afternoon."

"Agreed," Detective William Graves affirmed, his voice a low rumble resonating through the room. He leaned forward, resting his hands on the table, his gaze unwavering. "My team is prepared to work tirelessly through the night, if need be, to ensure a thorough collection and documentation of evidence. We must accelerate this investigation; these are undoubtedly perplexing circumstances."

The atmosphere buzzed with a sense of purpose as the team dispersed to carry out their assigned tasks. Senior Sergeant Roberts and Sergeant Smith took the lead, striding decisively toward the homestead, their steps resolute and self-assured. Graves observed them briefly, recognising their seasoned expertise and authoritative presence in such circumstances. However, not a word of praise would ever escape his mouth. These men needed to understand who held the reins of this investigation.

While Henry and Constable Mark Doomadgee made their way under torchlight in the opposite direction, Henry followed Mark's lead to the presumed location of the deadly nightshade tree. The scientist's profound knowledge of botany proved of great worth, as he conclusively identified the plant as Atropa belladonna, commonly referred to as deadly nightshade. This plant, categorised under the Solanaceae family and the genus Atropa, could be a linchpin in understanding the incident's circumstances.

The diligent process of collecting evidence was in full swing at the homestead. Graves scanned the scene discerningly, hoping to uncover the miniscule details that might unlock crucial insights. His team operated precisely; each member was well-versed in their assigned tasks.

Inside the fridge, illuminated by the sterile light, they came across a stash of XXXX beers, a partially consumed pavlova adorned with three different types of berries, steaks, and a medley of neatly stored vegetables in the crisper, aligning with Bruce's statement. These discoveries were bagged as potential evidence for further scrutiny, especially given the reports linking the men's illness to their evening meal. Once they carefully documented the fridge's contents, Graves and his team moved on to search the rest of the homestead.

Following that, they conducted a comprehensive examination of the kitchen bin. They gathered and carefully preserved the empty codeine boxes and the discarded fentanyl patches, placing them securely in an evidence bag. The team then turned their attention to collecting an array of hair samples, spanning from greying black, long, wavy strands to shorter grey hairs, along with thin blonde hairs and long grey ones that appeared to have been recently treated with peroxide to mimic a blonde shade. Finally, beneath the indigenous man's head, they found a pool of vomitus, a chilling reminder of the final moments that unfolded within these walls.

They maintained their diligence throughout the property in cataloguing fingerprints from various surfaces. Their focus on the plate holding the pavlova was particularly noteworthy, recognising its potential significance in the unfolding investigation.

Approaching the lifeless forms, Graves' instructions were clear and resolute. "Prioritise fingerprinting the deceased individuals," he commanded. These prints would serve as pivotal markers, allowing for comparisons with other prints found within the house, potentially revealing who else was present in the recent past.

The lights cast long shadows on the ground as the night wore on, creating an eerie backdrop to their work. The air was filled with a palpable tension. Hours passed, but Graves and his team pressed on, knowing their adversary was time. They worked through the night, their focus unyielding.

As dawn's gentle light began to wash over the landscape, the team gathered on the verandah to evaluate their progress. Graves, his notebook brimming with observations and promising leads, addressed his colleagues. "We've made significant progress, but there's still much ground to cover. Let's convene at the old homestead, confer with the rest of the team, chart our next moves, and approach this investigation with the same steadfast commitment after we all have a chance to rest."

Following a night of unrelenting investigation, the team returned to the old homestead. As they disembarked from the two rental vehicles, their steps betrayed weariness, yet their dedication burned bright. The rising sun hung like an ochre orb on the horizon, heralding a new day and a fresh beginning in their quest for answers.

Phil was the first to welcome the team as they arrived. Having woken an hour earlier, he was already washed and dressed in preparation to reach out to the doctor at Tennant Creek. He settled at the sturdy table that had become the focal point of their investigation, compiling a list of questions regarding Cindy Newman. As he heard footsteps drawing nearer, he saw a fatigued Graves standing in the doorway. The detective made his way to the table, followed by the other members of the squad. Simultaneously, the three local police emerged from their respective rooms after hearing the others arrive. Inside the homestead, the entire team congregated around the well-worn table, its surface cluttered now with scattered papers, evidence bags, and the tools of their exhaustive investigation. Graves, the weight of the night evident in his eyes, took a moment to meet the gaze of each team member. He noted their expressions bore the indelible mark of certitude, an indicator of their strength of character. He nodded, acknowledging their commitment.

"I commend each of you for your tireless efforts," Graves began, his voice tinged with exhaustion and pride. He made sure to include the four local officers in his address, recognising their invaluable contributions, "But we must not rest on our laurels. There's still a breadth of ground to cover, leads to pursue, and connections to establish."

As he addressed the team, the morning sunlight gently streamed through the curtains, painting a cozy radiance throughout the room. It illuminated the indomitable expressions on the faces of the collective team, underscoring the purposeful lines carved into their features. The atmosphere was electric with a shared sense of purpose, an unspoken acknowledgment that they stood on the verge of a significant breakthrough.

Phil leaned in closer to Graves, his eyes ablaze with tenacity, "Detective, we've compiled an extensive list of leads and potential links. I'm confident we're headed in the right direction, but a few crucial areas still require deeper investigation."

The detective nodded in genuine appreciation, recognising the sergeant's meticulous efforts. "Outstanding work. Let's prioritise those leads and assign teams to pursue them."

"Clearly, you've had a gruelling night, but do you have any updates to share before you all head off for some well-deserved rest?" Senior Sergeant Roberts inquired gently, fully cognisant of the fact the homicide squad had been working through the night.

Graves shifted his gaze towards Phil and spoke, "Our team has put in a considerable amount of effort, but there's still much ahead of us. I can report we managed to secure multiple hair samples and fingerprints from the scene. Notably, we found discarded codeine packets and fentanyl patches in the kitchen bin. I've also confirmed the contents of the fridge, and in line with Mr Hudson's report, there were indeed three types of berries on the pavlova. My team needs some rest now. If you don't mind, I'd appreciate it if we could reconvene later. It's been an exceedingly demanding night."

Phil nodded, fully aware of the gruelling demands of police work, often stretching into relentless, seemingly never-ending shifts.

Turning to his squad, Graves instructed, "Take a break, grab some sustenance, and be back here at 12 sharp. We'll regroup over lunch and outline our next moves." His directive was met with firm nods and a chorus of affirmations.

The team dispersed, leaving the four local officers at the table. Plates clinked as they shared a hearty breakfast and readied themselves for the day ahead. They were all acutely aware of the mounting police work back at their respective stations and the need to wrap this investigation up. The team was also mindful that this situation required their undivided attention.

Phil's phone rang as he completed his list of questions to ask Dr Daylight. It was an unexpected caller, none other than Mad Maureen—a figure notorious for her unpredictability and uncouth demeanour.

Seeing her name light up on his screen, Phil greeted, "Hello, Maureen," his voice steady, betraying none of the surprise her call elicited.

"I believe yous been lookin' for me. Words out. Whaddya want this time?" The rough, unrefined tone on the other end of the line came, Mad Maureen's signature brand of brashness.

"How good of you to call," Phil responded, his tone a blend of courtesy and calculated inquiry. "We know you were camping at Watson's River Station on Friday night. Can you tell us a bit more about that?" His words held a hint of scheming, a recognition Mad Maureen might hold a pivotal piece to this intricate riddle.

"Look. I know them two blokes are dead, and I also 'eard that Bruce 'as been yappin' off about them medications I sold 'im. Just tryin' to make ends meet, Sarge."

"I understand, Maureen," came the measured reply, "But we are dealing with a potential double murder, and we have to cross all the I's and dot all the T's. When did you leave the station?"

"Didn't stick around, did I? Just handed over the goods and made meself scarce," she grumbled, her tone a mix of resignation and defensiveness.

"Thank you for your cooperation. Did you spot anyone else on Friday before you made your exit? Perhaps John, Noel, or anyone else camping on the station?" Phil inquired, his tone measured and thorough.

Maureen hesitated momentarily before responding, "Nah, didn't see no one else. Was in and out like a shadow, I was. Just Bruce. He was a regular customer, like, 'cause of 'is back pain an' all. I knew 'e'd be good for the dough, 'avin' worked at the station all week."

"Nobody else? No trace of other campers? No one doing a bit of free camping?"

"Nope," she replied with unwavering confidence. "Like I said, I knew Bruce was set. He needed those meds, and 'e had the cash, so I unloaded the stuff I pinched from the doctor's bag. Go ahead and chalk up another misdemeanour for me. I'll sort it out when I'm back in Weipa."

Maureen's candid confession left Phil with a lot to consider. It was a significant piece of information, adding a new dimension to the investigation. Wayne also claimed he saw no sign of other campers, but perhaps some people were just exceptionally discreet. This revelation cast a shadow over Bruce's alibi, his claim of being out kangaroo shooting on the fateful night. The Queensland bush held its secrets close, and it was entirely plausible Bruce's activities were not as straightforward as they seemed. Once a steadfast pillar of his innocence, the alibi now bore scrutiny. As the gears of his analytical mind turned, Phil understood the imperative of a comprehensive re-evaluation. All of Bruce's statements and his alibi needed to be dissected with a fine-tooth comb. Each phrase and event were now a potential clue or a red flag, waiting to be revealed under the microscope of the team's scrutiny.

Next on the agenda loomed the task of contacting Dr Daylight. Phil carefully dialled the number provided to him in the email, anticipation coursing through him. The phone seemed to ring endlessly, each tone echoing in the recesses of his mind. A voice crackled through the line as he was on the brink of conceding defeat.

"Dr Daylight here," the voice rushed, urgency palpable.

"Good morning, Doctor," Phil responded, detecting the hurried cadence. "You sound incredibly busy."

"I'm terribly sorry, Sergeant," came the apologetic reply, the background noise suggesting a chaotic scene. "I've been called in early due to a major multi-vehicle pile-up. It's all hands-on deck here. Would tomorrow morning be suitable?"

"Of course," Phil replied, disappointment in his voice. He was so hopeful about this lead. He was convinced this young doctor held vital information that could shed light on their investigation.

CHAPTER 21

Plans were underway for Catherine to personally oversee the transportation of the gathered samples, prints, and bodies to Cairns. The scheduled forensic autopsies would be carried out at Cairns Base Hospital, ensuring the crucial evidence and human remains received the thorough analysis and processing they demanded.

Taking command of this critical body transfer operation, she swiftly orchestrated the deployment of essential resources. Her close collaboration with local authorities and medical personnel ensured a seamless and dignified process. An ambulance was promptly dispatched from Weipa to the station, its mission being the careful retrieval of the bodies. This same vehicle was designated to transport Catherine, along with the conscientiously gathered evidence, back to Weipa, where they would board a chartered plane for the journey to Cairns, marking a crucial phase in the investigation.

After traversing the rough road back to Weipa airport and, with all arrangements in place, Catherine and the local paramedics gently loaded the two body bags onto the waiting aircraft on the tarmac. Its engines emitted a subdued hum, signalling readiness. Under Catherine's vigilant oversight, the bodies were thoughtfully secured within specially designed containers for transfer.

With the doors closed and the engines roaring to life, the aircraft gracefully lifted off into the sky, carrying the weight of the deceased and the gravity of their circumstances.

Catherine sat in the cabin, her mind focused on the task ahead. She knew once she reached Cairns, the bodies would be taken to the pathology lab, where her team would press forward with the forensic aspect of the investigation. Catherine's mind wandered throughout the flight, reflecting on the lives lost and the families left behind. She understood the weight of responsibility she bore, not just in delivering the bodies but also in providing solace and closure to those grieving loved ones.

Her sense of purpose intensified as the aircraft touched down at Cairns Base Hospital. The humid, tropical air clung to her skin, starkly contrasting the icy grip of the case that brought her here. The investigation was far from over; in fact, it had just begun anew, guided by the litany of evidence and the unerring expertise of the forensic team. Catherine took charge of the comprehensive examination and analysis of the deceased individuals.

Within the pathology laboratory, she assembled her team of assistants. They gathered around her, eyes eager for guidance, as she recounted her initial findings from the grisly scene that unfolded. Faces taut with anticipation, they listened intently, aware their work could mean the difference between justice served and a mystery unsolved.

After dispatching the vomit sample for rapid analysis and sending the fingerprints, strands of hair, and other mysterious fragments to the main laboratory, Catherine embarked on a series of autopsies that would peel back the layers of death's enigma one by one. Her gloved hands, steady as a surgeon's, began with Noel Manson.

As she gazed at the strange blue tinge of the vomitus on the deceased's cheek, she yearned for a rapid analysis of that ominous substance, hoping for answers, looking to uncover the insidious presence of atropine or scopolamine or the elusive diagnostics of their breakdown products, tropine and tropic acid. It was a dichotomy that could swing from deadly nightshade berries to innocent blueberries, and only the precision of toxicological analysis could unveil the truth.

Catherine delved into the depths of the deceased's body, her every move methodical, her every incision purposeful. She extracted samples of stomach fluids and urine from the bladder. In the dimly lit autopsy room, she could almost hear the whispers of the departed, urging her forward in her quest for truth.

Purpose was not an abstract concept for her; it was a tangible force propelling her forward, a relentless drive to seek answers in science's cold, unfeeling realm. She believed the key to unlocking this mystery lay hidden within the intricate dance of chemicals and reactions, discerning the unmistakable traces left on the human body by the touch of poison.

In the sterile confines of the laboratory, she examined the extracted samples, her eyes trained for the faintest hint of a substance, such as undigested pill fragments, that could hold the truth. Routinely, almost one hundred chemicals would be rapidly assayed. She sent the samples to the laboratory technician for analysis, asking her to focus on narcotics, atropine, scopolamine and their breakdown products. Her heart raced with anticipation, envisioning the potential revelations awaiting her.

Returning to the body, her thorough examination unveiled a compelling narrative: The intestinal lining bore the telltale signs of congestion and inflammation, revealing small ulcers in the stomach and duodenum, their once pink surfaces now marred by dark stains. Within the thoracic cavity, evidence of pulmonary oedema - the lungs filled with fluid, sealing the tragic fate of these men as they succumbed to respiratory paralysis. Brain oedema was mild, while liver congestion further corroborated the narrative. To her trained mind, it was either deadly nightshade or opiates that would be the sinister agent of this man's demise. The conclusive evidence, so to speak, would lie first in the rapid and later in the quantitative analysis that would occur weeks or even months down the track.

Her thoughts resounded with the memory of the conversation back at the old homestead, where she'd been apprised of the ominous presence of the Belladonna tree as well as the discarded fentanyl patches and empty codeine boxes. The chilling pieces of this macabre puzzle seemed to be falling into place. The remnants of berry skins nestled within the digestive tract and the telltale congestion in the larger organs were eerie echoes of that briefing. It was a connection; she was sure of it. Carefully, she preserved those organic cobalt shards, each a potential key to unlocking the truth, placing them in a carefully labelled specimen bag for future analysis. These precious remnants, alongside the morbid harvest collected by the tenacious homicide team at the homestead, would now undergo closer scrutiny.

With this in mind, Catherine's gaze shifted to the remaining organs, her gloved hands deftly navigating the morose landscape of the deceased. There were no signs of recent myocardial infarctions, no telltale clues of a heart under duress. Likewise, no external trauma indicators marred the vital structures' exposed canvas. No darkening bruises, no punctures from bullets or blades.

Subsequently, she shifted her focus and conducted the post-mortem examination of John Granger. The eerie similarities were impossible to ignore: those ominous berry skins, like vestiges of a sinister feast, clung tenaciously to Granger's small intestine lining. The large organs were congested; pulmonary oedema, the silent witness to a final struggle for breath, painted a vivid picture within Granger's chest cavity. It spoke volumes, confirming the ruthless modus operandi claiming both lives.

With the examination of John Granger complete, Catherine's mind churned with the weight of the evidence. The parallels between Noel Manson and John Granger were undeniable, like chapters from the same sinister novel. As she left the examination room, her steps echoed down the sterile corridors of the hospital. The flickering fluorescent lights above cast unnerving shadows, a fitting backdrop to the two unexplained deaths now consuming her thoughts.

Back in the pathology laboratory, she gathered her team once more. Their faces reflected the shared understanding they were on the precipice of uncovering something monumental. She conveyed her observations with a resolute tone, emphasising the peculiar commonalities between the two victims. While certainly ominous, the discovery of berry skins could merely be a piece of a larger picture. The spectre of opioid involvement loomed as a viable alternative explanation for these tragic fatalities. She tasked her team with combing through every piece of evidence. She needed the items collected from the homestead refrigerator analysed ASAP.

In the coming hours, the lab would hum with the sound of activity, the air electric with the anticipation of revelation. Vomit samples, prints, hair strands - each held a potential key to unlocking the truth. Catherine knew that buried within these unassuming fragments lay the answers she sought.

As the clock ticked away, the rapid analysis reports began to trickle in. The vomit sample revealed traces of tropine and tropic acid, confirming Catherine's suspicions. The three berries on the pavlova were established to be strawberries, raspberries and deadly nightshade berries. The internal blood tests, however, held their own tale. They spoke of codeine and fentanyl, painting a portrait of opioid presence. Yet, the metabolites of deadly nightshade, the malevolent agents, were notably absent. The liver's swift breakdown of these lethal substances, atropine and scopolamine, could account for their elusive nature, a phenomenon not uncommon in cases that had seen days pass since ingestion. The fingerprints and hair samples bore no immediate revelations, but she knew they held secrets demanding patience and diligence.

With this crucial information in hand, she returned to the autopsy room. Her hands moved with purpose, guided by the newfound clarity of her discoveries. The cause of death was no longer shrouded in mystery; it lay within the insidious embrace of opiates and, more than likely, deadly nightshade. The chemical analysis provided the missing piece, damning evidence implicating a malevolent hand. The web of deception began to disentangle, and the shadows dispelled. Without delay, she needed to contact Graves and Phil to share the critical breakthrough that had just surfaced.

She dialled Graves' number, the rings carrying a tense anticipation. However, after two unanswered calls going straight to message bank, it became clear his phone was switched off. Frustration and a keen sense of purpose welled up within her. She couldn't afford to waste any more time.

The pathologist understood this was a matter demanding a direct conversation, not a message left in digital limbo. Phil, the next in the chain of the investigation command, was her immediate recourse. Their shared experiences at the station forged a bond; truth be told, she welcomed the opportunity to bypass Graves. Lately, his conduct and excessive familiarity were making her uneasy; there was an undeniably disconcerting quality about him. Fingers flying over the keypad, she quickly called Phil's number, the urgency palpable in every dial tone.

As Phil's voice crackled through the line, she could sense the flicker of hope in his tone. She could almost picture the gears turning in his sharp, analytical mind as if he was mentally slotting each piece of the puzzle into its rightful place.

CHAPTER 22

While the homicide squad slumbered, Phil and the other local officers gathered around the worn oak table. They had much to contemplate. Graves and his team returned earlier that morning, briefly updating Phil on their progress thus far. The crucial revelation for Phil was the discarded codeine boxes and four fentanyl patches in the kitchen bin. His curiosity was not confined to these pharmacological artifacts alone; he yearned for insights gleaned from the broader sweep of evidence gathered at the scene. However, he knew well the wheels of analysis turned at their own measured pace, and patience was the currency of his trade. He'd have to wait and wait, he would.

The homicide squad also confirmed Catherine departed to transport the deceased back to Cairns for post-mortems and further forensic analysis of the fingerprints and evidence collected at the homestead.

From Phil's perspective, these city slickers had descended upon their territory, with Graves swiftly assuming control of the case. However, in his estimation, they hadn't brought much to the table beyond what his team had already uncovered prior to their arrival. He understood the importance of adhering to established protocols and principles of sound police work, but he couldn't shake the feeling that these folks barged in, dictating the course of action without significantly advancing the investigation. Patience was crucial; the preliminary lab results shouldn't be too far off, and Catherine's post-mortem findings on the two deceased individuals were eagerly anticipated. With any luck, science would play a pivotal role in unravelling this mystery. Phil envisioned himself easing into the twilight of his career with a closed case, retirement on the near horizon.

Acknowledging patience wasn't his strongest suit, he took charge and contacted Catherine. It was nearing two p.m., and he held out hope she had completed the post-mortems and coordinated with the pathology team in Cairns for further analysis of the samples collected by the homicide squad. In his current optimistic manner, he dared to imagine she might even have received the preliminary lab results from the samples George took with him on the charter flight the day before.

He preferred to proceed without the hurried presence of the homicide squad, which tended to cloud his thinking and encroach upon the investigation. He simply wanted them gone. Phil was well aware of his own seasoned expertise in the realm of police work, and armed with the current information, he believed he could crack this case with just the local team by his side.

Poised to dial the number, he suddenly paused as his phone chimed to life. He glanced down and saw Dr Catherine Reynold's name on the caller ID. His brows arched in surprise, and then he smiled. The timing was perfect.

"Hello?" Phil answered, his tone a blend of anticipation and professionalism.

Catherine's voice came through the line, brisk yet focused, "Phil, I have some news for you. The preliminary toxicology report just came in." Her eyes scanned the document before her, a mix of concern and urgency in her gaze.

Phil's eyes widened slightly, his breath catching. He leaned in, absorbing every word. "Alright, go on," he urged, a spark of hope glinting in his eyes.

As Catherine continued, her brow furrowed momentarily, conveying the seriousness of the situation, "There are positive results for fentanyl and codeine in both men's internal samples," Phil's expression tightened, a mix of concern and contemplation crossing his face.

"I'm afraid it will take six to twelve weeks to get a quantitative assay result," she explained. "The extended timeframe is a result of the significant backlog of samples at the Queensland Forensics Department. This in-depth analysis is crucial in establishing whether the detected doses were potentially fatal."

Phil's gaze held steady, absorbing the information. He nodded slowly, processing the reality of the situation. His lips pressed into a thin line, signifying the weight of the task ahead.

"Thank you, Catherine," Phil responded appreciatively, "What about the nightshade berries?"

Catherine's weariness was palpable in her response. "I'm not entirely certain at this point. During the post-mortem, I did find some dark berry skins in the small intestine. However, they've been sent for further testing. They could be blueberries, nightshade berries, or something entirely different. Interestingly, I discovered breakdown products of the Belladonna berries in the indigenous man's vomitus, meaning they had to be ingested first. I also confirmed the third berry on the pavlova, a mystery to Carol but recognised by Bruce, was indeed deadly nightshade."

Phil furrowed his brow, grappling with the intricacies of forensics, a field that wasn't his forte. He knew Catherine was tactful enough not to highlight this. "But wouldn't they have shown up in the initial analysis if they were the cause of death?"

Catherine's reply was gentle, her expertise evident in her measured explanation. "Not necessarily. It depends on the timeline from ingestion to death. An adult would need to ingest at least ten berries. Typically, after initial symptoms such as drowsiness, vomiting, and diarrhea, the victim would progress to hallucinations, rapid heart rate, and thirst before succumbing to the poison nearly seventy-two hours later. Respiratory muscle paralysis leading to flooding of the lungs is the usual cause of death. Unfortunately, if this was the cause, the active substances in the berries, atropine and scopolamine, would have already metabolised and wouldn't appear in our rapid assay."

Phil absorbed this information, a concerned expression on his face. He appreciated Catherine's expertise and her willingness to navigate these complex details with him.

Upon learning this new information, Bruce was suddenly thrust back into the spotlight as a prime suspect. Phil considered the man's admission of supplying the deceased individuals with codeine and fentanyl patches. Graves casually mentioned the discarded patches discovered in the kitchen bin near the victims. Phil was aware of Bruce's lingering resentment towards both men due to their ties to the mining industry, and the fact he was present at the estimated time of death added another layer of suspicion.

However, Phil couldn't shake the nagging feeling Bruce might be innocent. Why else would he be so forthcoming and cooperative? Why willingly provide DNA samples and agree to an interview? It just didn't add up.

As the afternoon sun cast long shadows across the room, Phil sat in contemplation, the burden of the case pressing on him like a vice. Thoughts swirled in his mind, a maelstrom of leads, dead-ends, and half-formed theories threatening to overwhelm him. He could feel the pressure mounting, an invisible force threatening to shatter his composure.

Just as he teetered on the precipice of mental overload, the intrusion came, silent as a shadow. Graves, emerging from a restless slumber, moved with the stealth of a predator closing in on its prey. With a sense of purpose, he settled beside Phil at the expansive table, an unspoken insistence radiating from his presence. He looked at the wall clock and saw its hands read two p.m. Fury surged through him, a fiery mix of self-reproach for oversleeping and simmering frustration at his absent team. The moment arrived to summon the troops, to regroup and reassert control over the situation. This was a man on a mission. His eyes burnt with intense resolve, and now, as he sat beside Phil, he hungered for updates, for progress.

"Good afternoon, Sergeant," Graves murmured, his voice a subtle tremor in the charged atmosphere.

Phil's reaction was a display of flawless composure, his features betraying nothing of the surprise surging within him. "Afternoon, Detective," he returned, the neutrality in his tone thinly veiling the intrusion he felt into his domain, "I note you overslept."

"Yes," his voice terse, "I'll rouse the rest of the team now."

Phil's smirk danced at the corners of his lips as he met Graves' gaze. "Oh, I think you'll want to hear this first," he responded, his voice dripping with a self-assured satisfaction.

The detective sat upright, anticipation prickling at his skin.

Phil observed the detective, gauging his readiness, then continued with deliberate relish. "I've managed to track down Maureen and just got off the line with Dr Reynolds," he stated, a knowing glint in his eye; he paused, letting the suspense hang thick in the air.

Graves, eyes wide with intrigue, urged him on with an expectant nod.

"Mad Maureen herself rang me up," Phil continued, a grin tugging at the corner of his mouth, "She swears blind she was here on Friday, and apart from Bruce, there was no one else camped out on the farm," he let the revelation settle before delving into Catherine's latest findings.

The detective's furrowed brow bespoke his vexation, a testament to the prickling irritation gnawing at him. How could Catherine, the pathologist, have bypassed the established protocol? In this case, his authority was unquestionable, yet here he was, learning crucial information second-hand.

"Why didn't she come through me first? I'm the lead detective on this damn case," he muttered, a growl of frustration rumbling beneath his breath.

Phil met Graves' gaze, his own countenance a masterclass in restrained satisfaction. "I believe she attempted to," he offered, his tone both sombre and subtly triumphant, "Your phone, it seems, was off during your well-deserved and prolonged rest."

A sigh, laden with exasperation, escaped Grave's lips as he retrieved his phone. The screen blinked to life, revealing the evidence of missed calls from Catherine; two of them. "Damn it," he cursed under his breath, a begrudging acknowledgment of his own oversight.

He shifted in his seat; his gaze locked onto Senior Sergeant Phil Roberts with a laser-like focus. The room languished under the oppressive clutch of the afternoon sun, birthing elongated, ominous shadows slithering across their faces. They leaned in, their unwavering tenacity evident as they pored over the culmination of their investigative efforts thus far.

"Phil," Graves began, his voice low and authoritative, "We need to go through this methodically, no stone unturned. I want a comprehensive review of every piece of evidence we've gathered," a silent declaration of their shared mission.

Phil nodded in understanding. His features, a portrait of unwavering commitment, "Of course, Detective. We've got the tyre marks at the scene, bloodstains on the grass, those mysterious footprints near the deadly nightshade bush leading toward the homestead and a sweep of the entire house. We've also secured hair samples and fingerprints and even scrutinised the contents of the fridge," he paused, knowing the gravity of what came next, "And then there's what Catherine brought to the table."

Graves leaned back, the wheels in his mind turning as he contemplated the tangled web of information before them. "Indeed," he mused, "Catherine's findings have added a new layer to this investigation. Codeine and fentanyl were in the overnight analysis, but there was a distinct absence of other substances in the central blood samples. Deadly nightshade toxins in Noel's vomit and those berry skins in both deceased intestines."

He drummed his fingers on the table, clearly showing his frustration, "It's a damned conundrum, Phil. Were opiates the silent killers here, or was it deadly nightshade? And more importantly, who's pulling the strings behind this twisted dance of death?" Graves' stare bore into Phil's, the urgency of their mission resonating in the unspoken words hanging between them.

Phil's voice sliced through the air, sharp and urgent, punctuating the tension, "Add to that the unexpected death of Walt Henry and Carol's reports of blueberry muffins in the fridge. Those blueberries could have just as easily been belladonna berries, too, and suddenly, we're staring down the barrel of a serial killer!" His words reverberated off the walls, filling the space with a chilling sense of foreboding.

The detective leaned back in his chair, his eyes narrowed in contemplation, each word from the local sergeant setting off a chain reaction of thoughts in his mind, "Let's focus on the two deceased individuals here at the station," he began, his voice measured and authoritative. "Bruce harbours a motive, a festering grudge against the mining giant that devoured his community's land and against anyone associated with the profiteering, including John and Noel. He had the opportunity, based here throughout. He admitted to providing both men with codeine and fentanyl, sourced from Maureen. And then there's the matter of

Bruce's 'discovery' of those footprints and the deadly nightshade bush with its freshly plucked berries. It's all a little too neat, don't you think?" Graves arched an incredulous brow. He paused, letting the weight of his words hang in the air, "Now, throw into the mix the fact that Mr Hudson's alibi has crumbled to dust, neither Constable Reed nor Maureen glimpsed a trace of the elusive Jake that Bruce claimed was behind the wheel of the ute during his supposed kangaroo shooting outing. Seems our Bruce might have been painting a rather imaginative picture of the situation. We've got motive, we've got opportunity, and now, we've got a glaring absence of an alibi. I'd say the case is as clear-cut as they come," he asserted, a steely assurance in his tone.

He fixed his gaze on Phil, probing for any sign, any flicker of reaction; Phil, in turn, revealed nothing. The detective continued, "I place little faith in Bruce," his tone unwavering. "A man with a rap sheet for minor offences, a nomad on the fringes of society, holed up in a makeshift dwelling on the outskirts of a forsaken town. Bring him back in!" The detective commanded, the edge in his voice honed to a razor's edge. "Arrest him. He had motive and opportunity, and he confessed to supplying the very substances that likely led to the demise of those two men." The room seemed to pulse with the brutality of his words.

"Just a moment, Detective," Phil interjected, "Bruce has been fully cooperative with us so far, and I believe he's as keen on apprehending the culprits as we are. He's been happy to provide his DNA, and his fingerprints are on file."

Graves retorted with a derisive smirk, "He's only feigning cooperation to mask his tracks, my friend; the best defence is a good offence, they say. He roams these parts regularly, feeble alibis, unable to be backed up by anyone else, leading us astray."

"Hold on a minute!" Phil was angry now, his voice raised, "We can't just jump to conclusions here. This is a very serious matter, Detective! You want to charge a man with murder who has been fully cooperative to date and appears to mourn his own kin, his brother? This is preposterous!" He had not finished, "You can't just come in here, take over and demand we arrest the man. I understand you are busy and keen to return to Brisbane as soon as possible, but what about the three sets of tyre tracks, the small footprints, the blood, and the berry skins found inside the gut on post-mortem? What about Cindy Newman as a suspect?" He was visibly shaken; his face turned a deep shade of red, and his hands trembled.

"A convenient narrative spun by our suspect here on the station. There's a saying about lies often bearing the semblance of truth and vice versa," Graves concluded, his tone laden with scepticism, "Sergeant, I need concrete proof. Tyre tracks and footprints alone won't cut it; they're merely circumstantial. You have to make a compelling case for someone else deserving our attention. Show me!" He spoke with a pronounced impatience, his words ringing out loudly.

Woken from their rest by the escalating dispute, the rest of the homicide team swiftly convened around the table, their expressions reflecting a mix of curiosity and concern. Doubt hung in the air, casting a shadow over the room. The trio of local officers also joined the gathering, adding to the tension. The collective expressions on their faces made it unmistakably clear they had all caught wind of the heated altercation.

Phil felt the pressure mounting. "We can't afford to ignore what's right in front of us," he retorted, his voice more subdued.

Graves arched an incredulous eyebrow. "You speak of evidence? Pray tell, what evidence?" he inquired, his tone dripping with mock disbelief.

Phil's frustration was obvious as he stared intently at the papers before him, his mind racing with unanswered questions. "We can't jump to conclusions. We need a comprehensive analysis. Whose blood is it? And those tyre tracks; and the footprints?" His voice held a note of desperation, his eyes darting between the scattered clues.

A wry smile tugged at Graves' lips as he leaned back in his chair. "All conveniently presented to us by the very man we suspect; quite the performance, I must say," his scepticism hung in the air, casting a shadow over the room, "May I remind you? You were the one who said time is of the essence," Graves responded curtly, "Those who hesitate are lost, Sergeant. In my experience, we have a small window of opportunity to make an arrest before our suspect gets wind of our intentions and flies the coop. We already know Bruce Hudson lives on the fringes of society. He could just as easily disappear with no trace. I will not be held responsible for that! Bring him in! I demand it. That is a direct order!" The detective allowed his composure to slip.

Graves' suspicions lingered like a storm cloud. The investigation had taken an unexpected turn, and Bruce's involvement raised more questions than it answered.

Davo, known for his level-headedness and rational thinking, broke the uneasy silence, "Let's exercise caution here, jumpin' to conclusions won't serve us well. We require more substantial proof before we can make any decisions regarding Bruce." His words resonated, temporarily quelling the rising tension in the room.

Phil nodded in agreement, but Graves' steely gaze remained fixed on Bruce's file. "I understand the need for due process," he began, his voice measured, "But we can't afford to underestimate the severity of these findings. Mr Hudson has a motive, and he's been closer to this case than any of us realised."

A palpable silence settled in the room as everyone contemplated the weight of the detective's words. Clearly, the team was at a crossroads, torn between their duty to follow the evidence and their desire to believe in Bruce's potential innocence.

The homicide team were evidently eager to expedite their return to Brisbane. The prospect of an extended investigation in a remote town didn't align with their priorities or expertise. Judging by Grave's demeanour and words, he was inclined to close this case swiftly and attend to more pressing matters closer to their home base.

Phil couldn't shake his sense of unease. His instincts told him something was amiss. His suspicions about Cindy remained. Adhering to protocol, he knew he couldn't defy a direct order from a superior officer. With reluctance, he instructed Davo and Mark to locate Bruce and accompany him to the old homestead, fully aware Graves intended to press charges.

Davo and Mark exchanged uncertain glances before setting off to find Bruce, fully cognisant of the challenges ahead. They knew this task wouldn't be easy, especially for Mark. Bruce was one of his mob. He convinced himself he was merely doing his job. Nonetheless, he still felt like a traitor to his people.

The two policemen approached the donga; the area was eerily quiet, undisturbed. They choose to walk, allowing the rhythm of their steps to match the solemn weight of their thoughts. This undertaking weighed heavily on both men's minds, as they harboured a deep belief in Bruce's innocence.

Meanwhile, back at the table, Phil's mind raced. He couldn't shake the feeling they were moving too quickly, that crucial pieces of the investigation were being overlooked. He regarded the evidence laid out before them—the tyre marks, the bloodstains, the discarded fentanyl patches. It was all a mess at this stage. There had to be more to this story.

As the minutes ticked by, tension in the room reached its peak. Graves remained staunch in his position to bring Bruce in while Phil grappled with the sense justice was slipping through their fingers. The rest of the team exchanged furtive glances, torn between loyalty to their lead detective and the nagging doubts gnawing at their collective conscience.

Just then, a jarring phone ring broke the silence. It was Davo, his voice edged with urgency. Phil put him on speaker phone, "We've found him," he reported, "Bruce is sitting outside his donga. He's alone, but he looks," he paused, "distraught."

Phil's heart skipped a beat. Distraught? It was a word that didn't align with the image of a cold-blooded killer. He exchanged a pointed glance with Graves, silently communicating the need for further analysis.

The detective, however, seized upon the opportunity. "Bring him in," he ordered tersely, an obstinate look flashing in his eyes. "Let's put an end to this."

Approaching Bruce cautiously, Davo and Mark kept their eyes fixed on him as he sat on the verandah outside the donga, his eyes fixed on the horizon. His shoulders were slumped, lost in thought. They exchanged a glance, sensing a vulnerability contradicting the image of a hardened criminal.

"Mr Hudson?" Davo's voice was steady, attempting to strike a balance between authority and compassion.

Bruce turned slowly, startled by their presence. His eyes were rimmed with red, and it was clear he hadn't slept much. "What's happening?" he asked, his voice hoarse.

Davo took a deep breath, choosing his words carefully. "We need you to come with us, Mr Hudson. We need to ask you some questions back at the homestead."

The suspect's brow furrowed in confusion, but he didn't resist. He trailed after them, a measured pace marking his steps, his silence unbroken for the duration of the journey.

Back at the old homestead, the atmosphere was charged. Graves stood adamant, eager to wrap up the case. The rest of the team exchanged furtive glances before quietly filing out of the room, leaving Phil and Graves alone at the table.

As Bruce entered the room, the tension seemed to thicken, he looked at both officers, his eyes resting on Phil, who met his gaze with a mixture of empathy and curiosity, "Bruce, we'd like to ask you some more questions," the local officer began, his tone gentle, "Please take a seat," motioning to a chair opposite him.

Phil gathered his notes and turned to Davo and Mark, "Thank you, Sergeant, Constable," he said, addressing each of them in turn, "We'll take it from here." He knew this pivotal moment could hold the key to solving the case.

Inside the dining room, the air was charged with anticipation. Bruce sat, his demeanour a mix of stoicism and restlessness as if he could sense the shifting tides around him. Phil took a moment to survey the room, the stark walls and the single table separating them. It was a stage set for the unveiling of truths.

Then came Graves, entering the scene with the calculated intensity of a storm front. Adhering strictly to protocol, he intoned, "This is a formal police interview. Please state your full name and address for the record."

The suspect complied, his voice subdued, "Bruce Hudson, 84 Waum Street, Weipa."

The detective's penetrating gaze bore into him, a deliberate attempt to unsettle, to make him feel the weight of the situation. "You mentioned you were out kangaroo shooting on Saturday night. Can you walk us through your movements in more detail?"

As Bruce began to recount the events of that fateful night, Phil listened intently, his mind a whirlwind of analysis. He compared the suspect's account with Maureen's confession and Wayne's observations, dissecting every word, every pause, every nuance for any signs of deviation or inconsistency. Compliant as usual, Bruce responded once more to their questions regarding the circumstances preceding Diane's gruesome discovery. Every word seemed like an endlessly repeating refrain. The story was familiar to the local officer, recounted by Bruce in exact alignment with his previous testimony.

The detective leaned forward, his eyes drilling into Bruce's, unrelenting. His voice took on a steely edge, honed through years of experience in the field. "Mr Hudson, we have accounts from other witnesses conflicting with your statement. We need to get this straight. This story of a passing camper named Jake, driving your ute while you stood behind the spotlight in the back – that's what you're telling us, correct?"

Bruce's voice wavered, the strain of the moment creeping in. "Yes, that's exactly what I've been saying," he replied, his eyes darting between the officers.

Graves' tone remained uncompromising, "And yet, despite our thorough efforts, 'Jake' remains an elusive figure, a phantom. No other witnesses, no trace of him." His words hung heavily in the room, an unspoken challenge.

"Yes. That's correct. Just as I have repeated multiple times." Bruce's voice was beginning to show signs of strain.

Phil detected the tremor of unease coursing through Bruce. Years of experience taught him the importance of adaptability in these delicate moments. Leaning forward, he lowered his tone, his voice a gentle current amidst the storm.

"Let me make one thing clear," Phil said, his words deliberate. "We're not here to be your enemies. We want the truth and justice for everyone involved. We need your help to piece together what truly happened that night."

Bruce met Phil's gaze, uncertainty and weariness in his tone, "I... I don't want no trouble, either," he stammered, his apprehension palpable. "Maybe it's best if I just," he paused, "Say nothin' else. I've told yous all I know. I've tried me best." With those words, Bruce settled into silence.

The detective moved closer, his imposing presence growing even more pronounced. He leaned over the suspect, his posture intimidating, meeting his gaze squarely, eye to eye. "Mr Hudson," Graves's voice was a low, insistent growl, "We're not here for idle chit-chat. Two men are dead; your cooperation is not a favour; it's a necessity. Now, tell us the truth about that night."

Bruce's jaw clenched, his gaze fixed firmly on the table. He could feel the pressure building, the room closing in around him. But he held fast to his silence, a fortress of stoicism.

The detective pressed harder, each word a calculated strike. "You're playing a dangerous game, my man. Obstruction of justice is a serious offence. You might think keeping quiet is in your best interest, but believe me, it's not."

Bruce's knuckles turned white as he gripped the edge of the table. The room seemed to vibrate with the unspoken tension. He knew Graves was testing the boundaries, pushing him to the brink. Yet he held his ground, intent not to waver.

Phil watched the exchange, his own conduct a study in contrast. Where Graves wielded intimidation like a weapon, his approach was one of patience and understanding. He knew sometimes the quietest voice held the most power in this high-stakes game.

The local officer couldn't shake the feeling there was more to this story. As he observed, the suspect didn't fit the profile of a calculated murderer. His voice carried the weight of pain and regret, hints of a past marked by loss and hardship.

As he studied Bruce's face, he found himself drawn to the depths of those eyes. There was something in them, a raw authenticity tugging at his conscience. He knew the truth was often elusive, hidden beneath layers of complexity.

The oppressive silence was shattered by Graves' authoritative voice, slicing through the room like a blade through the darkness. "Mr Bruce Hudson," he declared, his tone heavy with authority, "you are under arrest for the alleged murders of Mr John Granger and Mr Noel Manson. You have the right to make a phone call. I strongly advise you to contact a lawyer. If you cannot afford one, one will be provided for you."

Phil was taken aback by this sudden turn of events. "Hold on a minute," he interjected, his tone one of disbelief, "There's still a mountain of evidence to sift through and a lot of leads to follow."

Graves shot him a steely glance, unmoved by the Sergeant's plea, "You can do that while the suspect is in custody. We have to move this investigation forward. Either he talks, and we get the real story, or he stays in jail and lets the court decide. It's as simple as that. I didn't come here on a charm offensive."

Those words marked the end of the lengthy, gruelling interview, leaving many faltering questions in the air.

Bruce's response was a chilling silence, an eerie stillness settling over the room; his head hung low in a gesture of dispirited acceptance, and his shoulders slumped in reluctant submission. With a resigned air and without uttering a word, he slid his hands behind his back, a visual testament to his surrender.

With a sense of choreographed timing, Davo made his entrance into the dining room, followed closely behind by Mark and Wayne. The air suddenly charged with a palpable intensity.

"Get those cuffs on him and escort him to the watch house," the detective commanded, swivelling to face Davo.

As Davo promptly carried out the directive, Grave's gaze was locked onto the suspect, a penetrating steeliness in his stare mirroring the definitive click of metal restraints securing Bruce's wrists.

Once the cuffs were in place, Graves relinquished custody of the suspect to Sergeant David Smith, who would oversee Bruce's transfer to the Weipa police station for further questioning and detainment. As the junior sergeant stood at the threshold of the homestead, the night air hung heavy with the weight of decisions made and paths chosen. Ever pragmatic, he broached the inevitable topic of discussion as if reading his fellow officers' thoughts, "We'd have to process the paperwork in Weipa regardless," he began, his voice practical and unhurried. "What say we call it a night? Leave everything be, and we'll pick up the trail in our respective stations?"

Still processing the sudden turn of events, Phil considered Davo's proposal. "Sounds like a logical approach," he turned to Mark and Wayne, extending a practical solution. "Leave your paperwork with us. It'll all be consolidated. I suggest that Mark accompanies Bruce in the back of the patrol car while you drive, Davo. Wayne can take the other car. You can all convene at the Weipa Police Station, and then the two constables can make their way back to Aurukun. I reckon you all could do with a night in your own beds, eh?"

Davo nodded in agreement, his gaze shifting to Phil. "What about you, Sarge? How will you get back?"

"I'll hitch a ride with Graves and his squad," Phil replied, his tone resolute, "There's no point in sticking around here any longer. We all have work waiting for us at our respective posts." He looked expectantly at the detective, "If that suits you?" Phil's voice held a subtle inflection, a question masked as a statement.

Graves, ever taciturn, grunted in agreement. "Yes, yes," he mumbled, his mind already plotting the logistics, "we'll rest up here and then organise a flight out. I'll give Senior

Sergeant Roberts a lift to the Weipa Station tomorrow morning."

The junior officers ushered the suspect outside. Every movement towards the waiting car was considered, every step punctuated by the hushed shuffle of resigned compliance. As the car's door swung open, Bruce hesitated for a fleeting moment, his gaze sweeping over the familiar surroundings of the station he came to know so well over the years. The earth and skies around seemed to pause, holding their collective breath as if gripped by the magnitude of the moment.

Sergeant David Smith gestured for Bruce to enter the police vehicle. "Let's go," he declared, his voice unwavering, revealing no trace of emotion. Bruce reluctantly obeyed, lowering himself into the back seat with a reluctant bend of his knees and a slight bow of his head, his actions deliberate, nearly robotic in their precision.

Graves watched the scene unfold, his expression unreadable. Internally, he mused, not many suspects could sustain this facade of silence for long; sooner or later, the dam would break.

As the car's engine roared to life, the headlights casting long, eerie shadows across the rugged landscape, the enormity of the situation settled in. Bruce knew his fate was now in the hands of the law, and the wheels of justice were set in motion. Suddenly, the night sky ignited into a tempestuous lightning storm, each flash charged with electric anticipation, foreshadowing the trials and revelations yet to come.

CHAPTER 23

The morning after, the atmosphere at Weipa station was subdued; a thick cloud of regret hung over Davo. Bruce, the man he held in custody, cast a long shadow on his conscience. The usual hustle and bustle of the police base was muted, replaced by an air of introspection. Outside, the sun fought to pierce through the thick clouds, casting sporadic rays of light that skulked across the grounds. As the clock neared nine a.m., a rental car pulled up outside.

Graves turned to Phil, "Our team will be taking our leave as well," he declared, his tone leaving no room for argument, "I will arrange for a charter flight back to Brisbane. If any fresh leads arise, I expect to be informed promptly. Understood?"

"Certainly, Detective. Crystal clear."

The Senior Sergeant stepped out of the vehicle and made his way inside the familiar station, the torments of the previous night's events clearly evident on his face. Davo, already buried in paperwork, looked up as the door creaked open. Phil's eyes betrayed the toll of the recent events on him; dark bags sagged beneath them.

The significance of the situation pressed on both men. They couldn't shake the feeling they had a member of their own community, someone they believed to be innocent, locked away. Davo stood and walked toward the holding cell, pushing a breakfast plate towards Bruce, it sat mostly untouched. No matter how many times he tried to bridge the gap with a conversation, Bruce's response was a hard-nosed silence. There was a darkness in his eyes, an abyss neither officer had glimpsed before, like a creature torn from its natural habitat, a wildness replaced with a hollow emptiness. He seemed adrift, a ship without a compass, a soul without a home.

The local officers strongly desired to sort this case out independently. The thought of an innocent man languishing in a prison cell, awaiting a trial for a crime they were convinced he didn't commit, was unbearable to them. The clock ticked relentlessly, allowing them a mere eight-hour window to detain Bruce for questioning within the bounds of the law before he was sent back to his cell.

No matter how hard they pressed, Bruce remained tight-lipped; they were intimately familiar with his stubborn nature; once he'd set his mind, there was no swaying him. Frustrated by their lack of progress, they reluctantly concluded the interview early, escorting Bruce back to his dim cell and closing the heavy door behind them with an ominous thud.

Upon returning to their desks, Davo immediately got to work, fixed on tracking down the elusive figure "Jake." He called various camping spots in Cape York, inquiring if anyone had come across Jake or his travelling companion. Meanwhile, Phil glanced at his watch, noting it was past eleven a.m. This seemed like an opportune moment to contact Dr Daylight. Phil dialled the number, his anticipation tangible as he held the receiver to his ear. Almost instantly, a warm and confident voice greeted him.

"Good morning, Doctor Daylight here," came the genial response.

"Good morning, Doctor," Phil replied.

"I've been expecting your call. I've already pulled some strings with the hospital administration. Now, I have the particulars of Nurse Newman's car for you; colour, registration, make, model; she divulged those to secure her parking spot for the duration of her stint," Dr Daylight's words flowed effortlessly, each detail meticulously gathered.

Phil diligently jotted down the information, a concrete lead forming before him. It was one less avenue to chase down, a small victory amidst the web of uncertainty.

"Thank you, Doctor," Phil said, savouring the exchange. After the ordeals of the past few days, this conversation was a soothing balm to his senses. "That is very helpful. I'm also curious if there were any unusual occurrences while Nurse Newman was stationed in Tennant Creek."

Dr Daylight's tone shifted seamlessly, cutting through the air with surgical precision. "Now, about any suspicious activities during the nurse's tenure?" The question hung, laden with potential significance.

"Indeed, any fragment of information that comes to mind might hold the key to solving this case," Phil responded thoughtfully. "Could you provide further details on peculiar occurrences during Nurse Newman's time there?"

"Absolutely," the voice on the other end affirmed with authority. "The potential link only came to light recently," he divulged, pausing for effect.

"What link?" Phil interjected urgently.

"It wasn't until news of the two deceased men on the station reached our town. It's been six or seven weeks since Nurse Newman abruptly ended her locum position, offering no explanation. One day, she was here, the next, she was gone. At the time, it didn't raise many eyebrows. However, six young indigenous men were admitted a day after her departure, exhibiting symptoms of anticholinergic poisoning."

"Forgive me, but I do not understand what this, anticholinergic poisoning, has to do with our current investigation."

"Of course, my apologies for slipping into 'doctor mode.' It encompasses a range of signs and symptoms resulting from the ingestion or inhalation of various substances. These include medications, insecticides, organophosphate pesticides, chemical solvents, and recreational drugs like PCP. Interestingly, it can also be triggered by consuming parts of the deadly nightshade tree," he paused, letting the information hang in the air.

"Interesting, very interesting," the policeman mused, "Six cases, you say? That does seem unusually high. Is this a common occurrence?"

"Unfortunately, it is. There's not much to keep young folks occupied in Tennant Creek, Sergeant. We often encounter this sort of thing: a few restless youths seeking a high. They'll ingest whatever they can lay their hands on—magic mushrooms, datura, deadly nightshade, even glue and petrol sniffing. You name it, we've seen it," the doctor responded earnestly.

"So, this incident went unreported to the authorities?" Phil inquired, searching for a link to his ongoing investigation.

"As I mentioned, none of us at the hospital paid it much mind. Just a few bored young lads fooling around."

"Until..." Phil prompted, urging the doctor to continue.

"Until Noel Manson's passing."

"But what's his tie to Tennant Creek? His people are up here," Phil observed.

"We received a complaint just two days ago from a local Indigenous woman. She asserts she is the mother of one of the lads treated for anticholinergic poisoning, and Noel Manson is the boy's father. This same Mr Manson recently met his end at Watson's River Station," he paused for effect, "The local woman contends Nurse Newman left a box of blueberry muffins for the boys in question as a parting gesture."

This revelation struck Phil. It hinted at a potential connection between the incidents and possibly multiple cases of poisoning, murder, and attempted murder. The complexity of the situation was becoming increasingly apparent. Empowered by this newfound revelation, Phil's will to vindicate Bruce surged even further. He needed to call the boy's mother.

"Do you have the mother's number, by any chance?" asked Phil.

"I can certainly look it up for you," replied Dr Daylight. "She came with the boys to the hospital so we have her phone number on our records as the boy was a minor. Give me a few minutes and I'll find it for you. Do you mind holding the line for a moment?"

"No, not at all," Phil replied.

Minutes later the doctor was back on the phone and gave the Senior Sergeant the woman's number.

"Much appreciated, Dr Daylight; you have been most helpful," Phil said before exchanging goodbyes and ending the call.

Immediately after ending that call, he called the mobile number of the boy's mother.

"G'day, Alice 'ere," came the rough voice on the other end.

"Mrs Alice Plummer?"

"Yeah, who's speakin'?"

"It's Senior Sergeant Phil Graves from the Weipa Police Station. I wanted to talk to you more about your son's recent admission to the emergency department in Tennant Creek."

"Whaddya wanna know?" she asked suspiciously.

"We have reason to suspect that the death of Noel Manson at Watson's River Station may be connected to your son's poisoning. Can you tell me more about that day, please?"

She spoke in the Kriol style of pidgin English, a contact variety common to the residents of the Northern Territory. This unique language likely originated from the influence of eleven convicts who were freed slaves from America and committed crimes in England. These individuals, with their diverse linguistic backgrounds, brought their speech patterns to Australia, blending with the local languages and dialects to form what we now recognise as Kriol. Over time, this new form of English developed, incorporating elements from both the English spoken by the colonisers and the various Aboriginal languages of the region.

"Sure, dem boys bin playin' soccer at da local ground wen dat nurse, Cindy Newman, drop some cupcakes by. Dey all got stuck into dem an den go missin', foolin' roun' in da bush. Four hours later me get a call from da local hospital sayin' me son's in dere, real sick an all."

"I understand you went to the hospital to visit your son," said Phil.

"Yeah, me did. Me son bin actin' real strange, telling me things like goannas bin talkin' to him, whispering all kinds of strange things. Dem goannas bin tellin' him, 'You goin' to cross over to spirit world.' Him real scared, thinkin' him gonna die. Him bin hallucinate, seein' all sorta things.

"Him say bunch of emus appear an' talk to him. Dem emus tell him, 'Wi bin see nurse at Watson's River Station.' Dem emus say, 'Dis nurse greedy, lookin' for power an' wealth. She got hidden motives, all tied up with ya family's sufferin'.'

"Den one old Elder from our mob bin talk to him. Dat Elder's presence bin strong, like ya can almost touch him.

'We know who kill ya father,' dat Elder say, 'an' dey still alive. Dey bin connected to Watson's River Station. Dey been dere, part of dis dark story in our history. Ya father's spirit can't rest till dat truth bin uncovered.'

"Dat Elder continue, 'Dis truth mus be revealed. Dis journey not jus for yu, but for all our people. Someone goin' go to Watson's River Station. Spirits will guide dem, dey will be brave. Da path will be hard, but ya father's spirit walk with dem. Tell our people trust in da signs ya see an' da voices dey hear. Dey will lead ya to da one who responsible.'"

Phil was deeply moved by this revelation. The story Mrs Plummer shared shook him to the core; it was unlike anything he had encountered before. He paused briefly, collecting his thoughts, before expressing his gratitude to Mrs. Plummer.

"Thank you for sharing this with me," Phil said sincerely. "It's a lot to take in, but your information is crucial. I promise we'll do everything we can to uncover the truth."

Mrs Plummer nodded solemnly. "Please keep me informed," she replied softly.

Phil nodded in agreement. "Absolutely. I will be in contact again if we have any further information."

With that, they exchanged parting words.

"Tank ya Sergeant, talk to ya later," replied Alice before hanging up.

Phil understood the importance of the information he now possessed. It was imperative that he relayed this crucial knowledge to Bruce's lawyer without delay. The pieces were fitting together too perfectly to be dismissed as mere coincidence. He was convinced beyond doubt that Nurse

Cindy Newman was the perpetrator they had been searching for.

*****

As the prisoner endured the harsh confines of the bleak, frigid cell, his future seemed to hang by a delicate thread at the mercy of the impending court judgment. Sergeants Roberts and Smith tirelessly utilised every available resource to expedite the trial proceedings. They held onto the hope the magistrate might be swayed by a sliver of compassion, perhaps granting Bruce the lifeline of bail. However, the grave charge of murder loomed large, casting a foreboding shadow, swiftly extinguishing any glimmer of hope for bail.

In the end, it was a journey to the heart of the bustling city, a transfer marking a profound shift in Bruce's confinement. From the remote confines of Weipa, he was now thrust into the bowels of Brisbane, a place so far from the familiar it might as well have been an entirely different world. Here, within the unwelcoming confines of a remand centre, he would bide his time, awaiting the date that would decide his fate in the hallowed halls of the Supreme Court.

Through it all, Bruce's silence persisted—a silence speaking volumes, casting a shadow of uncertainty over the future. The seriousness of the charges left him with no recourse but to steel himself for the long and arduous wait ahead, far from the comforting embrace of friends and family, in a place where time seemed to stretch endlessly, echoing the worry of his looming trial.

As the days passed, Bruce's stoic silence and refusal of food began to draw concern from the Brisbane officers. They couldn't help but wonder if perhaps they were holding the wrong man. A sense of weariness in his eyes spoke of a life burdened by something more than they could fathom.

Despite the inexorable pressure on the investigating police officers and relentless pursuit of leads, there existed a glaring absence of tangible proof linking Bruce to the double homicide. It was as if tendrils of uncertainty swirled around him, covering his supposed involvement in a veil of doubt. The absence of a direct link troubled not just Phil and Davo in Weipa but also troubled the minds of the officers in Brisbane, who were responsible for detaining him until the trial. They were left with a persistent suspicion there might be an alternative explanation for the deaths.

Bruce's rejection of a Murri lawyer and a Murri court only served to intensify the mystery. This choice resonated loudly. It bellowed of a man resolute in facing the system on his own terms, even if it meant confronting it alone. The officers couldn't help but experience a pang of empathy for him, an acknowledgment of the resilience required to navigate a world seemingly poised to perceive him as guilty.

In the blistering heat of Weipa, where the workload was ceaseless, Phil and Davo relentlessly pursued Nurse Cindy Newman. They understood letting this case slip through their fingers was not an option; it weighed heavily on their collective conscience, and it was imperative to vindicate Bruce. Fuelled by an indomitable spirit, they poured every spare moment into tracking down the elusive suspect. They spread the word within the local community and lodged a missing person's report, yet their efforts yielded no leads on her or her next of kin. Even reaching out to airlines proved fruitless, as Cindy Newman's name was nowhere to be found on passenger lists anywhere in the country.

Two months later, a crucial tip-off finally sparked a glimmer of hope. It led them to a desolate site a hundred kilometres west of Cairns, where a charred wreck of twisted metal and melted rubber stood as a chilling confirmation of a calculated and malevolent act of arson. However, there were no human remains, personal effects, or signs of those who once occupied the fiery tomb. The fire was deliberately set, erasing any trace of the vehicle's occupants. The VIN remained, enabling them to cross-reference it with the information provided by Dr Daylight. They verified the car once belonged to Cindy Newman, who was currently unaccounted for. Her name echoed through missing person reports, a haunting refrain resonating through the corridors of law enforcement.

For months, her visage graced screens and newspapers in the remote reaches of North Queensland, a ghostly presence lingering in the collective consciousness. Every police station remained on high alert, from the expansive Outback to the bustling cities. Cindy's biometric data flickered on screens, a digital sentry ready to flag any suspicious activity in the system.

Three months slipped by since the forensic evidence was gathered at Watson's River Station, and the trial date still loomed three more months in the future. Within the walls of the Weipa Police Station, Phil and Davo settled back into the rhythm of their daily tasks. The regularity held a reassuring rhythm, much like the gentle sway of tides along Queensland's coastline.

Then, on an unremarkable day, Phil's tranquil atmosphere was shattered by his phone screen's soft, otherworldly glow, signalling an incoming call. The caller ID revealed the name he had been waiting on for what felt like an eternity—Dr Catherine Reynolds. It was the call he longed for, the call he believed might finally provide the piece of information needed to close the case.

With measured anticipation, Phil answered, "Hello, Catherine. It's been a while," his voice was calm, but his curiosity simmered like an unquenchable flame beneath the surface.

Catherine spoke, "Hi Phil, how are you? It's been a while."

"Yes, it certainly has," came the somewhat expectant reply, "I do hope you have good news for me."

She hesitated before speaking again, carefully choosing her words, "Some good, some bad."

"Let me have it," he replied, eager to set the record straight.

"The qualitative analysis is finally back. The doses of fentanyl and codeine were not consistent with fatal doses. The berry skins in the intestine and on top of the pavlova came back as deadly nightshade berries. We cannot find a match for the footprints or the bloodstain near the Belladonna tree. As for the tyre marks, the forensics came back as a Yokohama All Terrain Tyre, 17 inches 265/65 size, one of the commonest 4WD tyres in Queensland, nothing particular about the wear marks or make."

This news left Phil somewhat dismayed. The forensics lent no further weight to the investigation. Basically, the trail was left cold, "I see," he responded, the disappointment evident in his voice.

"I'm afraid to tell you," her words cut through the daytime hum, "All the fingerprints and hair samples we've analysed, they're matches for individuals known to have been at the homestead in recent times. All except that first short blonde hair I collected from beside Noel Manson's head. We do not have a match. It may well belong to our elusive murderer."

Phil's heart quickened, and his thoughts immediately turned to Cindy, a vivid image of her with her short, pixie-style blonde haircut flashing before him. The connection was undeniable, a knot of dread tightening in his chest. The evidence was pointing in a direction he had feared since the beginning.

The police were not the only ones desperate to locate the nurse. Carol was also on the hunt. Her quest was twofold: to unearth Cindy and to execute a will harbouring secrets capable of reshaping lives. Her desperation manifested in a series of advertisements scattered across local newspapers and social media, a desperate plea for any inkling of the woman's whereabouts. In tandem with Phil and

Davo, they formed an unlikely alliance, pooling their resources and leads in a race against time.

Yet, with each passing day, Carol's hope waned. The harsh reality of an unrelenting chase loomed, and she grappled with the ominous prospect of executing the will should the nurse remain elusive. The convoluted legalities threatened to become an insurmountable obstacle, compelling her to seek professional advice.

Yet, another layer to her plight was a personal yearning tugging at her heartstrings. Carol longed to speak with Bruce, a man who, in her eyes, was deeply wronged and being punished for a crime he did not commit. She held a letter from Walt in her possession, a missive seeming to transcend the realms of the living and the dead. Its contents held the power to unearth truths long buried, and she was intent on being the harbinger of its revelation, to place it in his hands and watch as it reshaped the contours of his world.

Yet, for all her tenacity, Bruce remained an impenetrable fortress, shutting out the world beyond the confines of his cell. He steadfastly rebuffed all attempts at visitation, his silence an impenetrable barrier. He bided his time, locked in a cruel dance with destiny, awaiting the day of reckoning in the courtroom. He resigned himself to his fate.

As the trial loomed closer, his isolation became more pronounced. He sat in his cell, a solitary figure, his silence a fortress against a world that turned its gaze upon him. The potential consequences of the accusations hung heavy, but there was a stubbornness in his eyes, a refusal to crumble under the pressure.

In the quiet moments, the officers found themselves questioning their own opinions. Could they truly be sure of this man's guilt? The doubts lingered like a shadow in the corner of their minds, a reminder justice was a complex puzzle, and sometimes, the pieces didn't fit as neatly as they wished.

Phil and Davo displayed untiring tenacity in their quest to locate Nurse Newman. They diligently pursued every potential lead and followed up on every phone call, yet their efforts yielded no results. It was as if the nurse had vanished into thin air, leaving them with nothing but unanswered questions.

CHAPTER 24

The day of reckoning dawned, and the imposing doors of Brisbane's Supreme Court swung open with a solemnity befitting the occasion. Bruce, the central figure of this unfolding drama, took his designated seat in the courtroom, a portrait of resolute determination. He had shed his former self, emerging from the crucible of time, freshly shaven and adorned in a tailored grey suit. A crisp white shirt and a regal burgundy tie completed his transformation. To those who had known him for decades, he was a stranger in familiar guise.

In the hallowed halls of justice, the eyes of the gathered onlookers maintained their focus on Bruce, a microcosm of emotions playing out in the charged atmosphere. Suspicion danced across the faces of some, while others wore the mask of curiosity. In that pivotal moment, a pang of sympathy swept through the hearts of those who made the arduous journey to the capital city. Phil, Davo, Mark, Wayne, Carol, and Diane all traversed the distance to stand by Bruce's side, offering their staunch support in this pivotal chapter of his life.

The courtroom hummed with a palpable tension. The significance of the accusations against Bruce hung heavily in the air. The Supreme Court of Brisbane, with its towering columns and ornate architecture, bore witness to the trial of the century. The defendant remained tight-lipped, his silence a shield against the storm of accusations.

The double murder of John Granger and Noel Manson was a gruesome tale gripping the nation, its coils entwining around the remote corners of Watson's River Station. It was there, in that isolated expanse, that the seeds of this fateful narrative were sown. Bruce's statement, delivered to the police in those early days of the investigation, remained unaltered.

As the trial unfolded, the courtroom became a theatre of tension and conspiracy, with the prosecution masterfully crafting a vivid but circumstantial portrait of guilt. They wove together threads of suspicion and conjecture, presenting a narrative pointing directly at Bruce as the perpetrator of the heinous crimes plaguing the Cape York Peninsula for far too long.

In the solemn chamber of justice, the twelve members of the jury engaged in intense deliberations for a lengthy three hours, grappling with the responsibility of determining the fate of Bruce Hudson in a complex triple murder trial. As they emerged, the foreperson handed a sealed note to the vigilant bailiff, who promptly made his way to the judge, her stern expression betraying nothing of the internal anticipation coursing through the courtroom. With a commanding presence, Justice Reece-Jones accepted the note and, after a careful perusal, looked up to address the expectant onlookers and the apprehensive defendant. "I ask the defendant, Bruce Hudson, to rise," she proclaimed. The room held its breath as Bruce stood.

She continued, "The jury has reached a unanimous verdict, finding you not guilty on both counts of murder based on the compelling argument of insufficient evidence." A mixture of emotions swept across the faces of those present, from the gasps of disbelief to the palpable relief that washed over Bruce, who, at that moment, stood on the precipice between a potential life sentence and newfound freedom. He released a noticeable exhale of relief, and as the tension in his body eased, his shoulders dropped, accompanied by a subtle, wry smile.

Acquitted, he emerged from the courtroom a free man, his innocence declared in the eyes of the law. A collective sigh of relief swept through the room, a communal symbol of gratitude for a justice system that, in this instance, had done its duty. The small group of supporters who stood by Bruce throughout the ordeal now stood tall, their faces bathed in the warm glow of vindication. Phil and Davo concealed their smiles but couldn't hide their overwhelming sense of relief. In their minds, the verdict demonstrated the power of faith and the resilience of truth in the face of hardship.

Phil turned to Davo, "I think it's time for me to retire, mate; I've had enough, and this is about as close to closure as I think we'll get on this case."

"It's been a pleasure, a real pleasure, Phil. You've taught me a lot, and I consider you one of my closest friends. Don't forget to pop into the station from time to time to say hello."

"Count on it. And perhaps, when you find a spare moment, we might venture out for a spot of fishing together."

A smile crept across Davo's face, "I'll hold you to that," he said as he firmly shook his friend's hand.

"And one more thing," Phil said as he turned to leave the courtroom, "If you ever need a sounding board, you know where to come."

Davo's expression softened into a warm smile as he observed Phil's departure, a quiet certainty settling within him that this wouldn't mark their final exchange.

A chorus of mixed emotions echoed through the hallowed halls. The gathered supporters exchanged knowing glances that spoke volumes. Suspicion gave way to relief and vindication. They knew their unwavering faith in Bruce was well-placed. They understood sometimes, in the unforgiving realm of the law, the truth could be as elusive as a shadow in the night.

Bruce, the load of accusation lifted from his broad shoulders, walked with purpose toward Mark Doomadgee.

The two men shared a heartfelt embrace, their spirits connecting like the roots of ancient trees, their shared history and unspoken understanding binding them in a brotherhood forged through fire and trial. Bruce's calloused hand extended to the officers who investigated him, a gesture of respect for the duty they carried out, even when doubt clouded the path.

Bruce turned to Mark and spoke with genuine gratitude in his voice. "I knew you had to do your job, but thanks for believing in me," his smile radiant, lighting up his face. "Any leads on this nurse's whereabouts?"

Mark shook his head, "Sadly, none whatsoever. Occasionally, we get a call from someone in the Cape who thinks they might have seen her. All leads going nowhere, brudda."

Together, they left the courthouse and entered the streets of Brisbane. Their steps were lighter, their moods buoyed by the knowledge that justice had prevailed in the end. For Bruce, it marked the beginning of a new chapter, where the shadow of accusation no longer loomed over him and where he could finally rebuild his life with the support of those who stood by him through his darkest times.

CHAPTER 25

Bruce's return to Weipa marked the onset of a relentless quest for redemption. In the rugged days following, he painstakingly assembled the fractured pieces of his existence. The oppressive cloud of doubt surrounding his innocence, stooping his shoulders during the trial and the months of incarceration, began to relent, making room for a glimmer of hope. However, within the community, reservations still loomed, stains clinging stubbornly to the man in question.

Whispers wove a web of conjecture. Jude and Gladys were always at the centre of it. "I dunno, Gladys," Jude mused, her usual prelude to divulging something juicy.

"What don't ya know?" Gladys inquired eagerly.

"Well, where there's smoke, there's fire. Bruce did point the bone at old Walt, and now he's gone. Then, he happened to be at the station when the other two poor blokes met their end. No real alibi, they say."

"Now that ya mention it, Jude, this Nurse Cindy seems to be a phantom. No trace of her. And that Jake fella, too. Why haven't they stepped forward with all the fuss on telly?"

"Does make ya wonder," mused Jude. "I reckon this whole situation reeks. If Bruce was truly innocent, why didn't he speak up sooner instead of keepin' mum all that time?"

"You've got a point there," agreed Gladys, taking a contemplative sip of her chardonnay as they lounged in the Alby's beer garden.

Yet, it wasn't just Jude and Gladys casting dubious glances at Bruce. A small town is no sanctuary for a prime suspect in a double murder, especially one that garnered such widespread national attention. To this end, Bruce endeavoured to preserve a semblance of normalcy. For the initial months, he confined himself to his weather-worn shanty, shunning visitors and allowing the rumours of the ordeal to settle. His home became both his fortress and his prison. The creaking wood and worn floorboards held his secrets, bearing witness to the turmoil churning within him. He found comfort in the silent companionship of the windswept landscape, its untamed beauty a stark contrast to the chaos in his heart and mind.

As the sun-baked days marched forward, he sought support in the familiar embrace of old friends. First, he expressed his gratitude to the committed local police, Phil and Davo, who displayed unwavering belief in him. He embarked on a pilgrimage to the wise elders of his kin, the Wik-Mungkan people. After all the trials and tribulations over the years, he was grateful to find they welcomed him with open arms, their approval acting as a healing salve for his wounded ego.

In the heart of his Aboriginal community, he discovered a safe haven, a clandestine enclave shielded from prying eyes and murmured secrets. He found solace amidst the ancient traditions permeating the air. The elders, bearers of wisdom outlined in the sands of time, bestowed upon him a perspective transcending the confines of the present.

Once again, he ventured into the wild, a hunter and fisherman reclaiming his ancient birthright. His senses sharpened, and his tracking skills honed to a razor's edge. He became an encyclopedia of knowledge for the tribe's young ones and burgeoning men. The invitation to instruct was a lifeline, an affirmation of his place among them. In their midst, he discovered a purpose, a sense of belonging, stitching the fragments of his fractured heart.

With each dawn, his conviction grew stronger—his destiny intertwined with this mob, his family. His path to redemption was to teach, to guide, to become a venerated sage. The ambition to bestow his accumulated wisdom and skills upon the forthcoming generations became the cornerstone of his healing journey, a legacy that would echo through the annals of time.

Under the endless expanse of the star-studded night sky, he gathered the young ones around the crackling fire, weaving tales of ancient hunts and forgotten battles. His voice resonated with the weight of tradition, carrying the echo of generations long past. The flickering flames danced in their eyes, reflecting the fires of curiosity and reverence burning within them as Bruce served to maintain the oral history of his people.

He guided them through the ancient tracking arts with patient hands, revealing the country's hidden language. Once a realm of shadows and mystery, the vast Australian bush now unfurled its secrets before them, showcasing the interconnectedness of all life.

In the quiet rhythms of everyday life, Bruce unearthed forgotten joys, savouring the taste of untroubled moments. With every passing sunrise, he dared to let his imagination wander towards a future untainted by the looming shadow of suspicion. With its rugged beauty and steadfast community, the town of Weipa became the canvas upon which he painted the portrait of his own resurrection.

After what seemed like an eternity, the pivotal moment arrived. He could sense it in the air, a quiet certainty whispering through the timeworn walls of his shanty. It was time to open the door to Carol's steadfast presence. Her unwavering dedication, from the days of his incarceration to his subsequent exoneration, spoke volumes about her loyalty.

The gravel crunched beneath the tyres of her car as she pulled up to the shanty, a tangible echo of her resolve. With a subdued knock, she announced her arrival. Bruce swung the door open, his face illuminated by a genuine smile mirroring the gratitude he felt. He gestured for her to step inside, his silent invitation an affirmation of the trust they'd forged.

The shanty, humble and weathered, bore the scars of a life lived on the fringes. A lone bed stood against one wall, its frame sturdy but well-worn. Across the room, a small wooden table played host to two chairs, companions in solitude. In the corner, a cracked sink and a weathered bucket formed the heart of the makeshift kitchen.

With a delicate and purposeful motion, she extended a letter to him, its envelope bearing the seal of confidentiality. He looked at Carol, "Do you know what this says?"

"No idea, love. I haven't read it. Walt addressed it to you, and I have kept it for you all this time. Clearly, it contains some of his final thoughts. Once you've read it, I'd be grateful if you'd share those thoughts with me. It would serve as a cherished connection to the man we both held dear."

"Sure. I'll do that. Thank you," he said, looking earnestly at her and wondering what the letter might contain that required a seal of secrecy.

His eyes traced the words written on the page:

Dear Bruce,

I trust this message finds you in good health. There are matters that have been on my mind, and I feel it is only right to address them. I am aware of the past and the shadows it has cast on our relationship. For that, I am truly remorseful.

In light of this, I have taken steps to amend my will. I sincerely hope you and your community will benefit from the resources that have long been entwined with your ancestral land. Enclosed is a gesture of my goodwill and the deeds to a parcel of untouched bushland, which I entrust to your care.

Undoubtedly, you will steward this legacy with the same dedication you have shown to your traditions and community.

Warm regards,

Walt

Underneath, in blue rather than black pen, was a postscript, shakily written,

P.S. Bruce, there is something else weighing heavily on my heart. Cindy, the nurse who has been in attendance, may not be the ally she appears to be. My words may fail to convey the depth of my concern. Please exercise discretion and stay vigilant.

Wishing you good health and strength,

Walt Henry

The last words dwindled, descending towards the lower right corner of the page, as though penned hastily by a man in less-than-optimal condition.

Bruce let the words sink in before unfolding the small piece of paper folded within the confines of the letter. There it lay, an emblem of promise and power: a cheque inked with the staggering sum of ten million dollars. The magnitude of it left Bruce momentarily bereft of words, a profound awe washing over him. Carol broke the silence, her voice bearing the weight of a secret shared from beyond the grave. "Walt clearly wanted you to have this," she confessed, her gaze unwavering. "It seems as if it was his dying wish."

The room pulsed with the enormity of those words. Bruce's eyes met Carol's, searching for answers in the depths of her sincerity. He could feel the weight of a legacy, both burden and boon, pressing upon him.

"It's blood money," he declared, his voice resonating with the echoes of battles fought and ideals upheld, "I cannot take it. Everything I rallied against, everything I fought for, this represents."

He extended the cheque toward Carol, a symbolic act of resistance against the tide of compromise. Yet, in her eyes, he saw an unyielding commitment, a belief in the righteousness of this bequest.

"I insist," she urged, her voice steady as granite, "You can't deny a dying man his wishes. Think of the good it will do your people. The land is now rightfully yours, in your name. You can't hunt and fish freely without the mining giants controlling you."

His head drooped, and he stayed quiet, absorbing it all.

"Maybe stepping out into the sunlight will help clear your thoughts. It's a lot to process," Carol proposed as if she could sense his thoughts. Bruce agreed, and they made their way outdoors, finding shelter beneath the towering eucalyptus gums.

Bruce's heart waged a silent war, torn between the call of his conscience and the promise of transformation. He knew the path to salvation was never unblemished. Sometimes, one had to dance on the precipice of their convictions.

"I can't do it," he confessed, the consequences of his decision a tangible force in the room. His heart ached, knowing accepting this money was to court a darkness he had long sought to banish, "I can't take the money."

He stood at the crossroads of destiny, each step laden with significance; the cheque trembled in his grasp, its inked promise a beacon of possibility. He saw a vision of his people, shackles unbound, a future reclaimed.

"All money does is buy you opportunities," her voice cut through the heavy air, sharp and incisive, "Think of this as an opportunity. An opportunity to improve not only your own life but the lives of so many others."

Pregnant with both challenge and future prospects, her words seemed to loiter in the air. In that charged moment, he felt the weight of his past, the six months of confinement, bearing down on him. Within those prison walls, he forged a promise to himself during his bleakest hours: that if he ever tasted freedom again, he would embark on a new journey intertwining his love for the surrounding waterways and the wild bounty of the Australian bush.

This vision, now presented as a perceptible lifeline, held within it the power to shape his future and leave an indelible mark on generations yet to come. Starting a fishing charter and bush tucker business was a dream and a legacy in the making. It was a way to pass down the invaluable knowledge he accrued over years of challenges and hardships and imprint his essence on the land and the waters that witnessed his transformation.

As he stood beneath the eucalyptus trees, their leaves whispering secrets in the dappled afternoon light, he saw a path illuminated by this unexpected prospect before him. The scent of eucalyptus mixed with the earthy aroma of the Australian bush, grounding him in this pivotal moment. Each passing second held its own weight, each heartbeat a validation of the potential now lying at his feet.

The money hanging in the balance was a means to an end and a catalyst for a profound undertaking. It was the basis upon which he could build a venture that would sustain him and breathe life into his vision of preservation and education. It was the key to unlocking a future resonating with purpose and resounding with his promise to himself in those shadowed prison days.

With a deep breath, he made his decision; the die was cast, and the path forward was clear. He would seize this opportunity, not just for himself, but for the legacy he dearly wanted to leave behind, drawn in the sands and waters of a land that witnessed his journey from confinement to liberation.

Reluctantly, he accepted the check, tucking it away in the top pocket of his shirt, a token of gratitude heavy with implications, "Thank you, Carol," he began, his voice laced with a profound sincerity carrying the weight of the world, "Thank you for everything. I appreciate all you've done for me, especially in light of Walt's recent passin'. Ya didn't back down. Ya didn't let it break ya. Ya fought for what you believed was right and just. You're a woman of honour."

Bruce's hand found its place on her shoulder, and he locked eyes with her, his gaze immovable. "Thank you," he repeated, his voice firm and resolute, "I won't let you or Walt down. I'll see this through to the end; this money and land will not go to waste, no matter what."

As if a load had been lifted from her chest, Carol felt a rush of relief flood her veins. The decision to trust Bruce, to place her faith in him, now felt like a bright shard of light cutting through the suffocating darkness shrouding her world. An instinct, a gut feeling, whispered to her this alliance held the promise of something significant, something transformative.

She watched him, his eyes steady and focused, and knew she made the right choice. This man understood the nuances of their gritty, unforgiving world. In his presence, she sensed the potential for a force of reckoning, a force that could tip the scales back towards justice.

A subtle smile played at the corners of her lips, the expression a mixture of satisfaction and anticipation. She could almost taste the vindication lying ahead, the absolution honouring Walt's memory and the principles he held dear.

CHAPTER 26

The sun's brilliance painted the day in shades of molten gold, casting a radiant glow upon the waters stretching out before Bruce. It was a moment of pure elation, a symphony of light and warmth seeming to echo the newfound brightness in his life. Ten months came and went, each one a graphic illustration of the transformative power of fate.

One hundred and eighty-three days. That was the exact amount of time he had spent incarcerated. Each day was carved into the walls confining him. His tool, a crudely formed shank, the handle of a toothbrush; he swore he would never take another day for granted if he ever tasted freedom again. He saw the world with new eyes. The salty air tasted better, the trees' greens seemed brighter, and the sky's blue more intense. He would often reach down and grab a handful of ochre-coloured earth just to feel its texture on his skin. In that initial moment of liberation, Bruce uttered a solemn oath, vowing to navigate any distance and scale any height to elude the clutches of captivity once more. The flavour of freedom became a cherished refinement, an essence he would fiercely safeguard, relinquishing only with the utmost reluctance.

In the wake of Walt's generous bequest, Bruce's world unfurled into a kaleidoscope of possibilities. With those funds, he stepped into the proud ownership of a sixteen-foot vessel that now pirouetted gracefully upon the undulating surface of Weipa's waterways.

Bruce struck a pact with a seasoned local boatwright, entrusting him with the task of crafting a vessel to his exacting desires. The vision: a 16-foot aluminium dinghy adorned with a sprawling canvas canopy to grant refuge from the relentless sun. In its centre, a generous fold-out table designed for the delicate art of fish filleting. Six rod holders stood on the periphery of the vessel, three on each flank, poised to cradle the tools of his piscatorial pursuit. A spacious sanctuary awaited at the bow, earmarked for life jackets, emergency beacons and flares, and the anchor. It was, in every facet, flawless. Fittingly, he decreed the dinghy's outer surfaces to be rendered in a custom shade of resplendent crimson. Alongside this prized possession stood an array of fishing gear, each piece carefully selected as if woven with threads of adventure and sustenance - nets, rods, and tackle alike.

He sensed more than mere equipment as his fingers traced the lines of these tools. In this assemblage lay the seeds of a future for himself and the descendants that would follow. A legacy woven from the very fabric of the sea and sky, promising sustenance, adventure, and a continuum of purpose.

His vision, however, extended beyond mere possessions; he christened the boat "The Weipa Crocodile", a title steeped in layers of significance. It was a tribute to his totem name, bestowed upon him by the tribal elders in a ceremony cloaked in the mists of time. This name, gracing the very side of his fire engine red boat, stood as an enduring emblem calling to his roots, to the ancient ties binding him to the land, the sky, and everything dwelling in between.

Those who embarked upon his tours were greeted by the majesty of "The Crocodile" and by a living narrative, a tale whispered through the winds and the waves. They glimpsed the echoes of generations, felt the pulse of the rivers and sea beneath their feet, and marvelled at the unbroken thread weaving them all into the grand mesh of existence.

Today marked yet another memorable day for Bruce, who set out early, a ritual he never wavered from. His boat accommodated up to four eager anglers at a time, and on this particular day, he had the pleasure of hosting two couples. Shaun and Alice journeyed from Bundaberg, Queensland, a town renowned for its rum-making prowess, and Keith and Johnno, two mates hailing from Dunedin, New Zealand. Like countless others before them, they were embarking on a once-in-a-lifetime pilgrimage to the tip of Cape York. Bruce's tour wasn't merely a fleeting stop along the way; it evolved into an essential experience for many, a rite of passage for those passing through Weipa on their way to "The Tip".

A profound sense of gratitude washed over Bruce; he couldn't help but wonder how his life had taken such an unexpected turn for the better as he watched his passengers cast their lines toward the mangroves lining the estuaries around Weipa. His train of thought was abruptly interrupted by the unmistakable screech emanating from Alice's fishing reel. It was a sound that never failed to elicit his brilliant, toothy grin. A smile lit up his entire face, making his eyes sparkle.

Startled, Alice looked at Bruce, unable to contain her excitement. "What's goin' on?"

His own enthusiasm was infectious. "You've got yourself a real prize, I'd say," he replied, his eyes gleaming with anticipation. He cherished nothing more than witnessing the sheer elation of others when they hooked a coveted catch.

Eagerly, Alice sought guidance, "What should I do?"

Bruce, every inch the consummate professional, provided precise instructions, "When the fish takes a breather, pull up and start winding. But if it wants to run, let it. Patience is key. And always keep the tip of the rod up."

Alice's courage surged as she heeded his advice. Beads of sweat formed rivulets on her forehead as she grappled with the colossal fish, its formidable size pushing her to the limits of her strength and endurance. With each powerful surge, it threatened to wrestle free from her grasp.

The fish was a force of nature, putting on a spectacular display of its own vigour. It lunged and thrashed, repeatedly breaching the surface with a thunderous splash. Each time it did, a chorus of cheers and gasps erupted from the other fishermen, their voices echoing encouragement that ricocheted across the open water.

The sight of Alice locked in this epic struggle drew the attention of everyone on board. Their eyes were fixed on her, their faces a mix of anticipation and awe. It was a battle transcending mere sport, a contest between a refusal to give up and the untamed nature of the sea.

As the minutes stretched, her arms ached, her muscles screaming in protest, yet, she refused to yield. Holding fast with every ounce of willpower, intent on bringing this magnificent creature to the surface.

After what seemed like an eternity of relentless struggle, every muscle in Alice's body straining against the weight, she finally managed to bring the enormous fish alongside the boat. Like the seasoned expert he was, Bruce swiftly extended the net, expertly capturing the prize before deftly hauling it aboard.

Alice could hardly catch her breath, utterly drained from the monumental effort; despite her exhaustion, her eyes sparkled with the triumph of the moment.

"Geez!" exclaimed Shaun, his voice filled with awe, "That's bloody massive. Well done, Al."

"Thanks, Shaun," she replied, her breath still coming in gasps.

"Let's see just how big this one is," said Bruce, his eyes luminous with excitement.

With care, he lifted the barramundi from the deck, its large, impenetrable silver scales glinting in the sun's rays. The fish bore the scars of countless territorial battles, symbolising its tenacity and survival skills in this unforgiving environment. It measured an impressive one hundred and three centimetres.

"A true beauty," remarked Bruce. Beaming with pride, Shaun gave Alice a congratulatory pat on the back.

"Now, for the pictures," declared Bruce, a twinkle in his eye. "As ya know, to make sure them wild barramundi thrive, any fish over a hundred centimetres gotta be set free. But before anythin' else, we gotta capture this moment. Charlie, snap a few photos on yer phone," he instructed, gesturing to his crewmate.

As the deckhand readied his phone, the captain guided Alice on how to hold the gigantic fish to maximise its size in the photo. Meanwhile, Shaun was a flurry of activity, snapping pictures and recording every moment. He wanted to immortalise this achievement for posterity and, of course, for some well-deserved bragging rights.

This day unfolded as a resounding success, with Alice and Keith reeling in gigantic barramundi. Shaun was over the moon at his day's catch: a sizable threadfin salmon and two mangrove jacks. These were not just trophies; they promised a delectable feast. Not to be outshone, Johnno managed to reel in a barramundi surpassing the legal catch size.

Anticipation coursed through Johnno as he looked forward to the upcoming meal with Keith. He'd heard countless people rave about the delectable taste and robust texture of native barramundi, and finally, having the chance to experience it himself was a long-held dream come true. The joy in his demeanour spoke volumes; this adventure was a significant checkmark on his bucket list, and he was grinning from ear to ear. It was an experience that would undoubtedly grow more embellished with every retelling, evolving into a story to be cherished for years to come.

In order to provide an alternative source of employment for the young men in his community, aside from mining work,

Bruce sought the help of fellow individuals from his indigenous tribe to serve as deckhands. Today was no different; by his side was Charlie, a fervent teenager whose dedication to Bruce's teachings exceeded the ordinary. The young lad stood at the helm, diligently scanning the water for any loose debris, ensuring a safe journey back home. He also possessed a keen eye for detecting crocodiles. Bruce imparted this knowledge to him from a tender age—the territorial behaviour of the crocs, how to discern if one had recently fed by observing the swell in its belly, how the beasts move slowly and subtly through the water, using their powerful tails to navigate the waterways silently.

Over the years, Bruce had bestowed names upon the oldest crocodiles and would point them out to his passengers during the journey. They were Old Bob and Crafty Jack, always frequenting the same spots day after day. To his delight, the passengers would experience a palpable sense of thrill as they observed an elderly croc gracefully slip into the waterways from a sandbank. He also had to be vigilant to ensure the crocs didn't snatch the fish his passengers reeled in.

As the captain expertly guided "The Weipa Crocodile" homeward, he regaled his passengers with ancient tales from the Dreamtime. The story that piqued their interest most was one about the remarkable Barramundi fish, which possesses the extraordinary ability to change its gender.

"Is that so?" inquired Johnno.

"Ay, true that," Bruce drawled, his words dancing with the lilt of the Outback, "Our Dreamtime stories, they hold this truth, remindin' us that change is a part of life, deep in our Aboriginal ways. This change symbolises how we adapt an' stand strong, values we cherish."

Rapt attention filled the boat.

"Unlike our trip today, our ancestors didn't rely solely on rods to snare fish. To this day, elders amongst us craft cunnin' fish traps from the reeds flourishin' along the riverbanks. This is women's business - the art of weavin'."

The group erupted in laughter, tickled by the quaint notion.

"Jokes aside, within our culture, there are distinct roles for blokes and sheilas. Women weave these traps while blokes head out to harvest the fish. The baskets are deftly woven and shaped, lettin' fish swim in but slyly stoppin' their escape. Another ancient technique is spearfishin' - an art needin' equal parts patience and vigilance. A bloke must stand submerged in the waterways for long stretches, biding his time before grabbin' the right moment. It also calls for a sharp eye."

Ever the inquisitive person, Keith couldn't help but wonder, "And what about the crocs?"

"We've got a close bond with our environment, mate. Amongst my mob, there's a sacred ceremony, a shield against the mighty croc. But most importantly, we respect these critters, recognisin' their strength and the risk they pose. So, we approach 'em with reverence and a healthy dose of caution."

"Of course," nodded Keith, a newfound respect for the delicate balance between man and nature settling within him.

Under the sun's relentless embrace, the boat glided back towards the shore, leaving trails of shimmering ripples in its wake. The mood on board was jubilant, with laughter and stories intermingling with the salty sea breeze. As they approached the boat ramp, the captain kept a watchful eye out for Crafty Jack. It was a known fact he often loitered around the ramp, eagerly accepting any stray carcasses that might be on offer. This served a dual purpose—it provided some light entertainment for the passengers, hopefully concluding the fishing trip on a high note, and it ensured Crafty Jack remained well-fed, preventing any inclination towards a taste for human flesh.

As the vessel approached the dock, Bruce guided it into place, evidence of the countless hours he'd spent mastering these waters. Constantly eager to learn, Charlie stood by his side, absorbing every nuance of Bruce's manoeuvres. It was clear to anyone watching that this young apprentice was keen to be a charter captain someday.

With the engine silenced, Charlie set about securing the vessel. Bruce smoothly transitioned from the boat to the floating pontoon, assisting each of his passengers as they disembarked. Shaun, Alice, Keith, and Johnno gathered around their captain, their eyes gleaming with gratitude and elation. Each expressed heartfelt thanks to the crew for an unforgettable day on the water.

Turning to Bruce, Alice gently took his right hand in both of hers. "Thank you, Bruce. I believe I speak for all of us when I say it's been an honour to be part of such a unique experience."

"Here, here," echoed the three other men.

"It's been my pleasure," he responded warmly, adding with a chuckle, "and don't forget to spread the word to your friends back home." His face broke into a brilliant grin, radiating contentment. It was as if he was destined to share his expertise not only with his own community but with people from all corners of the globe.

It was Keith who spoke to Bruce next. He placed his right hand on the captain's shoulder, "I've got to say, your tours have become more than just fishing trips, haven't they? They've turned into transformative journeys, a real communion with the wild, a dance with the natural forces."

"I'm real glad ya see it that way. That's exactly what I'm aimin' for with me tours. I want me customers to get a taste of somethin' they wouldn't find anywhere else. It's more than just catchin' fish now. I want 'em to feel they've been part of somethin' greater than a regular fishin' trip. I want 'em to get a real peek into our ancient ways and history. Yer words, mate, they truly humble me. Thank ya."

As the sun dipped towards the horizon, Bruce and Charlie set to work, swiftly cleaning the day's catch. The routine was second nature to them, a choreography of precise, practised movements. After scaling, gutting, and filleting the fish, the bounty was evenly divided, ensuring each couple received an equal share of the day's spoils. A member of Bruce's mob would drive them the short distance from the Weipa Public Boat Ramp to the nearby caravan park, where they would settle in for the night.

The solidarity was obvious as Bruce and Charlie washed down the boat before escorting the group to the patiently waiting vehicle. Shaun approached Bruce first, his eyes sparkling with gratitude and contentment.

"Mate, this day ranks among the best of our lives, doesn't it, Alice?" he declared, turning to his partner, who responded with an animated nod and an infectious grin.

"Absolutely! I've had a total blast," Alice chimed in, her joy contagious.

Similarly, Keith and Johnno couldn't contain their indebtedness. They extended their heartfelt thanks to Bruce for orchestrating an unforgettable day out on the water. "A top-notch day of fishing, mate. Much appreciated," they chorused, their gratitude evident.

As the car pulled away, Bruce shifted his gaze to Charlie, a broad grin spreading across Bruce's freshly shaven face. Since the trial, he gradually reintegrated into his cherished community, now residing with his younger brother and wife. He took it upon himself to pay for the construction of a community hall, a sanctuary for their mob's collective gatherings as well as a cultural centre.

Bruce was awed at the stark contrast between his present reality and the dark days of confinement just a year ago. Then, he was held captive, like a caged animal, awaiting trial for a crime hanging heavily over him—a shadow that seemed insurmountable. Yet, here he stood, the taste of saltwater on his lips, the sun's warm embrace kissing his skin.

The whispering winds carried the scent of the sea, and the rhythmic lapping of waves provided a soothing backdrop to his reflections. Each breath was a testament to his resilience, a reminder that life's currents could shift dramatically, propelling one from the depths of despair to the pinnacle of contentment.

CHAPTER 27

Carol found herself in a race against time, with a mere two months left to fulfil the remaining provisions of the will, and each day seemed to slip through her fingers like grains of sand. Despite putting forth her best efforts and enlisting the help of both her lawyer and the local police, Cindy Newman remained elusive, like a shadow in the night. As uncertainty loomed over her, Carol grappled with a series of pressing questions that seemed to have no easy answers

Baffled, she made a pivotal decision to seek counsel from the very lawyer who summoned her to his office ten months ago, revealing the changes Walt made to his will in the days leading up to his passing. It was a time she would never forget, and now, she found herself in a situation where she needed his guidance once more. What steps should she take next? How could she possibly honour Walt's final wishes if this elusive woman, Cindy, remained beyond her reach? The conundrum was complex, and the path forward was veiled in uncertainty. She understood she needed expert assistance and guidance to navigate these intricate legal and personal challenges.

The receptionist's voice, warm and courteous, resonated through the line, "Hello, Mrs. Henry." Carol couldn't help but smile at the reference to her enduring connection with her ex-husband, a bond that time and circumstance could never sever, "How can I assist you today?"

"I wish to arrange an appointment with the lawyer. I require his expertise in finalising the remaining provisions of Walt's will," replied Carol, her tone as polished and professional as she could manage, a stark contrast to her upbringing as a true-blue far North Queenslander.

"Of course. Let's check his availability," the receptionist replied, her voice momentarily absent as she perused the appointment book, "How does early next week suit you?"

"That works well; I have ample availability," Carol affirmed, grappling to suppress the overriding nuances of her far north Queensland accent.

Following their discussion, a date was set for a meeting with the lawyer precisely one week from that day. It emerged as a mark of hope amidst the turmoil, an opportunity to untangle the intricate threads of Walt's final wishes and, perhaps, shed light on the mystery surrounding Nurse Newman's inexplicable disappearance. This forthcoming meeting promised a flicker of clarity in the midst of the ambiguity that gripped Carol's life since Walt's passing.

The week flew by, and before Carol realised it, she was in the lawyer's office. It was a sobering place, with shelves lined with leather-bound books and the scent of aged paper hanging in the air. She sat across from Mr Thompson, a man whose scholarly face spoke of years spent navigating the intricacies of the law. Carol found herself, yet again, captivated by the stark contrast between his appearance and his disposition. Though small and restrained, his mouth framed by pronounced nasolabial folds seemed incongruous with the radiant warmth emanating from his eyes. Far from diminishing his attractiveness, the receding hairline served as a subtle guide, directing one's gaze toward his brilliant emerald orbs.

She folded her hands in her lap, a sense of unease settling within her, "Mr Thompson, I've done everything I can think of to find Cindy Newman. Advertisements, social media, and even contacted the police. But there's been no sign of her."

Mr Thompson leaned back in his chair, his fingers steepled in front of him. "You've certainly made reasonable endeavours, Carol. It's clear you've put in a great deal of effort."

She nodded, grateful for his acknowledgment, "So, what are my options now?"

The lawyer cleared his throat, his gaze steady, "You have a few choices, but each comes with its own set of implications. The first option is to reserve Cindy Newmann's bequest in a fund. This means the bequest can be passed directly to her if she is eventually located. However, it also means your obligation to the estate could extend for years."

Carol considered this, the details of the decision pressing down on her. "And the second option?"

"If you choose to, you can divide her bequest among the other beneficiaries, with the understanding they will return the funds if she is later located. This option allows you to tie up loose ends, but it relies heavily on the integrity of the other beneficiaries."

She frowned, the thought of trusting others with such a significant decision giving her pause, "And the third option?"

Mr Thompson's gaze softened as if he was waiting for this question, "The third option is to apply for a Benjamin Order from the Supreme Court of Queensland. This would grant you the authority to distribute Cindy's bequest among the other beneficiaries."

She looked at Mr Thompson as if all her prayers were answered. There was an avenue whereby she could finally be rid of this headache once and for all.

He continued, "However, if the missing beneficiary later reappears, they may still have a claim to their share of the estate. The Queensland Succession Act of 1981 allows for applications to the court for a distribution that differs from the terms of the will. This might occur if the beneficiary was presumed dead and has now returned; they may have a claim to their share of the estate."

Carol leaned forward, "That sounds like the most appropriate option. How does it work?"

The lawyer explained the process, detailing the paperwork, court proceedings, and the time frame involved. She listened intently, a sense of certainty rising within her. This was the path that felt right.

In the following days, Carol embarked on the process outlined by Mr Thompson with a distinct sense of purpose. She gathered the necessary documents, filled out forms, and sought the required signatures from the other beneficiaries; each step brought her closer to the resolution she sought.

As the paperwork was filed with the Supreme Court of Queensland, she couldn't help but feel a sense of accomplishment. The court proceedings went smoothly. The judge overseeing the case recognised her diligent efforts and granted the Benjamin Order. It was a moment of triumph.

As time passed, she kept the nurse in her thoughts. How could someone disappear like that, particularly with such a sizeable sum of money in her possession, ten million dollars to be exact? Carol mused; Cindy must have known about Walt's sudden change of heart in re-writing his will. Why would anyone just up and disappear without claiming their bequeathed share of Walt's enormous estate? She spent hours pondering these thoughts and never got closer to the truth.

One ordinary afternoon, with the sun gently streaming through the curtains, Carol sat cozily on her living room couch. She brewed a delightful cup of tea, its aromatic warmth mingling with the comforting scent of homemade chocolate chip biscuits that had recently emerged from the oven. She was savouring the simple pleasure of this tranquil moment, allowing herself to get lost in the pages of a captivating novel.

Suddenly, her phone rang, piercing the peaceful ambience with its shrill melody. She reached for it and answered, her voice warm and inviting, "Hello."

"Mrs. Henry, I hope I haven't caught you at an inopportune moment," a voice, faintly recognisable, intoned, "It's Mr Thompson; I served as the probate attorney for your departed husband's will. Our last discourse was, if memory serves, some fourteen months ago."

Caught off guard, Carol's brow furrowed. What could he possibly want after such a lapse?

"It pertains to the will's beneficiaries."

"Yes," she replied cautiously.

"Just today, an email arrived from a lawyer in Germany. The absent beneficiary, Cindy Newman or Lucinda Neumann as she is known in her home country, appears alive and thriving. She intends to journey to Queensland to claim her portion of the estate. Fifty million dollars, to be precise."

It wasn't the staggering sum leaving Carol breathless; rather, it was the abrupt resurgence of this woman— someone she had never encountered or heard of until that day in Mr Thompson's office for the will's revelation. The fact this ghostlike figure now reemerged, seemingly from thin air, was as confounding as her initial disappearance.

"I understand," she responded, uncertain of the appropriate course of action, "What should I do now?"

"For now, nothing. In the near future, you will need to allocate the sum to a separate account if she proves to be the rightful claimant. One can never be too sure. In my line of work, we encounter all sorts, making grandiose claims about their identities. Especially when substantial sums are involved," the lawyer remarked with an air of nonchalance.

"Very well, I can manage that. No trouble at all," Carol felt unperturbed. She was content with life as it was, with her modest abode in Weipa. She lacked for nothing; she inherited the majority of Walt's estate and knew the wealth would always be there, but she harboured no hunger for material possessions. To her mind, her children were better suited to a life of opulence.

"I will keep you apprised. My next step will be to meet with Lucinda Neumann and ascertain the authenticity of her claims. I'll need to scrutinise birth certificates, passports, Medicare cards, driver's licenses, and any other form of identification. If she does prove to be who she claims, then I will arrange for the money to be transferred to her nominated account," he declared matter-of-factly.

"And the authorities? What of Davo and the new officer at the station? Surely, they'll want a word with her. I'm quite certain the double homicide at Watson's Creek Station remains an open case."

"That will be for the police to decide. I will certainly acquaint them of her impending arrival."

"Thank you," replied Carol, "Is that all for now?"

"Yes, at this stage it is. Rest assured, I will ensure this tiresome business is soon put to rest," replied the lawyer.

"I can't wait," her tone betrayed a mix of weariness and intrigue. Despite her yearning to wash her hands of this entire charade, as she disdainfully labelled it, she was equally anxious to set her eyes upon Cindy Newman or Lucinda Neumann. It was a need to ascertain what could compel the man she was wedded to for countless years to suddenly inscribe her into his last testament.

CHAPTER 28

Beneath the azure canvas of the Mediterranean sky, a gentle zephyr danced over the waves, caressing the cheeks of Cindy and her newfound paramour, ensconced in the embrace of the September sun just off the coast of the Greek haven, Naxos. The vessel they reclined upon was none other than Cindy's opulent yacht, yet another grand purchase in a succession of lavish whims. Like diligent attendants to royalty, the crew presented a prelude to their evening repast - libations teasing the palate and delectable canapés, accompanied by fine cotton robes to shield against the encroaching coolness that nightfall promised.

Her companion, sixteen years her junior and adorned with an Italian ardour, was a source of boundless delight in this latest escapade. Lips met, and the clinking of glasses resonated in joyous celebration against the backdrop of the setting sun's fiery descent.

The arduous days spent toiling as a locum nurse felt like a distant reverie. The ten million dollars bestowed upon her extended a life that once dwelled only within the realm of dreams. Yet, amidst this splendour, a singular dilemma remained, as is wont to befall one unaccustomed to sudden affluence. The wealth, once seemingly boundless, now coursed through her fingers like ephemeral mist – spirited away in the revelry of extravagant soirées, the thundering pulse of yachts, the adrenaline-fueled rush of exotic cars, and the whirlwind affairs with men who mirrored the transient nature of her riches.

For the first time in a span of months, her thoughts veered back to Walt Henry's will, a tangible echo of her hopes and desires. Safely ensconced in her topmost bedside drawer in Hamburg, Germany, a copy of it whispered promises of another fifty million dollars, a treasure trove to replenish her coffers, to grant her the freedom from toil she so ardently craved, and, to her mind, deserved. The prospect of such emancipation blossomed within her like a coveted secret, a tantalising possibility beckoning from the confines of her drawer.

Gone were the days when she would bend to the undignified task of bedpan duty or heed the urgent cries of patients, their voices a relentless chorus of "Nurse! Nurse!" once grating on her nerves like an incessant, discordant strain. The loathing for her occupation ran deep. While the public saw nurses as selfless paragons dedicated to their calling, the truth was far less glamorous. It entailed the unsavoury tasks of toileting, pill-dispensing, and the obligatory facade of amiability with doctors who wielded their orders like mandates from on high.

She had harboured a futile ambition to capture a doctor's heart for years. In her fantasies, she conjured a life transcending the confines of her profession—a life where she would ascend to the coveted role of "Doctor's wife". The title seemed to promise a liberation from the ceaseless grind holding her captive. It was a life free from the shackles of menial tasks, a life where she would no longer find herself tethered to the whim of a higher authority, but this was not to be.

Time had left its imprints upon her, erasing the bloom of youth that once held a firm allure for affluent men. Yet, in the twilight of her years, she possessed a certain affability and a shrewdness belying her age. These qualities, she discovered, were potent tools in her arsenal, enabling her to ensnare the unsuspecting heart of a lonely man in the far-flung corners of a foreign land.

Gone were the days of captivating wealthy suitors with her charm and looks. The mirror revealed a face lined with experience that spoke of years weathered by life's trials. Yet, she refused to let this truth define her. Instead, she summoned her wits, honed them over decades, and spun them into a finely woven web of deception that even the most discerning eye would struggle to perceive.

It was in Weipa, Cape York, Queensland, Australia, where the world's gaze seldom lingered, she found her hunting grounds. There, amidst unfamiliar tongues and customs, she wove her tales of destiny and devotion. With practised grace, she managed to ensnare Walt Henry. An unsuspecting man, a hapless, aging fellow who longed for companionship for a semblance of the forever he once possessed.

Under her spell, he came to believe their hearts had found their true home. His soul had finally discovered his lifelong partner. She wove these illusions with a skill born of necessity, for she knew in these isolated realms, she could reinvent herself, shedding the worn-out facade of a woman who had once been the object of desire for many. As the days passed, she rejoiced in the satisfaction of her art, knowing she had once again rewritten the narrative of her life, leaving behind the limitations of age and time.

She could not, and absolutely would not, return to nursing. The ten million dollars had rapidly slipped between her fingers in the last two years, and the prospect of returning to nursing to earn a living was anathema to her. Who, in their right mind, would willingly commit themselves to a vocation entailing the perpetual cleaning up after others? She despised the unwavering submission to a higher power, the menial tasks, and the shift work. The inheritance bequeathed to her brought with it the prospect of emancipation. It whispered to her like a clandestine promise, a tantalising vision shimmering within her grasp. Her copy of the will was a mere plane ride away.

As the sun dipped lower, casting long, golden coils across the rippling sea, Cindy's gaze wandered, lost in the ethereal beauty of the horizon. The cerulean waters seemed to hold untold mysteries beneath their shimmering surface, much like the paradox of her own destiny. She pondered the path that led her here, from the sterile confines of hospital wards to this realm of opulence and indulgence.

Basking in the lavishness of her yacht, a regal, navy blue Princess S60 spanning sixty-two feet of nautical grandeur, she cast an ardent gaze upon her lover. He embodied the vivacity of youth, a living artwork showcasing life's boundless energy, a stark contrast to the man whose company she once kept to pave her way to this lap of luxury. The memory of his flabby body, the clammy embrace, his pallid skin perennially drenched in cold sweat sent shivers down her spine.

Every inch of her fastidiously planned conquest had unfolded flawlessly. Every step was executed with calculated precision, from the strategic acceptance of a position with the RFDS in Weipa to the artful feigning of naivety at his opulent wealth. Their chance meeting in a supermarket aisle was the spark igniting the flames of seduction, a dance of fate setting her on this extravagant course. In his delusion, Walt truly believed an attractive, slim woman in her late thirties could be genuinely captivated by his repugnant habits and boisterous laughter. There were moments when she'd leave his mansion only to purge her revulsion near her parked car, a stark reminder of the pact she made with the devil.

Yet, as she looked around her now, ensconced in this world of unparalleled luxury, she knew every sacrifice was a worthy investment. Fate granted her the ultimate vindication—a discovery of Walt's infidelity, a revelation striking with the force of a lightning bolt. To catch him in the very act was a coup de grâce of monumental proportions.

She played her part to perfection, her feigned heartbreak and shattered dreams, a performance leaving no room for doubt.

In the tender embrace of her Italian lover, a plump, ruby-red strawberry hovered, a gem against the backdrop of the Mediterranean expanse. Tilting her head in anticipation, she felt the gentle caress of his touch, tracing the contours of her lips, leaving behind a fleeting trail of his exquisite cologne. He placed the strawberry in her eager mouth with a delicate grace, a morsel of sweetness in the mesh of their passion.

Her lover's embrace was a study in passionate tenderness, drawing her nearer in a fervent kiss, igniting the flames of their connection. The memory of their first meeting, a mere three weeks prior, surged vividly in her mind. He toiled shirtless, dark locks flowing down his back, beads of sweat glistening like liquid diamonds as he tamed the barnacles beneath another yacht's keel while it was dry-docked. At that moment, desire blazed within her like a tempestuous fire. An irresistible force consuming her.

The resonant laughter of her lover, a melody of richness and mirth, pierced the tranquil expanse, beckoning her back to the present. In the embrace of luxury aboard the Princess S60, she languished in her conquest, a queen of the sea, crowned in the splendour of her audacious stratagem. They say love is impervious to monetary influence, but wealth orchestrated a dance of transient elation and fervent passion for Cindy. Their worlds converged, an improbable union defying the confines of age and societal norms.

Her heart swelled with an intoxicating blend of joy and trepidation, for she was acutely aware this rapturous love affair could not endure indefinitely. Her handsome paramour embodied youth and allure in its most potent form, a turbulent combination whispering the inevitable truth: he might vanish like a fleeting wisp of cloud were it not for the allure of her wealth. Still, she was willing to make that Faustian bargain, to exchange riches for a taste of the ephemeral enchantment he wove around her.

In his presence, she felt like a nymphet, her age an irrelevant detail buried beneath the vigour of their connection. The allure of his youthful vitality infused her days with a vibrancy she hadn't experienced in years, and for that, she was willing to pay. After all, the money could soon be replenished, and she could return to bask in the invigorating energy he breathed into her world.

She knew there was only one course of action: to return to Weipa, Australia, and claim her inheritance. Fifty million dollars would be enough to secure a carefree future for the remainder of her days. She would be more careful with the money this time, forswearing the frivolities that once drained her resources. Every dollar would be invested judiciously, nurturing her aspirations with grace and foresight. She now possessed an evolved sense of financial acumen.

Her resolution coalesced into a plan as she relished the idyllic Mediterranean sunset. In the not-so-distant future, she would board a plane to her hometown of Hamburg and meet with her lawyer. She would instruct her to inform the estate attorney in Weipa, Australia, of her imminent arrival, where she would lay claim to the inheritance that was bequeathed to her.

A week slipped by, and Cindy found herself aboard a plane hurtling towards the distant shores of Australia. The journey was long and taxing, the hours stretching into endless stretches of cramped seats and recycled air. Yet, in her heart, she clung to the promise of a reward that would eclipse any temporary discomfort: a prize so grand it justified every ounce of jetlag and separation from her cherished Italian beau.

Cindy's thoughts meandered to the man she left behind as the plane traced its path across the vast expanse. The memory of his touch, the warmth of his embrace, and the whispered promises of reunion played like a sweet, inspiring melody in her mind. She took solace in the thought this voyage was but a fleeting interlude. She assured herself in just a matter of days, she would be back in his arms, a legacy of fifty million dollars richer.

Her firmness of mind only strengthened with each mile that passed beneath the plane's wings. She envisioned the moment when she would step onto Australian soil, claiming her inheritance, the culmination of a journey that destiny and a carefully executed plan lay before her. The anticipation swelled within her, eclipsing the fatigue and weariness clinging to her like a persistent shadow.

Cindy knew when she returned, it would be with a bounty that would reshape her life, affording her opportunities beyond her wildest dreams. The future beckoned, bathed in the golden glow of promise, and she was determined to seize it with both hands.

As she descended the gangway, Weipa Airport's humid, tropical air enveloped her, carrying with it the familiar scent of saltwater and eucalyptus. The journey was long, and weariness clung to her bones like an unwanted companion. She hadn't anticipated, however, to be met with such an unexpected scene.

Amidst the backdrop of cloudless skies and the towering silhouette of a palm-fringed runway, two figures strode purposefully towards her. One was unmistakable: Sergeant David Smith, a face she remembered from previous encounters in this far-flung corner of Queensland. His stern countenance was softened only slightly by the flicker of recognition in his eyes.

The other, his face made harsh by years of service, bore the marks of time. He was a stranger to Cindy; his facial features spoke of a lifetime committed to duty. His gaze bore no warmth, no trace of familiarity, only an air thick with foreboding intent. He wore the mark of a man indifferent to compassion, a callous figure in the shadows of authority.

As they drew closer, it was Davo who took the lead, his voice breaking through the hum of airport activity. "Lucinda

Neumann," he said, his tone a curious blend of formality and warmth, "I reckon this isn't the welcome you had in mind."

"No, not at all. How can I help you?" Her astonishment was palpable.

Davo pressed on, his voice firm, "Lucinda Neumann, you are under arrest. You have the right to remain silent. Anything you say can and will be used against you in a court of law. You have the right to speak to a lawyer and have them present during any questioning. If you cannot afford a lawyer, one will be provided for you. Do you understand these rights?"

CHAPTER 29

After retrieving her bags, Cindy was promptly escorted to the Weipa police station, a journey marked by a palpable silence. In the confines of the vehicle, Davo's thoughts wandered back to his recent conversation with Rutherford, a man to whom he harboured an intense aversion. No matter how hard he tried, an affinity for the man eluded him, replaced instead by a simmering resentment.

It was Davo who had taken the call from Mr Thompson, a call heralding Cindy Newman's imminent arrival in the heart of Australia. Without delay, he relayed this critical information to the newly appointed Senior Sergeant, Harold Rutherford. Yet, despite the significance of the situation, Davo couldn't suppress a familiar informality, "Harry, do you recall the cold case regarding the two murders at Watson's River Station a couple of years ago?"

"It's Harold or Sergeant Rutherford to you," came the stern reprimand, a sharp reminder of the changed dynamic since Phil's departure.

Davo couldn't help but yearn for the camaraderie he once shared with his old mate. Phil bid farewell to the force only a year prior, leaving an irreplaceable void, a sense of connection no newcomer could hope to fill. The arrival of the new officer and his equally vexing wife, Margot, felt like forcing square pegs into a round hole in Weipa. Harold's appointment was shrouded in whispers, tales of a rogue cop, a man susceptible to graft. His posting to Far North

Queensland was widely viewed as a form of reprimand, a sharp rebuke from higher-ups.

Finally arriving at the station, Davo took his place behind a desk in a private interview room, motioning for Cindy to sit opposite him. Sergeant Rutherford, true to his no-nonsense nature, chose to remain standing.

"Please state your name and address for the record," Rutherford intoned, barely glancing up from the file before him.

"Lucinda Neumann, Unit 42t 291A Elbchaussee, Hamburg, Germany," Cindy responded evenly.

"Should we call you Lucinda or Cindy?" sneered Rutherford, his tone laced with derision.

"Cindy is fine. But I must insist, what is the meaning of all this?"

"I believe you are well aware of why you are here!" retorted Rutherford, his voice raised, his posture an imposing lean, bringing his face uncomfortably close to hers.

"No, I truly don't. If you could please enlighten me, I'd be more than willing to provide any clarification and answers you seek."

Davo took the gentler approach. "Cindy," he said, looking warmly into her eyes with a familiarity, "It is about the murders of Noel Manson and John Granger at Watson's River Station two years ago. We believe you were involved."

"Murders?" she was taken aback, shocked, her mouth agape. "Mr Granger and Mr Manson. But how?" she asked incredulously. Cindy looked up to Davo, her eyes pleading, "And you believe I had something to do with it?" Her voice was incredulous.

"Don't play dumb with me, lady. Quit fooling around and cut to the chase," said Rutherford ruthlessly. He did not want to waste time; he looked through the cold cases when he took over as Senior Sergeant and was less than impressed at the police endeavours to find the true culprit. He felt the investigation had gaping holes in it, making it his top priority to swiftly address and resolve the situation.

In his assessment, all signs led to Cindy: The young men in Tennant Creek falling prey to anticholinergic poisoning, Walt Henry's abrupt passing in circumstances where this woman possessed both motive and opportunity and most recently, her appearance at Watson's River Station. The evidence of freshly picked lethal nightshade berries, the tyre tracks, the bloodstains on the grass, and the petite footprints supported his conclusion. He discreetly observed her shoes and estimated them to be a size six. In his mind, she was undeniably the one responsible.

Tension permeated the interview room, sunlight, unrelenting in the afternoon, seeped through the windows, further intensifying the uneasy atmosphere. Davo found himself uncertain about the situation at hand. Either this woman was completely innocent, or she deserved an Academy Award. She seemed oblivious to the fact the two men had even passed away. He drew nearer, his attention fixed squarely on Cindy, striving to discern even the slightest nuances or tells that might reveal if she was being untruthful or concealing something. Meanwhile, Rutherford, having already made up his mind, stood near the window, his gaze fixed on the solitary palm tree, its fronds weathered and brown from prolonged drought.

"Sergeant Smith," Rutherford rasped, breaking the silence, "Let's get straight to it. We're not here to dilly-dally around; the clock's ticking."

Davo looked at Cindy, "Tell us about the last time you saw Mr John Granger and Mr Noel Manson. According to our notes, Dr O'Leary of the RFDS informed us you paid a visit on a Friday, three days before they were found deceased."

Her eyes wide with disbelief, she sat on the edge of her seat. Her voice trembled as she began to recount the details of her visit to the station.

"Yes. It was a Friday afternoon," she started, her voice carrying a hint of wistfulness, "Noel was scheduled for a blood sugar check up. Being a diabetic, he checks his glucose levels but requires a blood test known as an HbA1c, which measures a person's blood sugar regulation over a long period."

"Go on," pressed Dave.

"I took his blood. He offered me a cup of tea, but I declined. I was keen to get on my way. It was my last appointment of the day."

"So, what happened next?"

"I bid my farewells and went to leave the station. It was nearly four, and I made plans to meet a friend at Bramwell Station. I didn't want to leave it too long. You know what it is like driving around at dusk in these parts, fraught with danger with all the native animals on the corrugated dirt roads."

"Can anyone vouch for this?" queried Davo expectantly.

"Yes. I believe they can. As soon as I finished at the homestead, I called Anthony Chalmers; he is a paramedic in Cairns. He recently moved to Australia from New Zealand and, like me, did not know many people in the area. We struck up a friendship and decided to take some time off and travel to the tip of Cape York together," she paused, "I also phoned him as I was turning in to the station to let him know it wouldn't be long before I would be on my way again."

"So, there should be telephone records?"

"I should think so," she replied, tears swelling in her eyes.

"If we called Bramwell Station, would there be any record you checked in?"

"There should be. Anthony and I registered our vehicles upon check-in, and we booked in for dinner there. They can vouch for our presence there that evening if they have kept the records."

"Did you make it to the tip?" Rutherford interjected icily.

"No."

"Please, tell us more," the Senior Sergeant was now smiling. He thought he had caught her in a lie, thinking back to the burnt-out car whose VIN matched that of Cindy's.

"Anthony and I got into a fight on Friday night. We both drank too much and decided to go our separate ways. While maintaining a casual friendship is one thing, embarking on a road trip together introduces additional stresses. That night exposed underlying personality conflicts, and we realised it was not a good idea to pursue a lengthy journey together."

"I see," replied Rutherford, his face a mask.

"We stayed the night in separate tents. I did not tell him anything about Walt's generous gift to me. The next morning, he headed north toward "The Tip", and I went south. I decided I would drive to Cairns and catch a flight home. Everything happened so quickly following Walt's sudden passing. I deposited the cheque in my German account and thought it best to go home, settle for a while, and clear my head. I never expected any of this to happen."

"We must contact Mr Chalmers and Bramwell Station to check your story. Would you like a cup of tea and a break? You must be exhausted after your long flight?" asked Davo with warmth and sincerity.

"Yes, thank you," she replied quietly. "That would be lovely."

As Davo turned to walk to the tea room, he turned to face Cindy, "One more question. Which name did you use when purchasing the plane ticket?"

"Lucinda Neumann. I travelled on my German passport. I have dual citizenship and possess two passports. For work purposes in Australia, it is much easier to tell everyone my name is Cindy Newman."

"I understand," replied Davo, making his way to the tea room.

Rutherford was not finished, "What happened to your car?"

"I have no idea. My mind was a blur. I was still upset about the fight and left it in the Cairns Airport parking area. It was an old bomb, and I figured I could buy a new one back in Germany. As far as I know, it is still there. I must owe a hefty parking fine, come to think of it."

He turned on his heel, returned to his desk and started making phone calls without another word.

After an hour's break, the trio reconvened. The Senior Sergeant breached the silence. With a hint of reluctance and disappointment in his voice, he said, "Well, your story checks out. Mr Chalmers happened to be on duty in Cairns today. He corroborated your tale. Bramwell Station managed to unearth archived records, validating your presence and dinner reservation on that particular evening. Regarding your vehicle, the parking manager at Cairns airport reported it missing two weeks following your departure."

Exasperation showed on Rutherford's face. After reading the file notes, he was certain that he could solve the case if he was ever given the opportunity to interview Cindy Newman. However, her alibi was watertight. If not her, then who did kill the two men? There was really nothing to pin this woman to Mr Henry's demise. For all intents and purposes, he could have died from natural causes. As for the young men in Tennant Creek, as the doctor pointed out, it was not unusual to see patients in the emergency department in various states of intoxication from a multitude of causes. He sat at the desk with his head in his hands.

Davo had questions of his own. There were still a few loose ends, and the deaths of the two men at Watson's Creek Station remained a mystery. Who plucked those nightshade berries and fed them to the unsuspecting men?

He decided to press further, "Did you see anyone else, Cindy? Anything unusual?"

Cindy took a deep breath, and her brow furrowed as she recalled the scene. "I didn't see John, but as I was leaving the homestead, there was a man. He looked startled."

Davo nodded, urging her to continue. "Where did you see him, and what happened next?"

"I saw him near a bush, about a mile from the homestead. He was picking berries; I stopped the car, and he looked at me as if I had surprised him. I recall the colour drained from his face," Cindy recounted, her voice tinged with concern. "I thought he might be unwell. I got out and walked towards him."

Rutherford's eyes narrowed, his scepticism palpable. "And what did he do?"

"He turned towards me," Cindy said, her gaze distant, lost in the memory. "Looked me dead in the eye. Then, without a word, he walked off."

A beat of silence hung in the room, broken only by the native birds chirping beyond the window. Her voice grew softer, recounting the rest.

"As I returned back to my car, I cut my leg on some cut grass," she continued, a touch of regret in her tone, "It was an accident."

Rutherford's voice cut through, sharp as a blade. "Describe him. This man you saw."

Cindy's eyes flickered, struggling to bring the details back to life. "It's been so long," she paused to collect her thoughts, "As I said, he was standing next to a bush; it was nearly shoulder-high. He had dark skin. He appeared to be of Aboriginal descent, with long, unkempt hair and a bushy beard. There was something around his neck, like a pendant on a necklace."

Davo leaned back, processing the information. "Anything else you noticed that might help us identify this man?"

"Yes. Now you mention it: feather shoes. I found it a bit odd." She said, uncertainty in her voice. "I couldn't quite make out any more details before he turned and walked away."

The room fell into a heavy silence. Davo was not sure they were any closer to the truth. He was present for the entire investigation, and still, the murders of the two men remained a mystery. The feather shoes or pendant did nothing to jog his memory. This elusive man could have been any number of people on the farm. As Diane pointed out, the station employed several farmhands who could be anywhere on the farm anytime.

Having explored every lead with Cindy, the officers convened in private deliberation before ultimately opting to release her without pressing charges.

"You're free to go, Miss Newman. We won't keep you any longer," Davo expressed, a note of regret underscoring his words, "We apologise for the inconvenience. Can we offer you a lift back to your hotel?"

"I'll manage. I'll call for a cab. I really need some rest. I'm utterly drained," she replied, weariness etching lines on her face.

"You'll be hard-pressed to find a cab in Weipa," Harold laughed sarcastically.

She looked at Sergeant Rutherford with a puzzled expression.

"There aren't any," he replied, a sardonic tone to his voice.

"It's okay, Cindy. I'll give you a lift. Where are you staying?" said Davo.

"The Albatross Bay Hotel."

"Hop in, let's go," Davo beckoned warmly.

Cindy complied, her energy sapped from the ordeal, longing for the comfort of her hotel room.

As they drove, she turned to Davo and asked, "Could you tell me how those men died?"

"They consumed deadly nightshade berries," Davo casually replied, then quickly added, "I apologise. I shouldn't have mentioned it. This investigation is ongoing, and we've kept the details confidential. Currently, only Sergeant Roberts, who's retired, Sergeant Rutherford, the Cairns forensic pathologist and her team, the homicide squad in Brisbane, the coroner, and now you know the cause of death. We haven't let it slip to anyone in this town. Gossip would spread like wildfire!" He chuckled, a release of pent-up tension.

"Don't worry. Your secret is safe with me. I didn't exactly make many friends in this small town in my four weeks here, especially after having a fling with the wealthiest man in town," Cindy said, smiling at Davo.

CHAPTER 30

Cindy stirred as the first rays of the unforgiving Australian sun pierced through the sheer hotel curtains, her body still grappling with the disorienting embrace of jetlag. Her senses slowly emerged from the depths of slumber, and she soon realised she had woken in a land where the clock danced to a different tune. It was morning in Weipa, Australia, but her internal body clock stubbornly clung to the late-night rhythm of her homeland in Europe.

She made a conscious decision to remain in Weipa for an entire week, granting herself a much-needed pause before resuming her globetrotting adventures. It was her oasis of solitude, an escape from the never-ending array of parties and exotic holidays that consumed her life for the past two years. Her beloved yacht rested in the Mediterranean, tended to by a seasoned crew who received one simple directive from her: "Take my Italian partner wherever his heart desires."

The looming daybreak wasn't just any ordinary morning for Cindy. Today marked her scheduled appointment with the estate lawyer, Mr Thompson. She prepared her arsenal of documentation, each piece carefully chosen to ensure the legality of her intentions.

The collection included both her German and Australian passports. Her Australian driver's license, a symbol of her connection to this land, a copy of her original birth certificate, faded and weathered like the memories of her youth, and then there was her Medicare card, just in case further identification was required to claim her inheritance.

Her appointment wasn't until nine a.m., so she showered, dressed and wandered out to the hotel's dining room for breakfast in a desperate attempt to reset her internal clock. As she settled into her seat, her ears caught wind of a conversation not meant for polite company. Two older women, their voices brazen and unapologetic, caught her attention.

"Well, doesn't she have the nerve, Gladys? Showin' 'er face around here!" exclaimed Jude.

"Who is it?"

"Don't ya recognise 'er, Gladys? It's that nurse. The one that's wanted for murderin' Walt and them blokes out at Watson's River Station."

"Oh, yes. It is her, too. Not many people dress like that in these parts. I wonder if the cops know she's back in town? I'm gonna 'ave a word with her. Tell her what's for," replied Gladys, her tone oozing vindictiveness.

Before Cindy could fully comprehend the situation, a sharp and accusatory voice pierced the air. "Oi, you!" yelled Jude, an overweight woman swathed in an ill-fitting yellow polyester dress, her face contorted in a scowl.

Cindy's heart raced, her mind a whirlwind of confusion. "Me?" she stammered, utterly clueless as to the identity of this stranger.

"Yes, you. You've got a bloody cheek, showin' your face around 'ere after what you've done."

A flush of embarrassment crept up Cindy's cheeks. There was no refuge in this moment; she longed to shrink, to fade from sight. When she'd embarked from Germany, she had no inkling that the town she remembered with fondness would greet her with such hostility.

"I hope the cops know you're 'ere. I'll have a word with 'em if they don't."

"If you insist on knowing," Cindy retorted, her voice measured, "I was interviewed by the police last night and was released without charge. Now, if you'll excuse me, I am quite tired and would prefer to be left in peace."

Jude shot her a withering stare before rejoining Gladys.

She refused to let these women see her crumble. She concealed her tears, swiftly retreating to her room where, once inside, the floodgates of emotion burst open, a tempest of feelings too overwhelming to contain. She let the waves of sorrow wash over her, knowing they would recede in time, leaving behind a fortified mindset.

As the minutes unfurled, the room seemed to comfort her in its silent embrace. It was a sanctuary, a place where she could gather the fragments of her composure. Though static, the walls bore witness to the serendipitous journey leading her to this moment. With a steadying breath, she composed herself. She couldn't allow this encounter to mar the purpose that brought her here. Mr Thompson awaited; no matter how insistent, the past couldn't monopolise her future.

Stepping out once more, she navigated the hotel's corridors with a renewed sense of purpose. The encounter with Jude and Gladys left a bitter taste, a stark reminder the shadows of her past loomed larger than she'd anticipated. Yet, she was determined to face them head-on, armed with the truth that exonerated her. As the appointed hour approached, she found herself at the lawyer's doorstep; the proof of her existence, distilled into passports, licenses, and certificates, clutched firmly in her right hand.

The receptionist, a paragon of professional composure, greeted her with a polite smile. "Lucinda Neumann? Ah yes, Mr Thompson has been expecting you. He won't be long," she assured.

Cindy settled into a chair, the anticipation hanging thick in the air. There was no need to reach for a magazine; time was of the essence, and the minutes unfurled with a steady, measured cadence. Then, like a harbinger of progress, the door to Mr Thompson's office swung open.

His presence was both reassuring and commanding. Emerald eyes, aglow with seasoned intelligence, met hers with a warmth, easing the tension coiled in her chest. "Miss Neumann, please, come inside and take a seat," he invited his voice a steady anchor in the storm of her emotions.

"Please, call me Cindy," she responded as she followed him inside.

Together, they stepped into the sanctum of Mr Thompson's office. The air was steeped in a palpable sense of purpose, the retention of thousands of stories whispered by the walls. As they settled into their seats, she braced herself for the potentially lengthy and complicated process that awaited.

With a practised efficiency, they delved into the intricate dance of identity validation and legal manoeuvring. Each document presented was scrutinised, and every question was answered with unwavering precision. The Benjamin order, a shackle on her inheritance, was dissected with legal acumen, a path to its reversal artfully mapped out.

"To reverse the Benjamin order, we'll need to establish a clear line of evidence attesting to your rightful claim," Mr Thompson explained, his words a beacon of clarity. "We'll proceed with filing the necessary documentation, and I'll liaise with the relevant authorities on your behalf."

Cindy inclined her head, her faith in Mr Thompson's expertise already well-placed. His aura exuded a confidence that washed over her, providing much-needed reassurance.

"As for your inheritance, once the order is reversed, we'll arrange for the funds to be securely transferred to a nominated bank account of your choosing. It's imperative you provide the details promptly to ensure a seamless transition," he advised, his tone a blend of professionalism and genuine concern.

As the conversation flowed, she felt the complications of the past begin to lift. She found a sanctuary amidst the paperwork and legal intricacies in this office. Here, her inheritance, both tangible and symbolic, was being wrested from the clutches of doubt.

CHAPTER 31

Bruce marvelled at his incredible stroke of fortune. His business had not only weathered the storms but was now thriving in a way he'd never imagined possible. This was happiness in its purest form, the kind that warmed his heart with every sunrise. With newfound confidence in his venture, he made a significant investment. Bruce acquired a second boat and, in an act of immense trust, promoted Charlie to the rank of captain.

It had been a couple of years since he took the young man under his wing, teaching him the ropes and instilling in him the wisdom of the waterways. Now, with a sense of pride and accomplishment, he handed over the helm, confident Charlie could steer his own ship. The apprentice had become a master in his own right.

During the off-season, when the law forbade the catching of barramundi to protect their breeding, Bruce found another avenue for his passion. He turned to the land Walt Henry bequeathed to him and set up bush tucker tours. It was as if a piece of the outback came to life on that patch of earth, beckoning visitors from afar.

The tours became a sensation, drawing in folks from every corner of the globe, eager to experience the raw beauty of the Australian outback and sample the unique flavours of bush tucker, lemon myrtle, wattle seeds, native plums and kangaroo meat. Bruce's connection to the land and his dedication to preserving its heritage were paying off, not only in prosperity for him and his people but in enriching the lives of those who undertook his tours and sharing a unique cultural experience.

As the dry season approached its waning days, he knew his fishing tours would soon conclude. The remaining available dates were already reserved, mostly due to his tour's widespread fame and favourable reviews. Soon after, he'd retire briefly to replenish his energy before embarking on his bush tucker tours.

The Weipa community held him in high regard, considering him a local legend. He had faced daunting challenges and emerged triumphant. His entrepreneurial ventures breathed new life into the town beyond the dusty mines as well as providing a renewed source of income and sustenance extending to the residents. Tourists enticed to linger in Weipa further enriched the town, contributing to the prosperity of the entire community.

Travellers found reasons to extend their stay in Weipa. They pitched tents beneath the starlit canvas in and around the local caravan park, cast lines into the surrounding waterways, and marvelled in awe at the kaleidoscope of colours painted across the Arafura Sea at day's end. These dazzling sunsets transformed into a must-see spectacle, a captivating attraction in their own right, offering a compelling motivation to journey to Weipa.

On a rare day off, Bruce relished a precious luxury. He journeyed to his bush reserve and settled quietly in the heart of a clearing. There, he rekindled the familiar pursuit of his youth: listening intently for bird calls and honing his tracking skills by studying the grass for signs of recent animal movements. As the sun ascended, an oppressive combination of stifling heat and clinging humidity enveloped him, foretelling the imminent arrival of the tropical wet season. The air was laden with moisture, an unspoken promise of the impending downpour. Bruce drew a deep breath, a seasoned sage of the natural world, finely attuned to the subtle cues of the elements. It was unmistakable: rain was on the horizon, a certainty coursing through his bones.

He allowed himself to drift through the corridors of his past, tracing the contours of decisions and their reverberations. A weight, a lingering shadow of doubt, crept into these moments of quiet contemplation. He could not deny, in the stillness, that he grappled with the knowledge of transgressions committed.

Yet, he was quick to quell any incipient pangs of remorse. The ends, he reasoned, justified the means. Here he stood, emancipated from behind prison bars and the shackles of financial worry, the architect of his own destiny. The business he built, the vast expanse of land unfurling before him, was not a mere possession but the rightful return of a legacy for his people. It was a reserve where he could hunt game through the untamed bush, ply the waterways in pursuit of elusive fish, and pass down the artistry of survival to those who would come after.

In the quiet sanctum of his soul, he sought solace in his own rationalisations. He did not see himself as a murderer but as a man who undertook what he deemed necessary to retrieve what had been unjustly wrested from his ancestors, from his people. Across the generations, many people pillaged and profited from this land, leaving wounds that cut to the core. To him, the mine and its beneficiaries were not innocent; they were entwined in a collusion of theft and deception. He refused to be labelled a criminal; he saw himself as a reclaimer of fractured birthrights.

He meted out his own form of justice, a measured response to those he held accountable. It was a punishment crafted to ensure they would never commit such crimes again. These actions were borne with a solemnity, a conviction echoing through the marrow of his being.

Walt, in his naivety, had been an easy mark. Realising the error of his ways, he sought to make amends. After the joviality of his birthday celebrations at the Alby, he paid Bruce a visit, a genuine attempt at reconciliation. However, Bruce hesitated to welcome him into his modest dwelling, deeming it too meagre for a man of Walt's stature. Instead, he suggested a meeting at the magnate's opulent residence, a setting more fitting for the significance of their conversation.

In the grandeur of the mansion, Bruce sat quietly as the mining tycoon once again pleaded for forgiveness. "I understand the significance of my actions. I can't undo the harm I caused to your people's sacred site. All I can do is offer this gesture and hope for your forgiveness. I've established an annuity in your name, providing five thousand dollars weekly for the rest of your life. Additionally, I've included you in my will. I've penned a letter for you, to be revealed only upon my passing. I believe its contents will bring you solace and serve as a generous reparation for you and your community," Walt's gaze remained downcast, his voice filled with remorse.

This disclosure set in motion a plan that had been years in the making. Bruce feigned forgiveness, concealing his true intent beneath a facade of reconciliation. He then artfully brewed a "special tea" using leaves from the deadly nightshade tree, a concoction hoodwinking the unsuspecting Walt into believing it to be a potent remedy for all his maladies, a sacred elixir of healing. Such was Walt's trust in Bruce to care for him in his time of need; he gave him a key to the house so he might check up on him. The old man swallowed the ruse whole, a gullible victim ensnared by the illusion.

Bruce attended to his needs with unwavering devotion, visiting him through Friday and Saturday. Unbeknownst to the ailing man, he introduced a measured dose of ordine, discreetly masked within Walt's food and drinks, to ensure he remained sedated. This powerful opiate elixir, a recent acquisition from the resourceful Mad Maureen, was obtained in a transaction just a few weeks prior.

Maureen was a shrewd and resourceful woman, possessing a knack for securing exactly what one desired, though never without extracting her due. If it wasn't in her possession, she'd unearth it through sheer tenacity and street-smart savvy. She navigated the world on instinct and a keen understanding of the underground networks.

Then came the fateful Sunday. As Bruce neared Walt's residence, he let himself inside. Looking around, he found no sign of him on the lower floors. He ascended the stairs, a sense of foreboding settling in. Entering the bedroom, he was met with the sight of Walt's motionless body. Bruce should have felt sorrow, yet instead, he was overcome with a strange sense of triumph. For all these years, he yearned for this moment, an opportunity to settle the score with a man who took so much from him, setting his own life on a path of decline while Walt continued flourishing.

The abrupt entrance of two intruders into the house jolted him into swift, albeit cautious, responsiveness. Urgency gripped him as he deftly and noiselessly crept down the stairs and unlatched the backdoor, ensuring its closure was as silent as a breath. With a survey of the surroundings, he scrutinised the vicinity for any lurking observers, ensuring that his movements remained concealed from prying eyes.

Taking deliberate steps to evade suspicion, he moved stealthily towards his parked car. Every motion was calculated, every glance wary, as he navigated the long shadows cast by the afternoon sun. The last thing he desired was to attract any unwanted attention. He seamlessly melded into the deserted Sunday streets, skillfully evading even the faintest sound that might reveal his whereabouts. Fortunately, the day played to his advantage, being a Sunday in a thinly populated town where the majority were either out fishing or enjoying a music session at the Alby.

Upon reaching his car, he executed a seamless unlocking, slipping into the driver's seat with practised finesse. The engine came to life with a subdued drone. Choosing a route that veiled his exit, he drove through the quiet streets, taking the first turn to vanish from potential watchful eyes. He had done it. After thirty-five years of nursing a bitter vendetta, he had exacted his revenge. Walt was gone, and Bruce was finally free from the wraith that haunted him for so long.

With each passing moment, the path ahead seemed clearer to him, revealing a clarity he hadn't felt in years. Within him, a festering resentment towards Noel smouldered like an ember, its fiery animosity building with every passing day. There was something about how the man carried himself—an air of unwarranted superiority that grated on his nerves. They were kin, bound by blood, but in Noel's eyes, it seemed Bruce was always relegated to the role of an underling, never an equal. It was a charade, a self-imposed delusion he could scarcely tolerate.

Yet, it wasn't merely Noel's condescension eating at Bruce's soul. It was the blatant disregard for their people's sacred customs and traditions. Noel, as an older male member of the tribe, held a position of authority, carrying with it a responsibility to uphold those very values. Instead, he shattered the sacred kinship rules when he fathered a child with a woman in Tennant Creek, an act severing the ties of that young man from his rightful kin.

He had forsaken the old traditions, stubbornly resisting the understanding of the land, its flora and fauna, and the ancient art of celestial navigation. He lived out here on the station, detached from the collective knowledge of the mob, never partaking in the sacred ceremonies where the invaluable oral histories and teachings were imparted. Bruce couldn't help but see it as a stark display of disrespect for the ancient ways, a rejection of the rich history of their culture.

In recent times, Noel's actions had taken an even more grievous turn. He succeeded in peddling shoddy, Chinese-imported didgeridoos and boomerangs to unsuspecting visitors and campers at the Station. He deceitfully passed them off as genuine artifacts, tarnishing the heritage that meant so much to Bruce. It was a betrayal, a desecration Bruce found utterly unforgivable.

In his eyes, Noel was more than just a disappointment; he was a disgrace to their people, a living affront to the legacy of their ancestors. The weight of this knowledge settled heavily on Bruce's shoulders, propelling him toward a reckoning he knew was long overdue.

John Granger, the proprietor of the station, unwittingly became collateral damage in the scheme. A pawn in a game of retribution, John stood in the way of what Bruce perceived as rightful justice. As he mercilessly plotted Noel's demise, he was privy to the knowledge of Diane's carefully arranged weekend retreat to Cairns. In the maze of his malevolent thoughts, he made a fateful assumption. He believed, erroneously as it turned out, that John would accompany Diane on her journey, leaving him free to execute his ominous design without the scrutiny of another pair of discerning eyes.

And then there was the fortuitous appearance of the nurse, a twist of fate playing right into Bruce's hands. Her presence would undoubtedly raise questions and sow the seeds of suspicion, diverting attention away from him. It was a masterstroke of misdirection.

As the sun sank low, casting long, creeping shadows across the land, he stood on the precipice of execution. In his hand, he held the nightshade berries, small but potent, intended for the pavlova Carol so kindly delivered earlier. It was a malevolent touch, a calculated gesture meant to finalise his plan. At that very moment, she appeared, unforeseen and unsuspecting. He observed her approach, the setting sun painting a golden halo around her silhouette. Their eyes met fleetingly before he turned away, melting into the shelter of the bush.

He was confident she hadn't ventured close enough to make a positive identification, should it ever come to that. He watched as she retraced her steps to her car, the engine's growl fading into the distance as she drove off. With a sense of cautious relief, he resumed his activities, keenly aware of

Noel's departure, off to rejoin John in mending fences in one of the distant paddocks.

Later that evening, when Bruce joined John and Noel at the homestead for a few beers, he couldn't help but hide a secret satisfaction. They had indulged in the pavlova, devouring its lethal contents along with the sweetness. He could sense the poison already taking its toll. Both men were suffering, vomiting and writhing in pain. Bruce offered them codeine and fentanyl patches, which they gratefully accepted, unwittingly hastening their descent.

Over the weekend, he paid them visits, administering liquid morphine to keep them sedated. They trusted him, believing he genuinely cared for their well-being. This act of killing felt disturbingly simplistic, its alarming ease leaving an unsettling impression.

Sunday afternoon brought him back to the house. John and Noel lay in their beds, their strength depleted, their defences compromised. Bruce prepared a concoction he dubbed "herbal tea," a lethal blend of nightshade leaves infused in piping hot water. He gently guided them to the kitchen table, suggesting to them sitting up and moving around might relieve their discomfort; they were both too weak to argue. He assured them he would call for a doctor, a promise he had no intention of keeping, before slipping away to his donga.

CHAPTER 32

Under the blazing Weipa sun, the brilliance of the day was undeniable, though the oppressive humidity hung in the air like a heavy blanket. The locals, accustomed to these conditions, were eagerly awaiting the forthcoming rains, a welcome relief from the mugginess enveloping the town. Emerging from her room, Cindy made her way down to the breakfast area, exchanging a nod with the hotel receptionist on her path.

"Good morning, Miss Newman," he greeted with a wry smile, "It's damn hot and humid today. This is the prelude to the wet season. By the way, the Barramundi season has only five days left. Have you ever had the chance to catch one?"

She paused, considering his question. "No," she admitted, "But I'd love to, given the opportunity."

The receptionist's eyes sparkled with fervent enthusiasm. "It's an experience like no other," he enthused, "If you manage to hook a big one, they put up quite the fight, and they're fantastic eating fish."

Her interest stimulated, she inquired further. "Are there any guided tours available in the area?"

"There are a few companies, but Bruce Hudson's outfit is by far the most popular. I can give his team a call for you. They frequently have cancellations due to the road conditions. Many people book months in advance, only to encounter a breakdown or flat tyre just before reaching Weipa. Enjoy your breakfast, and I'll see what I can arrange."

"Thank you, Henry. That sounds wonderful. I'm free for the next three or four days."

With her decision made, Cindy resolved to put the past two days' events behind her. The lengthy police interview and the uncomfortable encounter with the town's gossip mill at breakfast yesterday left her feeling drained. However, she wanted to enjoy her time here. After all, there was every reason to be elated. Mr Thompson oversaw the details of her bequeathment, and she still had five days to savour the charms of the town she had come to adore during her tenure here.

Taking her seat, she scanned her surroundings, feeling relief washing over her as the two old gossips from the day before were conspicuously absent. She perused the al-a-carte menu and settled on a full English breakfast, treating herself to a moment of solitude and the chance to recalibrate her internal clock, still adjusting to the new time zone.

Her privacy, however, was short-lived. Henry, the waiter, approached her table, breaking her train of thought. "Excuse me, Miss Newman," he began, "I have some good news for you."

"Finally," she mused, her mind reflecting on the challenging days preceding this one. She had weathered a storm of turmoil, from sailing the azure waters of the Mediterranean with delight just over a week ago to suddenly becoming the epicentre of small-town gossip and an unexpected prime suspect in a chilling double murder cold case.

"Mr Hudson's tours have had a cancellation for tomorrow," Henry continued, his eyes filled with anticipation, "There's a spot left if you'd like to take it."

A broad smile spread across her face as the memories of her recent tribulations faded momentarily. The idea of embarking on a new adventure, a little taste of Australia to carry back with her to Europe, was a welcome prospect. "Yes," she replied with unrestrained enthusiasm. "Sign me up," she declared, embracing the opportunity to be on open waters again.

At the crack of dawn, Cindy's alarm jolted her awake, punctuating the stillness with its insistent chime, diligently set for five in the morning. Today marked the commencement of her fishing expedition; the tour company's driver would collect her from the hotel and transport her to the Weipa public boat ramp. A surge of eager anticipation coursed through her veins.

After a refreshing shower, she dressed in practical attire for the day ahead, donning a long-sleeved shirt, a broad-brimmed hat, and comfortable trousers. In her bag, she packed the essentials for a full day on the water: sunscreen, sunglasses, bottled water, and a towel—a versatile companion for any unforeseen dampness or makeshift cushioning.

Right on cue, the driver arrived. As she swung open the door and entered the vehicle, Cindy was met with two amiable faces. Vicky and Colin, a Cairns-based couple in their sixties, extended warm greetings. Although familiar with Weipa, they were new to the "Weipa Crocodile" tours, drawn in by the hype surrounding them.

"That completes our crew for the day," announced their driver, an Indigenous man exuding a radiant smile and a gentle demeanour.

"Just the three of us," Colin said, his voice tinged with anticipation. "I have a good feeling about today. The barramundi tend to grow big toward the dry season's end. Hopefully, we'll all have a good catch," he added, the genuine warmth in his tone unmistakable.

Cindy reciprocated their smiles and extended her hand. "Hi, I'm Cindy. I've heard this is quite the experience."

"Ever reeled in a barra before?" inquired Vicky.

"No," she admitted, "It sounds like a very exciting prospect, I would love to experience the thrill of catching this famed fish."

"You'll never forget the day you catch your first ever barramundi, love," Vicky assured her, her smile radiating cordiality and camaraderie.

The sun was still low in the sky as Bruce pushed off from the boat ramp. His new deckhand, Johnny, had already set the rods in their holders and was busy getting out the bait nets stored underneath the bow of the boat. Their first stop would be to catch some live bait.

Following an hour's venture into the open waters, Bruce steered the boat onto a sandy bank nestled within the heart of the Embley River estuary. Johnny, barefoot as always, leapt from the vessel with boyish vigour. His lithe limbs, still buoyed by the exuberance of youth, found purchase on the sandbank's edge. With a skilful grace, he flung the bait net towards a shimmering school of silverfish, his movements fluid and deliberate. All the while, his body remained on alert, his attentive eyes prowling the waterways, his torso taut for the imposing figures of crocodiles, the undisputed apex predators of these waters. As Johnny expertly splayed out the circular, unfurled net upon the water's expanse, his actions reminded Cindy of roti cooks in distant Malaysia, expertly twirling and stretching the dough high in the air before deftly smacking it onto a gleaming, level metallic surface.

After landing the net directly over the school of bait fish, Johnny deftly manipulated the attached cords, guided by floats stationed at the net's periphery and coaxed the net into a constricting sack. He had enough fish to half-fill one of the ten-litre buckets he took ashore with him. He repeated this process twice more with equal success, and the crew and passengers were on their way again.

Bruce guided the boat towards the rugged shoreline with an expert's ease, where the water seemed to trickle from the heart of the bush into the waiting acceptance of the estuary. Here, the bank was a tangle of sticks and gnarled mangroves. To the uninitiated eye, it might have appeared an improbable locale for a successful fishing venture.

Johnny took charge of baiting all the hooks for the eager tourists, while Bruce, a seasoned captain of these waters, imparted his wisdom. "Cast as close as you can to the shore," he instructed, his voice blending authority and approachability. "That's where them mangrove jacks and barra hang out."

Vicky and Colin, well-versed in the art of fishing, needed no further encouragement. With proficient ease, they commenced casting their lines, each movement born from years of experience. Cindy, on the other hand, was a novice to the sport. However, under Bruce's patient and experienced tutelage, she swiftly transformed her inexperience into a respectable effort, her bait somehow finding its way into the vicinity the captain recommended.

The sun was still low on the horizon, casting long, golden flickers of light glinting across the water's surface. The air was alive with the symphony of nature—the distant calls of birds, the gentle lapping of water against the boat's hull, and the rustle of leaves in the nearby bush.

There was a sense of shared anticipation as the lines stretched into the depths. Then, it came—a subtle tug, a whisper of a presence beneath the water's surface. It began as a delicate vibration in the hands holding the rod, then grew into a lively dance of energy, humming and thrumming with life. The line taut and eagerly transmitting every nuance of the underwater world.

Colin's experienced hands felt the subtle shifts in the rod's tension, a signal a creature had taken the bait. The world seemed to hold its breath as the rod bent, a living extension of the battle between man and nature. A surge of adrenaline coursed through his veins, a thrill electrifying the air as the Mangrove Jack emerged, instantly identified by Bruce. It was a majestic display of power. The contest between man and fish was on.

With a fierce shake of its head, the creature executed a graceful somersault back into the water, then unleashed its might, its robust tail propelling it into the watery abyss. The line sang in response, a high-pitched squeal of resistance. Colin's hands moved in rhythm with the fish, a dance of strength and skill, as he regained control.

Minutes felt like hours, a timeless struggle between the angler and his quarry. The rod's voice changed, its tone shifting from the initial lively whistle to a deeper, more resolute cadence. It spoke of the contest, the rise and fall of power, the obstinate willpower of both fish and fisherman.

Then, at last, the moment of truth arrived. Bruce moved into action. Net in hand, he leaned over the edge of the boat, a testament to years of mastery on these waters. In one graceful motion, he scooped the fish from its watery realm and onto the deck. The first catch of the day, and the clock was yet to strike eight a.m.

The morning unfolded much as it began, with Vicky and Colin proudly landing two sizable barramundi apiece. Cindy was yet to land a fish. Despite the morning's triumphs, the relentless embrace of the sun and the suffocating humidity were beginning to take their toll on Vicky. Cindy glanced at her, noticing she was very flushed and did not look well, "Are you okay, Vicky?"

"A little light-headed. Perhaps I need a break?" she replied.

Cindy reached into the esky, pulled out a bottle of cold water, and handed it to her fellow passenger, "Here, pour some of this over your head and neck and take a few sips."

As the clock neared noon, Bruce, aware of the effects of the penetrating heat, proposed a welcome interlude beneath the canopy of swaying mangroves. He adeptly steered the boat to a secluded oasis of shade, where the dappled light offered a reprieve from the unrelenting sun. Here, they could all catch their breath, replenish their energy, and partake in a well-deserved rest.

Johnny, ever attentive, was quick to step in. With a nifty hand, he produced Tupperware containers and unearthed the well-stocked onboard esky, revealing an array of chilled refreshments. He presented a selection of sandwiches, all freshly made that morning.

Despite the tempting spread of food and the cool drinks, Vicky's head spun dizzily. Her cheeks flushed a deep scarlet under the relentless heat of the sun.

Cindy turned to her, "You don't look well. I think it is best if we call it a day,"

"No, please, I'll be fine," she responded, her voice revealed exhaustion and weakness, "We've all paid for a full-day tour. I wouldn't want a little heat stroke to ruin your day; and you haven't caught a fish yet. It's just not fair."

"I insist," responded Cindy, "You'll only feel worse as the day goes on. I think it best if we all head back."

Colin agreed, "C'mon, Vick, we can't have you pass out on the boat."

Cindy offered a comforting reassurance. "There's always another day," she gently remarked, understanding evident in her eyes. Bruce, however, held a different view. He proposed a solution ensuring Vicky and Colin's comfort and safety and affording Cindy the opportunity to catch a barramundi. He would return to the boat ramp, arranging for his driver to meet Vicky and Colin there and take them back to their hotel. He suggested Johnny accompany the couple to clean their fish for them. Bruce would then take Cindy out again and fish the waterways for another couple of hours in an attempt to catch the elusive barramundi.

Cindy found a sense of ease and trust in the boat captain's presence, making the decision entirely agreeable. Vicky and Colin, though apologetic, recognised the urgency of Vicky's condition. She needed respite, a soothing cold shower, and abundant fluids to bring down her body temperature. With unanimous consent, the course was set. Each individual's well-being was considered, and in the end, everyone found solace in the chosen path forward.

The tour resumed with renewed vigour once the couple disembarked at the boat ramp. Bruce did not want the day to end without Cindy reeling in at least one remarkable catch. With the wind in his hair and a smile on his face, he guided the boat's bow toward a well-guarded secret spot—a place he'd frequented for years that yielded bountiful returns for his dedication. This locale was shrouded in the secrecy known only to a select few, a hidden gem of Weipa's waters. He was confident they would have the place entirely to themselves, especially at this time of year. Most of the other fishing charters suspended their operations in anticipation of the forthcoming rainy season, leaving the tranquil estuary to the explorers and the spirited.

Before long, the boat glided to a halt within the heart of a secluded aquatic oasis, a preserve whose very existence hinged upon the whims of the tides. This hidden enclave could only be reached during the zenith of high tide; at other times, an impenetrable sandbar stood guard, steadfastly denying entry to vessels. The boundaries of this unique haven were delineated by sandy shores extending languidly on either side, while dense mangroves, with their gnarled roots and emerald canopies, stood as silent guardians.

The intimate setting on the water fostered a delightful afternoon with just the two of them. Bruce's seasoned expertise and personalised guidance transformed the outing into an enjoyable learning experience. Cindy swiftly grasped the intricacies of casting a line, finding the task considerably easier with fewer occupants in the boat, affording her ample room to manoeuvre the rod. Amidst their cheerful banter,

Cindy seized the opportunity to delve into Bruce's heritage, eager to glean insights into his people.

Pride gleamed in Bruce's eyes as he shared, "I hail from the Wik-Mungkan mob. Our ancestors have been fishin' in these very waterways for years."

"So, you're familiar with these waters?" she inquired.

"Yep, been comin' out here since I was knee-high to a grasshopper. This here's been my dream for a long time now. To own a fishing charter and share our culture with visitors," he affirmed.

"Well, you're doing a great job," commending him with a warm smile.

Their discourse seamlessly melded with Bruce's tutelage on the art of casting, and Cindy's excitement surged when she felt the telltale tug on her line. Yet, despite her efforts, the potential catch slipped away. Undeterred, Cindy rejoiced in the simple pleasure of being on the water.

As the conversation flowed, it eventually meandered into local affairs. "Forgive me for prying, but I only recently heard about the passing of Noel Manson and John Granger," a note of sorrow in her voice, "I was deeply saddened when I returned to Australia and learned the news. I might have been among the last to see Noel alive. It's such a tragedy, especially considering how young he was."

Bruce's response was lost in the clamour of the fishing reel, an ear-piercing shriek resounding across the water as a powerful force beneath the surface seized the bait and bolted.

"Let him run," Bruce advised, his voice rising above the din of the reel, "Then pull the line up and reel in on the way down."

She followed his guidance, muscles straining as she grappled with the immense weight on the other end of the line. The fish was no pushover, and she battled to maintain the perfect balance between control and yielding.

"Use all your strength," he continued his instructions, his excitement palpable, "Don't let the tip down too far, or you'll lose him."

It was a fierce duel, an epic contest of wills between human and fish. The captain's anticipation grew with each taut tug on the line, and then, it happened. With a mighty leap, a colossal barramundi soared out of the water, its entire length exposed in a dazzling display of power and majesty. Its silver scales erupted in a flash in the dazzling daylight as it contorted its body before plunging back into the murky waters below.

"Oh, wow!" Bruce exclaimed, his voice trembling with exhilaration. "It's bloody huge. It's a monster, keep reelin' him in."

The battle waged on, seemingly endless. Time slowed to a crawl for Cindy as her arms ached and her back began to protest under the insistent strain. The sun's remorseless heat bore down on her, yet her persistence never wavered. This fish was hers, and she was set on conquering it.

After what felt like an eternity, she finally brought the fish alongside the boat. Bruce stood ready, his net poised like a surgeon's scalpel. With deft precision, he plunged the net deep into the water. Cindy, physically spent but mentally resolute, allowed herself a moment of relaxation. She watched, beaming with exhilaration and pride, as he scooped up the colossal prize.

This experience, this epic battle of strength and will, now imprinted onto her memory like a vivid painting, was an adventure she would carry with her always. She was overjoyed. Her gaze remained locked onto the huge barramundi, its form glistening in the net, its head and tail extending beyond either side as evidence of its extraordinary size.

Bruce brandished the metallic ruler and carefully measured the fish, revealing an impressive one-hundred-and-five centimetres—a record for these waters! Both of them were overjoyed. Cindy handed him her phone, eager to capture the moment for an online post. She envisioned selecting the best shot to adorn the galley wall of her yacht. What initially promised to be a disheartening return to Australia transformed into one of the most exhilarating experiences of her life. Once Bruce captured images from various angles, it was time to release the venerable fish, allowing it to continue its lineage and potentially bring joy to another angler on a future day.

"I think it's time to head back now," Cindy declared, her grin impossible to contain, "Mission accomplished." She sat near the bow, which afforded maximum shade from the sun's harsh rays, while the captain remained at the helm at the rear.

"I don't think we could have asked for a better result," he remarked, his elation evident. She turned to look at him and smiled. It was an exceptionally fruitful day on the water, with all three of his guests landing remarkable catches. He beamed at Cindy, praising her, "Well done! What a catch. This one's unforgettable."

A glint, reflected in the sun's rays, caught her eye as he spoke—a white, polished object, smooth with age, suspended around his neck. She studied the object, inspecting it in more detail, and there it was: a crocodile tooth bound by a weathered leather strap. Years of wear burnished it to a brilliant shine, reflecting the light; triggering a memory. This was the same necklace she had observed on the man at Watson's River station—the one she had encountered after visiting Noel. She swiftly dismissed any connection, redirecting her focus to Bruce's face. The man at the station sported a wild, bushy beard and unruly hair. This man before her was clean-shaven, with warm, inviting eyes, a stark contrast to the individual's cold gaze at the station.

As they made their way back to the boat ramp, Cindy couldn't resist revisiting their earlier conversation about Noel Manson and John Granger. She turned to the captain, grateful, and spoke earnestly, "Bruce, I can't express how much today has meant to me. It's been truly extraordinary. I hope you don't mind me bringing up a gloomy topic, but I can't shake the thought of what happened to those two men at the station; I can't stop thinking about it, Noel was such a wonderful person."

Bruce's response was casual, but it hit Cindy like a ton of bricks. "Seems they must've eaten deadly nightshade berries by mistake. That's what folks are saying."

Time seemed to stand still for Cindy, her heart sank, her world crumbling in an instant. A surge of fear raced through her body. Sergeant Smith, the investigator, made it clear the cause of death had not yet been revealed to the public. How, then, could Bruce know? Unless...The connection struck her like a thunderbolt. Her eyes wide with shock and suspicion, she peered directly at the man before her. He met her gaze, and in that moment, he sensed her fear. But there was something more. His countenance underwent a noticeable transformation, shifting from an expression of relaxed contentment and genuine pleasure to one marked by a discernible mixture of doubt and apprehension. A hesitant uncertainty supplanted the ease that once graced his features, and the gleam of delight in his eyes gave way to a subtle shadow of fear. He realised he made a mistake, and Cindy saw it, too.

"It was him," she thought to herself, gripped with terror.

At the same moment, Bruce realised the woman on his boat was the same nurse who visited Noel on the farm the day he was picking the nightshade berries. Her hair was a little longer, and her skin was more tanned. She had gained a little weight, but Bruce had a good eye for detail and a long memory; it was definitely the same woman.

He contemplated his next move; he could not let this woman destroy what he had fought so hard for. He was living the perfect life now and he did not need someone to shatter his harmonious existence. So far, he had managed to get away with it. It was only her that now stood between him and the freedom and lifestyle he came to know and embrace. He had no choice but to act now, throw her overboard, make it look like an accident. Far north Queensland witnessed countless disappearances, swallowed by the vast expanse, consumed by its eternal silence. Swift thinking was imperative. He made a choice. Here, amidst the treacherous depths of crocodile-infested waters, she would meet her end.

He shifted his weight and gently eased the throttle down, a calculated move to gain the upper hand. Ever obedient to his command, the boat responded by slowing to a crawl, then eventually idled in the murky, foreboding waters. The moment hung heavy, pregnant with the weight of an impending act.

As if summoned by the dark nature of their situation, the sky shifted. Clouds swirled in ominous patterns, casting a blanket of foreboding over their surroundings. The encroaching rain clouds painted their world in dark grey, muted tones as if nature itself conspired to bear witness to this brutal act.

Bruce lunged forcefully at Cindy, aiming to subdue her and confine her to her seat. In the growing dimness, Cindy felt the stirrings of a primal force. Her heart pounded, the drumming rhythm of adrenaline quickening her pulse. Flight and fight, two primal instincts clashed within her, but the latter surged forth, a torrent of raw willpower. In a heartbeat, she shifted, the boat rocking in response to the force of his sudden lunge. He landed haphazardly with a heavy thud. The seat she occupied moments earlier now cradled him, sprawling and off balance.

Time seemed to stretch thin; each hastened breath measured in seconds. In that fleeting moment, she wielded her fishing rod, a makeshift weapon, aiming the base toward his eye with deadly precision. Her intention was clear—she meant to blind him, to seize the upper hand, but Bruce, driven by a savage instinct of his own, intercepted the strike, his grip firm on the rod's midsection.

He found his footing, the rod now a tenuous defence, but Cindy's will to survive remained unwavering. Her eyes scanned for another potential weapon, any edge to tip the scales. In a seamless motion, she claimed a gleaming filleting knife from the central table, its cold steel starkly contrasting with the fire blazing in her eyes. It was an unspoken declaration this had escalated beyond mere confrontation—a dance on the edge of survival, a struggle to the very last breath.

With the knife held firmly, she navigated her way toward the boat's stern. Bruce tracked her with the intensity of a predator closing in on its prey. He inched closer, each step deliberate, every movement a prelude to an end he was desperate to hasten. Cindy continued her cautious orbit of the boat, maintaining a distance that felt like the span of worlds. She made her way to one side of the boat, the table now acting as a barrier, a feeble defence against his lethal intentions. He lunged, a feral beast closing in, but she countered, the blade cutting a deep gash into his right forearm; pain fuelled his fury.

Her gaze darted toward the bow, where the anchor chain beckoned—a lifeline to her desperate gamble. With an almost preternatural grace, she dropped the knife and seized a mallet stowed beneath the table, its frightful purpose reserved for the unexpected intrusions of sharks. Bruce's lunge came once more, but the mallet met its mark with a sickening clunk. He crumpled, a figure struck down, blood cascading from his deep head wound onto the table and spattering the deck. The acrid scent of metal, so familiar from her hours as a nurse, hung heavy in the air.

With the same deliberate attention, Cindy moved to the stowage area of the bow, her fingers seeking purchase on the anchor chain. Bruce lay slumped, an inert figure, unconscious to the world. She ensnared his leg in the chain, summoning every last ounce of strength to lift and cast the anchor into the water. Tangled and weighted, Bruce followed, a shadow dissipating into the abyss.

In the frenetic dance of survival, victory was swiftly curtailed by a cruel twist of fate. His left leg wedged beneath the unforgiving seat, an ironic trap. Cindy battled against time's unrelenting march, straining against the inexorable pull of destiny, her efforts desperate and fevered. Sweat soaked her skin; breaths came in ragged gasps. Pulling and wrenching with every ounce of strength, she tried to free his imprisoned limb. And then, with a final surge of energy, she sensed a release and watched as he slipped away, vanishing over the boat's edge, leaving behind only ripples in the silent water.

After collecting the knife and concealing it within the confines of the helm, Cindy assumed command of the vessel, her grip on the throttle firm; she urged the boat forward. However, the engine betrayed her, sputtering and then falling silent. She repeated the ignition key ritual, toggling it on and off, her gaze fixed on the dashboard's illuminating display. She looked behind her and saw two fuel tanks connected to one engine. One tank must be empty, she thought. In a desperate bid to escape, her eyes hurriedly searched the display, looking for a clue as to how to switch the tanks over. With nothing obvious in sight, she leant down and started scanning both tanks for any signs of a shut-off valve. In her frazzled state, she failed to find any mechanism to change the tanks over. Her brow furrowed in frustration as she scanned the boat's interior for any conspicuous clues, but nothing revealed itself. With a sigh, she turned the key once more, only to be met with the same stubborn silence.

Her heart racing, Cindy reached for the VHF maritime radio, her trembling hand inching closer to the lifesaving device. But just as her fingers made contact, an unmistakable, metallic scent assailed her senses. It was the tang of blood, unmistakable and chilling. Her heart raced as she suddenly felt a vice-like grip encircle her waist, pulling her mercilessly toward the boat's edge. It was Bruce, drenched and stained with blood, his face contorted with rage. Weakened and dazed from a powerful blow to the head, he summoned his last vestiges of strength to wrest her to the brink of the vessel.

In a final, desperate shove, he propelled her toward the water, but Cindy, driven by sheer survival instinct, reached out and clung to his belt, dragging him down with her. The water churned around them, taking on a vivid crimson hue as blood mingled with the brine. They grappled in a macabre dance, their struggles a twisted ballet of life and death, until the merciless depths claimed them both in simultaneous descent.

And then, a sinister presence emerged from the depths of darkness. Old Bob, the ancient crocodile, crept from the shadows along the banks. Attracted by the smell of fresh blood in the water, his reptilian eyes fixated on the frantic commotion unfolding, observing with a calculated patience. His massive form, a relic of primordial terror, moved with deceptive lethargy as he inched closer to the ongoing fray. With every second, he drew closer. Old Bob could almost taste the promise of a savage feast, his anticipation growing with every ripple of the dark, foreboding waters.

CHAPTER 33

Davo relished the luxury of his rostered day off, savouring the freedom from duty. He picked up his phone and dialled Phil's number, a glint of anticipation in his eyes, "Hey, mate. Any plans for the day? I was thinking of swinging by for a good old catch-up.

"Absolutely," Phil's voice brimmed with excitement. Seeing his former colleague was like a lifeline to his days in the police force, a connection he held dear, coursing through his veins. "Let's make a day of it. Beers, a barbecue lunch, and stories from the good ol' days. When can I expect you?"

"Right about now," Davo replied, his enthusiasm matching Phil's.

"Fantastic, seeya in a bit!" the retired officer's grin stretched wide, his face radiant. The morning was a masterpiece - the sun danced in a cloudless sky, a promise of a few more precious days before the onset of the wet season. The rising humidity was a mere whisper against his contented morale.

Living within walking distance of each other in the close-knit town of Weipa, Davo made it to Phil's place in less than ten minutes. He barely had time to raise his hand to knock before his mate swung the door open, an eager grin lighting up his face. Their years of working side by side gave them an uncanny sense of when the other was near.

"G'day, mate," Phil enveloped his friend in a hearty, bear-like hug, "Good to see you. What's the latest?"

"Oh, you know," Davo replied, a casual air about him. "Just felt like dropping by to say hello."

"How's the new sergeant treating you?" he inquired.

Davo rolled his eyes before responding, "A real pain in the arse."

He chuckled, "Sounds like things aren't like the good ol' days."

"You've got that right," the younger man affirmed with a wry grin.

"On another note, I hear Cindy Newman's back in town," Phil said. "Gladys and Jude have set the rumour mill in motion yet again. I assume you've had a chance to talk to the nurse. Must feel like a weight off your shoulders, finally closing that case that's been looming over this town for two years. I was expecting a call from ya sooner, informing me of the good news."

"Well, actually," Davo began, his tone measured, "She's not our killer."

"What?!" Phil's astonishment was palpable, his pupils dilated, his brows raised.

"Yeah, it's a real head-scratcher," he confirmed. "Harold and I drilled her for over four hours when she first arrived. She's got an alibi as solid as a rock, and she hadn't even heard about the murders. Apparently, she jetted back to Germany on the Tuesday after Diane found John and Noel."

"Well, I'll be," came the stunned response. "What's your next move, then? Did she let slip anything that might help track down the real culprits?"

"I'm not sure. I've been racking my brain over what she said, and none of it adds up or brings us any closer to a resolution."

"Tell me everything. Even the tiniest detail could be a lead. Does anything seem off? Anything catch your attention as odd?"

Davo recounted Cindy's words to Phil as best he could, emphasising the only new information was about the man she spotted near the bush when leaving the station, "She mentioned she saw some indigenous bloke with a pendant around his neck. The way she described it, he was probably close to the deadly nightshade bush."

"Many locals wear pendants, often tied to their totem animal. Doesn't narrow things down much," Phil mused.

After a moment of contemplation, Davo added, "Oh, I nearly forgot. She mentioned he was wearing a pair of feathered shoes. That struck me as rather odd."

The retired officer's eyes ignited with recognition, a distant memory flickering to life within him. "The only bloke I've ever seen in a pair of shoes like that is Bruce, down at the Alby that night when he pointed the bone at Walt. They're special ceremonial shoes, designed for stealth, leaving no trace or tracks."

Davo's expression became grave, grappling with the implications. "You think Bruce might be our man?"

"It's the only scenario that lines up," Phil replied, his voice tinged with certainty. "He might have been the one to end Walt's days, too, but we're short on evidence for that. Let's consider it. He had motive and opportunity, and that alibi about 'roo hunting with Jake never held water. Everyone knew he had a grudge against anyone who profited from the mines. Plus, he's got a solid grasp of native bush plants and knows how to track like a pro," he paused, "I hope we are wrong. Graves would be bloody delighted if we were. Snide bastard."

Davo's face furrowed with concern. "But we've already tried him once for murder, and he was acquitted. What options do we have now? What about the double jeopardy rule? We can't subject him to another trial for the same crime, or can we?"

"Double jeopardy was once the norm in most states," came the reply, his words steeped in the foresight earned from years on the force and countless hours with trial lawyers. "But now, we'd need to present new and compelling evidence that couldn't have been brought up at the initial trial. Personally, I don't believe we've got much else to tie him to it. Any lawyer would scoff at us—relying on a pendant and a pair of shoes? It wouldn't hold up in court."

"So, he just walks away, scot-free?"

"If he is our perpetrator, I'm afraid so. I must say, he did a bloody good job at pulling the wool over our eyes," Phil commented with a heavy sigh. He couldn't shake the feeling of letting the system down. "Let's keep this between us. Let bygones be bygones. If anything similar comes up down the line, we'll know who to turn to first for a closer look. There's not much else we can do at this stage."

CHAPTER 34

The turbulent waters frothed with a gruesome mixture of mud and blood as Cindy and Bruce grappled desperately. Old Bob, the cunning behemoth, slithered through the depths, inching closer, an ancient predator on the prowl. They breached the surface for a gasp of air, only to find the colossal reptile descending upon them, a grim reaper in scales

"Stop, we don't have to die!" Bruce's voice tore through the chaos, a desperate plea. Cindy's instincts screamed at her, warning of a trick. She placed her hands firmly on top of his shoulders and pushed him beneath the water, feeling his resistance surge against her grasp. Time was their merciless enemy, and they had none to waste.

Cindy kicked hard at Bruce and started swimming the short distance toward the boat. Despite the ongoing blood loss and his resultant weakened state, he managed to catch her by the leg and draw her back toward him. She kicked to no avail. His grip was tight, and she felt herself going under again.

Bruce looked around to see the crocodile closing the space between them much faster than expected. He let go of her leg and made a dash for the boat himself. Cindy took the muddy, bloody water into her lungs and was struggling to breathe, coughing and spluttering. In a last-ditch effort to save her own life, she made a final push to the boat, arriving just in time to see Bruce clear himself out of the water, "Help me!" she shouted desperately, "Help!" she screamed as old

Bob drew precariously closer, attracted by the bloodied waters and the commotion.

"Why?" he asked with a menacing grin, "So you can stab me again?"

"It doesn't have to be this way, Bruce. We both got what we wanted. Now help me onboard, and I'll disappear from your life forever," she turned. The reptile was mere metres from her now. "Hurry!" The desperation in her voice was evident.

In a brief surge of empathy, he offered the net's handle to Cindy, reaching out to assist her aboard the boat. Her gaze met his with feigned warmth, a calculated effort to deceive him into thinking they might forge an alliance. Yet, in an instant, she summoned every ounce of her strength, clasping the handle with a fierce grip and unleashing a powerful tug, aiming to drag him into the opaque, treacherous waters. He, however, proved too nimble for her scheme. Swiftly discerning her intent, he countered by forcefully thrusting the net back in her direction.

As Cindy fought against the relentless pull of the water, her strength waning, this sudden action threw her off balance. The weight of exhaustion pressed heavily upon her limbs, urging her towards surrender. Time was slipping away, sliding through her fingers like water through a sieve. Her desperate gaze sought out Bruce, her eyes a mirror of pleading, hoping to find a glimmer of salvation. Yet, he stood there, unmoving, a statue carved from the conflicting emotions swirling within him.

"Bruce, please!" she implored, her voice tearing through the tempest, a raw plea for help echoing in the storm-laden air, "Help me, please!"

In those agonising seconds, Bruce's world hung in the balance. He knew the gravity of his choice. Leave Cindy behind, let the ancient hunter claim its prey, and ensure his own escape; it was his only choice. He had worked tirelessly to build the life he now secured, and Cindy threatened to shatter it all; she held the power to ruin everything he held dear.

She made a last-ditch lunge at the boat, but Old Bob was on to her instantly, taking the entirety of her right leg in his gigantic mouth and chomping down. A blood-curdling scream emanated from her mouth. A cry never heard before, as if it came from the fiery depths of Hell. She still had time to plead as her lifeblood drained away, "Please, I beg of you, please,"

Those were the final words Bruce heard as Old Bob embarked on his ominous death roll. With a powerful surge, the massive reptile veered towards the murky depths of the river estuary, drawing his captive prey into the chilling depths. The water churned and frothed, bearing witness to this primal struggle between predator and prey, until finally, silence descended, leaving only the gentle undulations to mark the spot where the ominous dance took place.

Bruce watched as the thrashing, boiling mud and blood slowly dispersed before returning to the helm and dialling into channel 16, the international hailing and distress frequency, "Mayday, Mayday, Mayday. This is Weipa Crocodile urgently reporting a woman overboard at Evan's Landing, Weipa. There's a grave concern a crocodile may have seized her. Our position stands at approximately 12.6 degrees South and 141.9 degrees East. Immediate assistance is desperately needed. Over."

He looked over the boat; it was a mess, and blood was everywhere. It truly did resemble a crime scene. He had no time to clean it, knowing the Coast Guard would be here in a matter of minutes. He must think quickly and act fast. He looked valiantly for his filleting knife, to no avail. He opened his tackle box and removed a small scaling knife. It would have to suffice. He stabbed at his own arm, piercing the skin deeply in the arc of a crocodile's mouth. He roughened up the straight cut made by the filleting knife earlier by boring the knife down into the cut and twisting it, forming jagged edges. He placed his worn Akubra hat over his head to hide his recent injuries before taking a quick glance around for any other craft; he saw none. Rapidly grabbing one of the fishing rods, he threw it overboard; he then started vigorously punching the tabletop. The pain was excruciating, and his energy was depleted. As he heard the sounds of an approaching vessel, he looked down at his bruised, abraded knuckles and deep, jagged, bloodied cut on his right arm. He was pleased with the results.

The Coast Guard came up beside Bruce and noted the bloodied vessel, "What happened here?" he asked. By now, Bruce had become an expert liar. He looked the man straight in the eye and said, "Sir, one of our passengers, Cindy Newman, to be exact, was pullin' in a massive barramundi. She was real excited. To the point of distraction. It was huge, a real monster of a fish, and she struggled to land it, bein' so small an' all. Just as she reeled it near the boat, a big old croc emerged from the waters and frightened her good. She leans over, loses 'er balance and plop! Straight in the water."

"And what happened to your arm?" Asked the guard.

"I tried me best, Sir. I tried.." he choked out, his voice fading into a painful silence. His gaze turned misty, the corners of his eyes pooling with unshed tears. And then, unable to hold it back any longer, he broke down, his sobs echoing around the waterways.

"I know this is hard. When you are ready, please continue."

"Right, that big ol' beast, he came right up alongside the boat. I leaned over and gave 'im a poke in the eye. That's when he had a go at me arm. I somehow wrangled it free before usin' both fists to give 'im a good whack on the snout," he paused for dramatic effect, "I should've done more."

He held his head in his hands and sobbed a heartfelt, deep cry. The tears ran freely and fell to the deck, mixing with the blood on the boat. "The croc got hold of her leg. There was nothin' I could do to stop it. He took her, he killed her. Oh God, please forgive me." The pain was obvious in his voice; he was a picture of wretchedness.

The Coast Guard then said, "Any sign of her since?"

"No, none. She went under; there was a splash of the ol' croc's tail, some bubbling of the waters, then nothing."

"Are you okay to steer the ship back to the boat ramp? I'll call ahead and have the paramedics waiting for you."

"I'm sure I can manage," replied Bruce, pretending as if he were attempting to regain his composure. His face was blotchy, and his eyes inflamed from crying.

He followed the Coast Guard back to the Weipa boat ramp to a waiting ambulance. They patched him up but decided he needed to be medically evacuated to Cairns Base Hospital. The wound was far too deep and extensive to be dealt with locally. Transport was arranged, and he was flown by helicopter out to Cairns, returning two days later to a town expressing their collective joy that he survived such an ordeal.

In the aftermath, as emotions swirled around them, it was Gladys who couldn't suppress her final, cutting remark. Seated beside Jude at the Alby, she raised her glass of chardonnay to her lips and took a measured sip. Turning to Jude, she spoke with a tone of vindication, "Looks like justice has had its day," her words held a sour satisfaction. "I always had me suspicions 'bout that nurse. I'd wager me last dollar she had a hand in John, Noel, and poor ol' Walt's passings. It looks like no one's truly safe 'round these parts."

CHAPTER 35

Eight years had slipped away, and Bruce awoke from a broken sleep, drenched by the persistent rain, in the well-known clearing. He pressed his back to an old eucalyptus gum, and the red earth sat beneath him. He wore nothing but the "possum" loincloth, his crocodile-totem pendant and ceremonial paint. He was ready.

This was the very spot he prepared for Barlang's sorry business on Watson's River Station, a memory that seemed as distant as the ancient hills that framed the horizon. Spring blossomed in all its glory, painting the landscape with vibrant crimson waratahs and luminous golden bottle brushes. Majestic eucalyptus gums stood tall, enclosing him in their embrace, while the kookaburras, faithful heralds of time, boisterously announced the arrival of dawn. Their laughter echoed through the bush, once a comforting companion. This morning, he no longer found solace in their mirth; instead, he interpreted it as a cruel jest, a punishing reminder of the path he had chosen.

As the sun's rays pierced through the dense canopy, casting dappled patterns on the floor of the clearing, Bruce slumped, seated in the dirt, shoulders hanging forward, with a heaviness in his heart matching the leaden clouds above. The once familiar ground now seemed to bear witness to the weight of his past, the memories carved into the very earth beneath him.

He turned, his gaze drawn upwards to the towering eucalyptus tree, its ancient presence commanding the clearing. His fingers, weathered and calloused, gently grazed the bark, the rough texture a tangible connection to the past. Each crevice, every knot, whispered of decades and centuries gone by, secrets held in the very fibres of the tree. They were silent witnesses to the choices one makes in life, stories etched into the wood, and they unsettled Bruce, sending tremors through his heart.

The burden of those tales pressed upon him, each a reminder that he could not turn back the clock and undo what had been done. In their presence, Bruce felt the enormity of his own actions. The wounds cut deep, a painful testament to the wrongs he committed.

The night had painted a collage of vivid dreams into the fabric of his consciousness, where spectral figures of ancient ancestors had materialised, bearing solemn reckoning upon his weary soul. In the ethereal realm of slumber, they whispered truths cutting through the haze of his waking life, leaving indelible marks on his soul.

Yesterday, when he first arrived at the clearing, triumph surged within him. The familiar ground seemed to echo with the footsteps of history, a validation of his endeavours. Yet, the visitations of his ethereal ancestors altered the landscape of his thoughts, casting a different light on his achievements. Their spectral presence reminded him the passage of time held power beyond mortal understanding.

He had built a thriving business and owned his own land, land that could no longer be controlled by the mining giants. He fought to preserve his heritage, to pass on his knowledge and the custodial rights to his land, a legacy he was determined to bequeath to those who would come after him.

The ghosts of his past cast long, haunting shadows over him. Four lives were selfishly taken, leaving a bitter taste of remorse and doubt. What had it all amounted to? He rationalised those actions, weaving a narrative of cultural preservation as his shield, a last stand against a world that appeared hell-bent on obliterating his heritage. It was easier to deflect blame outwards than to confront the man staring back at him in the mirror.

Colonialism, the relentless march of "White-fellas", the ceaseless clamour of mines—these had all become convenient scapegoats in his desperate bid to justify the unforgivable. He clung to these notions, allowing them to absolve him of the guilt constantly gnawing at his moral core. It was a dangerous game of self-deception, a futile attempt to rewrite history with his own hand. An emptiness reverberated within him, a void appearing to stretch to infinity. His vitality withered under the chains that bound his choices, and in its place remained a mere husk, a shadow of the man he once was. His self-perception now reflected a figure stripped of character—a hollow vessel.

As the years marched on, the gravity of those lost lives grew heavier, a constant reminder of the irreversible choices he had made. The passage of time had not softened the harsh reality nor dimmed the faces of those he had wronged. Their voices echoed in the chambers of his mind, a haunting chorus of accusation and pain.

Admitting culpability felt like drowning in a sea of regret. The first murder had been for vengeance. The next two were a crusade for heritage. The fourth was to preserve the life he felt he deserved. Now, as an elder, he saw the cruel irony. His own people no longer held their traditions sacred. The Wik-Mungkan language languished, dismissed for fear of ridicule. The younger members of his tribe could speak only a few words; not one of them could string together a sentence.

English emerged as a formidable bulwark against the jeers and ridicule his people faced, both in the classroom confines and the workplace's unforgiving terrain. It became more than just a language; it became a lifeline, a means of survival in a world demanding conformity.

The relentless pressure to assimilate served as a constant reminder of the cost of standing out. It was a tug-of-war between preserving a heritage and blending into the dominant culture. The echoes of ancestors' wisdom, once so vibrant, now seemed to fade against the backdrop of this new reality.

Even the national anthem, a rallying cry for unity, underscored the prevailing sentiment. "We are one and free" declared a powerful message of togetherness but one carrying with it an implicit call for homogeneity. It was a dichotomy tugging at the very basis of his identity, a struggle to find a balance between honouring the past and embracing the present.

The allure of assimilation into the larger Australian society morphed into his mob's collective ambition, eclipsing the traditions that once stood as their guiding light. Bruce, who dedicated his life's labour to safeguarding his people's culture and heritage, observed with a heavy heart as it seemed to crumble like weathered rock formations. The ancient practices of navigating by the stars, interpreting the language of the land through man-made rock formations, and imparting to the younger people the profound interconnectedness between humanity and the cosmos all felt like fleeting whispers in the vast expanse of time.

The once-thriving flame of tradition dimmed, its radiance subdued by the powerful pull of modernity and the tantalising promises of progress. The song lines of ancestral wisdom that once echoed through their community now seemed to dissolve into the windswept landscape, lost amidst the rapid currents of change.

Shortly after that fateful fishing day in the waterways around Weipa, his tribe bestowed upon him the title of "elder", a mantle of honour. It was a recognition of his insight and his deep connection to the land. Yet, with each passing day, weariness eclipsed elation. The youth no longer cradled the old tongue or revered the oral traditions. They sought to carve their own paths, leaving behind the ancestral ways binding the community for thousands of years. Inscribing their stories of culture and heritage into books to shout their own truth-telling to the world. For Bruce, this shift in priorities cut deep; it was a source of profound inner conflict and sorrow, akin to a betrayal of his people's timeless traditions. A sacrilege. To see their cherished history and age-old customs revealed to outsiders was like a wound cutting straight to the bone. In his youth, such actions were strictly forbidden, and he himself paid a steep price for transgressing these tribal laws. With every word they wrote, every story they shared with the world, he felt a piece of their collective spirit being laid bare.

He approached the grave task with composure, clutching a bottle of oral liquid morphine, or "ordine," procured from Mad Maureen's hidden reserve. The previous day, he navigated through the shadows to reach the deadly nightshade tree, its gnarled boughs laden with untold secrets and heavy clusters of fruit, each one teeming with its own lethal power.

Seated beneath the sprawling canopy of the ancient gum tree, he raised the bottle to his lips and let the sedative elixir flow, its bitter taste a communion with his chosen fate. The liquid slid down his throat, each swallow a deliberate step towards the reckoning he had long avoided.

One by one, he took the berries he gathered earlier, their glossy exteriors concealing a potent darkness within. Placing them in his mouth, he crushed each one between his teeth, ensuring the seeds were broken to unleash their venomous power. It was a macabre reflection of the fate he dealt to those three other men, a solemn acknowledgment of the inescapable cycle of retribution.

The weight of his deeds pressed upon him, an insistent force threatening to suffocate him. Once, he was ablaze with purpose, driven by convictions that now seemed distant and hollow. The justifications providing solace crumbled to ash, leaving him alone with the harsh truth of his actions.

In the moment's stillness, he knew he could no longer bear it. The ember of remorse smouldered within him, its heat consuming the remnants of his former self. Though fraught with pain, he could no longer evade the path of redemption. He became a prisoner, shackled by his own choices, and now, he would face the ultimate reckoning.

As the nightshade's poison coursed through his veins, he welcomed the embrace of darkness, a fitting end to a chapter defined by the shadows he cast. In this final act, he sought a semblance of closure, a reckoning with the deeds defining him. And as the world faded around him, he knew, in the end, he chose to pay the ultimate price for the lives he had taken, a painful step towards a fragile, uncertain peace.

www.ingramcontent.com/pod-product-compliance
Ingram Content Group UK Ltd.
Pitfield, Milton Keynes, MK11 3LW, UK
UKHW042157171224
452513UK00001B/164